THE

DICTATOR'S WIFE

The Dictator's Wife is published under Reverie, a sectionalized division under Di Angelo Publications, Inc.

Reverie is an imprint of Di Angelo Publications.
Copyright 2024.
All rights reserved.
Printed in the United States of America.

Di Angelo Publications
Los Angeles, California

Library of Congress
The Dictator's Wife
ISBN: 978-1-955690-77-5
Paperback

Words: Hollie S. McKay
Cover Design: Savina Mayeur
Interior Design: Kimberly James
Editors:

Downloadable via www.dapbooks.shop and other e-book retailers.

For educational, business, and bulk orders, contact distribution@diangelopublications.com.

1. Fiction --- Thrillers --- Political
2. Fiction --- Thrillers --- Psychological
3. Fiction --- Romance --- Suspense

THE

DICTATOR'S WIFE

HOLLIE S. MCKAY

CONTENTS

For my childhood best friend Kirra, who taught me the art of compassion

PROLOGUE

December 24, 1983: The slice of time before one's memory has begun to patch together the fragments of a life too young to recall. It is only with the letters and anecdotes that arise decades later that I can stitch these moments–Anna's infancy–into a narrative sense.

She is just thirteen months old and lives on the edge of the earth–the village of Vea in the Middle Eastern Island country of Tucana. Vea belongs only to women; there are no men left, and no new men allowed. One winter's night–Christmas Eve–several women huddle together in a single clay shack for warmth.

"Can you see it? The scar?" Hala asks the others, tears streaming down her pale face. The women, including her mother, aunties, and cousins, all pull their hair back to emphasize the scarred flesh protecting their right brain. They raise the same rhetorical question without answers.

"From the soldiers," Hala weeps as the solemn faces nod in agreement.

Hala wills the tears away, holding baby Anna tight in her arms. Her long raven hair flows around the infant like a blanket, a bulwark against the frozen night. As it is Christmas Eve, Hala extends a hand to say grace before the feast. All she can whisper is that the smell reminds her of the burned flesh of a baby under the sun, shock overwhelming her.

Gasping for air, the tiny Hala–much too tiny even for a teen, with skin stretched around her rib cage–presses the baby against her chest as she manically, rushes out into the frost-dusted night in a place barely holding on to its sanity.

The legend goes that the country belonged to Mesopotamia in the centuries before Christ– the first vestiges of human life, the first place kissed by the morning sun. Years of severe and ceaseless storms, however, caused Tucana to eventually break away from the mainland, creating an island unto itself.

Three years earlier, all of Hala's home country was merely an impoverished island insignificantly dotting the Mediterranean Sea: a multi-ethnic, multi-religious peninsula beset by delicately cracked, stony plains in washed-out hues of gray and beige. It has little more than mud hut homes stippling towns and villages that roast in the summer and freeze in the winter. Until recently, Tucana had been a little-known parcel with little-known value.

Then, a dictator took control after the passing of the King. Explorers found oil, and subsequently insurgent violence ravaged the capital city of Cyra. The little villages outside the lair, however, were never subject to the unrest that engulfed the metropolis. They were sparsely populated with peaceful farmers who kept to themselves, paid little attention to politics, and plied the sea like perpetual children.

Despite barely making ends meet, the villagers of Vea were the type of people who looked to God to save and be saved, never taking a penny that did not belong to them. They couldn't speak English as fluently as the city folk. Instead, the villagers conversed in their ancient tribal tongue of Rasa, a soft melodic dialect that echoed the softness of their humble demeanors. It is a language that is fast becoming extinct, and no longer commonly spoken in Cyra or the larger towns.

On a sweltering August morning in 1981, and without a word of warning, one hundred angry men overran Vea, stampeding up to the little village balanced at the hoof of the mountain. It was not immediately clear who the intruders were or where they had come from, but all wore black robes and brandished smuggled weapons.

These peculiar men tossed grenades and opened fire into frightened faces, their gunshots drowning out the symphony of screams. With wild eyes, the outsiders wrenched all the village girls – and the women who loved and protected them – and threw them into open cattle trucks by the ends of their long strands of hair. The invaders seared their muzzles into their captives' right temples, leaving black and blue markings on their flesh.

The girls could only watch helplessly as the fighting forces all-black lined the trembling boys and men of Vea along the mountain ledge–the sons, the fathers, the grandfathers, and the lonely shepherds, all forbidden to own weapons themselves and left like lambs to the slaughter. In a matter of minutes, they were all executed. One by one, their limp bodies fell into the vacuum of nature below, into the wooded gorges–their scooped-out, bullet-battered heads submerged into mass graves.

The perfume of gunpowder, burning bodies, and the blood and sweat of a searing summer's day dug into the pores of the stolen women and girls, never to be washed away. The trucks meant for cattle drove them toward the unknown. Some women were held captive for days, others for weeks, and a few died in fits of distress as the men watched over them in a windowless room.

Gradually, the women were released and sent back to Vea, but the captors forced Hala to stay the longest, deeming her the prettiest. When she was freed more than a year-and-a-half later, she returned to her home village with a face depleted of color and a small baby in her bony arms.

The black-clad men and their dirty arms clutching rifles gathered again just before Christmas, more than two years after the first invasion–this time to target the terrified Hala specifically.

Hala dashes down to the same patch of wet ground where she found her baby in the fetal position a day earlier, frying on the open coals. The smell has dived into the depths of her memories, rattling her demons to life. All Hala can do is let out a primal scream, half wolf and half human, as the other concerned women—never far behind—ready to hold her when she falls.

"I cannot save him," Hala weeps.

She crumbles to the ground, and her wet-eyed mother rushes over to lift her up. Nobody says a word. Nobody knows what to say. Nothing can be said.

Hala allows herself to be helped up. She slowly walks back toward the mud hut called home, her bare feet sinking into the ice-pebbled track with every step. She does not wince. Her feet calloused long ago.

By the time the women make it back, the candles have burned to the ground, and Vea has fallen asleep.

"They will come for me again," Hala trembles. "First the baby, and then me."

She tucks Anna into the thin mattress and kisses her rosy cheek, creased with the impression from her nightgown.

"I love you, even if you are half evil," Hala whispers. "I still love you."

There is no anger, no affection, just an emptiness that mirrors her wounded existence. Yet Hala's premonition is already unfolding. Somewhere between darkness and light, she disappears.

Christmas morning arrives with the jingle of donkey bells and an ethereal sunrise that can only be seen by those who stand in the place of time's beginnings. Snow flies down like sinking stars and sprinkles the hilltops. Pink streaks break through the cloud cover, reaching down to illuminate the pastures that still boast a hint of green.

And when Anna's childhood memories return to concrete life, it is almost five years later, and her existence revolves around a faraway and dreamy place called the Beverly Hills Hotel.

It is a hot and muggy summer day in 1988, with the smoky scent of Fourth of July BBQ padding the air. My father Bobby is home for the rare occasion. I cling to his side, dripping wet in a swimming costume that sparkles a glittery green in the sunshine outside the Beverly Hills Hotel.

I hold on to his now soggy pant leg, afraid for the day when he will leave us again. Then it would just be my mother and me, the nanny, and a big home poised all alone in the unlit crevice of Mulholland Drive.

Giddy with the sugar rush of candy and thickly iced cupcakes, the term LAX floats around my burning ears as my father continues his conversations. I roll across the warm pavement, duck between my daddy's legs, and reach out to swing from his bulging waist, a warm gun tucked inside his shirt resting against my cheek. The cool metal never frightens me like it should scare most small children. Dad once said it could kill me and stop me from being killed.

My father is a strapping man at 6'5, towering above most others, a Hollywood spaghetti westerner type with Elvis hair, a black beard and light eyes. He looks the kind who belongs on a horse riding bareback into the sunburned plains. He chews fresh tobacco and commands a room, even though he says little. But Dad holds his head high, even though there is a slight limp to his swagger.

Josie calls it the Saigon stomp. One time, I asked why, and she whispered that we do not talk about the Saigon stomp. And I don't call Josie mom. She told me never to call her mom.

"It just makes me feel younger forever," Josie once insisted in a bird-like chirp, not meeting my gaze.

I know my father travels the earth inside slim jets and talks on a giant brick-shaped phone that, to my innocent eyes, is ethereal. But every day, he wears his cowboy hat and boots–if only to remind himself, amid the feast of lavish pool parties and Hollywood superstars, of his humble beginnings in a cocooned mining town dug deep inside the American south.

Most nights, I don't want Josie to read me childish bedtime tales. I want her to tell me, over and over, the love story of how she and my dad met. Josie's mind glides elsewhere, and she talks to me as if I am a grownup, a friend.

Dad left the nest of his childhood ranch at sixteen, learned a thing or two about oil excavation as a junior apprentice at an energy firm for four years, and was preparing to launch his own small business when he spotted Josie at a Houston café near her new ballet studio. Her ash leotard glued like a youthful layer of raw skin to her lithe frame, her shiny blonde waves swept into a slick bun, with just a glint of sweat on her long neck.

It seldom snows in Houston. But it snowed that day.

Josie had relocated from France to the United States years earlier when she was seventeen, carrying only a wooden gripsack and a wrinkled, un-precedented paper offer to be the youngest principal ballerina with the Houston Ballet. Josie still spoke little English, but after Bobby introduced himself, they communicated with eyes and wandering hands. She was a paragon of grace and drama, battering the long chocolate lashes that rimmed her ebony eyes, enamored with the burly man in boots and a cow-boy hat. They sat together for hours that day, the afternoon playing out like a romantic Shakespearean fantasy with milky coffee and cigarettes and nervous laughs in the nucleus of the red, white and blue.

For two months straight, my father took a break from work every afternoon, running two blocks to the studio parking lot to see Josie. Even if all they had time for was a sweaty, stolen kiss in between rehearsals. He was in love. She was in love too. Only she is the type of person who was just in love with the idea of someone being in love with her.

"Love is going where you are wanted," Josie once told my confused eyes, drinking aromatic red wine at the foot of my bed. "Otherwise, you spend forever seeking lovers who will never love you back. When a man loves you, you take it. You must go where you are wanted."

But one morning–after being scolded by the ballet's artistic director at a weigh-in and in a weeks-long state wavering between lethargy and motion sickness–Josie visited the doctor to discover with a routine pee-in-the-cup that she was pregnant. Horrified and paralyzed, she waited before telling anyone, even my father. He eventually found out in a heated screaming match after they shared a whole bottle of wine.

Although a man of irrefutable God-fearing faith, Dad was willing to stand by Josie's adamant decision to "take care of it." Only she had left it too long in her mad state of denial. It was too late. Josie loves me, not in a maternal way, and my heart belonged to my father.

With the luck of striking a small fortune in a discovery expedition somewhere in the Middle East, my father's small business has quickly grown into an illustrious oil company. I don't know much about it, but I have a red cap with the logo RUSCO that I wear to the park on sunny days. I love it because it is the same patch he wears on his shirt. We match.

Father is home for thin slithers of time, and each time he returns he drives Josie and me through the winding West Hollywood streets in his open-top convertible and to that exquisite hotel. The Beverly Hills Hotel is our happy place, where the worries of the world are washed away by polo games and glamorous people, buckets of champagne and a piano player, retro cabanas and palm trees that reach up into the clear California skies.

I have always been an offbeat child, but I do not understand what strange is, as I am never really privy to children my age; I never go on play dates. Instead, I fondle inflated swans, swim with strangers, and chase the reflection of palm trees in that big, blue Beverly Hills Hotel pool.

When my father is here, I want him to hug me more. But every time he does, he squirms like a kid waiting in the chair to be vaccinated. And whenever that curious, giant portable phone shrieks, I know it means he is about to fly far away again. I'm constantly holding my breath, waiting for that big phone's inevitable piercing ring and vibration to send darts into my chest.

Leaping over the wooden table of Fourth of July food, I trip in a tangle of thoughts; the waxy white bun of an uneaten hot dog descends to the damp ground.

"Little, behave," is all father says. His eyes refuse to meet mine, instead fixating on the stars and stripes that distend across my swimsuit, all puffy with pouches of water.

There are no goodbyes. There are rarely goodbyes. Josie trails behind in her leopard bikini, her permed, bleached curls bouncing as she rants that her life is like a single parent. She rants until Dad dissolves into the porous sunlight.

Josie returns, composed, downing more Martinis by the pool as she giggles with the mob of men who have gathered to be in her magnetic aura.

I float through those waters, artificially tinged teal by the LED bulbs. I float until the sun plunges and the moon comes out, until my skin shrivels around calcified fingers, until everyone else has dried off and done away with their beer bottles and the bones of the chili-spiced wings. I float until a jerked, pull-of-the-plug mid-song stops the Frank Sinatra vinyl. I float until the plastic American flags are torn down and tossed away to flap in the piles of trash.

I want to stay here forever in the nook of paradise, made up of make-believe and glamour. The five-year-old life, already laced with horrors, wants to stay in this storybook life.

Josie shakes out the chlorine from twisted hair with a familiar slur of her words. She shuffles me inside, past the plastic-like palm trees and into the dimly lit yellow ladies' room. She plops me on a floral sofa so plush that my small body sinks, and the gold-framed mirror hovers over at a contorted angle. Josie swivels like a swing-dance star through the room, touching up her painted face and changing into tight red leather pants to match her voluptuous, lined lips.

In a cab bound for home, Josie lights up a cigarette and puffs and puffs. But those red lips never utter a word. Instead, her spare hand pats my head the same way I stroke my Barbie dolls before I rip off their heads to see if there is anything inside.

"You go in, Anna baby, and get ready for bed. Josie has to see some friends down on Sunset," she asserts with a distinct Parisian snap, depicting herself as a distant character as we screech to a halt in front of the driveway. "Lolita will make you some dinner and run you a bath. I will be back before you know it."

I pause. I hate making that journey alone. It is not just the darkness. The driveway, the idea of an unlit trail that snakes to our house at the canyon's rim, prickles my nerves.

I slowly step out.

It isn't always, but sometimes a black shadow chases me down. I can feel it, grand and grotesque, like a hot breath burning my neck.

Most pronounced of all, I can smell it. Burning hair, rancid blood–the peculiar scent of a charred body. Its oversized head materializes, a vague silhouette on the pavement, and then the tiny frame. Even with limbs not mature enough to run, it comes for me. It comes for me in a way that climbs into the grooves of my brain. It is already waiting in the bushes by the driveway. I feel it; I smell it.

The cab is already turning to take Josie far from me. I cannot linger alone, still wrapped in a towel adorned with American flags and faded words of an American Dream.

I steel my jittery self and sprint down that driveway and toward that lonely mansion erected from the earth, a house so dark in the thickets of the canyon that I cannot make out a single light from a neighbor's window. Even the stars look dead above the gray stone architecture.

I run and run, hot vomit rising in my throat. It takes every ounce of my mind not to let the shadow drag me into the burgeoning fire, where the flames would lick until I surrender into a fetal position to die slowly.

For seconds that masquerade as minutes, I bang and prostrate myself against the locked door in abandon, hoping somehow my physique can bust it free. Lolita–my nanny and our ever-doting housekeeper–recoils at my panicked face and jumping legs when she eventually appears behind the heavy oak door.

I trip over the doormat, tumbling onto the toffee-colored carpet. Lolita's wobbling arms pull me up and into the groove of her chest. It is not the first hysterical episode and will surely not be the last.

"Oh Anna, my little petal," she whispers, pressing my face into her bountiful flesh. "You are a special one."

"The shadow," I gasp. "The shadow, Lolita."

The shadow dangles my sanity from its invisible mouth.

"It is only in your mind," Lolita assures me, strands of her silvery dark hair combing my lips. "The shadow is not real, my little green-eyed petal."

Lolita has green eyes too, but she blushes if I ever mention them.

"Green eyes can be a curse," she once said. "But yours, I will make sure yours are always protected."

Josie staggers in hours later, lipstick smeared across her lips like blood, her chipped pink nails clutching a small glass that smells more like cleaning products than water.

"Anna, you should be asleep," she hisses, spotting my wavy shadow hiding pathetically behind my bedroom curtain as she peers into my room.

Her body slumped against the door frame, Josie whimpers about the wrong child dying, wailing that I should not have been born, until Lolita, rattled and sweating, leads her into the sounds of a running shower.

Still wrapped in the curtain, I stare at the ceiling, afraid to turn the light off in case the shadow surfaces from the obscurity. I stare up with wide eyes, terrified to close them until Josie's moans wither into unconscious murmurs down the hall. Lolita tiptoes into my bedroom, saying nothing as she brushes out my long black hair and folds me into the giant waterbed.

"What did Josie mean?" I ask, just before our kiss goodnight, before the lamp goes out.

Lolita hesitates and then seems to retreat into a trance.

"It was before my time working for your father, but they said when Josie learned she had to go through with the pregnancy because it was too late. So, after giving up her ballet contract, she drank half a bottle of vodka and she fell down fire exit stairs," Lolita explains slowly, enunciating every word with an odd focus on articulation. "Splashing with a breathless, slow-motion thud onto every step."

Perhaps she thinks a small child cannot understand. Does Lolita want me to understand?

"Then the bleeding started," Lolita continues, eyes glazed. "And so did all the regret."

I envision Josie drowning at the bottom in a pool of blood that washed away all but none of her over-dramatized emotions.

"Did she kill another baby? Was I going to be a twin?" I ask. "Why was I never meant to be born?"

Lolita hesitates. And then she talks, and she does not stop.

Josie had screamed and commanded my father to relocate RUSCO and that they move far away. Josie wanted to live only in Hollywood with its all-year sunbeams and attractive people, as if to thrive in a bubble she would never feel the need to burst.

On the winding way, they rerouted through Las Vegas and, naturally, got hitched at the Little White Chapel. But, before their appointment time and even with a burgeoning belly, Josie drank a whole bottle of cheap Spanish wine, smoked a packet of cigarettes and wailed in the casino bathroom of Caesar's Palace. She persuaded my father to upend tradition and change his last name to hers when she eventually came out.

Paradis, she insisted, is far more alluring than Russell.

Smitten with her every ruthless demand and whipped into fear at the thought of losing his love, Bobby conceded. They never made that switch official. But Dad was a man of his word. As their child, I would be Paradis.

Lolita snaps out of a verbal trance, panic-stricken.

"You will upset Josie if you keep asking about this," Lolita says, wrapping my little hands into her flat fingers and dropping her voice. "Please, no more, sweet Anna. Josie just had a bad night."

Lolita leaves. I close my eyes. But I still remember.

Sometimes I wonder if life would be different if I were Anna Russell. How much is in a name? Would I have sought out a more mundane, straight-and-narrow existence if my name was more buttoned-up and less memorable?

Josie has often told me that the great prima ballerina Anna Pavlova, her favorite of the golden era, inspired my name. Like her, Josie continues, I will be a star. I nod enthusiastically.

Josie often dresses me up in sparkly tutu and tights and spends hours perfecting my hair and makeup. Then, whenever I think it will be the day, I will go to the stage. Only we never go anywhere. When I try to twirl, Josie's face falls.

"Stop. Stop right now," Josie demands, like a toddler throwing a tantrum over a forbidden cookie.

But once her flames subsided, she jingles her bracelets and continues, softer this time.

"Anna baby, you can be anything you want to be when you grow up," she coos. "But you are not a ballet girl, eh."

I pretend to be asleep on gallons of purified water, entangled in a web of satin sheets encased by a life that should feel safe. But I'm gutted with fear over being lost in the dark, sick over smelling a burned baby, and feeling like all this confusion and uncertainty will never end.

CHAPTER

TWO

As an only child, I find companionship in the sandalwood bookshelf in the attic study. I read and re-read all the classics, the children's books, the adult ones—anything I can get my hands on, even if the words are too big and the phrases too convoluted.

Before my tenth birthday, I discover Maurice Sendak's *Where the Wild Things Are,* as well as Sylvia Plath and Ernest Hemingway. I continue, over and over, to read Peter Pan. I learn author J.M Barrie's brother died in an ice-skating accident the day before his fourteenth birthday, and the idea of a child never growing old–of remaining frozen in time–was of great comfort to his mourning mother.

Lolita gave me the book for no special occasion, making me promise not to tell anyone. It is our little secret. Dad is hardly home now, and Josie is always dressed up and lost somewhere south of Sunset Boulevard.

I read *Helter Skelter: The True Story of the Manson Murders* by the lead prosecutor Vincent Bugliosi while hidden away in my attic bedroom when I am supposed to be at school. I don't care much about school. I don't care much for friends, sports, parties, or anything in between.

I am not well-known like the daughters of directors and rock stars. Nobody at school teases me, but I'm not popular either. Oil is the commodity that fuels the Porsche, of no worse or more significant standing than the salesman who closed their parents' deal when they upgraded. Each personality and net worth have a place within the Hollywood Hills, built upon layers of old mystic power.

Then beneath all the layers of characters, there is the core. The core is for all those who want to be left alone. That is okay, too. Nobody questions those who seek to be left alone.

In the attic, school library, or against the wallpaper of painted greenery at the Beverly Hills Hotel cabana, I love soaking in words and worlds of weird people who seek solace in something extraordinary. I love smelling pages that, to my young mind, are thousands of years old. And I love wrinkling the pages of a paperback as I read–the deeper I plunge into a book, the more pages are behind me to thicken the cackling noise.

Since I relegate death and despair to my imagination, they never disturb me. They are safe there. Those real moments, the ones outside my mind–of running up the steep driveway in the darkness and being too afraid to turn around–are the things I cannot safely hide in my head. Those are things I can never run from fast enough.

I read *Findings* by Leonard Bernstein. ". . . some say he never found his foothold . . ." In the next breath, I find old inscriptions by Bob Dylan and the poetry for "Mr. Tambourine Man" at the bottom of the return trolley swamp in my school library. I love the library, which smells of old air conditioning units and cheese sandwiches. Maybe other people sneak their cling-wrapped lunches inside too. If they do, I never see them. No one is ever hiding between the shelves but me.

That afternoon, as I finish the Dylan collection at home, burrowed beneath a desk lamp even though the sun washes over the attic study like a sprinkler, I decide, like Bob Dylan, I must learn an instrument.

An old rustic piano sits closed in the living room. I always thought it looked out-of-place, too special to sit among the floral lounge chairs and hefty fake ivy drapes and stacks of dusty vinyl. Yet, it has been here for as long as I can remember.

Lolita is the only person I know who can play a real instrument. The only other musician I have seen is the piano man in the Polo Lounge at the Beverly Hills Hotel, although I see others when I watch MTV with Josie on Saturday mornings. With a cigarette and her hair in rollers, she constantly raves about how she knows all these hotshots like Vince Neil and Madonna's backup dancers from her nights down the road at Sunset Strip's Whisky-a-Go-Go.

But Lolita is the only one I know.

Sometimes, when she thinks nobody is near, her thick fingers frolic along the keys that time has colored camel. She sometimes sings in this velvety language I do not understand, sending chills across my skin like freckles.

"Anna darling, I don't have time to teach you," Lolita says that afternoon when I first ask to learn, looking a little sheepish that I discovered her hidden talent. "I don't think Josie wants me to teach you."

But I persist, sending her paper planes with phrases like "the answer, my friend, is blowin' in the wind" across the room after supper for several nights. Then one evening, when Josie is out in the world, she relents, telling me airily about when she was a little girl in the woods somewhere far away.

"My father came back with an old piano, and I listened to the notes of the wild parakeets, their voices floating up and down," Lolita whispers.

By the time we have the second lesson a few days later, my undisciplined mind is already bored. Instead of pleading to play, I beg to look inside the piano as Lolita plays, fascinated by the inner workings.

"Look, each little hammer has its own string, and it vibrates! Do you see this? Lolita," I shriek in delight. "Have you seen the way the hammer hits the strings?"

Ahead of the upcoming third lesson for the following week, Lolita promises me that I can look inside that magnificent beast again and examine those hammers at a closer angle. It will be my reward after I memorize the keys for "Ode to Joy."

We only ever have those two lessons. I wake up early on the day of our planned third session to the rustle of banging doors and the tremor of a truck in the driveway. I watch through the bay window as the old rustic piano is loaded and carted away. Josie grunts in French and supervises the removal like a bulldog in her fuchsia pink robe. Somehow, she found out about the lessons.

It may remind her too much of those ballet days and the grail she had left behind. Or is she scared I will be good at something? Too good?

Two nights later, Josie creeps into my room as I am half-sleeping and draws the blinds–shutting out the shards of night light–before sitting on the edge of my bed in pitch black.

"Take your nightgown off," she orders, her finger pressing into my breastbone. "And put this on."

As my eyes adjust, I can barely make out the deep red bodice made mostly of lace, with asymmetrical strips of glowing organza. I do not understand for a moment, and then comes the whiff of age. The sweet, musty smell of something abandoned long ago.

"My first company performance," Josie says flatly. "Now, your turn. You must learn elegance, my Anna, to be something better."

I flick on the fairy lights that loop over the brass bedhead like a never-ending Christmas, pull my nightgown over my head, and change into the teeny costume. It fits like a glove. I dissect myself in the full-length mirror, transformed, transfixed. Josie's eyes bore into me from behind. Through the reflection, I can see she isn't smiling. She isn't proud that it fits so immaculately.

"Okay, Anna, get it off," Josie flares suddenly. "Now."

The pendulum of moods might have disturbed most children. I do not flinch, but I shrug. I also idle for a few seconds, wanting to rebel against the routine paradoxes, wanting to leap across the room, somehow proving my innate, untapped skill.

I take it off without a word, ripping open the weak seam until it is almost a two-piece. I toss it to the floor and haul myself back beneath the covers.

Glaring at the broken costume with sadness, Josie doesn't say a word either.

Two days later, she disappears.

Josie rises breathlessly and early one Monday morning–dressed like Farrah Fawcett in a white pantsuit almost the same color as her drained face–and then climbs into a black helicopter. It hovers low for a few minutes in the backyard, then chops up and through the Los Angeles smog.

Lolita, who usually clucks her tongue and nods whenever–or however–Josie flitters from home, swallows stress with every breath. There is something different this time.

I sit at the foot of the stairs, watching Lolita's silhouette make endless phone calls to all the bars, cafes, and clubs Josie frequents. I listen to her yell to nobody in particular that this is not Josie's normal departure.

"What if they take Anna away?" Lolita sobs to herself, scarfing down chunks of pound cake.

After she leaves the kitchen in a frantic shuffle, I also grab a fistful of cake, savoring how sweet the fresh cream tastes on my tongue. My comfort. My acquired taste. My secret. From that moment.

Dad returns home the following afternoon with a suitcase in tow, a suitcase he never bothers to unpack. He keeps it by the front door by his shiny black handcrafted boots, ready to run when the ring comes.

"I've hired the best to find her, so far nothing," he hisses to Lolita when he thinks I was outside. "You better work harder to sort this out."

Lolita tapes a number for pizza delivery to the fridge and announces she is off to find Josie.

"Someone has got to get Josie," Lolita weeps before she leaves.

There is a maternal concern, of course. But I sense something more profound than that. Something larger feels at stake. A flight risk. A woman who could leap without looking or kiss and then tell. I should have been confused. But my childhood is confusing. It makes sense for nothing to make sense.

Then it is just us. Dad Saigon stomps and makes that head-tilting gesture I understand to be a signal to hop into his Corvette for a whirl to the Beverly Hills Hotel. The distraction. The rescue. Where all is green and pink, pretty and perfect, but I have another idea. Josie is not here, and I am sickly scared and excited.

I beg my father to take me to a windowless dance studio in the basement of a Rodeo Drive shoe store.

"Just this once," he mutters, eyes rimmed with too much exhaustion to argue.

Can I prove to Josie that I am a ballet girl? Perhaps I could be good enough to be proud of but not quite good enough to be better than her.

Dad drops me off at my first ballet class, and I hate it.

I curse when I can't tie the ribbons on those floppy canvas shoes the teacher loaned me. I pout when I have to look at myself in the mirror, and I curse when my bun pins fly because Dad had not known how to do my hair correctly. He just bunched it all up and stuck pins into my scalp, spreading soap across the top instead of hairspray. It is all wrong.

I curse because I know at once that I never want to return to that class. My chapter on talent closes before it ever opens.

Lolita returns to the Mulholland Drive house a day later, bearing lots of "everything is fine" variations to Dad, even though her face sags with sweaty wrinkles. Every time the doorbell chimes, she freezes, her face ashen. Nobody answers when I ask where Josie is—nobody knows, or they do not want to know. Or they do not want me to know.

Dad grows more distant with every hour she is gone, more agitated, his mind drifting further away.

Then, poof.

Josie returns a week after she boarded the helicopter. She wafts through the door in a wispy yellow sundress, with a proverbial halo balanced over her much shorter blonde bob. The word rehab springs up in a few conversations over the next few days. She assures me she no longer drinks; her nights on the Sunset Strip are over, and she vows to become a better wife and mother.

I have never seen my parents show affection toward each other. But that night, over Lolita's handmade pasta and basil sauce, and when Josie thinks no one is looking, she grazes her hand with his–Dad does not resist. Their secret affection is safe.

Dad takes off again less than sixteen hours later. It is as though nothing had even happened, as though Josie had never vanished and miraculously reappeared all shiny and new.

Soon, she starts joining him on occasional overseas work trips. Neither explains where they are going, other than Dad has big projects spanning the globe. I do not mind the mystery. It is as though I live in the confines of a thriller that will all unwind when it is supposed to, and if I don't ask them questions, they don't ask me questions either. The characters of my adolescent mind are unhindered.

On my brooding bookshelf, somewhere between my eleventh and twelfth birthdays, with wild hair and mood rings on every finger, I find the Bible. Yet the only part I learn by heart is the Ecclesiastes . . . "a time to plant and a time to uproot, a time to be born and a time to die . . ." We don't attend church regularly, and only ever when Dad is home. And still, it is rare, sporadic, and never planned. Maybe only when Dad really needs it. Lolita would drag me early from Sunday slumbers, with the pillow still impressed into my cheeks, and wriggle me into stockings and a smocked dress. Then, off we would go into the beachside morning mist.

I am uncomfortable singing in public. And still self-conscious of what Josie might do there. In the days before the black helicopter took her away, she would almost go back for a second–a third, or fourth sip of sweet wine from the priest, igniting stares and whispers from the wide-eyed faces through the pews.

But every time I step inside that lovely, old St. Monica's Cathedral in

Santa Monica–where Josie likes to stand behind Arnold Schwarzenegger–I fall again for the ritual of lighting candles. My fantastical notion of disseminating light into the dark world is born, and I marvel at how the tangerine glow seems to wash over everything around it.

Soon after I memorize that passage, "a time to be born and die," Dad orders us all back to the charming church near the sea. Rather than the hymns, the flickering illumination across the sidewall, all those candles clumped in a burning cluster grab my attention. Inhaling the scent of old wax and lemons, I breathe a sickening whiff of leather tanning over a fire, the human body baking, cries drowned out by the choir's hymns.

A fire, the fire–it could start at any interlude; it is starting. Soon, it will be too late.

"What about the baby? Would it burn too? Why didn't God save it?" I squeak out, turning to the old Sister who stands behind my father, her back bent crookedly in deep prayer.

The old Sister cocks her head in confusion, glaring at me and then glaring at Dad–his eyes blistering into his leather-capped western boots, Saigon-lilted to one side, unable to return her gaze.

"What baby?" Sister asks, eyes darting between both my father and me.

I glance back at the fire, now just candles twitching blandly in the sallow light.

Dad does not answer, and neither do I. I know it is the same baby that chases me like a tornado down the gloomy driveway, the same enkindled infant that visits on odd occasions and constantly cries in my mind, dying but not dead. Dad knows about the baby that only I can see. He knows of the nightmares and visions, but he never tries to tell me it isn't real like Lolita and Josie do.

I storm out into the Sunday sunshine, jumping over the church's side barricade, and never return to that House of God. I even give it the mood-ringed middle finger as I wander off and rip off that knee-length violet tulle dress to reveal a punkish mini skirt bouncing over my unshaven legs.

Those steely hairs are the ugliest sight north of 90210. I need to start shaving.

On my twelfth birthday, I discover the erotic Roman elegies of Johann Wolfgang von Goethe. And after that, I notice how men stare at me—the strangers in the bakery or the rockers at the hotel, who tell me that long black hair, green eyes and long, pale legs are unique in the bleach and tan tumble of Tinseltown.

"Get your towel, little," Dad asserts after I emerge from the Beverly Hills Hotel pool, still in my childhood bikini a size too small for a protruding chest. The few cigar-smoking men nearby must have said something to arouse an angry demeanor.

"Cover the heck up, now," he growls in a way I had never heard before. "And put your sunglasses on. Cover your eyes."

I reach forward to grab one of the cotton terry Turkish towels, planning to stamp off in a huff over being told what to do, dashing inside the lovely ladies' room with its soft lamps, gold mirrors, and rosemary soap to melt with embarrassment. But instead, like a woman has possessed my adolescent body, I wring out my dripping lush hair. I tilt my backside a little farther to widen the gap between my pencil legs and accentuate the high cut of my zebra-print bikini. I grab a hand towel to wrap only around my neck and strut slowlytoward the cabana as if on a catwalk, copying Naomi Campbell in the Versace fashion shows on TV that Josie loves to watch.

I do not dare meet my father's harsh stare.

Until now, I have always felt like a blundering girl who blends into backgrounds and behind book covers. But, in the dawn of my teenage years, it's not necessarily the need for attention that overcomes me, but the desire to feed a growing fire. A desire to go against the grain, a part of me that knows something is missing. Secrets are hidden in the hills, far from Mulholland Drive.

It is my thirteenth birthday when I find the book that will impact the woman I am becoming: oil and blood, a match and an extinguisher.

This is the *Book of Tucana*: the land where life was first born, where the sun first touched the earth.

THREE

The last Tuesday of November 1995. Nothing much happens on Tuesdays. Except this is my first proper day as a teenager. I am getting ready to go to school, intending to attend my first few classes, leave before lunch, and hide out at a café on Melrose with the new Joan Didion book. The school is increasingly sending home letters regarding my absences, which Lolita discards with a sympathetic nod.

There are times when the administrative office calls to speak with my parents. With Josie's extended work stints with Dad, neither are home. Those calls and letters never phase me. What are my parents going to do? They are not home to punish me, and Lolita avoids ever making me worried or upset. All she wants is to cook for me and soothe me with tight hugs that are starting to become annoying.

So here I am on that birthday morning in a Rodeo Drive-type rapture, delving into my mother's extensive wardrobe, pressing the padded fabrics and scents of designer goods against me. I find a pair of her silky, cream short shorts, the kind the dancers would have worn to Whisky-a-Go-Go on the Sunset Strip on a Friday night. I slip them on beneath my baggy jeans so that when I make it across town to the café, I can easily shed a layer, perhaps catch the attention of the tattooed types with tangled hair, who hang out discussing Zeppelin and Chris Cornell.

I think of Josie in patent leather Jimmy Choos tottering around the pool's edge at the Beverly Hills Hotel, men making no effort to avert their gaze from her svelte ballerina body with that disproportionate bosom. I should want that, shouldn't I? Josie sheds layers like a snake when my father isn't around. It is just what women do. Isn't it?

I clutch a fistful of her costume bangles and stroke the little mounds of brass and color, opting for just one dainty gold bracelet that I secure around my wrist. But as I turn to walk from the wardrobe, the twinkle of something else cloaked in jewelry catches my eye. A glint of metal pings onto the light and sends sparks across the ceiling as if the room is on fire.

I edge closer, afraid that if I move too fast, the little room will erupt in a fireball of fury.

But here, immersed in clashing gold and rose gold, is a tiny, sterling silver handgun, elegantly camouflaged. Touching it launches electricity through my spine. I caress it, remembering what it is to have it nuzzle my scalp as if tucked into my father's waistband. Fingertips at first, and then my whole palm presses into the shaft. The muzzle smothers my cheek, dragging down my skin to my lips, running across the peaks as though applying lip gloss. I smell it, inhaling a deep whiff from its insides, my nose petting the trigger, the curved metal hook skirting my nostrils: rustic, charcoal, wood fire, blood, smoking tires, pine trees, sulfur.

I glare down the sculptured cylinder of the muzzle merely an inch from my eyes, intrigued, into the vacuous hole for several supple seconds. I am waiting for something to burst up at me, like a spider that spasmodically bounces up from the toilet bowl and hooks on for the bite.

Tick, tick, the strikes of the old clock rebounds against my ears.

I grip the trigger, my head elevating–lighter and lighter–drifting into a dream. The black hole stares back at me. My Revlon-chipped fingernail curls around the polished strip of metal, easing it back as if manipulating the crescent moon.

That pull, that tug, that slow-motion drag. The ceiling starts to cave in. My brain floats out–rising pensively over my lithe frame, mesmerized by the girl with a gun pointed to her face dotted with little specks of sunshine, finger firm on the trigger.

Pulling . . . pulling . . . pulling . . . silence . . . *SNAP.*

My head jolts, and my mind blasts back into my skull. The pistol tumbles from my limp hand, thudding onto the wooden stool before plunging into the plush carpet.

I gasp, my hand flying to wipe the fluids from my face. The sticky substance that clings to my fingers is not blood. It is sweat. I drop to the floor, panting, trying to make sense of what just happened and how quickly the mind can leave the body. But nothing had transpired other than the weapon slipping from my fingers and hitting the floor. I touch my limbs, still intact. I smile, invincible, exhilarated. I touch up my moist brow with a dash of translucent powder, throw on my beloved lipstick, and toss that silver metal ornament into my denim backpack. It feels safe to me, somehow.

"Good morning, Anna," Lolita sings, enveloping me in a tight hug as I scramble into the entryway. I kneel, hauling my feet into my beloved floral Dr. Martens boots. Then I see it. The little room, flooded with morning light, illuminates a small ceramic statue of two cherubs that nearly blends into the blush wall, wedged into the corner beside the heavy oak door.

Twins? Twin cherubs? How did I miss that statue before? Is it new? I tread closer. The cherub eyes. They stare back at me.

I jump. Lolita is behind me, her warm hand on my shoulder.

"That was in my home as a little girl," she says wistfully, staring at the delicate ceramic before I can even pose a question. "One of the few things I brought when your dad flew me here to work. I keep it in the garage. Josie doesn't like it. But she is away for a little longer . . ."

I don't like it either. But I am mesmerized by how piercing the eyes are–open like the dead have open eyes–riddled in shock as it all ends.

"Happy Birthday, sweetheart," Lolita says, yanking me from my statue fixation and into her motherly embrace. "Growing up so smart and beautiful."

That's right. I had almost forgotten. I am officially a teenager.

Lolita's hug lingers, her overbearing bosom pushing into my more un-developed chest. Her hand travels down to my backpack, drawing me even closer, and I freeze. The gun. The hug is too tight, too long. Her stubby palm pushes harder and harder, resting apathetically onto the cold alloy rubbing the small of my back, clenched into a hardball. Can she feel the gun? What if she finds it? Or worse, what if she–

I hold my breath and count one, two –

Lolita abruptly releases, looking into me with tears welling as I let out a sigh of relief.

"Anna baby, look at you all grown up," she continues softly, touching my nose. "A young woman now, smart and so independent. You have sur-vived so much, so much."

Lolita spins me, so we both face the mirror behind us. She strokes my cheek, smoothing back the wisps of hair falling into my eyes. It feels like a Brothers Grimm moment of pondering my fairness and my fallibility: mirror, mirror.

"The men will offer you wine and try to win your heart but bury it, Anna. Don't let them catch you into their dream," Lolita murmurs, still staring at my reflection. "Catch them into your dream; only let the special ones see those green eyes."

I smile shyly at her. Then her voice lowers.

"When someone hugs you, you still hold your breath," Lolita observes. "Breathe. I will not let anyone hurt you, my girl."

I head off to school with a bit of reluctance. At the shriek of the lunch-time bell, I jump over the fence, peel off a layer, and hop on the bus bound for Melrose–showing off my springy legs in those teeny cream shorts. While sitting on the alfresco café seat, I notice him staring intensely across the terrace–his gaze never veering.

Him. Attention. A stranger. An alluring stranger. Prey or predator? It doesn't matter.

I laugh. I laugh like Josie. Then he stands up slowly. Luke Perry meets a

Hell's Angel with a twist of Kurt Cobain. He casually plops beside me, his thick notepad knocking against my espresso, eyes adverting to my shiny, shaven legs in the sunshine.

It is that easy.

"Anna," I say nervously, extending one hand and using the other to remove my sunglasses so he can shoot his daggers into my emerald eyes.

I caress the cheap notebook coated in his messy cursive.

"I'm writing a new song," he mumbles, waving a sculpted, tattooed arm toward that chunky file of notes on the table. "When we make the music video, maybe you can be in it."

"I don't act," I declare, leaning forward, not breaking my gaze.

"I can teach you," the mystery man replies, not breaking his gaze either. "We can start now."

He jumps up, chugs down the remainder of my expresso in one potent gulp, scoops up his notes and keys, and tilts his head for me to follow. I do so without hesitation.

I am a teenager now, after all.

Without a single transfer of words, I climb on the back of the imposing gunmetal black Harley Davidson and lean against his dirty white cotton shirt; my arms wrangle around his tapered waist. We roar and weave through the dense Los Angeles traffic, my hair erratically blowing in the beach breeze as we etch closer to Venice Beach. It is early afternoon, and the sun is just beginning to stab through the veneer of Westside gloom.

He—the man whose name I still do not know—leads me inside a small, lightless studio fastened below a string of tattoo parlors and souvenir shops along the iconic boardwalk. A thin mattress, crumpled clothes, empty beer bottles, and old pizza boxes cover the rest of the room.

There is no time to shed my backpack or loosen up before he shoves me against the wall harder than I anticipated—an aggressive kiss and his tongue all over mine. For all my posturing, I have never even kissed a boy before. His tongue feels captivating, then disgusting, and while riddled with nerves, I do not want it to stop. Schoolbooks poke into my spine, and my blouse rips open, like a movie scene defined as heat and passion.

"Amy, just don't tell me how old you are," the mystery man mutters, his voice so deep and husky. His sweat deluges into my pores. Before I can correct him on my name, he reaches down to my silky cream waistband, his firm hand ready to rip it off. He wrests me from the wall and pushes me down onto the mattress, and then–

BANG.

A firecracker explodes into my eardrums, a lilt through the air, his body paralyzed over mine. For a second or two, the intensity ushers in a surreal ecstasy. I see it before I feel it: his hand is covered in wine-red; and deep red splatters abstractly over his crisp white shirt.

"Oh no," I whisper hazily. "That is going to be hard to clean."

"That was a gunshot," he croaks, eyes bulging as he heaves himself off me.

A hole has ripped through the base of the faded denim backpack, charging down and grazing through the silky cream. Now, a trickle so warm and sticky weeps from my left bottom cheek–a small casing and the grazed bullet blushed red beside it.

I wriggle up my shorts, somehow trying to preserve whatever dignity remains, smearing a larger pool of burning red liquid across the creamy material. Oh shit. This stain will be too hard to clean, and Josie will kill me for ruining her clothes. And that tear, will Lolita be able to sew it up and make it look as though nothing happened?

Numbness. More numbness.

Boom. I feel it. Did he pinch me? Damn. I still do not know the guy's name. The agony of a hundred wasps stinging into my backside so savagely I want to vomit. The muscles in my legs are contracting and trembling uncontrollably before my eyes.

"It wasn't me!" the man with the husky voice suddenly screeches like a high-pitched child. "I didn't do it!"

I slowly sit up, dropping my fastened backpack from my shoulders, the fabric at the bottom now blown to bits. In slow motion, I crawl on my hands and knees onto the muddy boardwalk, the horrified faces of tourists, surfers and skaters, and the Jamaican drum circle staring back at me like a mosaic in a hazy horror movie. Or a crazy carnival by the bay. There it is–the burning baby. The hollow-eyed infant scalds beneath the short shadows of a winter afternoon, mouth open in a final plea for air. Too far gone for any sound to come out.

Choking on my anguish, I reach for the inflamed flesh–

When I wake up, I wake up draped in necklaces of pearly white tubes and bright lights. A woman in a white coat stands over me, lips pursed in a half-smile.

"Anna Paradis," she says, touching my shoulder, not bothering to wait for me to stutter out some inquiries of confusion. "Anna, you are at Saint John's Hospital in Santa Monica because you suffered a gunshot in the backside earlier this afternoon. My name is Dr. Amanda Cohen; call me Amanda. Or even Mandy, if you would prefer. I'm taking care of you."

"What? How?" I stammer.

Amanda smiles fully this time, squeezing my hand.

"That's why some people will come by tomorrow morning and talk to you. But for the rest of the night, the only thing you need to be concerned about is resting," she continues. "You will be fine; the wound is superficial and missed any major tendons or nerves. The muscle tissue will take a little time to repair, but you should be back to normal in a few weeks with some care and quiet time."

I pause, trying to drink in the enormity.

"Try not to overthink right now, Anna, and get some more sleep. Your nanny is in the waiting room, but I have urged her to go home and get some rest," Amanda says. "It might take a day for your parents to get here, given that they are in Cyra and the airport has been closed with the unrest.

But they are chartering a flight out, so don't worry. They should be here by tomorrow afternoon. I spoke to your dad a couple of hours ago and assured him you are doing well and will be fine."

Wait. Cyra? As in the capital of Tucana? My mind dashes back to some chatter in history class that I didn't pay much attention to—an island in the Middle East that had broken away from the Syrian border long ago. My parents are in Cyra? I had heard names like London or Dubai as passing places, but Cyra?

"Would you like to speak to them? I can arrange a call if you would like," Amanda offers. "Lolita is also still here; I can tell her to come in and see you if you feel up to it. Everyone is worried about you, Anna."

I shake my head, bubbling with an accelerated flood of shame and intrigue.

"Can I get you anything before I leave for the night, Anna?" Amanda asks.

"Yes," I reply hurriedly. "I would like to read . . .you know, I love books about faraway places and would like something on Tucana, seeing as though it is such a big part of our family's life."

Amanda discreetly taps my hand.

"Anna, I can't always fulfill every patient's request, but I can fulfill that one," she responds as if stamping an imaginary badge of satisfaction on her shoulder. "One of our former doctors here just left to volunteer in Tucana. Out in the villages, I believe. He read incessantly about it before going and left a few books on his desk."

Amanda returns with *The Book of Tucana* and a United Nations guidebook on Tucana. There is no author listed, but it is filled with pictures, historical data, and stories of the governing family, the Amsa family.

As the lights in the hallway dim and the conversations in the corridor dissipate, the dull pain in my left side almost subsides as I switch on the bedside lamp. I open to the first page and plummet into a rabbit hole, into *The Book of Tucana.*

CHAPTER
FOUR

The rumbles of a morning storm and the humiliating blot of the past twenty-four hours dip to the wayside as my mind swaddles in the lore and legend of Tucana. This existence is so far away, yet so alive. I devour every word, every fact, every anecdote a little at a time–scribbling alongside the volunteering doctor's notes.

As *The Book of Tucana* informs me in long-winded passages and effervescent descriptions, the country is an island sculpted from the land where all civilization sprang to life. There are scattered villages and one lovely big city called Cyra, a cross-section of the world's wealthiest and those who will forever roam and work with their hands on mountain tops and tiny villages.

Foreigners discovered the largest proven crude oil reserves, virgin and unexploited, in Tucana during the great oil boom of the 1970s. In 1977, the long-running King died of old age, conflict broke out in the family as to who was the rightful heir to the throne, prompting the United Nations to intervene. The bloated bureaucrats installed the well-spoken General Rian Amsa as the "caretaker" President, impressed by his willingness to work closely with the West and his almost impossibly full academic degrees and credentials. The book claims this military man retired to become an astrophysicist and polyglot and that he speaks Arabic, French, English, Aramaic, the dialect of Jesus Christ and, of course, the native language of

Rasa. Eventually, the term "caretaker" withered away, and General Amsa took the reins for good.

Dollars from the West had flooded into the petroleum-teeming Tucana. Especially Cyra, which, at a dizzying speed in the early 1980s, evolved into a mecca where old meets new, and gold meets hard cash; where open-air markets meet massive malls, and where mud huts meet hotels dripping in diamonds and Michelin star restaurants.

The UN is a little more brash in its assessment. The President General, as he insists on being called, initially welcomed international development and investment. That was until he realized that keeping it almost entirely state-owned would reap more rewards. He would first win the game of public perception, convincing Tucanese that outsiders exploit their resources, and then swoop in to save the nation's soul. But, of course, it would also be a substantial victory for his personal wealth, an unencumbered ability to siphon off government revenue. So the politically connected rich get richer; the poor get weaker. The Palace grants a few well-positioned foreigners permission to explore and extract every year, and only if they serve the state.

Every few years since 1977, even with government-subsidized healthcare, education, and food rations for Tucanese families, there is a dust-up between the powerful and the poor, whose standardized salaries continue to slip more and more below the basic poverty line. When gas prices rise and baskets don't contain enough bread to feed a family, the impoverished and enraged assemble like an informal militia to protest the President-General.

They wear bandanas and carry hand-painted signs with the words "freedom fighter," chanting for Amsa to step down and allow them to cast their votes. Military forces sometimes retaliate by shooting bullets into the air. In other instances, bullets are fired directly into their bodies. And then some are dragged off into ambiguity, only to emerge again at their hanging in Cyra Square.

By contrast, according to *The Book of Tucana*, the island is "falsely" considered a totalitarian hereditary dictatorship by the international community. Indeed, Amsa family members vehemently deny this accusation, citing the periodic elections and stressing how much the President General is loved, typically scoring at least 99.2 percent of all votes. Although I don't know who or what the international community is, I do come to believe that Tucana is an unbeautiful and incredibly beautiful place—a metaphor of extremes, a mirror to my contradictions.

"Anna, we would like to speak to you," a voice outside says sternly, yanking me away from thoughts of alleyways made of ancient stone and smells of freshly turned earth. For some reason, I shove the books behind my pillow, my subconscious secret, and wipe the pebbles of sleep from my sleepless eyes as two uniformed police officers enter with notepads in hand.

The men introduce themselves as Frank and Gary, ask how I am doing and announce they have just a few questions about what went down a day earlier on the Venice boardwalk.

"I thought it was just a replica, a gift Josie saved for my dad," I explain nervously. "I found it in the jewelry box. I thought nothing more of it. It was my birthday, so I wanted to leave school early for a sea breeze, sat down on the boardwalk and bang. A terrible accident."

The more I emphasize my recklessness and sheer devotion to the well-being of others, the less the officers quiz me. And the more sympathetic they become to my plight.

"Thankfully, only I was hurt," I ramble, faking something akin to a cry. "I could never have lived with myself had I harmed someone else."

The officers stop writing, and one of them, I think it is Frank with a curly mustache like an immutable frown, pats my shoulder and looks at me once over with warm eyes. But I am just getting started, reveling in my performance.

"God was watching over me," I stammer, turning up the theatrics a touch. "However, I will walk away with the life lesson never to touch a gun, not even what I think isn't a real gun."

Frank pats me again as if I am a three-legged dog and declares the case closed–swallowed, hook, line, and sinker. Gary, a little grayer with a belly bulging over his holster, nods.

"Well, we know you live on Mulholland Drive. We know you folks living up there in the misty hills all need to protect yourselves," he says, trying to convince himself that there is nothing more they should know. "We ran the serial, and it is a legal gun belonging to your mother. Of course, it is a mad world out there, but your folks should tell you it ain't a toy, some Hollywood prop."

Life is easier when it is fantasy, I think, my mind transcending at a dizzying speed through the pretend red carpet at the Beverly Hills Hotel, through the Corvette drives toward the hills that slouch toward the Santa Monica seas and then up the winding hills to our home, our home that looks out over the city that sparkles like a permanent Christmas tree.

"Oh, Anna," Josie suddenly shrieks, flying into the room and to my bedside.

She kisses me on the head and theatrically inspects my bandages before turning to the police with a polished smile. She shakes their hands and thanks them for coming, her voice dripping like syrup, asking if they have any further queries.

Gary twitches his mustache as he shakes his head, clearly mesmerized by her thick coating of Elizabeth Arden perfume.

"No, ma'am," he replies. "No further action is needed at this time. However, please properly store all firearms in the home so this doesn't happen again."

The officers wish us both well and then depart. With the sight of their backs, Josie's posture transforms from slightly tilted toward me to upright and stiff. Lolita and Dad enter sheepishly. Lolita shuffles behind him, hunched over, perhaps worried she will face retribution for what arose.

We all sit in the uncomfortable pit of our thoughts for a while, unsure which of those thoughts we want to fuse with articulation. Josie glances over at the fresh bouquet Lolita brought me. Her face softens for a few seconds. Then, she pushes her shoulders back like a swan-necked dancer, eyes suddenly shellacked as if staring into a blinding stage light.

"I used to get flowers–opening night. Your father . . ." Josie's words trail off. She bites her bottom lip. "You brought these, Lolita? Anna does not need flowers. She does not need rewards for misbehavior," Josie snarks, stopping herself from an outburst as the nurse enters, carrying a tray with some soapy-looking rice dish, a banana, and juice that I immediately push aside.

"You have to eat, Anna," Josie states, mild irritation creeping into her jet-lagged yawn. "You won't heal without nutrition."

Lolita offers to bring me something home-cooked or to pick up the chopped salad I love from the Polo Lounge in the Beverly Hills Hotel, or a burger from Jerry's Diner in Westwood.

"That won't be necessary," Josie snarls, striding over to my bedside, where she begins braiding my hair so roughly that I wince. "She can eat the food we're paying for here."

Lolita stares mournfully at me, the whites of her grass green eyes as red as her flushed cheeks. She backs away slowly as Josie demands she follow her out the door. Dad, arms folded in the corner, stomps over after they leave. Saigon stomps.

I want him to get angry, yell at me, and react in some way. He barely frowns. The cowboy hat casts sinister shadows under his eyes, contouring his sun-tanned complexion.

"I'm sorry, little. I know everybody likes to shoot . . . but nobody likes to get shot," he says dryly, looking through me, not at me.

I stay for a few more days at Saint John's Hospital, immersed in the seductive but bruised copy of *Tucana*. Once I finish those books, Dr. Amanda quietly ventures out to Barnes & Noble on her tea break and buys me more:

a Rasa language guide, an in-depth history of Middle Eastern wars and rulers, and an overview of Tucana's religion which I learn is a melting pot of Christians, Zoroastrians, Muslims, and Buddhists.

Then, under my bedcovers at home, I recuperate for several more weeks. I slowly walk again, the stitches in my butt cheek self-dissolving. I am almost myself again–maybe an inch taller and a few pounds lighter. But my head feels much heavier, swimming with my new, quiet dedication to a faraway place.

Like a boomerang, Dad flies off on a plane, comes home, and goes again. Thanksgiving arrives, but Josie instructs Lolita not to prepare a turkey feast because she is on Madonna's newfangled vegetarian cleanse and does not want the temptation.

December rolls in, and the days grow darker. Los Angeles is cold. They don't tell you it gets cold in Hollywood movies. Josie and Dad are fighting again.

We attend Bob Seger's holiday party in a private room at the Beverly Hills Hotel. I assume Dad knows him from whisky nights in the Polo Lounge. I sit quietly in the back, observing the expanse of tuxedos and swinging dresses swish before me as their well-dressed offspring wait in line for the fake Santa Claus photos.

The night is only getting started, the ballroom filling with famous people drinking champagne in flutes and glancing over one another's shoulder for the next person to rub elbows with when Dad declares we are leaving.

"Those two men not drinking near the stage," I overhear him mutter to Josie. "I've seen them before. At the airport lounge, down the bottom of Mulholland Drive, at Tony Romo's café garden on a random day."

It is the first time I have seen the Bobby Paradis mask crack just a little–he stomps a little more heavily than usual, and I worry his shaking leg will buckle beneath him.

Dad proclaims again that we are leaving.

Josie rolls her eyes.

"You're losing it, Bobby," she responds curtly, sauntering calmly toward coat check to collect her giant mink wrap.

Then her black-rimmed eyes, like an owl's, swivel to me.

"Both of you," Josie snaps as I limp over. "Well, Anna, baby. I can see who you got your imaginary friends from now."

This is the first time Josie ever acknowledges my fears with words, the burned baby that twists in my mind at the strangest of places and oddest of times.

"I don't have imaginary friends," I protest, lowering my voice so as not to cause a scene in a happy place.

What I see is real. I am so sure of it, even if nobody else can see the charred child.

I try to block out Dad and Josie's bickering that night, drowning it out with my Discman and books below the duvet.

"Fine, Bobby, I will tell you. But if I tell you–I kill you, or you leave," Josie shrieks.

As sunlight splays through the cracked window, I rub my eyes groggily and throw off the covers. I take for granted the gurgling of the waterbed fluids, unaware it would be the last time I hear them. At some point amid the darkness and the daylight, two giant crocodile skin suitcases–red-trimmed with a red ribbon–were placed at the foot of my bed.

It is weeks too soon for Christmas morning. My eyes gallop around for a note or card or–

"*She's awake, Robert . . . Seren bi vada eki,*" squeaks Lolita's voice, tempered with tiny weeps, near the half-opened door.

I'll handle it.

"Oh, *seren bi vada ek,*" Dad hisses back.

No, I'll handle it.

Dad knocks, and I welcome him inside.

"*Sera siana,*" I state flatly. *I understand.*

My ability to recognize Rasa, the native tongue of the Tucanese, should surprise him. His eyebrows do not even arch.

Had he even noticed?

"It isn't even taught to the kids there anymore. It's all English. It's all-new Tucana," Dad notes, flicking off the language exchange as he would a fly on a glass of Scotch.

Dad crosses his arms and swings his foot over the other, leaning against the doorframe, his hulking figure a configuration in the dull light. Stoic. Unafraid.

"Little, you can't go back to school. They won't have you at Beverly Hills High because of the whole bringing-a-gun-to-school-in-your-backpack thing," he says, choosing his words carefully. "I'm off so much and have little business left here in the U.S. Josie is helping with things more and more, and I need Lolita to start coming on some business trips too and going back to her assistant duties. You're old enough now not to need her."

He tugs his hat down farther, trying to hide his eyes.

"It's too much for her to take care of you all the time," Dad elaborates. "So tonight, I'll fly with you to boarding school in New York; check you in before I continue flying on again. You will have lots to do and people around you."

As my father's words wilt away, so does any sadness or surprise.

I have no friends I am leaving behind. Nobody at school ever pays much attention to me or acknowledges my ascending tendency to dismember the rules or lock myself so intently into other worlds real Hollywood life could never penetrate. Is "real Hollywood" an oxymoron, anyway?

New York City, I think. *Freedom. Real freedom.*

I trifle through my closet, flinging my most precious items into the suitcases.

"Are you going to Cyra?" I ask loosely, realizing it is the first time I have questioned my father directly about his work ventures.

He pauses, straightens his posture, then nods.

"I have a lot of business there now, little. It's booming with oil," he replies, with what I detect as mild pride. "Bigger and bigger every day. The only foreigner allowed by their government to stay."

I smile, also realizing that this is the longest my father and I have conversed with honesty, just the two of us in a room exchanging life.

"I would like to visit there someday," I press on. "It seems like an interesting place."

Again, Dad looks through me—no "yes," but no "no" either.

"When it's safe and steady enough, I will try to send you a ticket," he fumbles. "Regardless, we will have to meet somewhere outside of here."

"Why?" I probe.

Dad stomps forward and pivots to face me as if prickled by my raised eyebrows.

"I must stay there in Tucana for good this time. It's too risky coming back," my father states, his voice lowering as though he is talking to himself and not me. "Be packed and ready by 5:00 p.m."

Lolita chokes up, her face like a balloon trying not to burst into hysterics as I drag my bags down the stairs. In an act of self-flagellation, she strikes herself softly with both hands on her right temple.

Dad glowers, evidently angry at her act of unbridled emotion. Lolita jolts to attention, yanking herself together in a split second, her hands lowering from her head and into prayer. Then Josie snivels, exhaling gentle sobs as Dad and I climb into the waiting car, bound for LAX. I do not cry. My favorite books are with me, which is all that matters to me. I am hollow, or am I hardened? Can I be both?

I wave a floppy goodbye, anesthetized by the uncertainty of my new life. My father and I reel away through the Los Angeles twilight, the vision of Lolita crying so much that she cannot speak fading from the rear-view mirror.

The curtain, it seems to me, is falling on my childhood.

Most other girls are still away on winter break when I arrive at the Athena Academy for Girls, a stately pre-Second World War building overlooking Manhattan's Central Park from the West. I marvel for a minute under the flickering dawn streetlights, fresh snow crunching beneath my feet. It is my first time seeing snow, feeling snow. I gape at the way the milk-colored pebbles nip at my ankles like tiny tadpoles, idling on the soles of my thin Los Angeles shoes.

A large clump of white spreads across a bald patch in front of me. I step right in, knowing from books how special it is to step on snow that no one has stepped on, especially in a place like New York, where people swarm the streets and live in coffin-sized studios stacked one above the other.

Dad rings the doorbell of the frosty brownstone. I pivot one last time to take in the blanketed ivory ground before maneuvering into another time and place—chandeliers, wrought iron statues, polished parquet floors, high ceilings, and narrow hallways.

Dad and I linger by the fireplace, watching as the flames sample the logs. The embers start minuscule and grow in intensity.

Wait. Wood?

I want to turn away, to run. But my limbs will not cooperate, and my eyes will not move.

And there it is. A whimpering burning baby buried between the logs withering away at warp speed. This time, I am close enough to grasp the open-eyed child. This baby I can save. I reach, my arm outstretched, my fingertips sweeping above the cauldron—

A firm hand taps me on the shoulder, and I jump.

"Cold? This isn't Los Angeles. Don't get too close to the flames," an Amazonian woman with fiery red hair piled carefully on her head states sharply but not unkindly. "You must be Anna Paradis. Welcome."

Looking back at the fire, I cannot see the baby.

Most likely burned to ash. Why is nobody reacting? Is it them? Or me? Is it jetlag? Am I dreaming? Is this all too much at once? No, I am here.

This is real. I know what I saw, and I am not crazy. It takes every ounce of strength not to burst into tears.

Ms. Daphne, as she introduces herself, leads my shaking legs up two flights of stairs and into my new room, my new chapter. Two thin wooden beds, crisp white linen that smells like all sorts of sour notes. A pressed and shapeless dress, my weekday school uniform, is folded neatly on the stiff white sheets alongside black slacks, alongside a white blouse strictly to be worn on weekends and after-hours.

"Males aren't normally allowed beyond the first floor. But because you're just moving in, Mr. Robert here can take your suitcases just this once," Mrs. Daphne asserts. "Please allow ten minutes for your goodbyes; breakfast is in twenty minutes. It is at 7:30 a.m. on weekends, at 6:30 a.m. during the school week. 7:00 p.m. for dinner each night. A review of the rules will take place later today after you have settled. Your roommate will return tomorrow."

Dad stays just three more minutes. I gulp, not ready for him to leave. I feel the pang of wanting to hold his leg and gain his attention like that breathless child at the Beverly Hills hotel.

"Little, behave," he stammers, a strong man in crocodile-skin cowboy boots.

"I lo– I will," I utter, refusing to recognize the tears that stir somewhere deep down.

Bobby glances at the small, sparse room and out the small window open enough to keep the white flurries outside.

"You, little," his hoarse voice continues, his eyes on the floor. "You will be okay here."

The door closes without so much as an echo.

The next time it opens, Mrs. Daphne is summoning me downstairs to learn the rules and regulations that will govern my life for the next twenty-one seasons.

The next time my door opens after that, the folded arms and pursed lips of a girl about my age–olive-skin, a platinum Twiggy-like pixie cut with feline-like gray eyes, and long lanky legs–strut inside.

"My parents tried to buy the whole room out so I wouldn't have to put up with this roommate shit for my second semester here," the girl says airily, popping her gum and nudging past me with a bulging Louis Vuitton suitcase in tow. "But seeing as though that was not possible–don't eat my snacks without asking and then throw them up in the bathroom because we all have to share. Last year a girl did that, and the smell went through the air ventilation, which was gross . . ."

The model-thin girl proceeds to strip down right then and there, clearly unfettered about nudity in front of a stranger. She shifts from rigid leather pants into deep purple Baby Phat sweats.

"If you get all homesick, don't slit your wrists inside; there is a big park across the street for that," she continues like a chortling bird. "Whatever it is, I won't tattle if you don't tattle. You fuck up enough to the point you deserve it, and I'll stab you in the front because I don't do back-stabbing. Keep it real. I expect the same back of me. Deal?"

This is Taya Taylor. My first real friend in this hurricane of life.

Together, five years of competing to be top of the class, giggling as we learn to eat with the correct fork and balance books on our heads as we parade up and down the creaking hallways. Five years of equine therapy and weekly group sessions of learning to love our inner beauty. Five years of sneaking out to meet the boys from the boys' school and soothing each other after our hearts bounce from our burgeoning chests and then broken apart by feckless boys. Five years of occasional weekends horse-riding on the Taylor family's sprawling ranch in Connecticut in the spring and wading through the still waters of South Hampton in the summer. Five years of sharing study notes in the bay-windowed school library. Our heads go down and then up again–five years of freedom even within the confines of the stuffy but divine boarding house.

Josie comes to New York to see me twice a year on her way to and from Cyra. And Lolita, who went to live in Tucana as Dad's assistant as soon as I left, stops by just once that first year. She hugs me in the visitors' lounge on a weekday evening in the late spring, covered in a thick fawn coat, at a time when bare legs and sundresses have just started to occupy the sardine streets, fidgeting and looking about nervously.

Something is off. More off than normal.

Lolita's fingertips caress my face as though confirming I am real, just like she had done on my thirteenth birthday.

"I am not supposed to be here; your dad had some business in the U.S., and I snuck out of taking notes at his meetings to find you," Lolita whispers, pressing my fingers into her tender temple. "I can't say what I want to say. The wrong people are always listening."

I hear her say she loves me, and then, like a perishing mirage, she rushes off.

Over time, Lolita ebbs from my life. The calls become more infrequent, and then entire seasons fly by without so much as a letter. I tell myself that she will come again; surely, she will come again. Then the years sail, and she never does.

"She is so busy working as your dad's assistant, Anna," Josie answers when I ask her if everything with Lolita is okay. "Being at your father's beck and call is more than a full-time job. He needs her to stay silent and focused on all the tasks. He is making a lot of money in Tucana now."

I refuse to imagine that Lolita, always with so much–often too much–heart to give, is too busy to talk to me. The thought leaves me wounded.

Eventually, I stop waiting for my father's plane ticket. The infrequent calls with my father come and go, with little substance beyond work and weather. Josie lets it slip that she has stopped going back and forth to Tucana to see him.

Over strong black tea at Café Lalo, Josie–a flimsy pink scarf over her fried platinum curls–explains brusquely that she and Dad are over. They are not getting a divorce because he does not want to return to the U.S., hire lawyers, and sign the paperwork. Apparently, she says, they have both agreed they are free to move on.

I am not all that surprised. Our family fractures have always been apparent to me. The pieces never fit together in a wholesome puzzle, so the divorce news doesn't hit me like a ton of bricks. Indeed, there is something–many somethings–that fester in the pit of my stomach, things for which I have no words.

"I am selling the Mulholland mansion," Josie continues, looking out the frosted window into the wet streets and the black umbrellas piled up beside the heaping black hills of trash. "To retire in a small beachside studio in Malibu."

"Retire from what? I didn't know you ever worked," I remark with a quarter smile.

But it is a semi-serious question. I have never known Josie to have a real job other than to follow Dad abroad. Josie looks at me with a little anguish, recovering with a dramatic pucker of her pink-lined lips.

"Helping your father with the business was always the vocation," she retorts. "Now, let's go listen to some jazz, Anna."

I graduate high school in the late spring of 2000, on a gusty morning in May. With an immaculate, ladylike posture, I pack up my little life in a few cardboard boxes. Taya and I spend our first summer week in her parents' vacation house in South Hampton, perfecting our tans by the hourglass pool by day and dancing in the opaquely lit bar with the well-dressed in the overflowing cafes by night. But I am itching to get back on the Jitney bus bound for the city, to start padding the pages of my new chapter, losing interest in ocean breezes and rubbing shoulders in a place that feels like life on a perfect pause.

My years in the boarding house in perpetual sleepover mode has enabled me to bypass the desire most people my age have to live on campus and play beer pong every night. I am ready for rent checks and actual adulthood. With a modest money dump from Dad, I move into a shoe-box-sized studio apartment atop a noisy nail salon with strobe lights in the East Village.

Still, I miss the girls—now women—from the Academy. The sisters I never had, the drama, the bonding, even the pranks, gossip, and fighting. I never had to sleep alone, a roommate unknowingly protecting me from the horrors of the burning baby after twilight. All those years and the fire with flesh never returned. The sensation of being surrounded and wanted seems to nearly make the afflictions go away.

But what is the saddest word in the English vocabulary? Nearly. It gets so close but ends in -ly, in a lie.

An artist had lived in my new studio before me, painted the walls and fire escape a fire engine red, and retiled the small kitchen all black. I adorn the apartment with strange statues and potted plants I find dumped on the sidewalks, as well as a leather-upholstered couch from the vintage store on the corner. I drive a U-Haul to Queens to pick up a wrought iron-framed futon and matching bookshelf I find through a friend of a friend on Myspace, who was selling it for a few bucks. I line every shelf with my favorites and the dusty secondhand finds from the Strand Bookstore. It takes up the only wall space where most would have put posters, art, and photos. That swarming black rack of shelves is my artwork.

To my young and untraveled eye, the tiny apartment is exotic and otherworldly. Not pretty, mostly gritty. I feel as if I am gliding into another dimension. Taya sublets a fancier studio apartment in a building with a doorman two blocks away just for a month. We bounce between each other's abodes so much that it still feels like the golden Athena Academy days.

Sometimes, I walk the unrefined blocks with nowhere to go. But when I do know where I am going, it is to the glorious public library on 42nd Street. That is what a New York summer does to us: it makes us crazy, oozing with passion and no purpose, ready to plummet down those restaurant holes only to rise back up like it is the most normal thing in the world. The dimensions of physical space and the skyscrapers rooted in concrete soil choke us, compressing our ability to think clearly. New York makes us gasp for the open air and yearn for nature and non-human creatures that aren't rats, bed bugs, or roaches caught in the cracks of our lives.

New York–with its overwhelming stench, its dripping fire escapes that serve as balconies like oven doors left open and the fear that rusty window air conditioners would topple you to death at any moment–hates us all. But she holds us close and nurtures us all the same.

Taya and I meet for Happy Hour sushi in late July, a typical week when storms roll in from the East and rain drenches even the brightest days. Perhaps the twilight of summer cleanses us like tears. They both rinse us and then let us go. I cannot believe Taya is moving away from me. She will no longer be down the road.

With tears, she hugs me goodbye, giving her signature, "now you have your own pad; you can bring all the boys back!" before departing on the Amtrak to D.C. She has already lined up White House internships and is preparing to volunteer on Senate press campaigns to mesh with her grandiose plans of taking over the globe. She wants to be the next It-girl publicist like Samantha from *Sex in the City*.

I enroll as an English literature major at New York University. I score my first real job from a Craig's List ad, making coffee and copy editing for ten dollars an hour at a small publishing imprint, Extreme Press–just an office tucked inside a peeling old warehouse overlooking a cast of crazy East Village characters.

Once an avid mountaineer, big-wave surfer, and bareback horse rider–to name only a few items on his adrenaline diet–a broken femur-and-heart-condition-rendered fifty-something Cliff Walker is little more than confined to carving out his niche publishing adventure books and tales of how human beings can push beyond physical limits, conquering goals that most of us mortals would perceive as impossible.

Cliff refers to it as casting light onto the scariest of scary stories. His toned body reverberates when he talks about those tales of triumph and tribulation. When he finds his voice rising with too much excitement, he sits cross-legged on the floor and closes his eyes like a consummate yogi retreating into a serene mental place I can only imagine.

"Because people don't realize how far they can go," Cliff constantly reminds me. "They don't want to accept how far you can go; it is all in the mind. What's a boundary? We make up boundaries."

I quickly consider Extreme Press my little oasis amidst all the madness and Cliff a kind of father-figure confidante teeming with alluring stories and pearls of wisdom.

One later summer night, Josie calls me. I can hear the waves crashing ruthlessly from her Malibu balcony.

"Anna baby," she says. "I need a great favor from you. Something big is happening, and it is great news."

"What is it?" I query from my moth-noshed red couch, snuggling into a half-dozing Todd—my quasi-boyfriend whom I met three weeks earlier when he was dispatched to my building after the deli next to the salon directly underneath caught fire.

"President General Rian Amsa's middle son just arrived in New York to complete his medical degree at Columbia. It would be wonderful of you to show him around. I can't imagine he would have too many friends this side of the pond," Josie gushes. "I don't have his U.S. cell yet, but I'll give you his email, and you will reach out tonight, yes?"

Josie doesn't have to tell me. I already know. She is referring to Rian Amsa, the embattled ruler of Tucana. The name dominated my adolescence but slipped from my radar during boarding school when I realized my father was never going to send me a ticket there. My heart pulsates for a moment.

"Ah, sure," I respond, kissing Todd guiltily on the nose as I make my way to the kitchen to scribble down the address. "Do I . . . ah, do you know him?"

"No need to mention me, don't mention me. I mean that, Anna. You had better be listening," Josie says hurriedly, her tone losing its chirp. "Your dad does important work over there, and I don't want to . . . but I thought it would be a lovely gesture. It must be daunting for him to have come so far from home, with no family or people to lean on here. A very different life. I'm sure he would love to hear from you."

Todd is already snoring over the *Friends* episode on repeat. I quietly open my laptop–drafting and deleting the email so many times.

"Hi, Saif,

I hear you made it safely to New York. Happy to show you the city sometime. Tucana occupies a special place in my heart.

Best,

Anna Paradis."

I click send before I can backspace it all again. Then I kick myself because "occupies a special place in my heart" sounds far too romantic and pathetic to write to a member of a First Family.

Todd stirs a little as I flutter back beside him, the electric fan blowing furiously but not furiously enough to stop my nightgown from sticking to my damp skin.

He and all his gym-pumped muscles had promenaded into my shoebox, leaned over, and rescued me from impending doom with a hose and big rubber boots, like a hero in a romance novel saving the damsel in distress. Despite the fire being theoretically a tiny one that barely left a mark on the nail salon's kitchen, he rescued me from a fate of fiery flames and tragedy.

It could have been something life-threatening, I reason.

I spread the blanket over us, shoving away the empty plastic Chinese takeout boxes. I could stay here, snuggling in those bulging safe arms.

But I do not. I fall for danger.

I am eighteen and I do not yet understand that this is the last time I will ever date and lust over someone so lightly, without consequence, drama, or complications.

In the end, I send Saif two emails. There is that cringe-worthy first one and then a friendly follow-up three days later. But I do not receive a response.

CHAPTER

FIVE

Several days later, I am leaving a Myspace-founded book club meeting at my favorite Greek diner in Hell's Kitchen. A storm brews in the background as a familiar man wanders into the black-fronted Silver Legs next door. Wait. Could it be?

In even the thickest crowd, I would recognize that familiar face. I had typed his name into Ask Jeeves enough times over the past week. I know I am not mistaken: wiry, thin, straight mustache and almost colorless gray eyes to complement his curly, coarse, brown hair. I had studied that goofy, handsome, awkwardly attractive face photograph again and again.

This is my Josie-like or Taya Taylor moment, to not hold back. I impatiently wait until the other students abscond down the subway steps and sneak next door. I follow the man's footsteps into a cosmos of neon lights and heavy cigar smoke.

And there you have it. I meet a slightly tipsy Saif Amsa all alone at a strip club in Hell's Kitchen on a Monday afternoon. Inappropriate for a member of the First Family? Perhaps. Alluring? Most definitely.

He is sitting front and center, staring open-mouthed like a fourteen-year-old boy at a curvy young woman with long, fish-netted legs and an acne-mottled face plastered over in discount Maybelline.

I am too awestruck to be nervous.

Without hesitation, I stride over and take a seat at his table—folding a twenty-dollar bill into the dancer's bra, prompting her to shift her attention from swinging cleavage at him to greeting me with a leg spread and swivel.

Tips from Taya's arsenal, I think with a slanted smile, reflecting on our sneaky Saturday nights tiptoeing from the boarding house with fake IDs. I lean forward into the oily-skinned dancer, drawing her close and whispering seductively into her the dried hairspray stuck to the insides of her ear.

"Give us a moment, will you?" I purr, plopping in another ten-dollar bill for good measure.

"Sure, baby girl," she says with a wink, grinding her way over to another lone overweight male on the far end.

I peek over at Saif—endearing and fumbling, his thin, adolescent-like mustache twitching ever so subtly—and I smile.

"Saif Amsa," I say, tilting my chin just enough from the spotlight to contour my high cheekbones the way Josie did while lounging at the Beverly Hills Hotel. "What are you doing here?"

His jaw drops, but only a little. He picks it back up and grins, leaning forward just enough for me to hook on to his bourbon breath.

"I could ask the same thing about you," he responds. "I won't tell if you won't tell."

"Oh, I know it's not proper practice for the President General's son to be in a strip club, even if this is a novelty you don't get at home. But me? Whatever I want."

"I also know you aren't twenty-one, and getting in with a fake ID is illegal. But I won't tell if you won't tell . . . Anna Paradis."

"You got my email, then?"

"I got two emails . . . I had my people at home run a background on you. You're even prettier in person. And I saw your dad does business with my dad."

"Is that a good or bad thing?"

"I don't know; I haven't heard from him to ask."

"Do you always play by the rules?"

"Amsa's make the rules."

"Not here, they don't. Land of the free."

"Home of the brave. That's why I'm here."

"In the strip club? Or in America?"

"First time for everything."

"Including me."

"I should call the driver."

"No, you shouldn't call the driver . . . Cabs are already waiting outside. Much faster."

While leading Saif onto the glittering wet pavement, I feel his deer-in-the-headlights gaze latch onto my behind. I hail a cab with no place for us to go. A café? A whisky bar? A museum? My place? His? Todd enters my mind and then evaporates. Should I be riddled with guilt? Some guilt? There is none.

"Excuse some unpacked boxes. Newly arrived and all," Saif murmurs as we vault inside the yellow vehicle.

"Last thing on my mind."

In this moment, life's road rolls out before me. First, the well-trodden tar leads to the conventional life of marriage and motherhood and once-a-year vacations to the Bahamas and Europe. Then, this alternate path—inky and still wet—materializes in my mind, ascending so high that I cannot see what is on the other side.

"My place," Saif says, rummaging through his wallet for an address he has not yet burned into memory.

Before I know it, I am at the starting line of a wild one-night stand in Saif's spacious sublet loft—enhanced by his constant words of validation.

"Pure and giving," he says beneath the sheets. "Like Mother Mary caring for the cherubs."

Cherubs? My mind freezes. What an awkward thing to say. But Saif is awkward, and that is part of what whips me up and spins me closer to him.

I let the remark go. At least for now.

And I never want to spend a day without him, ever again.

"Isn't it funny," Taya notes smugly over the phone the next afternoon after I reveal my ardor-charged encounter with a President General's middle son. "How we give everything to a stranger, and yet it's too intimidating to talk to them on the phone for two minutes the next day?"

I can hear her pouring a glass of wine from her Georgetown apartment.

"Girl, we've all been there," she continues matter-of-factly.

Taya is right. We can spend a night naked with a stranger and then be too skittish to text or call the next day. But Saif never felt like a stranger to me. All of the adolescent Tucana reading and those nights in bed memorizing Rasa words create that deep connection.

But this beyond-superficial bond makes it harder to call him, because he might say the night was all empty fun, and no real conversation follows.

I pace up and down my red-and-black shoebox for minutes, maybe hours. Then finally, the long-awaited text message materializes, flashing in front of me. So desired, so manifested, it is hard at first to believe it is even real.

"I have been thinking about you all day, Anna," it reads as I flip open my palm-sized Nokia. "Up for some Joe's Pizza?

And, like that, I flop head-over-heels for Saif Amsa. We spend as many waking and sleeping hours together as possible. I miss him when I am not with him, and I miss him when I am with him, thinking about when we will need to separate to take on our life chores. He is thoughtful and tender, a cocktail of the seven love languages stirred into one. He knows things about the world that I do not. He promises to take me out of the country someday. I have never left this country.

Saif is six years my senior, a Gemini, studying to be an ophthalmologist. His charisma and attractiveness would not appear particularly impressive to most outsiders. However, when I am with him, the emergence of a burned baby never returns. He protects me with every embrace.

Saif blends in with the melting pot of New York City. He is studious and quiet, relishing the fine things like the opera and wagyu in a dimly lit brasserie, but seeks no extravagance or attention. Like me, he is more of a loner who loves getting lost in this concrete jungle. Over the next few weeks, we study together over takeout Italian in his downtown summer loft and take Sunday morning strolls over the Brooklyn Bridge, sharing intimate nuggets about our favorite songs, books, and memories.

It is his simplicity, his clumsiness, which draws me in and does not let go. But there is also mystique to his almost flat-lined persona, with the sudden spikes of naughty adventure that has me wanting more. It is the lust-poured honeymoon phase I am so sure will never end.

Yet back in his homeland Tucana, the cycle of civilian uproar is loaded; it is a cannon waiting to explode.

"My father just won't return my calls," Saif admits one night as we sip cocktails at a rooftop bar, sucking in the New York skyline. "Mother keeps telling me everything is alright, everything is handled, but . . ."

The front page of today's Wall Street Journal depicts President General Rian Amsa as a brutal dictator. According to the article, he rounded up scores of innocent university protesters who had staged a peaceful sit-in around the Palace a week earlier, demanding better healthcare, cheaper housing, and free and fair elections. Images show men and women the same age as us with bullet wounds gaping through their faces, tear gas ripping through their wide eyes as they clutched one another. They are the faces of those who are not seeking glory but some chance at a different life; faces now charred into memory but whose names we do not know.

Survivors told the Journal that they were stripped naked by the secret intelligence unit, forced to falsely confess to "concocting plots to over-throw the government and planting car bombs in civilian neighborhoods so they could loot and fund their terror campaigns." And then their geni-tals were beaten to a pulp by officers in underground rat-infested interrogation rooms.

"Do you think they're terrorists?" I ask softly, squeezing his hand.

"I don't know," he replies, equally as demure. "And I don't know what I can do about it either way. It is not as though my father talks to me, let alone listens."

We suck in more of that New York skyline in silence, harder, more frantically.

"Hey, fuck you! Fuck you, Saif Amsa," a loud voice bellows from behind. "Go the fuck back to where you came from."

Standing a few feet away is a massive Middle Eastern guy frothing at the mouth.

"Your fucking father killed my cousin this week," the man screams as his two friends try to pull him away.

"And you," he fumes, suddenly turning his attention to me. "You fucking whore with this piece of shit. How do you fucking sleep at night, hey?"

To prevent Saif from leaping, I grip his svelte frame tightly, his Rolex digging into my arm. But Saif breaks free from me, he flies toward the heated patron. The men exchange a couple of punches, a few Rasa curse words. Then, as Saif catches his breath, he snaps back into controlled anger.

"Don't you ever speak like that to a woman–let alone my woman," he hisses, unclenching his fist.

Then he spins toward me, kissing my trembling lips and wrapping his whole body around me. It is the sexiest thing I have ever seen. Saif is safety. The budding doctor looks into my eyes and does not break away until the stranger spewing profanities is booted out by the security guard–his screams of "fuck you, you killed my cousin" ricocheting through us both.

Saif's cloak of anonymity as a student in the U.S. is fast fading. He claims he has no place or purpose in Tucana, but worries he is beginning to stand out like a swollen red eye in the crowds of New York.

A week later, on an early September night, Saif and I find ourselves unable to sleep, tangled in a lattice of his satin sheets. We toss and turn. Every time I glance over at him, his forehead is crinkled deeper than the flesh of a twenty-six year old ever should be, his fists clasped beneath his chin.

I don't know if there is a certified definition of what it means to fall in love; I don't know if most people know it is happening. As I realize what has happened, my stomach jerks.

"Babe, are you alright?" I whisper.

It is a stupid question. Saif is not alright. The drama unfolding at home and the headlines that ensue are wearing him down. He flips open his mobile phone and tries again to call President General Rian. Only it beeps and goes straight to a voiceless voicemail. Then my phone vibrates; I have four missed calls from Josie. I roll my eyes. She has been persistently calling since I let it slip on her follow-up call about my meeting Saif that we have something going on beyond the friendly token of tourism.

"Babe, it's not your problem. Get through school and make a career for yourself. Remember, you are the lucky one with choices," I tell him. "It's your father's and brother's cross to bear, not yours. The weight is not on your shoulders."

As the middle child, Saif has a lot of options unlike Firas, his older brother by five years. As the eldest and thus his father's successor, Firas has undergone intensive grooming since childhood. He has no alternative but to attend five years of military academy, including a final year in London training to be a fighter pilot. He then must return to Cyra to serve as an officer by day and by night to earn a Master's in Public Diplomacy and Homeland Security.

Saif has freedom, if not the attentive eye of his father. His mother, Madame Sara, however, urged him to make the family proud by becoming a western-certified doctor.

I reach for Saif's hand, and he lets me furl his fingers into mine. Then, just as quickly, he pulls away, retreating into the bathroom. The sink water runs for at least five minutes. I pretend to be asleep–but I squint, my eyes open just enough to observe his thin frame outlined by the city lights, shoulders slumped forward, as he lumbers back beneath the covers.

Observing Tucana from afar, I can tell Saif cares deeply about his homeland. I can see it in his heaviness. But for him, it is as if he is standing on the other side of a bulletproof window banging on the impenetrable glass. I see the soul, the layers, the burden that I wish I could help him carry.

"I need to stay and finish my school here to do some good," Saif mutters, his voice cracking to combat his fermenting tears. "But it's safe, too safe here. I should be at home; I should be helping my country."

And at that moment—

"I love you," I whisper, the potent phrase escaping my lips before my brain can squash it.

I mean it. I mean each of those three words fused as a lightning phrase. I love Saif's vulnerability, his pain, his heart, and him. The realization overwhelms me, and I drift on a weightless high, gently cascading from a rooftop, but never hitting the ground.

He pecks me on the cheek. And says nothing.

Hours later, after the night has brightened into an immaculate clearskied morning, Saif rolls over and draws me closer.

"I love you too," he whispers.

Slowly, I exhale.

And then the illusion of our romantic safety net is blown apart. *BOOM.* A piece of glass soars from the chandelier and cracks the mirrored closet. I fling myself from the bed and dash to the glass doors of the balcony. A gaping hole has been carved into one of the Twin Towers, smoke curling into the deep blue sky. Then, a faint object slices into the adjacent tower.

It can't be. Is this real?

I leap onto the balcony towering over the growing crowds, crowds blanketing the first signs of auburn leaves across the pavement. Life upends, and I watch, frozen. One tower breathes in; its ribcage lifted like mine with an inhale, then it lets go–a stunning, dizzying exhale to the surface below.

The skyline recedes into the bright light, into something I no longer recognize.

"Saif! Saif!" I scream as the smoke billows and sirens bellow from every direction. "Saif, something is wrong!"

He dives to the balcony, staring in disturbed shock not at the battlefield that had uncoiled before us, but at my unclad body on display. In my fog, I had not even realized I had run from bed without clothes. I doubt anyone is paying attention to me. Not a single person glances up at me, at least not as figures tumble from the high windows of the Twin Towers, like grains of sand soundlessly slipping through an open hand.

"What the hell do you think you are doing?" Saif yells, his eyes bulging and his cheeks inflaming in a way I have never seen before. A single vein beetles from his otherwise enamel-like skin, and his upper lip jiggles furiously.

Saif gruffly lifts me, my head spinning as the sixty-six floors below liquefy, gusts of wind whipping my hair across my face. My back thrashes against the balcony railing, the metal slapping my backside as my head cranes backward, the pavement far below overwhelmed with smoke.

My body is propelled forward toward the open glass door. I spin once— maybe twice. Dizzying speed tempers slow motion. I crumple into a fetal position of shock and tears as Saif releases his grip on my waist. It was like a kiss, a rough kiss that had morphed into a protective love bite.

"Anna, I cannot believe you would do that," Saif pants. "Naked out there for the world to see. Don't you ever do that!"

Saif leaves, slamming the front door behind him. The sirens grew louder as I lay on his polished floor. An ear-shattering thud echoes from the second tower as it collapses to the ground.

Our lives as we knew them have just come to an end. This volatile aftermath could be the end for Saif and me as well. But I choose to make it a new beginning because I love him. Even if love feels not just hard, but hard work.

He returns a minute later with tears in his eyes. He benevolently pulls me into his chest, stroking my mangled ebon locks. He runs a tissue over my eyes and holds me in a way neither he nor anyone else has ever held me. There is apology in the way someone touches you.

"I love you, Anna. I hope you are not hurt," Saif murmurs, his low voice thick with emotion. "I didn't mean to hurt you. I just wanted to bring you inside, protect you."

It is a divine phrase. I am wanted. Josie always told me to go where I am wanted.

"You must go where you are wanted," I remember her telling my little girl's eyes.

All those years I spent immersed in silly, self-indulgent, and stupid romance novels coalesce into shame as smoke rises into the empty Manhattan skies. Had I removed myself too much from the real world?

I sob most of that night when downtown's once stunning spectacle of lights remains dark. Then and there, I vow to burn every fiction book I own and not purchase another. There is only one thing that matters: the real world. There will be no more sci-fi or fantastical existences.

What eventuated on the balcony the morning of September 11th, Saif and I put behind us in an unspoken agreement. I was in shock. So was Saif. We look to the future. There is power in forgiving ourselves from the past.

After that September morning, no one I know seems to care about Tucana's calamity and rebellion. The U.S. government does not believe Tucana to have extremist ideologies. Despite sectarianism and a large class divide between rich and poor, there are no known Al Qaeda cells in the country. In a sense, Tucana is an island unto itself.

Saif and I lose track of the days, rankled by insomnia and the ghosts of an era gone by. Months grind on like a crusty black-and-white movie featuring our city united in mourning–all of us collectively trying to remember and trying to forget at the same time. I transfer out of my once-beloved English literature major and into Economics, harboring a new desire to perhaps work for the United Nations to structure microfinancing initiatives to help impoverished and wounded communities get back on their feet.

I turn twenty on a nondescript Tuesday spent at Extreme Press, thumbing through a submission from a middle-aged woman from Nebraska who overcame her drug addiction to summit Mount Everest twice in one year.

"Do people still care about this stuff? I mean, we're at war," I note bluntly, her long passages about sweat and tears and pining for divine strength to get through bouncing off the computer and into my anxiety. "People are dying every day in Afghanistan."

Cliff glances out at the now jagged Manhattan skyline where the towers once were and then turns his eyes to me.

"Anna, people are dying every damn day, and nobody cares, and we don't hear about it," he replies, his voice dropping.

Cliff seems to drift into the ruts of memory, back to some atrocity he witnessed while the rest of the world ignored.

"So then, what happens when the bloodshed doesn't want the bloodshed anymore? Will the bloodshed reach the finish line? Who decides when it is all over?" he continues, not waiting for my response.

I click save on the open document and swivel my chair away from the screen.

"What happens if the fight inside our fight stops fighting? Do we give up on ourselves?" Cliff persists. "What happens when we stop telling one person's story because it isn't part of a binder of big numbers? What happens when we stop giving ourselves as individuals permission to have the last word?"

CHAPTER
SIX

In early April 2002, Saif and I sign a lease on a Chelsea loft together. Previously a classical ballet academy, the loft bestows ivory ceilings and natural light that splashes in from every direction. He wants to get away from downtown, where the smells of tragedy haunt every aperture on the sidewalk.

Saif can't tell his family in Tucana that he lives with a girlfriend who is not his wife–that is a strictly forbidden concept–so he carries that detail with him. The lovely loft is our secret, our porcelain village of togetherness. Shielded in his arms, we celebrate our first night with white wine and gentle silence–studying all the colors of the sky as they deepen, dripping down into darkness. Moments with Saif often seem wordless. I tell myself it is because we are real lovers, and presence is enough.

Meanwhile, Josie seems slightly excited and a little apprehensive when I eventually tell her the news of us sharing an address.

"Oh, Anna. Send pictures of your place," she responds, hardly surprised. "Has Saif spoken to his father? Have you heard what just happened there? Is it going to happen again?"

I can't get a minute with Josie without her asking me a million questions about my boyfriend. While I don't want to answer, sometimes I can't answer all her questions about him, us, and the country he left.

When Josie and I finish our call, when I am sure Saif is in the living room writing his thesis, I open my laptop and search for news about Tucana.

I try not to talk to Saif too much about his homeland. He is here because he wants an existence far removed from that isle of blood and beauty. He talks about setting up a medical practice to prove himself in a different way from his family. Instead of slotting into a symbolic First Family role, he endeavors to be a well-respected doctor and family man. He wants a less stressed, idyllic life, far from the threats of a car bomb erupting or the possibility that a dissident covered in unhealed wounds could kidnap him on a morning run.

In less than half a second on Google, images of men blindfolded with black scarves piled on the Tucana roadside, faceless in the dirt, permeate my screen. Then there are women in long dresses, some with headscarves and some without, howling in heartbreak. The more photos I see, the more I wince. Headlines flash across the news sites, "Massacre in Tucana Province Kills All Men," "Government troops open fire in Tucana Town of Mana," "Amnesty Calls for International Investigation Over the Wiping Out of Village Men by Dictator Amsa," "The U.S. to Sanction Tucana President Amsa after Murder of 252 Civilian Men," "Worst Attack in Tucana History Carried Out Under Tyrant Orders . . ."

My eyes fog over. My stomach churns, and my right temple throbs.

I do not hear Saif come up behind me. I gasp, partly in dismay and partly in guilt, when his heavy breathing prickles the hairs of my neck. When I slowly swivel to see his reaction, I first notice the mustache identical to all the pictures of his father.

"They are terrorists," he states bluntly, grabbing my hand delicately. "They won't report it right; the press will never report it fairly. But those men were planning an uprising."

There is a defiance in Saif's eyes, a certainty that did not exist when we first met. He kisses each finger silkily at first. Then harder and harder, until his teeth clamped down my trembling thumb.

"They wanted to overrun the Palace, kill my family, and have Tucana to themselves," Saif continues, his voice steady and calm. "The informants infiltrated. Imagine if the terrorists had succeeded; it would have been a bloodbath."

Our response to hurt and consternation is always the same. Saif insists I pack a small bag, and we go to peculiar places to meet peculiar people. This time, we hop on a plane and fly to Oklahoma City. In a place forgotten by the cell service, we discover an old bed and breakfast tucked behind a back road.

We ride horses with the old cowboys, who have never met people who reside in New York City before. We smoke cigars, sip whiskey, and eat tender beef burgers. We fool around in a rustic shack garnished with buffalo heads affixed to the slanted stone walls.

Saif tells me again that I am beautiful, like the mother of cherubs. I wince. I say nothing. Then, tucked in bed early the following morning, he mutters that he thinks we should break up.

"You can keep the apartment," Saif says dryly, without remorse, to my surprised and abhorrent face.

He rambles that he must focus on his career, on getting the most prestigious job possible, so he will not be deemed a total fuck up in his father's eyes. I can barely register what he is saying. I am too shocked to cry, yell, or do what romance novels tell you to do when your love no longer wants your love.

"And do you think I wouldn't want that for you?" I stammer. "You think I wouldn't support you and want you to be the best you can be? That is the stupidest cliché when people say that. 'Oh, I can't date because I have to focus on my career.' If you are with the right person, they will want you to have a great career. They'll support you and add to you having a great career, not detract from it."

As he was busily learning to fix the eyes of others, my love for him became blinder. I constantly grope for him out of thin air. I need someone,

I need him, to hold. I would rather exist in his world than be alone in mine. The thought of ever living without him causes thorns to sprout in my throat, tearing through my vocal cords and severing each fold of tissue one by one.

Saif pauses, his lip twitching the way it does when he is adrift in reflection.

"Support through everything? Are you sure you can commit to that?" he asks, softening. "Because I only want the best for you too. I want you to trust me, Anna."

"I trust you."

"But I don't always trust myself. There's this thing, this anger—this other person in me. I don't know; I will never hurt you, Anna."

"I trust you. I don't trust myself, either. Sometimes, all that matters is that someone else does."

Gawkily, Saif drops to his knees as the sun rises over the vast plains.

"Marry me, Anna," he says suddenly. "We will build our life together, me as a doctor and you as the most philanthropic financial advisor . . . Children, trips around the world, quiet magic."

One moment Saif is ending it, and the next, he asks me to be by his side for life. Is he mad? Am I mad? On that rollercoaster, my stomach has already lifted outside myself, leaving me with only my exasperated adrenaline left.

I do not say yes right away. I do not say anything. I roll over and pretend to slide back to sleep, half wondering if I am still dreaming. When the morning heat begins to burn, Saif takes the brooding truck we rented into town and returns with an unwrapped diamond rock that glistens, rough-cut and unvarnished on a narrow rose-gold band. Just as I would have wanted—perfectly imperfect. A little rough at its immaculate edges. Saif is the most romantic man I ever knew.

I hold the diamond to the light, sending a spark across the near-barren walls.

A spark. A flame. A smell. That smell. Burning flesh, a baby's cry and–

"Yes," I respond giddily, a little too loudly, sitting up straight with the crusty linen sheets over my bare-skinned body. "Yes!"

The infant's shrills melt away; the smell eradicates in a split second.

I am only twenty. Saif is still a few weeks shy of twenty-six. But I have never been so sure of anything. I love him. He loves me. We have prospects and a place to live; that is all the glue we need.

We hold our engagement close for a whole year, our secret, and those months blur in a succession of ecstasy, work, and dreams. But I can't keep anything from Taya. She takes the Amtrak to New York after I share the big news, insisting on taking Saif and I to Cipriani's for a celebratory meal. It always feels awkward to me when my two favorite people are together. Civil and polite, but distrusting, unsure, a struggle to dominate the conversation and then they both fight over the bill.

After the cherry blossoms spout to life on the shaded Manhattan streets, Saif declares he plans to go to Tucana in the late summer to introduce me to his family. We will attend a garden party soiree in our honor and hold a press conference announcing we are engaged and to marry over the next couple of years. There is no urgency in our bubble of courtship. The visit will only last three days. We both have exams in New York and can't stay longer than that.

Saif kisses and pats away my nervousness, and each night before bed and when we wake up, he goes out of his way to assure me that everything will be fine. Some days he returns home with fresh flowers from the deli downstairs; other days, with our favorite cherry dark chocolate.

At work, Cliff hugs me when I show off the ring. The hug he gives feels more melancholy than excited.

"Don't worry. I am not going anywhere. Saif and I will permanently live in New York City," I promise him.

Cliff smiles.

"No matter where you are, Anna, always make your money so that you can marry for love," he says, looking over at the photograph of his smiling wife on his desk, the wife he lost thirty years ago to an avalanche and never once looked romantically at a woman again.

I tell Josie the news the night before we leave, anticipating at least a little happiness to ring in my ear. She says very little and does not offer her congratulations. Assuming he is still in Cyra, I email Dad to inform him of the engagement and invite him to the garden party. Despite calling me after the September 11th attacks to make sure I was okay, I haven't heard from him in months. The email I send Lolita bounces back.

"Little, Tucana isn't safe for you," my father cautions in an email that comes through just moments before we board the plane.

For me? For everyone? I shake it off. Dad never followed through with taking me to Tucana, and now he is upset I am doing it on my own.

My worries weaken as the jet takes off, soaring into Manhattan's skyline, my country vanishing below the clouds.

A man with a cracked leather jacket, a dyed-black mustache, and aviator sunglasses–like something out of a terrible Soviet-era spy film–is waiting for us in Cyra as we step off that first-class flight. I don't need a visa stamp or an interview with passport control. I don't need to collect my bags or wait in hour-long lines. The waiting man ushers us past all that seamlessly, singing like a tour guide as he leads us into the armored limousine.

Cyra has the incense I had always imagined: desert with the tang of a tropical sea.

The first time I leap into the island capital, I could not have imagined discord ever touching this land. Everything is gold and gleaming. As the statuesque towers rise into the clear sky, patches of flowers dot the fertile earth, blending with dense foliage of maples, pines, and bamboo flutes strategically placed to soften the summer's sting.

To my flabbergasted eye, it oozes with fun and freedom, and of the new and the historic. Bulletproof limousines and wide streets are wondrously open for our convoy as we glide through. Heavy traffic comes to a standstill, and every car pulls to the shoulder so we can pass as if we are something exceptional. Something worthy.

It is unusual for a little girl who grew up in a privileged Los Angeles life, but is not a movie star or royalty, who was always second fiddle to the kids of Bruce Paltrow and Goldie Hawn. What did I do to deserve such respect, other than meet a man born to a powerful family?

Nevertheless, I embrace it, even love it.

We curve through quaint alleys dotted with street sellers hawking soft fabrics and roasting sweet almonds, past sidewalks adorned with painters poised in front of colorful canvases. Soothing classical music sounds spill from the villas, where all have balconies wrapped around their pastel-colored exteriors.

Saif is busy texting away on his new Blackberry when we arrive at the fortified grounds, disinterested in the Palace he once called home. In the meantime, I am swimming through a fairytale that had occupied so much of my primitive mind as a teenager. This is Tucana.

As we approach the high black gates–slicing into the sky like swords– and glide into another time and place, it takes extraordinary self-control not to laugh or weep, run away or pinch myself so hard that my skin splits.

The Amsa Palace, designed by famed Russian architect Sergey Vladimir Chekov in 1982, sits on 3.2 million square feet of once-voluptuous forestland. Its 505 rooms glisten in white and gold, dwarfing the guards and workers milling about.

I close my eyes, remembering all those pictures of gold-encrusted fittings, diamond door handles, imposing gravel structures, and giant swimming pools that stretch out to a place so far, I'm sure it is where the river meets the sea.

The piercing rev of a Lamborghini shatters the Chopin-like melody of my mind–a blacked-out Murcielago–smoking as it careens through the snaking driveway, hovering just inches above the ground, and comes to a sharp break just inches from where Saif and I stand.

"Yo, little Saify long time," the voice from inside booms. "This is your American girl? Dude, she's smoking.' Looks like one of us."

I had expected Firas Amsa to be a General Patterson-like archetype—strong and all-encompassing in his masculine camouflage, with a mustache chunkier than all his comrades. He is a carbon copy of his stern-faced father—with a lot of Italian-type playboy mixed in for good measure.

Firas swings his legs under the car's scissor door and strides toward me with a charming smile. He extends his hand, kisses my hand, and holds it for a little too long. Then, a creature the size of Labrador bounds from the Lamborghini and lumbers to Firas's side. Only it isn't a dog. I yelp and grab Saif's arm.

"This is Montana," Firas coos, leaning down to pat the young tiger. "Not the stupid American state—after Tony Montana."

A low noise rumbles from the pet tiger's broad chest as Firas ruffles its brindled fur. I can't tell if it is a growl or a purr.

"He loves pretty girls and me, and only bites if you're into that sort of thing," he continues.

Firas winks, and I give myself a second for my heartbeat to simmer to normal, before studying his enormous grin. Firas, I admit, is astonishingly good-looking. Like a male model with a hand-carved, symmetrical face and penetrating wide-set raven eyes.

"You got any sisters? 'Cos girl, you are fine," he drools on, smiling at me seductively, the raven eyes running from my top to my bottom.

I glance at Saif, expecting him to say something—to at least denounce his hyper-flirtatious brother and put a protective arm around my waist. But, instead, he looks glumly at the manicured ground. Everyone around us freezes, their eyes fixed on the velvety stone pavement.

"I am sorry, I do not have any sisters, Mr. ah—Firas," I respond a little pathetically. "I have no brothers either."

It doesn't matter; he is not listening to my words.

"Want to go for a ride? I've got others you can pick from," Firas boasts, staring directly into my chest, covered by a green blouse. "Custom Aston Martin DB7 Vantage Volante Convertible, a Maserati coupe to match your green . . . eyes . . . A tour of this town, and don't worry, I promise not to touch."

He lights a thin cigarette and continues smirking at me. Montana flops onto the ground, luxuriating in the warmth of the driveway.

"If you change your mind and want to marry the future President, not this little eye doc boy, I will take incredible care of you and defend you for life," Firas croons. "Emma, right? Better than any of the Russian girls who've been hanging in my bed."

I arch my eyebrows gawkily back, not bothering to correct my name. He has already averted his gaze to Saif's reddening face.

"You scored fucking good, Saify," Firas says, bending down to nuzzle Montana's ear, the two strutting off like a mirage into a puff of smoke.

When I glance over at my fiancé, he is flushed with that deer-in-the-headlights expression I remember the first night we met at the Silver Legs. Then he squeezes my hand ever so softly as if to say 'here goes the ride.'

And so we ride–on a shiny white gold golf cart–into the main mansion.

Three butlers assist us out of the cart and lead us into the massive dining room. The two of us sit in the living room and sip tea for a few minutes, and then for another few minutes. The jet lag slowly seeps in, an unfamiliar but draining brand of tiredness. If only I could drown inside the assortment of white fluffy pillows in the guest quarters that look like clouds on earth.

"Mama—Madame Sara—is coming," Saif assures me, although not apologetically. "It is just Tucana time . . . It's a Middle East thing; you have just got to go with it. 2:00 p.m. means 4:00 p.m., or even 6:00 p.m., that kind of thing."

Then, an elegant older woman with a long neck, varnished in a sapphire-colored scarf and smelling of lavender soap, enters the gold-walled room with arms open like a prima ballerina. I instantly follow Saif to my feet.

"Oh, my joyous one," she hums eccentrically, not meeting my eye as she draws her middle son close and douses him with kisses. "How I have missed my doctor, oh how proud I am of all your studies. Hurry up and finish so you can come back here and take care of your mother's failing eyes and help all the people of Tucana."

I shoot Saif an imaginary eye dart of puzzlement. He has not told his mother that we do not intend to reside in Tucana.

"Mother, I want you to meet the most amazing woman in the world–equal to you, of course," he squeaks politely, more anxious than excited. "This is my fiancé, Anna Paradis."

Her narrowed eyes shift to me, pretending to suddenly notice my presence. I twist into a half-bow, half-curtsy, unsure how to greet the First Lady.

A graceless few seconds tick by before Madame Amsa extends a hand to shake mine.

"Pretty, pretty you are, Anna. Welcome to Tucana. We are all most excited for your short stay," she says distantly, her long, clawed nails coming together in a prayer position. "I wasn't sure what to expect when our Saif here said he was marrying an American girl, but you look–nice. And he is lucky, unlike his big brother, who must by our constitution marry a Tucana lady . . ."

Madame motions for us to sit and sip more tea from the delicate China cups. A plain, matronly woman with a ballooned face and untamed eyebrows–whose name tag reads Millie–hurries in from a side door to check if everything is okay. Madame dismisses her with a wave of the hand, and not so much as an acknowledgment. Millie, who could be between forty-five and sixty, clumsily bows straight down into her flat feet, with her rump hanging oddly in the air. Then, with her eyes on the ground, she shuffles away as quickly as she had entered.

I want to call out to the plump-faced woman to let her know that I know she exists. I see her. Instead, I say nothing.

"Saif told me," Madame continues slowly, articulating every syllable like a queen delivering a televised message to the nation. "You are almost ready to graduate and move into the financial sector?"

I nod enthusiastically.

"Do you plan to further your education?"

"Yes, ma'am, ah, Madame. I will work for a year and have already applied for my MBA at Harvard."

This time, Saif shoots me an alarmed look, evidently not wanting his mother to latch on to the timeline and realize that Cyra will not be home for us.

"Please, call me Sara," she chimes, oblivious, focused on feigning a bond with her future daughter-in-law.

"MBA? Economics? You must be busily radicalizing yourself with the capitalist principles of what the world should be," Madame Sara says, stinging me with every dripping vowel. "You must come here and think we live in some terrible communist society."

Opening and closing my mouth like a fish, I want to respond but don't know what to say.

"And because you Americans don't know the difference, our policies are far from communist. Socialism is not bad either, although McCarthyism was a wicked abuse of whom too many innocent lives suffered," she continues. "You will see the streets here and how people are taken care of with the world's finest foods, medical care, and vocations. Very different from America."

Then, Madame Sara excuses herself with a flick of that sapphire scarf.

"I need to take a bubble bath to moisten my skin for the evening," Madame states. "I will see you both tonight. And Saif, your father's Chief-of-Staff notified me this morning that his plane will leave from his duties in

Baghdad at 1600, so he will touch down here at 1700, just in time for the intimate gathering tonight. He will be making the toast. Ciao."

I peer over at my fiancé. I know he knows his mother isn't the most pleasant. She is, frankly, a bitch. But if he isn't going to say it, maybe not in those stark words, I am not going to either. So, I brush off the poor first impressions and return to our guest quarters, where a borrowed black Versace sequined gown and a makeup artist and hair stylist eagerly await.

The so-called intimate meet-and-greet gathering of at least a thousand well-dressed people spawns across what they call the "East Forest" wing of the Palace lawn. It is a sunset soiree in our honor fluffed with fine wines, perfectly paired curated meats, and a soundtrack of violins and chit-chat. The event extends beyond the two hours listed on the invitation until the sun sinks into the mountains.

Firas surfaces late with a gang of muscled-up men and a gaggle of duck-lipped Eastern European girls. He hangs out for a bit, tells me I look hotter than Kate Moss, and dissolves into the night with a Macallan Select Reserve Single Malt Scotch Whisky bottle.

I meet Willard, their youngest brother. Saif has spoken little of him; they had an awkward three-and-a-half-year age gap, and it seems they aren't very close. But Saif looks down at him, nonetheless, with big brotherly love. He always described Willard as a good kid, if not precocious, who uses his smarts to melt the hearts of all the adults in his path.

"Where Firas flashes his Uzis and his big biceps, Willard is all about the words and the suave seduction," Saif once explained.

Willard is just nineteen and in his sophomore year studying international relations and public diplomacy at the University of Tucana. He wears gray skinny jeans and oversized glasses, a Hugo Boss-meets-Williamsburg-hipster prototype who speaks in intense, verbose sentences, dissecting everything from the quintessential philosophies of Heraclitus to Belgium's colonization of the Congo and Rwanda.

"My future is in public diplomacy and serving Tucana in either the foreign ministry or abroad as an ambassador in a highly adverse nation," he emphasizes at the party as we watch well-dressed folks mingle stiffly across the freshly cut lawn. "If we can agree on the fundamentals of sciences and technocratic principles of governing, any tense relationship can find an amicable solid ground.

A savvy smile spreads across Willard's face.

"But if I had a choice, I'd go live in Thailand and crack coconuts," he enthuses. "And run a business offering elephant rides. At least it would be a circus-like job, unlike this side show of horrors. Maybe someday."

I smile. It is a relief to know that I wasn't the only one with my toes on the sidelines of a world so exotically lovely and terrifying simultaneously. Every so often, Saif introduces me to another dignitary, another distant family member, another face staring curiously at mine. Then there are those he rushes off to talk to alone. Being watched by so many is more exhausting than speaking to them. Is my posture upright? Do they know anything about me? While sipping my wine, I pretend I don't see the flashing light bulbs suddenly surround me.

Still no toast, still no President General Rian. As 10:00 p.m. approaches and some in the crowd start to move towards the exits–until the guards hurriedly stop them–Madame Sara takes to the podium instead.

"To my son," she choruses, raising her imperial glass of bubbles. "May we wish you happiness and prosperity. We are so proud of you, Saif. Becoming a doctor. All of Tucana is proud of you!"

Everyone raises their glasses jovially. I do, too–to him, not to us.

I stand alone on the lawn, watching the faces dance by. Saif whizzes past to kiss my cheek, then dissipates into a smoky bar far down the lawn, the section only for men.

The sequins are already shedding from my long, form-fitting black gown, a size too tight. I momentarily contemplate retrieving them, but the uncomfortable grimaces of those multiple leather-jacketed men from within the bountiful garden bed loom behind me. Are they surveilling me?

Or my backside? Or both?

"Don't worry about them," Willard conjectures, casually walking toward me. "They're everywhere, always trying to appear tough, but most of those guys barely know how to holster a gun."

I laugh a little.

"Thanks for the reassurance; it's a lot to take in," I admit, relieved to have at least one apparent ally in this staggering structure of Palace formations.

That smile. A little gap-toothed. A little Madonna, perfectly imperfect. Willard did have an exceptional smile. Boyish, innocent, not yet roughened by the responsibility of manhood and the First Family.

"It's not so complicated, although it seems it," he continues flippantly. "The ones to watch out for aren't the ones in those hideous jackets. Those are secret ones dressed like us. The ones you don't know about. They are cunning and nimble, knowing and resourceful."

I must be modeling a quizzical expression because Willard hooks his arm into my elbow as a symbol of comfort.

"No need to worry. They are just keeping us all safe," Willard says, cocking his head to the growing cluster of leather-jacketed men. "The impalpable we call the Shush Police; it means 'ununiformed' in Rasa."

Eventually, the quartet packs up, and the fairy lights dim out. Guests exit in their expensive cars with in-house drivers. The crystal trays of leftover caviar and local salmon from the seas are scraped into bags and wheeled away into the waste bins in a matter of minutes.

"It was a pleasure to have your presence tonight, Ms. Anna," Willard adds. "It means the cosmos to our small family to have you join us in bringing a timorous heart to the Tucanese people."

He politely kisses my giddy hand goodnight before leaving.

I remove my impossibly high Manolo Blahniks, also a size too small and borrowed from the Palace stylist. My bare feet feel soothed against the lush grass, I walk around and around, looking for my beloved fiancé. I wait almost an hour, with only staff left to clean up the party, for Saif to reappear in the garden. He seems a little down, so I dare not ask where he has been. I can see now why he loves his home but wants to give his heart to a different kind of life five thousand miles away.

We stand together beside the moon shimmers, bouncing off the pool until our eyes swing between open and closed. He is waiting, quietly crossing his fingers that his father's plane will touch down even after the celebration has drawn to a close. I had re-emailed my father and Lolita an invitation as soon as I touched down in Cyra. Dad wrote almost immediately that he would try to make it but could make no promises. I still cannot reach Lolita, her email bounces back again. But Dad assures me she is well and busy.

Saif strokes my hair, fingertips caressing my neck and sending goosebumps through my body like the night we first met.

That is why we bond in ways that no words, only chemicals of commiserating souls, can explain. We are just humans whose childhoods had been glutted with shiny things, when all we want is the respect of the first man we ever loved.

I close my eyes and take in the past twenty-four hours, the mountain of affluence I never properly understood was possible and feel a twinge of guilt.

"This seems so surreal . . . Remember how I burned all my fiction books after September 11th and pledged that only the real-world matters?" I say softly to the stars and to Saif.

"This is the real world, Anna," Saif replies, putting his hand on the small of my back. "I hope you never have to see how real it is, though."

CHAPTER

SEVEN

I wake late, snoozing soundly until mid-morning, sinking deeper into the 1800 thread count Egyptian cotton sheets. The California King bed on Saif's side is hardly rumpled, although he is already up and gone. Even though the morning is in full swing, the Palace is quiet. I peer down from the Jalousie window slats as the staff moves in robotic motions through the maze of walnut-colored paths across the lawn.

The buzzer at the bedroom door chimes, and a chubby redhead emerges sporting a gray uniform with the tag "Head Chef." Had she been keeping an eye on me, waiting for the exact moment I awoke?

The woman sails in with a steaming silver mug of medium-roast coffee and frothy almond milk with a dash of unrefined brown sugar. My exact Starbucks order. How did she know? The steaming silver mug has cherubs engraved on both sides.

"Why the cherubs?" I ask hesitantly.

"Cherubs, twins," the nameless lady responds warmly. "They are the national arts symbol of Tucana."

And then she shuffles out again. I crane my neck, noticing cherubs staring down at me from the fixture on the ceiling, and I gulp. Does everyone in this palace come and go like puffs of smoke?

The coffee drips down my throat like liquid perfection. Beside the saucer on the tray, swaddled in a dainty pink paper towel, is what appears to be the brand of multivitamin I take each morning. I hadn't packed my home supply for Tucana since it was a quick visit. Had Saif told them? Saif didn't even pay attention to the brand of multivitamins on my side of the bathroom cabinet.

I examine the thin red capsule, mystified. I set aside the gnawing tingle in my stomach, reasoning that my attentive fiancé must have told her. Still, I chose not to take it—*The Matrix* and all.

Once the caffeine rush kicks in, I throw on my gym clothes–which someone already removed from my suitcase, washed, pressed, and laid out at the foot of the bed. A glasshouse gym with state-of-the-art equipment is on the other side of the lawn.

The imposing machines glisten in the quiet space–quiet until Firas saunters in for some show-off iron-pumping exhibit with the free weights. He does not acknowledge me; I do not acknowledge him either. I run a few miles on a sleek treadmill that will not stop talking to me about scenery, goals, and weight management, as though an actual trainer is trapped inside the handlebars, tracking my every move.

I stretch on a thick yoga mat in the far corner and cool off with a gallon of water.

And as I turn my heel to leave, a thick hand clutches a fistful of my ass. The left side, the gunshot side, and I squeal a little.

I whip around. Firas grins and leans his sweaty body into mine, as if it were the most normal thing inscribed on his daily to-do list.

"You know you want me," he taunts. "I'm more than my piece of shit, brother."

I freeze, terrified to move. I don't stop it. But I don't kiss back. Firas's forthrightness frightens me. And it ignites me. Our sweaty bodies plunge to the rubber floor.

BANG.

A dead baby lurches over Firas's defined body, orange flames in the sockets where eyes should be—a melting shadow rolling closer to my neck. Firas grabs my gym shorts; his hand moves up to yank down my sports bra.

I let out a half-yelp. What the hell am I doing? I jump up and yank my sports bra back down. The burned baby is gone. I draw a shallow breath and tread backward toward the door, trying to act normal. Desperate to act normal.

"I almost got you," Firas says coolly, still sprawled out and dripping. "I will get you. Or someone else will."

It is the last I see of him on that virgin international trip. Frazzled, I stumble back into the main Palace, taking the long way to hide my flushed face behind the towering garden beds. I am hungry, dizzy, searching my mind for that burning baby who needs me. I rip off a newly bloomed white geranium, running it along my trembling skin, desperate to eliminate Firas's scent. Can Saif smell him?

Saif is not perfect, but the thought of ever being without him is a terrible torture I cannot survive. When he returns from his duties for lunch, he kisses my cheek twice, but does not elaborate on what he has been doing. Official meetings are all I know. He is relaxed, smiling, and doting on me a little more than usual. Still, I pick at my raspberry-glazed duck breast like a petulant teen as we sit by the Roman-style fountain that cooled like an oasis in the developing heat.

The Palace Chief-of-Staff, a stiff man with a British accent and a deep blue bow tie everyone calls O, approaches as we take our last sips of Far Niente Chardonnay. Saif kisses me again on the cheek and recedes into the blaze of the sunshine. O takes his seat and informs me that there will be a press conference in the late afternoon to officially announce our engagement to the press corps.

A flamboyant man wearing an ivory suit, snakeskin loafers, and an oversized Rolex introduces himself as Neo. His job is to style the First Family.

"Anna, I hope you liked the Versace dress I left for you last night. I have some samples for you to choose from for the press conference," he muses, pursuing his lips and examining my seated frame with an attentive eye. "I'm thinking Lagerfeld for you, but we should consider some local designers, too, for aesthetic sake. Of course, it will have to be solid, neutral tones, as we don't want to overshadow your soon-to-be-husband at the conference."

He whips out a pair of aviators from his pocket and motions them over his black-lined eyes, peering closer at my raven tresses as if I were a cub in a zoo.

"But because you aren't going to be the First Lady," he exclaims. "We can have a little more fun! A plunging neckline or a little ankle on display."

I take a closer look at him too. He has long, surfer-type locks: a sprinkling of facial hair, big biceps, and a high-pitched voice. He drags over a seat from the adjacent table, and man spreads, clicking his fingers. A techno rumble choruses through the sound system, and suddenly a dozen glum-faced young women strut by me as if they were on a runway in Paris Fashion Week.

Then I realize this is indeed a fashion show, and I am in the front row. I am the target audience. It is all odd–but what is most peculiar is how eerily the women resemble me. They are all around my 5'8 height with a similar sylph-like frame, pale skin, big green eyes, and thick manes of hair swept up into high ponytails and parted down the center, just like mine.

The music eventually stops, and the women stand stone-faced and statuesque, hands-on their left hip as they glare past me.

"Bravo!" Neo shrieks, jumping to his face and clapping in delight. "Aren't your decoy models fantastic?"

Before I can question what decoy models are, O glides in beside me, changing the topic. Neo flounces around, explaining the different designers and fabrics and the inspiration behind each part of the collection. However, before I can decide between the Gucci or Pucci dress, O returns to unapologetically inform me that the communications department has canceled the press conference. It's as simple as that.

"Madame Amsa suggested the image we craft of you should be a little more low-key," he states. "The American money girl is leading a quiet, ca-reer-centric life. We will tip the paparazzi off instead, and they will see how pretty you are."

I don't ask questions; O leaves before I can. Neo glances at me with disappointment, then orders the models to the changing room and pounc-es after the Chief-of-Staff. I am left alone to the sounds of the fountain, growing ever louder against the throbbing of my head. Where is my spine? Why am I not questioning anything?

My voice trails, hollow and isolated, as if it had tumbled into that rab-bit hole.

While I'm somewhat relieved there won't be a press conference, I'm also embarrassed. Moreover, I do not know what to say or do next. I do not have to think for long, as with most things beneath the Palace canopy. I am learning each facet has its own time and place, and there is an agenda for every day.

"Don't worry about the press conference thing, the press here will get to know you soon enough. Let's enjoy our day instead. We are going to ex-plore Cyra," Saif texts me. "Meet me at the gates in thirty minutes."

Again, I do not question where he was all morning. So many things I configure will never be my business here. Towards the end of the after-noon, Saif and I navigate through the affluent, government-loyalist neigh-borhoods around the Palace.

The Rolls Royce limousine floats through the wide streets tinged with the smell of new money, freckled with expensive cars and fresh markets, and children playing in the stubby oak trees that unfolded into the skyline.

The vehicle weaves us into the newly dubbed "Madame Sara Boulevard" in honor of the First Lady—where designer stores from Paris and Milan lay bare their treasures for the ever-evolving oil money coterie. I can't under-stand why the western news media persistently decries the evils of the "un-rest." The people of Cyra could not have been kinder and more hospitable as we pause to take photographs and sample the local honey-drenched delicacies. They make no secret of their worship for President General Rian Amsa.

I observe young boys and girls stop to admire and salute the giant billboards of him–in military camouflage—stoic on a pale Arabian horse. Then, when people recognize Saif, walking beside me in a tailored suit and glasses, they lavish him with praise about what a charming family he hails from and what a fierce protector his father is of their land.

Saif wants to show me how open-minded and tolerant his country is and prove that all the reports in western media labeling his father a tyrannical autocrat cracking down on dissidents, dipping them in baths of acid and shooting them square in the face, are wrong.

We venture to the dazzling, gold-tipped mosque in the heart of the Cyra. I remove my shoes and cool my feet in brass sinks of purified water. I slide through the blue carpet orientated toward Mecca, marveling at how the light rains through the high trellises and sprinkles across a frail man deep in prostration.

Then we pass through the narrow alleys of the Old City piled high with brass pots and spices, and entire rooms stuffed with brick ovens, wooden paddles, and soft bread that smelled like a warm blanket on a winter's day. We drive to the medieval monastery off Vea Road on the outskirts of town, sprawling over the green hills like a collection of toy chalets veiled with low-hanging clouds and breezes whispering from the East.

It is one of the oldest structures in Tucana, built in the early 15th century. The monastery is a faded stone place that shivers in January, blisters in July, and blooms with life in those eons of time in between. The angst I felt at church as a teenager toward God fizzles away. A time to be born and a time to die. A time to plant and a time to uproot.

The space is primarily barren, except for the lingering sweet curls of incense smoke and a few nuns bowed over lit candles, so buried in prayer that they do not even notice we are at the door. A beam of sunlight strikes the marbled gold statues, sending powerful splinters of ecclesiastical light to the arched ceiling.

We wade in the mellow obscurity, taking a seat at the dark front pew. We sit until the sun outside thickens from pastels to navy. Saif sits so close, his breath drumming slowly beside mine.

I glance over at his almost boyish face and close my eyes.

I can feel one foot wading through the door of this majestic new existence. But the other foot remains outside, pointed back toward the Big Apple life with my lover, the life I thought had been laid out before me.

When I open my eyes again, it is to examine the colored mosaic high beneath the arches. I repent my guilt over what accidentally ensued with Firas that morning; at least, I attempt to. I can feel Saif also letting go of something. I am not entirely sure what. Ever since the violent balcony incident on September 11th, he carried something with him that he always wanted to shake. Every time he touched me, it was with extra tenderness. A fear. A restraint. An apology. Is he letting that guilt go?

Saif is the kind of person who could walk out of that church, leaving all his sins behind. And I am a person who cannot help but take them all with me, tattoo them to my body, worrying that I will only add to the file of things that I have done wrong.

I call my father's mobile one last time when we return to the Palace. I called it many times before. The line is always busy, or it just rings out. I email too, but I am still waiting for a further response. This time, I telephone from the secure Palace line, and to my surprise, he answers. To his surprise, there is my voice at the other end.

"It's your last night? Oh, I thought you were staying longer, little. We would have more time," Dad stammers.

My heart both sinks and simmers, pumping misery and anger. I have not seen my dad in so many years, and here I am, in his city, and he is not chomping at the bit to embrace his only daughter. His only child. He has not even met my fiancé. My father needs to meet the man I will spend my life alongside, who will one day father his grandchildren.

"Of course, little, I want to see you. It has been a bit difficult with contracts and things," my father says slowly, the chomp of tobacco echoing down the phone line. "I fly to Sana'a late tonight. But please, if you can, come over first. My residence is not far from you. Let your driver know. They know where I live."

Before I properly disconnect the call, a staffer pipes up that a designated driver is on standby to escort me to the home of Mr. Robert Russell. The name jars me; he had always been a Paradis, even if it had never been made official.

Ten minutes later, with Saif sitting anxiously by my side, we ride just a mile down the road to a lovely ranch-style mansion, hidden behind a high gate with an English garden and a fountain in the front yard. Bobby greets us under the porchlight, aged from my last memory, but unchanged in his cowboy boots with a southern drawl.

He beckons us inside, that signature Saigon stomp as pronounced as ever. More pronounced than ever, perhaps.

I open my shaking arms to hug my father. He just put his heavy hand on my shoulder. I introduce him to Saif, but there is a flash of knowledge in both of their eyes. They shake hands with a familiarity I cannot quite understand. Then I remember when I first met Saif at the Hell's Kitchen strip club. He had mentioned his father vaguely knew my father or knew of him, but we never mentioned it again.

Surely, Saif would have told me if their paths had ever directly crossed. Surely, he would have said something if he knew my father. Dad guides us into the living room, the décor a throwback to Texas. A place I know Dad so profoundly misses. The room smells of sandalwood and cumin. There are hunting trophies hanging high over exposed brick walls and plush blankets draped over rocking chairs.

I totter into a creaky seat, the back-and-forth cadence reminding me of childhood. I wonder if I was ever encased in my father's arms and rocked to sleep under the lull of his deep voice.

The moments are long and awkward. I want my father's approval, but instead what I get is a non-rejection. Are they the same thing?

Dad and Saif engage in small talk, primarily banter about the oil industry. Dad has become one of the most prolific industry figures–the original foreign license holder–who swept through in the late 1970s, building up Tucana's energy sector to all it has become today, ripe with natural resources and ripe for the world's attention. I learned that little by little over time.

Despite this, Dad maintains he has not returned to the United States and does not intend to do so. I shift uncomfortably, and Saif reaches for my hand and holds it reassuringly. I ask my father if he still communicates with Josie.

"My life is here now. I can't go back. Well, I have no reason to go there," he murmurs. "Josie and I haven't talked in a long time; we can't talk. It's, well, not safe."

I dare not use the word divorce, but the word hangs over us like the elephant that needs no further explanation.

"I never could go back to sign," he continues, shaking his head, knowing he had said too much. "We–we don't speak much anymore."

Dad's eyes dim with that starry glaze born out of losing something you still love.

"I would have done anything for Josie," he says.

In my periphery, a shadow emerges at the hallway entrance. Lurking, hovering, listening. An unrestrained shriek bounces off the walls, and the figure tiptoes toward me like a little girl breaking the schoolyard rules.

My heart jabs me. Lolita bursts into tears as we embrace, drying my tears with her soft cheek. I have not seen Lolita since that one hasty visit when I was a teen at boarding school.

"You still hold your breath when you hug," she whispers, before touching all over my face, assuring herself that I am real. "Grown-up, so beautiful. You look so much like–"

Lolita stops suddenly, and smiles with shimmering eyes. After all these years, Lolita still makes me feel like I am not alone on this island. Lolita is still home. The only staple in a fleeting childhood.

"I wrote to you so many times, Lolita," I tell her softly. "You have no idea how much I missed you."

Lolita opens her mouth to speak, but only nods.

The four of us sit in the large, open living room, talking without saying anything. But none of us want to stop talking, and none of us want to be the ones to say the first goodbye. As if on cue, Saif's phone rings, and we are informed dinner is ready and guests are waiting at the Palace.

I invite Dad and Lolita to join us. I do not expect them to come, and they do not fail to surprise me. My father embraces me stiffly, his booted feet at a distance. Lolita sobs a little more as I prepare to walk away.

"Have you met my father before?" I ask Saif casually as we drive back to the Palace.

"Ah, a long time ago," he responds quickly. "You know, we've talked–well, not really. It is just he knew–knows–my father from back in the day and things. Setting up the infrastructure here for the refineries and what-not."

For a moment, I feel like the kid left unpicked during gym class sports. I am on the sidelines, watching a game of which I do not know the rules.

"I knew he knew your father, but you never said anything about meeting him yourself," I scoff.

I am annoyed, but I try not to show it. It was a slip; I internally rationalize, as Saif put his hand lovingly on my thigh, sending electric pulses through my body.

Madame Sara's dinner party is another extravagant affair of handmade pasta imported from Florence and fresh fish caught from the tiny village of Vea. We sit at a giant table gifted five years ago by the French President in the Versailles Baroque ballroom. All that boarding school training, and I am still determining which fork to pick up first.

Diplomats dance in and out of the dining area, and so do high-ranking generals and dazzling young women with tiaras and beauty queen sashes around their necks. Sara relishes every moment when another young model-esque beauty joins the table and ensures they meet all the military men and Saif.

Then, he appears.

Despite the dozens of suited guards and the quietude that washes over the hall as he surfaces, the audience rising and bowing in unison like a silent Greek chorus, seeing President General Rian for the first time in the crude flesh is a little underwhelming. All the books I've read about Tucana portray him as a monumental and giant man with a thin mustache and a cigar dangling from his lips.

The President General—still in his military regalia—is technically all those things. More than six feet tall, boasting a signature Cuban, a narrow mustache, and a comb-over, just as the descriptions and pictures implied. But he is as one-dimensional as he is imposing. Chilling, but pitted, a caricature of a Middle Eastern authoritarian. His face looks half handsome and half hound dog. He looks like a wax figure that belongs in a museum more than he belongs commanding an oil-swathed island.

The President General does not bother to introduce himself to me. But he stares at me uncomfortably for a long stretch of time, his brother Tig whispering something into his ear that causes him to glance at me and then the exit door multiple times over.

President General Rian stays at the affair only briefly, shoveling down the main course of porterhouse steak and butter-whipped potatoes artlessly, ignoring all the members of his immediate family—except for Firas. The eldest brother is on his best behavior and much more subdued than I had seen before, as he obediently follows his father. The two leave with a bevy of burly men after an urgent call and before the orchestra begins.

While Saif does the rounds of socializing, Willard moves to sit beside me, ever so calm and collected, sensing that I am on the outside looking in.

"Anna, don't let this all get to you," he says under his breath. "My mother will come around. You don't need to be part of the hoopla. These parties are an embodiment of the hippodrome component of international statecraft. The indulgent puerility. You are better than this."

I thank him with my eyes. Willard gets it; Willard gets me. I blush. I am sure he blushes too.

There is gossip teetering across tables about Firas having invited a dozen beauty queens from Lebanon to the affair, and the butler is stressing where to place them. I can't bear the thought of looking him in the eye if he returns without his father to keep him in check, and I worry about what he might say to me in his loud, obnoxious tone.

I glance up at the chandelier. It is pretty at first—the folds of teardrop glass clinking above the sipping of wine below.

I notice something tiny and flashing clinging to the column. The longer I stare at it, the more a minuscule red dot blinks back at me. I gulp down the Chateau Lafite Rothschild. Perhaps, it is the red of such fine wine reflecting. Suddenly, a hot, steaming clump of undigested food shoots up my throat and crashes back into my chest. I politely excuse myself.

Instead of going to the bathroom to quietly mobilize my mind, I run back to our guest room and pace for a few seconds. I dry heave over the sink, but nothing happens. I splash my face with cold water, urging my floppy mind to get it together. But what is together? What is going on?

I try to jot down the thoughts and memories when they surface, only I have not been all that attentive over the last few whirlwind months. But this is a moment I need to remember. I open my laptop and the Word document I had been slowly adding to, chronicling my memories of everything from my childhood to boarding school to my wild love affair with Saif that has led me here.

"Your account is locked," the banner screams at me, indicating too many incorrect attempts at entering my password.

Was it Saif? Madame Sara? Who the heck has been trying to get inside?

I must transfer all my personal files to the special encrypted server Cliff uses to protect all the manuscripts. I need to be smarter about having a backup.

Figuring nobody will miss me with Madame Sara to carry the room, I wait another hour, lost in a morass of unsettling thoughts, when I can log in again–with the correct password. I breathe a sigh of relief that my document is still there, seemingly untouched.

Almost.

The description of Willard and the rough notes I entered on my way out the door this morning are gone. Maybe I was in too much of a hurry and forgot to press 'save.' With fresh details in mind, I retype my observations, click save, and email the document to Cliff for direct upload.

I sign in to my email and several frantic messages from Josie pop up, asking if I am okay and when I am coming home. My hands shake. I had barely finished my wine. The walls blur, and the painting skews. A message from Lolita's old email account pops up on my screen, then vanishes. Gone. What? Huh? Am I imagining things?

It dawns on me to open the junk folder. There are hundreds of emails from Lolita. As far back as my first year at boarding school, every email is marked as read. This doesn't make sense to me. And then, before my very eyes, they disappear too.

Heart racing and right temple flaring, I shut down my laptop lid and flop onto the bed, wafts of laughter and a violin churning from the lavish dinner downstairs reverberating through my spinning mind. Eventually, I fall asleep with the pale pink of my Chanel slip dress clinging to my body, Saif's side of the bed still empty.

On the following day's drive to the airport, we weave through the peaceful streets as people go about their business in a mixture of tradition-al, flowing dresses and tightly tailored suits. People buy halal street food from the sidewalk, and others stroll in and out of high-class cafes with briefcases tucked beneath their arms.

I read about all the discord in the Washington Post and heard analysts discuss it on NPR back home, but being here now; that all seems fabricated. The food is plentiful. People are working and happy. Only, I can't wait to be home, to walk on the streets of New York, to be any person I want to be that morning or at that moment.

As the vehicle swerves into the main road approaching the airport, the traffic halts to a standstill. I am curious to know how the people of Cyra know that it is a car of importance. They've probably undergone extensive social training to recognize and react to elaborate convoys with heavily-tinted windows.

Except one. A single beaten-up old Honda wracked with dents and rust honks a few times, evidently puzzled why all the traffic has stopped. What transpires next is the worst thing I have ever seen in my two decades of life.

"Out! Out!" screams several guards, storming from the armored vehicle directly in front of the Honda, AR-15 rifles strapped at their necks. There are at least six of them, and they jerk the crooked-back old driver by the silver strands of his balding head. Realizing that he had honked at a Palace VIP, the man looks ashen.

As if watching a silent horror film, I sit pathetically as his coke-bottle glasses crash to the gravel. Doom washes over his wrinkled face, now squinting in the broad sunlight, his mouth opening and closing, begging for mercy.

I stare out at the motionless pedestrians, helpless, curdled in fear. *Crack, crack, crack.* I can feel the nausea rise again as guards hammer the head of a barely five-foot man into the road. I fling my head into Saif's shoulder, his arms bringing me in tighter. *Crack. Crack.* Squinting my eyes, blood soars and plunges like a child squirting hose water on a summer day. I shut my eyes.

I could say something to stop it, but I don't. I could say something to Saif to stop it, but I don't. Saif could have gotten out of the car to stop it, but he doesn't.

I do not see the old man die. But I hear it. His croaky yelps and the pops of his skull against the pavement go on and on. And then they stop. When I gather the courage to uncover my face from my fiancé's shoulder, there is only a mangled body with limbs jutting at odd angles left. Guards quickly scoop the remains into giant garbage bags and push the Honda to the side with their raw strength. Now that the road is clear, we speed forward, and traffic resumes.

"I'm sorry," Saif says softly, brushing away a loose strand of hair before drawing out his Blackberry to casually tap away again as though nothing unusual had happened.

Is he only sorry I had to see it? Or sorry it had happened at all? Silence envelops the remainder of the drive. An airport employee opens my car door and I almost fall out, struggling to find my footing, shaking. The piercing heat has given way to a cool breeze as I float into the VIP entrance, barely registering where I am. The weather is beginning to shift in Cyra. Autumn is arriving, and winter will soon be on its way—the heaving season of perseverance.

Tucana is the state-approved story I read and dreamed about as a teen in all those books. However, Tucana is still a partially told story.

For almost the entire flight home, I lapse into a strange rapture. My eyes are asleep, but my mind is awake. Tremendous remorse trickles through the chords of veins in my body, rushing towards my heart, replaying the old man's bird-like cries for help while nobody dares to do a damn thing. Unperturbed by the incident just hours earlier, my fiancé assiduously takes notes while reading an ophthalmology textbook.

In the minutes before our descent into New York City begins, Saif slips into a light snore and I stand up to pull down some of my own financial planning NYU textbooks from my suitcase. But when I open the overhead compartment, something isn't right.

Reaching aimlessly into the black hole, I feel for my duffel bag of books when–

SLAP.

A burned baby tumbles from the suitcase–whacking me in the face and slamming into my seat underneath. I jump just as the plane drops in a random fit of turbulence. The baby disappears. Where did it go?

To calm myself, I rush to the bathroom to splash water on my face. A puffy red blotch stands out above my eye, exactly where the head of the burning creature fell.

Saif will make it okay, I tell myself. For so long, he made it okay.

Josie telephones me an hour after I land. I expected her to call, requesting details about everyone I spoke with or observed entering or leaving the Palace. But she has statements to make before there are any questions.

"Anna, I was doing a little–well, research–looking ahead to your wedding, and I didn't know before, but," she pauses. "It's in the Tucana Constitution that anyone who marries into the First Family with foreign citizenship must relinquish it; they can only be Tucanese. This wouldn't be good for you. Nothing is worth losing your U.S. citizenship and ability to be here and safe."

Josie could be contradictory and confusing at times. So much of my childhood is punctuated with her silly insistence on my stardom, only to rip the ballet shoes off if I ever became what she did not.

"You were the one who told me to go where I am wanted," I snap.

Jealousy again, I reason. Josie is jealous that I have the attention, the dresses, and the glamour she so rampantly sought in her itty-bitty bikinis and late nights on the Sunset Strip. Josie wanted something grand for me, but then again, she did not. Josie loves me, but it came with the conditions of her ever-oscillating ways.

I sigh and collect myself.

"It's okay, Josie, that's a provision that only comes into effect if the couple in the First Family lives in Tucana as their primary residence," I patiently explain. "Saif and I have agreed to build our lives here in America.

We love America.

"Our life is here. Tucana is not Saif's problem," I continue. "That's a Rian and Firas issue. We want a different life, far from politics."

A sigh of relief comes from the other end of the line.

"Good then, Anna. I was a little worried for a while. But, as charming as Tucana can be, you're safe in the U.S. It's a passport you never want to lose and always want your children to have," she insists.

For the first time, Josie sounds like a mother. Her seriousness perplexes and worries me. But just as quickly, her voice kicks back into the familiar, high-pitched chirp.

"Soooo, walk me through step-by-step! What new stores are there on Madame Sara Boulevard?" she enthuses.

A few more weeks roll by, and summer transitions into fall, the perfect time to wander through the city streets in rain boots and a light jacket, a city still coming to grips with the magnitude of loss. Saif studies hard while I score a college-accredited Wall Street internship, setting up philanthropic funds for European banks in the United States.

On the nights Saif is at his ophthalmology residency, I continue to work for Cliff in his tiny office. I pour over his manuscripts, ones he wrote from the Kachin State jungles of Myanmar about how humans are no different from birds in our cycles of limping, flying, singing, and dying.

And I spend hours writing and recording my own anecdotes.

"If you are not speaking, you are storing it," Cliff tells me over and over.

I transmit my diaries, files, and computer contents onto his private server. I record more voice memos. I trace childhood moments into threadbare fragments that only make sense to me.

"I will let you know when I am ready to put it all together," I say to Cliff. "When I am old and in the twilight of my life."

I don't need to continue working at Extreme Press. It is hardly any money and a departure from my Harvard MBA dreams. But there is something about Cliff—a father figure, a straight shooter, someone I trust in a world where it is hard to trust.

"I didn't mean to overhear you; my headphones were on," Cliff says one evening, almost apologetically. "You recorded what you saw that afternoon in Tucana on the way to the airport."

I am unable to meet his gaze. Cliff would never have stood by as a bevy of strong men murdered a defenseless old man. I feel his warm hand on my shoulder.

"I know you feel it, Anna. I know you feel a lot of things," he continues. "What if a teacher sees bullies beating up another kid in the classroom, but does nothing to stop it? Does that make them complicit? You can't change the past, Anna. But you are an incredibly smart woman, and you can learn."

I lumber through bridal websites, searching for the perfect bright white dress. Saif and I have yet to discuss wedding plans, other than he promised I could choose the destination.

The cold is rushing in fast. My mild annual cold develops into a flu-like virus. Unable to sleep, I hover over the sink, throwing up the few bites of Magnolia's cupcakes Saif brought me home for a treat when the tragic call that would shape our lives buzzes.

"What do you mean, an accident?" Saif croaks out, almost dropping the phone to the floor.

CHAPTER

EIGHT

The following hours pass in a miasma between this world and the one that looms ahead. My gut crisscrosses, and a mound of hot vomit surges in my throat and sinks back down like a yo-yo. Saif is ashen, striding from the dining table to our plush white couch–too overwhelmed to speak, too conditioned to cry.

Once he has finished pacing, he trudges into our sprawling bedroom and methodically begins placing his finest shirts and shoes in his suitcase. He is less like an unflappable man and more like a kid hurt by the idea of moving to a new town, a terrifying new school. I sit motionless on the wooden floor of our Chelsea loft. The snow waltzes across the shuttered window, drowning out the constant sirens of Manhattan living below.

Firas is dead, and that means my fiancé is next in line.

"I'm here for you, Saif," I sob.

Since the news broke, I don't think anyone he loved thought of saying those words to him, especially not his father. My insides yearn to comfort him, but I am afraid to touch him. It is as if he is a shell that could shatter. When I get up, it is to fetch water to drown out the nausea, light candles, and power the CD player to hum "Winter" by the Rolling Stones.

"I wanna wrap my coat around you" –sometimes, I heard Mick Jagger's voice waft out of Josie's bedroom on scratchy vinyl in between her heavy sobs. But the music always comforted me in uncertainty, a place for my melancholy to nest. When I return from the kitchen, O is talking to Saif rapidly on speakerphone. They coordinate his immediate flight to Tucana via a private jet from Teterboro, a private airport in New Jersey.

"Be prepared for a lot more security on you now. You are the successor, Sir," O continues.

My fiancé's status in the ranks of the VIP soared in an instant. I want to be by my man's side. I should be by his side. But perhaps selfishly, I am closing my first major deal between a hedge fund and a massive AIDS vaccine laboratory in Gibraltar, the product of a full year of tireless work.

Before I even mention my place in all this, Saif insists I stay and take care of work and studies. O reiterates that it probably isn't necessary for me to join, stressing that "a lot of official business between the President General and Saif" must be conducted after the funeral. It feels callous, yet I suppose that is what it takes to run a country. There is no moment to waste weeping over blood, never thicker than water.

I know Saif, still in shock, won't ask how his big brother died. But I will. The writer in me must understand how this man spent his last hours on earth. Taking his time, O pieces together the tragedy.

A blanket of obscurity and bruise-colored clouds covered the sky in the early hours of the morning. After days of partying without sleep, Firas decided to take a spin in his new crimson McLaren, which he had freshly imported from the United Kingdom. According to Palace security, he drifted through the jade plains toward Vea, a small Tucanese village. The only route passes through winding mountains, which makes racing even more exciting.

In an unfamiliar car, O speculates that perhaps the brakes failed, or the speed was too high. In the end, the future ruler's life–feigned as invincible to everyone around him–amounted to a plunge off a ledge into a fiery mound far below.

I throw up again over the toilet bowl, too frazzled to comprehend what this all means for the Amsa family. For Saif. For myself. For us.

Early the next morning, the sun gracefully pools into our sleepless abode, and flurries latch onto the window. Saif does not kiss me goodbye. But he holds me for a little longer than usual. Then, he pulls out loft keys from his briefcase and hands them to me. I do not ask why he is not taking his keys, but I understand.

The door closes, and I stare at its back for a while, the brass security chain swinging like a charm on a bracelet. And then it stops.

My office room is eerily quiet after Saif leaves, and I notice his medical journals and notes buried in an extra-large trash bag. He walks into the city's snowstorm, where the snow has already crusted into stained muddy strips stuck to the pavement, and begins a new life. I refuse to call it reverting to an old life, because this was never supposed to be his path.

I purge wildly again. I love Saif too much to let him walk out on me too.

Just two hours after emergency workers recovered Firas's fried body from the wreckage, I read on AOL that President General Rian took it upon himself to amend the Tucana Constitution, lowering the Presidential minimum age from thirty to twenty-seven: the age of his second son.

I telephone Saif three or four times a day over the next two weeks. Our conversations are always brief, only a fleeting minute or two. Training already consumes him, learning everything he can about the military, governance, diplomacy, and history. For his entire life, Saif could not get his father's attention. Now, suddenly, all he has is the President General's scrutiny. It is grooming. It is baptism by fire.

I nudge the rough diamond on my finger. We still need to address what our future will become. I ignore Josie's persistent calls, typically checkered with questions about the Amsa family and what I would be doing, followed by an almost begging that I do not surrender the life I–we–have built in New York. But without Saif here, New York is no longer my home. He is my home. My job feels less critical. What I wanted washes away.

My period is late. Stress, I tell myself. I am on birth control. Did I take it diligently? Yes. Had I forgotten? I rush out in the frozen day and buy a pregnancy test from the Duane-Reade pharmacy across the street. I pee on the stick and watch two pink stripes materialize before my eyes. I rush back out and buy more. A dozen more, every box they had left on the shelf.

I drink water and pee all afternoon. And the following day. And two days later. The double stripes stare at me every time.

"They want me to marry somebody here, someone from a wealthy family here," Saif blurts out during one of our late-night calls a few days later.

Even though we know certain things are coming, they can still catch us off-guard when they arrive.

They must be his parents, the Chief of Staff, the ministry heads, Palace Communications—the people with fancy titles and the bricklayers for the house Saif will someday head.

"An arranged marriage?" I ask, voice quivering.

"Yes," he says. "I can't expect you to give up everything you have wanted for this. I am about to take on something never destined to be mine."

"How do you love if it is an arranged marriage?"

"You learn to love, they say."

"Is that what you want?"

"It's not about what I want."

A long pause.

"I'm pregnant."

A longer pause.

"How far?"

"I just found out yesterday. I was waiting for the right time to tell—the doctor says about six weeks."

"Do you want to keep it?"

"I don't want my child. I want our child."

"You know what this does to me, right?"

"What do you mean to you? I'm boxing you in now without a choice?"

"No, baby, you are my choice. But I am not supposed to have a choice."

"Well, you do. And we are going to do this. I want to do this with you. I don't care about my life here. Home is you."

"Give me a few more weeks to get through pilot training. Then, I'll have the assistant craft a plan for us to meet for a weekend in Paris. I don't want the fanfare; it is a country in mourning here."

I do not wantto ask more questions, too anxious about the answers. I am afraid to call the doctor, afraid to call Saif, and afraid to listen to all of Josie's voicemails begging me not to move away. Emails and calls flood in from the New York Times and The Guardian, and a bossy CNN crew has been camping outside my building for three days.

"There is no need to complicate your life more than it is," Cliff tells me on the phone when I seek his advice. "We all tend to complicate our lives much more than we need."

I hide inside and survive on the sourdough bread loaves left in the freezer, the only thing I know I can keep down for at least a few hours. I mayo-lather each slice with great purpose, sometimes for hours, watching the delicate whitish cream melt into the slightly singed pores like face cream.

"Carbs will make you fat," bellows a familiar voice. "The doorman let me in. I worked my charm. He said you haven't been answering his calls."

Looking like an immaculate supermodel in a form-fitting black fur coat and skin-tight pantsuit with feline eyes accentuated with thick mascara, Taya breezes into the loft with a basket of farmer's market-fresh foods and a clipboard.

"Do you think I would let you spend your 21st birthday alone? Not a chance, baby girl," she states.

Like some angel in red Giuseppe Zanotti boots, fresh off the express Amtrak train from Washington D.C., Taya opens my laptop, guesses my email password, and begins tapping away–handling the press queries with her right hand and navigating my blackberry messages with her left. During the moments in between, she roasts chicken and chargrills broccoli. She vacuums and scrubs the entire apartment without a word, intuitively understanding that I do not feel comfortable with someone I did not know coming in to clean the apartment.

I can't be certain that the National Enquirer wouldn't pay the stranger to steal secrets covertly. I cannot be sure that a stranger in my home would not shop around pictures of my haggard body over the toilet bowl.

I haven't told Taya I am pregnant; I barely digest the news myself. But in our kinetic friendship, she knows–pouring red wine only for herself and filling my glass with fresh cranberry juice, which she hands me with a wink.

I watch a little of Firas's funeral on television: the grand procession and the Tucanese mourners choking the freshly paved streets. My gut aches with both relief and longing. I should be there. But guiltily, I am grateful to be safeguarded by the wandering brown leaves of New York City. Then the shiny Sepia coffin reaches Verte Square. In this historical place, teenagers ordinarily hold hands, and tourists feed the pigeons and walk solemnly around the frozen-over fountain and quiet cafes.

Many don't notice the rusted noose still swinging from a looming, decaying pole. But when we were there, I saw it. Of course, public executions are a relic of a time long past, exceedingly rare these days. At least, that is what the books by Tucanese writers told me. I wonder why they kept it there. Perhaps a reminder never to return to such barbaric cruelty. Or to stay in line.

Days grind on. Taya continues to work her alchemy on my behalf. Then I snap with an insatiable need to feel the fresh, invigorating New York air on my skin. I throw on a hoodie and ripped jeans and ride the subway to the only place outside the house where I can breathe: Cliff Walker's Extreme Press office. I don't text him first, but I know if he will be there. He is always there.

I turn the key, and sure enough, Cliff is sitting beneath the shivering lamplight, rubbing his beard deep in thought, while he types late into the

December evening. His simple, sustainable timber desk is barely visible beneath the mounds of books and loose papers, broken pens and ripped magazines.

What must it be like to love what you do so much that you have sacrificed everything else for it? And that every second of every day, you are pining to dip back into devotion, where nothing feels like work and everything feels like love and duty mixed as one. I love my work, but I love Saif more. Does that make me an ordinary, unambitious woman?

"Oh, Anna," Cliff says sympathetically, in a way that tells me that I do not have to say anything.

Since I don't want him to see that I am almost crying, I focus my attention on the walls of Extreme Press—news clippings and magazine covers cover every inch of space. Cliff's certificates for skydiving and ski instruction, and rodeo championships hang at off angles. Photographs of Mount Everest and Byron Bay are frameless and taped up, blown up to the point where the colors have waned, and his face on them is no longer recognizable.

My favorite is the Polaroids Cliff took on horseback sometime in the mid-1980s. At first glance, he is moving at a lightning pace through an alpine village. However, when I press my nose closer, I see something wrong—large holes burrow into the ground, shattered windows, and a panorama of mountains surrounds the shrapnel that once was a fence.

I trace my finger around those pictures and notice, for the first time, a "V" in a dull marker at the bottom of one. Maybe it is Cliff's code, his secret.

I don't know why I am even here. Cliff already knows my password to the encrypted voice recordings. There is a drawer I packed with all the notebooks from my childhood and boarding school. They are all labeled by date and collecting dust. I want to show him again, I suppose, to remind him to keep my memories secure because I can't trust myself to do so. He pours me a small glass of aged whisky, but I politely push it to the side. We chat about book sales and the internet, his plans to live for a month with the Bedouins in Petra to write an article for "Outside" magazine, and all the poetry submissions coming in from Alaska and New Zealand.

I could stay here forever with Cliff, a gentle father figure in an oversized Siberian hand-knitted sweater and a zest for life and stories without a mere mention of money that I had never known was possible.

"I have to go now," I mumble, looking achingly at the chipped gray door I would have to walk out and through.

Cliff fishes out a ridiculously small black recorder from beneath the desk rubble—barely the size of my pinky finger, with a simple on-and-off switch and jagged holes serving as a speaker. He says it was courtesy of a former Israeli intelligence official and what he planned to take to capture thoughts when running up mountains or skidding down glaciers on the earth's edges. He makes me promise to dictate every languishing memory, assuring me it will be transmitted through encryption back to his private server here.

"You will have many eyes on you, Anna," Cliff continues. "But this is the sort of technology that the Tucanese don't even have yet. Keep it tucked in your bra or pocket when whispering into it; make sure you keep it well hidden, and your voice will be safe. Nobody can erase this."

In all his worldly wisdom, Cliff understands the arena I am heading into much more than I could have possibly imagined at that moment.

"That way, no one can hear or delete your soul," Cliff says, somewhat cryptically, staring down at my diamond. "You are marrying a man who will not belong to you, but will belong to everyone. This outlet is for you."

The depth of those words is beyond my comprehension, and I do not know if I could ever comprehend them. But I vow to whisper and whisper into that minuscule microphone, continuing what I have already started: the little girl, the memories, the moments, and the magic. Yet at that moment, there is no doubt that something ominous has crept through the window, sneaking in with the breeze.

"You still have choices, Anna. Remember that," Cliff says gently.

"The only choice I have is Saif, and Saif no longer has a choice," I reply defensively.

"Yes, he does," Cliff notes firmly. "We all have choices, and he is making his."

We bid each other a long and silent hug goodbye.

When I close the door, I close something else. Cliff knows I am never coming back. I know I am never coming back. And when I wait for the subway home, I wait for the last time.

A peculiar man in a leather jacket strolls along the platform, his eyes bouncing between me and the opaque subway tunnel where a train should arrive at any moment. His gaze traces my back, outlined beneath the flickering 40W bulbs that have long passed the point of replacement. There is only the hissing of a rat on the moldy tracks as the wind batters through the dim tunnel. His footsteps creep behind me but then halt, interrupted by the blinding lights of the oncoming train bustling around the corner.

The shadows. The hot breath on my neck. The train screams closer. A baby. Burned and bleeding eyes before me on the tracks. My heart races. The train is screaming closer, and the tiny baby, too tiny, starts wailing out to me with an outstretched arm. What can I do? I shriek uselessly at the conductor to stop. *STOP!* But it will be too late. Maybe I can leap and then press myself against the gap of the platform, just in time for us both to survive. I indecisively allow the seconds of stiff thought to linger for too long. One, two . . . I think I can do it–then a gloved hand yanks me back from the platform edge.

The man with the leather jacket. His eyes meet mine as I stumble onto the safety of the cold subway platform in a stupor of disorientation and an ominous gurgle in my stomach that I cannot shake.

The burning baby vanishes from my view.

"Oh, Anna, I am so sorry," Taya says as I rush in, her French-manicured nails resting on my shoulder. "The leader. It is confirmed. President General Rian passed away about an hour ago."

What? My eyes unsteadily swerve to the television. The ticker at the bottom bounces out at me that the authoritarian leader of Tucana "died suddenly of a massive heart attack on a flight from Riyadh to Cyra." I hear it on the television, not from my fiancé. I cannot believe I have to see and hear it on television.

When my momentary anger subsides, I bury my face into a stash of tissues. I can only begin to imagine Saif's pain.

"Baby, I love you," I choke down the phone line when he finally picks up.

"I love you too, Anna," he responds, his voice deeper than I ever remembered. Stronger. More commanding. Not cracked with emotion the way I expected. "It is not too late to–take care of things."

I don't ask questions because I do not want answers, a trait that is becoming more and more ingrained in my daily life. In the long silence that permeates the other end, Saif gives me one last chance to walk away, to retain this life that was mine. I am only 21. Motherhood will surely come again.

But I want him, and that comes with accepting his life. I want our child. I want his child.

"I should be there," I stammer.

"Everyone is a wreck, mother, Willard, the pool cleaners . . . Nobody was ready for this," Saif says, his voice slightly breaking, before coming together again. "But Anna, we will have to move this up. This wedding won't be the fantasy–but I think we're both okay with that. We can both be in Paris in eight hours. I have to take care of a few things here, but the office will make your arrangements, and I will meet you there a day late . . . The Palace will forgive me for not marrying a local woman once everyone understands why."

I pause. Does Saif want to be a husband, or does he need a wife? Does he want to be a dad, or is he just going with the motions of being a father? I push down the swelling tears.

"And I love you," Saif adds.

These are the words women must hear. *Click.* I spread my fingers wide over my tumultuous yet still flat stomach.

"It's going to be okay," I repeat to the growing speck inside me.

"You have to stay strong, Anna," Taya says soothingly. "You have a growing little one to protect now."

"How do you know?"

"You're my sister. Nothing escapes me."

A rash of nausea once again injects itself into my abdomen. I dry-heave and fall asleep fully clothed, waking at sunrise to Taya pressing a warm washcloth onto my forehead and Karl Lagerfeld at the foot of my bed. Well, a flotilla of his unique creations, at least.

The morning passes in a flurry of white tulles and slicks, like pearls forming the string of my evolution. Of course, Taya knows Karl and called him personally to have dresses shipped in the night for me to choose. A burgeoning Washington woman, Taya knows everyone in the industries where it is essential to be somebody among everybody. So, amid a mental fog, dresses come on and off.

The showing ends with a simple, long-sleeve wrap dress resembling an overpriced Grecian robe carefully hung into a silver bag by Taya exclaiming, "This is it!"

"You are gorgeous," she assures me for the tenth time that day, squeezing me in tears and waving me off from the private Teterboro airstrip.

I touch down in Paris in the heart of the sleet-bitten night, inhaling my first European adventure with all five senses. I wander alone through the icy streets rich with cafés and cigarettes, laughter, and Christmas carols, sworn to secrecy over what is to come, settling on a quiet bookstore nestled by the River Seine. It is all bridges and booths teeming with handmade trinkets.

I am alone, but never really alone. The leather jackets roam a few yards away, never making eye contact with me, but never far from my gaze. Are they watching me? Do I just not notice such leather all around me?

I shake the slivers of paranoia from my mind and study the river that flows at the crux of coup attempts by the Romans, then known by its Latin name Sequana. I pick up random books, but the words buoy in front of my eyes, not sinking below the surface. I think about how I am technically half French, but sitting here, I do not feel it.

My phone rings again. I cannot ignore Josie's calls any longer. Begrudgingly, I answer. She rattles off everything without me saying anything—where I am and why.

"I can't tell you what to do, Anna. But it is not too late to walk away. Please think long and hard, because you will never be this free again," she declares feverishly, the familiar sound of the Malibu waves lapping behind. "You don't have to live this life if you don't want it."

The burden falls back onto my shoulders. I get it. This moment is it. I have a choice, but Saif is my choice. He is home now, and wherever he is, that is where I want to be.

In my silence, Josie understands my decision.

"The night before you marry is the saddest day of your life," Josie continues, returning to that rare maternal mode. "You have to say goodbye to your family. And you can't be your father's daughter again. You say goodbye to your family, whether you know it or not. No one ever wants to tell you that. The safety net goes away. I can't keep you."

Jealous. I reassure myself. Just jealous.

"There is always William and Harry," she posits, but without the chuckle that usually accompanies a joke. "Might be a better fit."

Is she that insensitive?

Despite the double-tragedy ripping at the seams of the Amsa family, I am happy. I tell her so. Josie is wrong. Josie is writhing with envy; I continue telling myself. She is always jealous. My future husband is powerful, wealthy, and has enough money to keep our fairytale intact.

"I am the star," I state, my voice rising. "You wanted me to be the star, and now I am, and you can't handle that."

"It's not that simple," Josie remarks.

That old saying about blood being thicker than water, well, so are wine and milk. I end the call.

Before flagging down what will probably be my last inconspicuous cab ride, I stroll toward the Four Seasons Hotel George V, poised just off the Champs-Elysees, through the city of light, crowned by an opalite fog.

I arrive at a penthouse hotel suite doused in red roses and chocolate, and my fiancé fresh from his plane from Cyra, idling by the window in the shadows of the Eiffel Tower.

Saif looks a little beefier than before, but when he smiles, I see him—I see the man who buys flowers from the deli and uniquely unvarnished rings. That boyish smile will never fade. I race toward him with open arms. There is no turning back. And I do not want to turn back.

We have broken every rule in the book, from living together before marriage to conceiving a child and plotting a private wedding. And we will keep breaking more. That means getting dressed together the following day with croissants and coffee, evading the rule that the bride should never see the groom on their wedding morning.

For only a bit longer, Saif is all mine. We talk arbitrarily about the leader he wants to be.

"I will not be like my father," he pledges, looking me dead in the eyes.

He glimpses through the window into the browning trees, frosted white, and stretching into the thick tendrils of morning mist.

"I will be proud. I am proud. But Tucana will be a free place. I will address the concerns of the dissidents. Nobody has ever really listened to them. Tucana will have a strong economy. We want positive relations with the United States of America, open up the economy in more ways than just oil," Saif continues, gaining momentum. "We want tourists from all over the world to see the beauty of Tucana, not just visitors from Russia and China. Anna, we are a young first couple and western-educated. We are different."

I curl my hair and do my own makeup, all actions that would later be folded into the public image of "the people's princess," so to speak. But the most critical task right now is keeping our nuptials as far away from the press as possible. Saif zips me into a silky layer of Lagerfeld white and pins a single pink rose into my hair.

"My beautiful cherub mother," he murmurs into my lips.

A state-appointed photographer, flown in from Cyra, captures our private moment of exchanging vows and rings. These images will remain in the vault until the powers-to-be decide it is time to make the big announcement. The happiest day of my life hastens by in a blur, a brief private ceremony beneath the Arc de Triomphe, built under King Louis-Philippe in the early 19th century to commemorate his victories.

We have done the deed. It is momentous, but the earth does not move.

The kiss comes last, and Saif makes me promise to spend a few days to myself in Paris—where all I will do is swill around the grand boulevards and wrap up the loose ends of my old life. I promise.

"And then you will follow me," Saif says with a long kiss goodbye. "To Tucana."

My husband leaves again, and for a second, I remember that little girl squeezing her father's leg by the Beverly Hills Hotel pool, her cheek pressed close to his concealed weapon, wishing he did not have to leave. But Saif must hurry back to Tucana to take care of a leaderless country.

I send an email of resignation to the banking firm in Manhattan, terminating my paid internship. I am not bothered about the bonus I came so close to cinching with an AIDS vaccine laboratory ready to sign on as a client this week. It would have been my first major deal; one I had constructed from the beginning almost to the end. Nevertheless, I walked away.

I surrender my citizenship at the U.S. Embassy before the close of business that afternoon to arched eyebrows of official surprise, a long black coat covering my wedding dress. I'm not yet ready to take off that beautiful gown.

I promise myself that I will not be bitter about parting ways with my homeland as I slowly walk along the Parisian streets. However, a great deal of discipline is required to stay away from the windows of travel agencies selling vacation packages to South Carolina and Vegas. All the places I once could go to without a word.

But they say deaths happen in threes.

It is over a lukewarm pot of mint tea at an open-air café—reading *Freedom from Fear* written by Aung San Suu Kyi while on house arrest in Burma—that I notice reddish smears on my clothes. Oh no. Can a dry cleaner remove the stains? As a dull ache convulses in my stomach, I rush back to the hotel.

Then more smears and some more. The dress is stupidly expensive and on loan under Taya's good graces.

With complete clarity in my trembling tone, I telephone the concierge downstairs for an immediate doctor's appointment. Oblivious to the impending snowstorm, I make my way across the windy street into a modest gray clinic as the sky grows darker. . Chic Parisians wait with their lovers. I am ushered in before them, insulated from what suddenly becomes sheeting rain and snow outside.

An older man, maybe seventy, with hairy hands and magenta spectacles prods around the sullied swaths of my ruined wedding dress, before inserting an object between my legs and examining my swollen belly with a wearied eye. The thump of the beating heart, the cherished sound I read about in all those first-trimester forums, is replaced by silence. Seconds that tell me everything I need to know.

The doctor purses his lips and, in roughened English, instructs me to rest until the bleeding stops. Was it the flight? Was the dress too firm against my growing waist? The cup of coffee? I think about everything I have done wrong, panic clogging my mouth. I think about asking the doctor all these questions calmly and articulately, but when I speak, he shakes his head as if to say that I make no sense.

In those few dreamlike days drunk on the honeymoon of grief, alone in my elaborate suite, I wonder if the bleeding will ever stop. I speak myself through the pain, guilt, confusion, and pity into that little recorder Cliff gave me. I tell the untold story inside me, immortalizing the moments, and I speak of the child that could have been.

I stare at my phone. But I do not call my husband. It is strange to think of Saif this way. My husband. He is dealing with too much already.

In a weird way, I had erased my past. I left the only book I had with me, the one by Ayn Sang Suu Kyi, at the open-air café when the beginning and end of that past life started. Anything that had taken place in my old life as an American is now gone. The page is blank and open.

Then, the bleeding stops. The pain goes away too. I leave Paris for Cyra with tender breasts, a broken heart, and an unfamiliar diplomatic passport.

"When you do those long climbs, do you still feel phantom pain, even a long time after it has subsided?" I text Cliff before I board.

"There is no such thing as phantom pain. If you feel the pain, it is real," Cliff writes back almost immediately. "And you might want to consider going back to some fiction books. Sometimes, we understand more about the real world when it's written in make-believe."

A husky smog blots out the sunshine, as if somewhere President General Rian Amsa still presides over the weather with a switch. It is my first official public engagement with Saif, but nobody–at least publicly–knows he is married.

Saif holds me the moment I arrive–he needs the embrace just as much as I do. I do not want to let him go.

"I'm so glad you are here, my love," he whispers. "I could not do this without you."

If there was any hesitation toward this new existence, it evaporates. Love doesn't come by every day. I open my mouth to tell him what happened with the miscarriage, but with the funeral proceedings of his father ongoing, I close it again.

The suited people around us now call him Doctor Amsa. Saif hasn't finished his medical degree, but it seems that doesn't matter, and the Tucanese people don't need to know that. As far as Tucana is concerned, if he says he is fully qualified, he is fully qualified. Saif will soon be the President Doctor who will rule their isolated little land.

I trudge, subdued, beside my husband, following behind the flag-draped white coffin in a black mink coat, Valentino glasses, and a black veil issued to me in one of Neo's tissue paper-protected shopping bags with a note reading "FINAL FUNERAL."

The snow has melted into somber puddles on an unusually warm winter morning. Saif and I sweat beneath layers of clothing and the billows of humidity. Willard walks to our left, holding his tear-streaked moaning Madame mother. The Army Chief of Staff is positioned directly to our right, in front of a band of high-ranking military men. They stampede around the cavalcade of black Mercedes and tanks designed to detect and destroy roadside bombs. Men in green uniforms swarm the barricaded streets to ensure nobody breaks through.

President General Rian's carefully crafted face glares down at us from every billboard towering over the crowded streets—a bushy mustache and canonized eyes of strength and openness. The paradox of a loved and hated leader.

Now comes the final funeral service for the dear leader. The first occurred at dusk the day before, a very private procession on the Palace grounds, with trumpeting and scenes of his heroism displayed on moving vehicles. The only press allowed in was state television Cyra24 and the Tucana Times state newspaper, the President General's mouthpieces, and national treasures. While I was somewhere in the skies from Paris clutching my depressingly empty stomach, there was an escargot de Bourgogne-filled diplomatic reception in the Palace for the arriving foreign dignitaries. I could tell from the photographs that the service was smaller than Saif had anticipated. I quietly configured the low turnout is due to the murky standing Tucana had acquired as a growing pariah in the international community. The second was an open casket viewing at dawn this morning for men of the military and intelligence branches.

And now I watch the farewell in the company of high society while the common people languish behind fences on the sidewalks.

French President Jacques Chirac is the only Western head of state to have undertaken the journey. The United States is keeping a distance, careful of appearing too close to a regime accused of long-standing human rights abuses. Richard Armitage, the Deputy Secretary of State, has been sent in place of President Bush. Probably to snoop or to make sure the last drilling license for Chevron makes it through, I muse to myself.

And here we are, a nervous bunch, all waiting for the swan song to start.

Before the formal speeches commence, the dignitaries are left to mingle for a moment. My first instinct is to walk over and say hello to the Deputy Secretary. He ambles alone at the edges with a water bottle in hand, staring out at the thick mourners in a kind of artificial oblivion. But with an internal shove, I remember the United States is no longer my country. What would I say? Hello, I surrendered my citizenship a few days ago?

The Russians, meanwhile, have sent an entire delegation. When I pivot, a tall figure in a cowboy hat–the outline of my father–stands out in the entourage of friends and family allowed in the procession. I blink. Once. Twice. Dad? And then the figure wanes into the weeping masses.

I mentally shake out the creases of my mind and inch closer to Saif, his eyes protected by wrap-around Ray-Ban sunglasses. He shakes visitors' hands calmly, seeming to forget I am even here. I want my new husband to turn back and brush my arm or at least lock eyes, but he does not. From inside my mesh veil, I observe a sea of black-cloaked mourners, collapsing on the sidewalks, sobbing for their leader.

Beefed-up guards sweep the gridlocked crowds, randomly dragging mourners aside for an intense pat down and scan. When a guard's eyes focus on a person, their feet suddenly shuffle in exaggerated grief. The taut faces around them begin to tremble as if they too are trying to convey as much distress as possible. It is as though they are all performing like their lives depended on it–did their lives depend on it? Even in death, the President General is perhaps more feared than loved.

I can't think of a single person I know who would be as upset over the death of my President–my former President–Bush.

A swollen sea of bodies stretches as far as the eyes can see; arms extended in anguish toward their dead leader's coffin. They are raucously propelled back by the sweating and suited guards. A firmly controlled regime has no room for protest or opposition or any person that does not appear distraught. There is nothing but pure loyalty and devotion to the dictatorship.

The procession arrives at the Palace gates, which looks like an explosion of color and bouquets. My new home is where the leader will eternally rest beside his eldest son, buried beneath a hill of fresh soil, a searing reminder of the other wound that still oozes.

There, amid the enormity, I hear myself saying goodbye to myself. I am on the outside of my body, looking through the dark veil's holes at the life unfolding before me. I could never have imagined such a life in my wildest childhood dreams. I am about to become someone. Someone of importance. Someone famous. Someone wealthy. Not just anyone.

I am supposed to feel that I have made it; I am a success. But I only feel like a fraud. What have I done to be victorious, other than to fall for a foreigner at a strip club and forget to take my birth control one night? I haven't done anything of significance to earn my place of power. Marrying into government seems too hollow to be considered an achievement.

I peek over at Saif's blank stare at the massive crowd, his eyes clouding even more when he catches my stare. He knows he hasn't done a thing to warrant triumph either.

I can sense my husband's pain, but cannot feel my own. I am about to be part of the leadership of an island nation I have long been fascinated by, even though I possess only surface knowledge. I think about Josie's warnings and her vehement worry about me giving up my U.S. passport. My out. There is no longer an out: this is it. This exquisite property, poking up from the fertile patches of soil, is my house. Saif is my home. My everything. I have nothing else left but him.

Hours pass with trumpets, speeches, prayers, and self-flagellation into the muggy sky. Then, under a chorus of cries, the pristine gold coffin is lowered into the earth. In spite of Saif's tearless face, he seems trapped in a web of complicated emotions he can't fully grasp. I clasp my husband's hand. Although I may seem so far away in his mind, I am here.

A sudden realization dawns on me: this could have been our honeymoon. There is a part of me that wants to console Saif. There is a part of me that wants to rip his clothes off. And then there is a part of me that longs to throw off my heels and run away with him. Far, far away, never to return to the sprawling lawn, the throngs of humans, and the invisible layers of responsibility.

Following the formalities, men smoke thin cigarettes on the opulent Palace grounds and drink tart black coffee passed from palm to palm, all the while making no attempt to conceal their admiration for the scantily clad young women. I remember one of the women from our engagement garden party, a former Miss Tucanese called Eva. To me, they are all Evas, fluttering around, offering the men a shoulder to cry on. I wonder how all the Evas manage to get inside the wake in the absence of Firas.

On the other side of the main residence, I hide beneath an awning for a few minutes. Then, a familiar round face, balancing a heavy water jug and a clipboard, bounds toward me awkwardly. That's right, Millie. I recall the name and pudgy face from a brief encounter on my first visit to Cyra.

"Miss Anna, are you okay? Are the food and drink okay?" she asks in a high-pitched tone that reminds me of a child, her eyes wide open in concern.

"Yes, Millie," I respond, touching her arm in a reflex to ease her apparent stress.

"Good, good," she gushes. "I am the director of food and beverages. If you ever need or have any special requests, please come to me. I will do anything I can for you, Miss Anna. Welcome, Miss Anna. Hello."

Something about her innocent begging, the way she carries her excess weight with a lilted gait, makes me feel as though I can confide in her.

"Millie, I have no idea what I am doing here," I confess. "What happens next? How long does this go on?"

This short, wrinkled woman with a sweating brow and strands of silver hair leans close to my shoulder, simultaneously putting down the objects that occupy her arms.

"We mourn each death for twenty days," Millie says, voice low and quiet, unraveling the cultural ritual like a game of Chinese whispers. "Someone dies, and for twenty days we wear black and pray, cry, and lean on each other. We remember them and talk to them. And on the twenty-first day, we awake, and the life has re-started."

The days of mourning for Firas have passed, and it has been ten days since the sudden departure of the President General. Ten more to go. In eight days, I promise to stop dwelling on the budding life taken from inside of me.

Against the apricot sky, as the bright parakeets glide back to their homes, I return to the pile of black designer clothes and the soundtrack of well wishes. I ask the waiter for a glass of whiskey neat.

With the glass at my lips, a black-gloved hand yanks it away.

"What are you doing, Anna? You can't drink, remember?" Saif mutters into my ear.

All I want is for him to hold me and tell me everything will be okay. Grabbing his tux, I draw him close, close enough for my aching breath to touch his ashen face. My knees want to buckle, but I must stay upright. I stare into his bewildered eyes for a moment. The elastic seconds. I shake my head.

Saif's face twists into a knowing look.

"Just a few hours after you left," I explain hoarsely, surprised that I even have the strength to say it. "The bleeding started."

His face resembles a silent movie of anguish cross-fading into anger.

"The heck," he grunts. "I married you. We agreed to have that child."

I am immediately perplexed, wounded. Is it the stress? The grief? Why is Saif acting so cold?

"Don't you dare take this out on me," I hiss back as angry tears spring from my eyes.

This time, it is Saif who draws me closer. He might kiss me in a gesture of apology, his lips moving toward my neck. But, instead, he exhales heavily into my ear, the fire of his breath persisting. And then he walks away without a word.

Standing there with a half-full glass, I remind myself that love should know no bounds. I remind myself that Saif is hurting too. His brother and father passed before he could say goodbye, and now the child he thought was coming is dead too. I gulp down the glass and venture with feigned confidence into the crowd, blending in with the famed and fortunate with whom my new life chapter is centered. Madame Sara is wheeled up alongside me, holding Willard's hand as a Palace staffer pushes her in a gold-plated, diamond-encrusted wheelchair. Two younger staffers fan her dramatically and pass a tissue for every rolling tear. Madame Sara's delicate bones protrude through thin skin, much thinner and more drawn than I remember.

"What did you do to my son?" she scoffs at me. "It's you who is making me sick. Don't think you will be taking my place in presiding over Cyra. You know nothing. American girl who doesn't understand our economy, what is best for our people."

I freeze. Willard glances at me regretfully, shaking his head in irritation. My right temple burns into my scalp again.

"You don't know me, and you don't know what I know, Madame Sara," I respond with all the self-respect I can muster, leaning on one Yves Saint Laurent heel and swinging my hips, determined to peel my man away from that growing collection of beauty queens filtering through the crowds.

I can't believe what I just said, that I had dared talk back. Madame's firstborn and her husband had just died. I could have said nothing and apologized for making her so upset. What had gotten into me?

But the truth is, I am not sorry. Madame Sara does not even want to give me a chance. So, I will have to show her. I have no choice but to prove how popular I can be and how much good I can do for Tucana.

I don't know if Willard–standing a respectful distance behind me with eyes cast out at the thinning crowd–thinks it appropriate to stand up to his mother. Nevertheless, he is at my rescue the moment she is wheeled away like the withering Wicked Witch of the West, fighting for her relevancy in a modernizing palace.

Willard–with his wholesome radiance–appears like a suited knight. He says nothing and yet says everything with a thoughtful and prudent shoulder squeeze that sends a tingle through my spine. Calm and thoughtful, and wet-eyed in grief behind those Delphic frames. He stands beside me, where Saif had been hours earlier. My husband's youngest brother is the only one who is calm, collected, and seemingly able to hold the weight of the world.

"You are going to do an incredible job, Anna," Willard whispers.

Jetlagged and on the verge of tears each time my hand touches my hollow stomach, I thank him with a quick embrace and quietly exit the wake before it reaches its depressing conclusion. I feel the same pang I felt as a child crawling out of the Beverly Hills Hotel pool when my fantasy dissolves into the bitter reality of leaving those pink walls and palm trees behind. In the same way, I want to hold onto this moment because I'm afraid of what lies ahead.

Willard kindly walks me back to my quarters.

"Saif was always the quiet one," he remarks tenderly. "Stood back, did as he was told. Leading Tucana isn't going to be an easy ride–but he's a lucky man to have you by his side."

Willard hugs me goodnight, a real hug without the tense or distant protocols.

I curl up in bed in anticipation of my husband's return, relishing the moment of resting my swollen feet. I wait. And I slip into a dream state while waiting.

I am surprised when I go downstairs to the entry foyer the next day to learn—and see—that Josie has sent condolences to the family in two incredibly large bouquets of vibrant roses. Quite a budget, I think dryly. A few minutes later, she calls and asks if the Palace received them and, in her throaty voice, implores me to vow that if I ever were scared for my safety, I would inform her immediately.

"I will use every resource I have to get you out of there," she whispers. "Tucana is not safe. Trust me, Anna baby; I know it is not safe. And we can't have this conversation again. The Shush police do not want you drifting out of their control."

I feel shaken. But Josie does not need to know it.

"I am fine, Josie," I say. "I am just fine."

Josie's sporadic motherly love manifests in the oddest of ways. She questions me about imported foods, the new designer stores, my drivers' nationality, and the mourners' actions.

"Had any of them received threats of things that could happen if they didn't cry enough in the streets for President General Rian adequately?" she asks, trying to sound calm and collected. "You know, well, I read that senior intelligence closely examines all the footage, and if anyone doesn't look mournful enough, they typically end up in jail."

Josie talks about the crime thrillers she is reading and the new season of "America's Most Wanted." The cabin of Malibu amplifies her zany ways, and even though she insists Tucana is dangerous, I can't tell if she misses the tiny island she wandered in and out of so frequently during my childhood. I am sure she must, after all, it is one of the most exquisite places on earth. Or perhaps she misses the man she once loved but pushed away.

Saif and I do not discuss the miscarriage again, and in his unspoken regret for how he had behaved, he takes me out to the Cyra Christmas markets, one of the most romantic things in the world, at dusk.

"I want you to see how magnificent your new country is, Anna," Saif says excitedly, spinning me around and dipping me backward as if we were inside a Louis Armstrong jazz club.

The entire market is shuttered to the public so that we can drink mulled wine and wander hand in hand through the crooked paths looking for spices of cinnamon and rosemary as several leather-jacketed men trail behind. We kiss beneath the mistletoe and pray with old Christian pilgrims in the monastery. My husband guides me to the roof of his favorite restaurant, where we sit like Sultans on sturdy cushions, swaying to the beat of musicians sent to serenade us with island harmonies and instruments created from shells on the beach and sticks from the jungle. These are the precious days of the in-between of our lives, shrouded in bliss, before the inauguration, the labels, the folders of burden and the feeling that tragedy was never far away.

I married a man who is married to everybody, Cliff's warning chimes in my ears.

A few days later, as I am snuggled between coats of fine cotton and blanketed by flicks of the blue moon, the right side of my head pounds. It is the nothing time allying night and day—the gray time just before the dawn broke through—that it pounds the hardest.

I am only twenty-one. I am married and a First Lady. I thrived in a short career in finance and book editing, and I left them both behind. Only I have never backpacked around Europe, danced under a full moon in Thailand, or even visited all the chic clubs in London. I cannot afford to make a mistake, misstep, or howl with abandon. Did I grow up too quickly? Or am I even grown up at all?

On Christmas Eve, a designated staffer raises the Palace flag from half-mast, and the twenty days of mourning for President General Rian are over. My husband strides out of our bedroom, his shoulders pulled just a bit farther back. He carries a confidence that screeches he is headed for the first time to host a meeting at the President's board room. I follow and slip into a chair unapologetically at the end.

"You don't need to be here," O whispers. "The First Lady is normally more involved in, well, social meetings."

I glare at him.

"Thanks for letting me know, but I will stay," I respond courteously.

O nods and walks off, distracted by the meeting agenda.

"We want to be modern leaders, inclusive leaders. So, I'm doing things differently," Saif tells O and a cluster of other staffers in the dimly lit room with a marble table and fine Tucanese art on every wall. "And Anna will do more than host elegant parties and wear nice clothes."

Christmas Eve is also the day my life stops belonging to me.

Hours before the inauguration, a simple black-and-white photograph of our ring exchange is released to state television, informing the universe that Saif and I were wed in a private and non-denominational ceremony in Paris. News reports and tabloids rewrite our love story to claim that we met through mutual friends at a Manhattan diner, where we were both studying at top universities. However, back home Taya expresses her dis-appointment—she hoped the Palace would bolster my brand to one of in-tellect and intrigue by releasing wedding photographs and a story exclu-sively to the *Economist*.

"The bride wore a custom Karl Lagerfeld and did her own hair and makeup, showing her desire for less excess and fuss," the social column of the Tucana Times waxed on the front page of the next day's paper. "She grew up in Hollywood, a child to the stars, but declined an acting career for finance and philanthropy."

As pandemonium unfolds beyond the Palace with waves of anti-gov-ernment demonstrations and security forces pitching clusters of tear gas and arbitrary bullets from rooftops amid the change-of-power, Saif and I are transferred from the east quarters to the master grand bedroom and living quarters, with no mention of the resurging anarchy, deeper into a life that is as confusing and dreamlike as it is enticing.

Madame Sara's protests reverberate across the hall. She is screaming about why she has to switch rooms with us. There is no point in appeasing her. Her reign has ended. Moreover, protocol staffers did not ask if I wanted to move; they told me. The senior protocol officer, a gangly man with olive suspenders whose name I do not know, tries to calm Madame Sara down as the boxes are stuffed and shuffled out.

Unflinching, I stare at her as straight-faced workers wheel my clothes inside. Despite Madame Sara's lack of words, her stare of return is deadly.

After a while, I avert my gaze and move out onto my heated deck, craving an escape from this new life for just a minute. My mind tries to process who is who, why, and the nuances I need to carry into my new role. I take out the manila folder O gave me, brimming with names, titles, and faces I must remember, along with a calendar of significant events and mission statements of charitable organizations. I shut it as quickly as I opened it, trying to stave off a throbbing right temple.

"The inauguration will take place on January 1st, 2004," O informs me briskly, guiding me down to my private office, anchored by a magnificent grand staircase connecting the ground floor and the upper-level library, outfitted with locally upholstered benches and beams of light that dramatically pierce the mammoth origami structures holding the ceramic desk.

"And Madame Anna, we need to fill the position of your Communications Director as soon as possible," he continues. "Your right-hand man or woman to handle your diary and image. I have already collected some pre-vetted resumes for your perusal. But ideally, it should be a trusted confidante, someone you trust. So, have a little think about it."

I do not need to think about it. There is only one person in my life, outside of Saif, that I trust.

"Taya Taylor," I respond immediately. "We will need to make her a strong offer. She is a rising D.C. star with endless opportunities as a political press secretary."

A flash of concern lights up in O's eyes, perhaps disapproving of Taya's

American credentials.

"She is the only person for the job," I continue, surprised by my bossiness.

Taya arrives on the eve of the New Year–tottering into the Palacein leopard print Givenchy heels–taking up residence in a spacious loft in the southern quarter, having stopped in London on her way to collect a metallic boucle tweed skirt suit from Alexander McQueen as my inauguration outfit at Neo's request.

Saif half rolls his eyes as he welcomes Taya in, and she eyes him up and down, impressed with his sudden status, but in her own way ready to show off what she can accomplish.

"Let's see now who gets to spend more intimate time with your woman," Taya tells Saif, half-joking.

Still, they kiss on both cheeks and move along with their business. Meanwhile, I am ecstatic. The missing chunk of my home is home again. Taya has a way of comforting me and calling me out at the same time. It is love and protection the way Taya knows how. She seems to slide seamlessly into Tucana life, not missing a beat, absorbing all that the cushioned Palace life has to offer.

The morning of the inauguration, Taya pinches and yanks the McQueen zipper so sharply that it takes my breath away.

"An extra rumple or two, Anna, Madame Anna," she commands, pressing my abdomen, the only person aside from Saif I have told of my tragedy in Paris over wine the night before. "You're living the high life now. Emotions are high; the parties are endless. And when you get back down to a supermodel weight, I'll have you on every fashion magazine cover worldwide."

The technical mourning for what I have lost is over. I cannot eat away the emptiness anymore.

Taya possesses an honest breed of ballsiness that makes me both envious and grateful–jealous that she always states what she wants and, more often than not, gets it. I'm also thankful that I don't have that same nerve. To always be that forthright and formidable is to be constantly vulnerable. The constant need to speak your mind and purge your thoughts means everyone else can see the heart on the sleeve–when it is beating and when it is dead.

"I'll see that the trainer gets you on a two-hour plan. But first, I need to make sure you fit the sample size," Taya reiterates, not unkindly but more matter-of-factly. "I got you, Anna. Listen to me and you will be the best darn thing that ever happened to this little country."

I hold my breath, notice the new vase of the twin cherubs in our room, and promise myself before I head out to the inauguration that I will not break into a million pieces. Tucana is the sort of place where the weak are eaten alive. Taya holds my hand, and we go.

Once again, the streets swarm with security and adoring Tucanese, bused in from villages far and wide.

"Everyone is here, everyone is here because this is a nation that adores the Amsa family," O tells my fascinated face, whizzing by and barking orders to his staff.

My husband's oversized, half-smiling face shines back from a few bill-boards. I also notice giant advertisements for McDonald's and Levi's jeans. Strangely, the men in the streets now seem to model my husband's features. Saif's mustache is much thinner than President General Rian's, and his hair is a little shorter with a square cut.

"I thought we agreed on a simple, modest inauguration," I mutter to Saif as we climb into the open motorcade, simultaneously waving to the screeching commoners as the etiquette coach had instructed.

"This is," Saif shoots back. "You should have seen my father's. I was just a little boy in a diamond-encrusted open-top Ferrari."

We step out and I compel everything inside me to switch on. I smile and wave elegantly at the crowds, cupping my fingers at a slight angle. Am I doing it right? Yes, I think so. The etiquette coach, ordered in by O from Buckingham Palace, told me in our few quick lessons this past week that I am a natural. It was obvious to him that I had gone to boarding school.

I wave until my hand feels like it will flop off. Then, cheers and shrills of excitement bounce back to me. Perhaps I am a natural; maybe the coach didn't tell me a lie.

Proceedings begin from the specially erected marble podium outside the Palace gates. There is palpable stillness in the dense crowd. The scene around me is the apotheosis of what many young women consider life to be: designer clothes, adoration, a title.

The crowd falls silent as the commemoration begins.

"Anna! Anna!"

I swear I hear my name. I am sure I hear my name. I glance around. Nobody is looking at me.

"As I stand today, I must begin by thanking the Almighty God for granting us the strength in this resolute country during such a time of heartbreak and tragedy in all that has befallen us, losing two of our most beloved," declares President Doctor Saif Amsa into the microphone, with the perfect blend of stoicism and compassion. "I respect the people's will and will gladly carry out the mission I have been given and shoulder the burdens. I thank you for electing me as the trusted leader of Tucana."

The line disturbs me. But I dare not flinch as I stand behind Saif. They are revering faces, except one: several rows back, long dark hair, pale skin, fidgeting, the only person not looking adoringly at my husband. Instead, she is looking at me and clutching her right temple. Unblinking, burning. Like a mirror. Only me. I worry for her; what would they do if they notice she isn't paying attention to the President Doctor?

And then—out of nowhere—flames flare at my husband's feet, smoke ripping into the silver sky. I wait half a second for the commotion to swell like a sea before me, silenced by the armed forces lurking in every corner like spiders in their web to fan the fire.

However, the ocean of faces remains transfixed on my husband, and now I can't see that lone face staring at me.

In a few fractured seconds, I realize the inferno is creeping toward Saif's ankle, along with the growing smell of the burned baby. Does anyone else realize what is happening? With hundreds of thousands of eyes on me from all directions, I am immobile in fear and unsure of what to do. The infant surfaces, a charred shadow in the dull light.

"We must not fall into the improper trap of thinking our great Tucana must overnight become a western democracy. What is true democracy? True democracy stems from our history, our culture, and our civilization. It stems from us as Tucanese, and it is up to us all to create a country that exists in freedom and tolerance to all ethnicities and religions," Saif says, not missing a beat. "We must work together to support women's rights and take a stand against waste and corruption."

Who will stop the fire? Who will save the baby? The President Doctor does not even know he is about to be burned. I draw a shallow breath and plunge to my knees, the designer dress tearing, flinging my hand forward, fiercely pushing him from the blaze with a scream.

Time slows, and an open expanse of blurry and befuddled characters stare back at me. Everything stops. Saif's knees buckle and he clutches the podium to remain upright, glaring down on me in horror; the fire and burning baby I saw evaporates before my eyes. I feel a leather-gloved hand reach for my elbow, propelling me from the podium floor to the armored security vehicle by the stage, like a crocodile mutely seizing its prey.

"What the fuck?" a gruff voice seethes.

I see the bearded man now as he whisks me into an armored security vehicle and slams the heavy door so violently that the roof rattles.

"The fire was about to burn him," I argue as he folds his considerable height into the backseat beside me. I can hear the panic shaking in my voice. "Did you not see it?"

There is a tap at the window, the passenger door swings open, and Taya squishes between us.

"Get your hands off her, and I will handle this," Taya announces curtly, shoving the guard away and embracing my trembling soul with her mere presence. "Anna, don't worry about this. I will tell the press it was a little mild hypothermia. But, sweetheart, we need you to take better care of yourself through this transition process."

Where did the fire come from? The scene seemed so real. But Saif had not even flinched.

That evening, still shaken and embarrassed, I make only a brief appearance at the fancy inaugural ball in the grand ballroom adorned with twenty-five antique Solstice Comete chandeliers. I want to slither in and out. But as the harsh laws of nature have it, I encounter Madame Sara just as I am about to execute a silent goodbye.

She smirks at me, grinning from ear to ear, delighting in my anxiousness, questioning my ability to step into her potent stilettos.

There is no escape. Madame opens her mouth–

"How incredible you look this evening, Madame Sara," Taya's lofty voice enters the fray, her eyes glistening as if determined to win the old first lady over.

Taya's loyalty to me is unwavering, and I take advantage of her distraction to steadily head toward the exit. My mouth involuntarily gapes as I glide across the polished floors and look up to see Josie, ever-regal in an emerald number.

"What are you doing here?" I stammer.

Josie looks a little older than I remember, her skin a little stiffer from the sun, courtesy of a beachside balcony.

"Anna, baby, I wanted to surprise you; Taya got me a ticket to the ball," she explains, her eyes swollen with oily tears. "What happened today–I'm glad I can be here for you."

I grab Josie's arm, leaning in with intensity.

"You saw the fire too?"

"No, Anna, I just saw you—never mind. This is a lot to cope with so quickly."

I prepare my head for what is coming next: a barrage of questions delivered with Josie's usual low-volume intensity.

"Have you seen your father or Lolita since coming back? Did they say anything at the Embassy when you renounced your citizenship? What will you do now if the marriage doesn't work out? Has Saif changed since taking on the role? Is he serious about being a better democratic ruler than his father? How did they train him for the role? Has the issue of releasing political prisoners been raised yet?"

I am at a loss as to where to begin. Josie seems to be talking about something I don't understand. As for answers, I don't know anything more than what is in the media.

I am hungry. I power-walk away and scoop as many sea-salt caramel and brie tartlets from the buffet table into my crocodile-skin purse. As strangers hang around to make small talk, I hurry into the bathroom and shove the sweetness into my mouth so quickly that I might have been sawing my throat with cardboard edges. Choking, barely breathing, spluttering, savoring, swallowing, tasting the dry air, and a dash of expensive sweetness.

Taya's words dance in my head, warning me to get back to a sample size to score covers. And so I panic some more, running tap water through my mouth as my pink lipstick smears down my chin.

I don't use one finger. I use two. Then three. I can almost get my fist down my bleeding throat as nebulous globs of dessert protrude up and out from the raw flesh, with a lingering sickly satisfying euphoria.

How will I survive a lifetime in a palace overflowing with gourmet goodness and party after party? Will I feel safe and obscured from the constant threat of dissolved willpower? My knees cave onto the cool tiles for a moment, willing myself to hold it together. I must armor up. I have armored up. I must do what I am supposed to do. I wait for my eyes' red-ness to ebb before returning to this strange real world.

Taya and Josie are right outside the door, foreheads creased with concern.

I scowl at both of them, storming toward my grand primary bedroom.

When I turn back for just one glance, Taya thoughtfully advises Josie not to follow me, holding her back. Taya smiles reassuringly at me. She understands I must do whatever is necessary to survive this public limelight.

In the safety of that sprawling room, I wrench off the dress so voraciously it tears a little, and I throw it over the small statue of the cherub twins in the bathroom.

I crawl naked into bed and wait for Saif to return. I still have not talked to the President-Doctor since the morning podium incident, since I embarrassed him beyond the point of return. And when he doesn't return, a dreamless repose envelopes me, and I suppose I simply accept that his new duties take him far and wide. At least my curious incident disperses into the files of the forgotten within the next 48 hours, as if it had happened to someone else at some other time.

And when I do see the him again two days later, I reach for his hand across the breakfast table, but it is too far to touch. I wait a moment for him to reach over from his side, to meet in the middle like in the old days. But he doesn't look up from the newspaper.

I stop this senseless waiting for him and busy my hands stirring tea, suggesting he request a call with the U.S. President and offer Tucana's whole-hearted help in fighting the War on Terror.

His father had failed to make that gesture out of hatred for George W. Bush and the American way of life. However, it would now demonstrate to the White House that this is a fresh start. Now that a young and hip renegade is behind the wheel, with a Hollywood-bred woman next to him, friendly relations are not impossible.

To my surprise, Saif agrees and immediately instructs O to schedule the call.

Afterward, when headlines spawn the international news cycle using descriptions such as "Heroic Modernizer" and "The Middle East, We Want to See," my husband suddenly sweeps me into the freezing ocean for a celebratory moonlight swim. Only it isn't freezing. Saif had a section of it portioned into an Olympic-sized pool and heated to a perfect 78 degrees just for our special night celebrating a successful call and media blitz.

Later that night, with Saif fast asleep by my side, I whisper into that little recorder that this is finally starting to feel like an adult fairytale watered to life, the grown-up Beverly Hills Hotel I do not have to leave.

"We are coming into our own," I add.

CHAPTER
TEN

The first months in the Palace buzz with meet-and-greets, white caviar facials, the Mariinsky Ballet guest season, and a never-ending waltz of diplomatic dancing. My husband does most of the talking. O instructs me to smile a lot, so I smile. A lot.

I learn to wake up with the *muezzin*, the Call to Prayer, as the sun rises blood-red from behind the hills. A chime of the church bells from the monastery outside follows. When I take in the sounds, I round the edges, at least temporarily, of my jagged days of trying to fit into the new world.

Sometimes snowflakes grace the green lawns that never turn brown. Sometimes, the sun stings so harshly that I could bronze my fair skin within minutes. It is that unpredictable interval between winter and spring when our island is tilting–an instability, a sense that anything could happen.

I pass my NYU finals via correspondence, but only by a small margin. Studying was pointless.

A week later, I receive a lump of mail from our old Chelsea apartment, including my acceptance letter for Harvard's MBA program. I almost forgot I had applied. The days of New York seem like a lifetime ago. I tell myself that I don't want that old life. I, however, cannot bring myself to send Harvard a declining email. I throw the glossy acceptance letter in the trash along with CVS coupons and discounts to the Guggenheim Museum.

I busy myself whispering out these scattered thoughts into Cliff's device—filing away chapters of memories, recorded and released from my mind. To better engage with those who aren't privileged enough to speak fluent English, I take private lessons in the native island language of Rasa. As the lesson ends one afternoon, O lurks around my office door and strides in.

"I wouldn't waste too much time on that," O scoffs just after the retired professor, my Rasa teacher, scuttles from my office. "It's only the people far away who speak it. It's all English for the younger generation and the cosmopolitan. It's the language of the peasants."

Even Saif has lost what bit of Rasa he once knew somewhere while growing up. The loss of an entire language bit by bit, generation by generation, seems to me a massacre of memory, a torching of history.

I am stubborn. I persist, encouraged by Taya, who analyzes my efforts through the hungry eyes of publicity. I am the people's princess, the wealthy wife of the nation's leader who can conveniently masquerade as approachable.

Guided by Taya, I practice public speaking—flowing between two languages—over sips of wine and portion-controlled slivers of goat cheese pizza late into the night. But, despite our efforts, O routinely makes it clear that he prefers it if I do not make any public speeches yet, insisting that I only commit to a few brief appearances like slicing the ribbon at the opening of a school or congratulating the national winner of the Annual Peace Project.

The light approach to First Lady duties is to Taya's fierce objection. She constantly reminds O of my finance skills and ability to do more than look good.

"Anna is the new generation of First Ladies. She is a woman who can stand with her husband and stand alone," she snaps at O during an afternoon tea in my office.

"Don't forget, the Tucanese people are used to Madame Sara. Madame

Sara was their Queen equivalent for three decades, and the transition must be slow and smooth," O responds.

He turns a discerning eye toward me.

"We must be sure you are up for it," O continues, inadvertently reminding me of the humiliating inauguration.

That's not all there is to it. Madame Sara is determined not to let me overshadow her.

As the days fly by, the mechanics of a new government are coming together.

Saif's administration fills its cabinet positions. The President Doctor hand-picks most of his staff, but I mostly learn about new appointments in the morning newspapers. I am not privy to the ongoing discussions and decisions made in the most shadowy meeting room of them all in the bunker below the earth.

In the 1970s, President General Rian renamed the highly classified room the Guerra room, the Spanish word for war, after buying a sculpture of a burning aircraft made by a Spanish Nationalist commanding officer. The legend is that the respected officer and self-confessed artist applied the final touches of clay as the bullets entered his head north of the Guadarrama mountains in 1937. His blood is crusted into the paint on the fixed wing.

Those high-level positions remain mainly within the Amsa family: uncles, cousins and cousins first removed. Despite still being a student and only twenty years old, Willard becomes Prime Minister. O—who I learn is Madame Sara's sister's London-born eldest son, who got his communications start at Buckingham Palace decades ago fresh out of Cambridge—is to remain the Chief of Staff. He is also designated to oversee the directorate of communications.

Saif's uncle Tig Amsa, President General Rian's younger brother, who had long presided over the shadowy Shush, is the hardened new defense minister. He is a broad-shouldered silver-haired man whose face is a spider's web of wrinkles. I have never had a conversation with Uncle Tig. We would not have had much in common to discuss. It is well-known that he, like his late big brother, believes women belong either serving tea or sipping it.

The President Doctor eliminates many once-esteemed political positions. The inner circle of Cyra is shrinking and tightening. Yet the perks for those inside the lines are certainly substantial. There are a few women in cocktail ambassadorship roles or leading committees, but this feels more like optics than serious leadership. Madame Sara takes over the tourism ministry—another vanity title whereby the underlings do all the actual work.

"That is just an excuse to host garden parties for press people and supermodels offered free trips," I tell Taya with an eye roll as I skim the *Tucana Times*.

My finger slides down the list.

Oil Minister: Bobby Russell.

Then I reread it. Saif appointed my dad to the position of oil minister. That is a hugely critical role. Oil is the lifeblood of the country, the region, and inside a volatile world. Oil earnings account for about 85 percent of government revenue.

Saif or my father should have asked me, or at least, informed me in advance.

I pace outside in the sunshine until my annoyance subsides, and then call downstairs for an oriental harmony massage and wine bath to ease my accumulated tension. I would have felt guilty for such fuss and indulgence in the past. Now, I use such treatments to deal with the hollow haze.

Over and over, I call my father to congratulate him—and to question him—about his newly sanctified government position. It is not surprising that he does not answer. The voicemail box is always full.

It is still unclear why my father has never given me much of his time in this life. I've always felt something was off. I can hear Cliff emphasizing that it is because something is off. Despite this, I can't imagine he has reached a point where he has completely given up on communication.

I go to bed, and for the first time, I dream in Rasa–watching myself as a fair-faced small girl in the island's choppy seas, reaching for a stray dog that was always a step out of reach, and calling for help that would not come.

And this is the night my life as the Tucanese First Lady truly begins.

Not far geographically, yet a seeming psychological cosmos away from our small island parcel of peace, Iraq is erupting with bombs and brutality. Almost a year has passed since the U.S. invaded the country, and it is months since Saddam Hussein's execution.

"Do you think that could ever happen here?" I probe Saif in a rare moment in his crammed schedule of showering together.

He pauses, pulling me closer.

"The U.S. has no reason to come here," Saif responds tepidly, warm water streaming onto his face like a rash of tears straying from his eyes. "We are a tolerant place, a peaceful place."

A few weeks later, when the Iraqi refugees start arriving in wispy dingy boats and handmade rafts–a perilous journey I am sure nobody would make unless they feared gravely for their lives–I insist on traveling to the shores in a formal capacity. I am determined to ensure that the Tucanese welcome weeping Iraqis warmly, and all the children, with wet clothes clinging to their bones, have shoes.

However, the communications department denies my request, with no explanation other than I should not get too close as "we do not know who these people are." I also learn that the Palace denies the United Nations' request to work in Tucana under the formal statement that Tucana will use its own resources and not allow foreign spy groups to operate on its soil. Whenever I ask about the refugee camps' location or what happens to the refugees once they arrive, nobody in the office can provide me with an answer.

Increasingly, I am reluctant to raise controversial topics with my husband. When I see him, I want to keep the peace and remind him that he is loved. But one night, as we read under dull lamps by the bedside, I pluck up the courage to ask Saif what is going on.

"We don't know who they are," he echoes with a shrug when I press him about allowing the refugees to obtain work permits, rent homes, and rebuild their lives, at least for a short while in Tucana. "Iraq has turned into a shitty country. They could bring drugs and crime. Some could be rapists."

"And some, I assume, are good people," I conjecture, rolling over indignantly.

My first few months as the President Doctor's wife are marked by a growing popularity with the local media. Daily headlines—I assume it is again Taya's public relations prowess—paint me as the pleasant and personable American beauty who looks and acts like one of them: a smart and sophisticated woman accepted into Harvard but followed her heart, not her head. A young woman who longs to serve the Tucanese people, a populace steadily becoming her own.

"It is as if she were Tucanese," one of the columnists for the *Tucana Times* writes. "It is as if she has grown up here her whole life."

The pundits on Cyra24 rave about my poise and style, artfully discreet makeup, and approachable yet high-brow demeanor. Pundits and expert contributors spend hours of screen time raving about my endeavors to be more than just a social extravaganza. Perhaps this is a veiled dig at my predecessor, Madame Sara.

Articles and television segments describe every detail of my outfit whenever I step outside.

This new phenomenon called 'blogs' crop up, some dedicated entirely to chronicling my sense of style: a mixture of local designers and top ones from the western world, occasionally accented with an affordable or mainstream piece, hand-crafted courtesy of Taya's super-powered phone book. Always a mix of high-end and slightly more mid-range. Neo prefers me to wear only tailored, high-fashion concoctions that commoners cannot buy.

The Palace institution still turns up a powdered nose to anything that can be purchased by those who do not belong to the Tucanese First Family. O and his cadre served in the era where the rulers must flash their money, an age where the upper echelons dressed in the finest furs and snakeskin slippers for even a short flight or a steam-train ride from one sea to another. They are part of the Old Guard, where there is no blurring between the rich and the poor.

Saif and I are changing that. Are Saif and I changing that?

The days drift, and I do not see much of the President Doctor. Instead, he is busy reforming his land, promoting the economy, encouraging trade, and winning over the people by increasing the monthly food boxes and offering a broader range of free medical services and state-run clinics.

I wish we did more together, like the modern-day leaders he promised me we would be.

There will be plenty of time for that, I console myself. We are still in the challenging transition period. So, I miss my husband quietly. I recall what Cliff said: I married a man who was married to everybody.

Early one morning, before my husband flees the bed for a dizzying pile of duties, I point out that free internet in homes would be a fantastic way to promote democracy. It would enrich and educate the population. It would position Saif as the consummate reformist, unlike his father, who exercised tight control over his people. Like a little girl with a wish list for Santa, I've been waiting weeks to offer my suggestion.

"You're brilliant," Saif gushes, kissing my forehead.

A team of top technicians is on their way from Istanbul within minutes. They set about clearing out all the porn and abandoned Hotmail accounts from the antiquated dial-up system and introduced the concept of wireless to most Cyra homes. Still, it must be advanced enough to reach the remote villages near the island's edge.

Saif spends more time in oil fields, at military bases, in Cuba and China, and along the Black Sea. Nevertheless, when he returns, we are reunited in waves of intensity and passion. We are like lost teenagers suddenly burdened with enormous responsibilities. In my drawers, I always have different sets of La Perla lingerie. The Bologna showroom ships them to me weeks before the retail floors receive them. It's difficult to read my husband, but I am always there for him.

Those moments when he is home, lying beside me under the sheets before the indigo sky slices through the skylight, are moments that I would like to freeze. Together, we exist in an imperfect bubble that cannot burst.

My cell phone shakes.

"Let's meet as soon as possible in your office," Taya writes. "We must discuss the most appropriate level of jewelry for you in public appearances with Neo. He just got the new Tiffany collection from New York."

I spend considerable time crafting an image. What initially thrilled me, like writing a script, quickly gave way to a lot of yawning. Every day, Taya insists we go through the newspaper and brainstorm keywords about my image. Like a girl wandering with a wild imagination, distracted by and discarded by shiny things, I quickly bounce between mild excitement and boredom.

Taya often writes notes and makes suggestions, and then the covey of press secretaries reporting to O take more notes and offer even more suggestions. Then both would review them for approval, and the process would repeat itself.

"I know you want to do good things; make the role yours," Taya conjectures over pressed lemon and cucumber juice one afternoon in my office. "But the most important thing is optics; it's okay to do good. But it's most important to be seen to be doing good."

For weeks, I've been chanting that I want to establish a foundation to eliminate poverty and advance girls' education. But it has been decided for me that I will instead be at the helm of the pre-established, mostly inactive, Amsa Foundation. It is re-registered in my name and Saif's, alongside a mission statement to "enhance the wellbeing of the Tucanese people and culture."

"It is too broad," I object to Taya.

Nobody, including Taya, adequately addresses my concerns. Words project from my lips to the air and evaporate. Being new, I am still trying to figure out when and how much I can speak out of turn, even to all those who technically worked under my wing, without it getting back to Saif and igniting a rift.

"We have a lot of material to work with, you can jump onto any convenient cause, and we will make you stellar–the master of everything," Taya enthuses back. "Remember Anna, while much of the Middle East is experiencing terrible war and violence, Tucana is peaceful for everyone. We are a society that deeply loves and respects its leadership, as much as its leadership deeply loves and respects its society."

So, I do as I am told and throw myself into that position the way I threw myself into my work with Cliff. I read and study the people and places who needed help the most. When I am not in my office or the "other" office designated for me among the people–an ivory studio lodged atop a small hill overlooking the Old City–I shop along Madame Sara Boulevard and the adjacent streets that reek of oil money. Of course, that all unfolds late at night when nobody is around to watch assistants carry out bags and bags of luxury goodness on my behalf, courtesy of the highly taxed Tucanese. The secrecy is for my security, and Taya announces it is to protect my image.

I host dinner parties for foreign dignitaries and the winners of the Tucanese poetry grants, and for the affluent subsect who drape the national flag around their shoulders in praise, slowly freezing Madame Sara from the high platform of social stardom. I smile with my chemically whitened teeth; I diplomatic dance all over the Palace, from the trees that encircled the outdoor parties to the inside scenes of sequined dresses and side-eyes.

The production of my social life does not stop.

One late May night, a rush of panic sets in, my insides bursting from the buckets of creamy, spicy sushi I jammed inside when nobody was looking. I race into the private bathroom as the guests clink glasses and sway to the quartet's sounds in honor of a rescue cat charity. A fatter reflection of my face laughs at me from the gold-framed mirror.

Fingers–then a half-fist–slither like a snake down my throat until the mental gymnastics gives in to the soup of chunky salmon and seaweed sheets, hot from the belly, burst through my lips and into the toilet bowl, splashing my nose with indignation along the way. I tickle and punch the dry latch on my throat until the fish is blood-soaked.

I collapse on the tiled floor in exhaustion and euphoria. I can control at least one thing in my grandiose but insular world. I want to escape the food, the parties, the chefs, and the ever-overflowing kitchen. But what choice do I have?

The food will be perpetually fabulous, the compliments overflowing and gracious, yet the sample size will remain the same. With the vision of Taya frowning at my lack of willpower, the calories are often expunged in fluid firestorms when the lights go out.

Whenever it is over, I whisper out loud that it will be the last time.

A week later, I'm back in the bathroom during one Greek-themed book launch luncheon at the ballroom, centered on oily fish and dolmades. With my hands ungraciously covered in bits and bile, I notice a slight red glint from the engraving where the wall meets the ceiling.

The ceilings are tall, but low enough to trap, to cramp one's thoughts and close their mind. They need to be higher, I think, absently. Yet, for the first time, I also observe twin cherubs subtly carved into the roof beside that blinking dot, the eyes of those infants piercing down into mine.

I tense, a sudden gust of wind whipping around me from nowhere. I panic. Who has been watching me in the bathroom all these months?

A burned baby drops from the roof, loud and wailing. I gasp, contorted over the sink like a reptile giving birth. I close my eyes and shudder as the baby's breath spews over my neck and back into my gaping dirty mouth like death. The hot air streams into my body, engulfing my barren stomach's vacuum.

When I open my eyes, that dying infant disperses. Maybe they all think I am insane. I know I am not. I know what I saw. Once again, I glance up.

I have seen that red blink before. Then, in a type of measured madness, I sit rooted for a second, maybe a minute, tear off a too-small, red-soled heel and toss it at the minuscule camera–observing triumphantly as the pulsating stops.

When I march back into the fog of unfamiliar faces and fine wines, I storm over to the center chandelier, glaring up, zoning in on the squinting red. Another camera captures my moves.

I hate the ballroom. The Versailles Baroque Ballroom. I loathe those hideous twenty-five antique Solstice Comete chandeliers. And I detest the adjoining dining room in all its gaudy gold and porcelain glory. It reeks of the YSL Opium perfume Josie stashed in her purse and of old money and too much of it–the outlandish design ambitions of Madame Sara early in her tenure.

I resent all these nonsense dining rooms. What would they all say if I hurled my Louboutin's at all the ceilings in here too?

CHAPTER
ELEVEN

On June 5, my husband turns 29, a day engulfed in fog until midday. The President Doctor promises me he will return from Moscow in time for a celebratory lunch. As a naughty surprise, I wear a French maid's outfit with a black satin apron. I plan to tell Saif I have learned to bake after hours of practice just for him. But, of course, it is Millie who slaves for seven hot hours to bring to life the Irish crème cake. This cake is crafted not with any ordinary cognac but with an exquisite Remy Martin Black Pearl Louis XIII.

I ambulate nervously through the main house and then through the garden. I wait until the morning burns into the late afternoon. I succeed with every ounce of willpower not to scoop the cake up with my bare hands.

Then there he is, idling alone near the gates, sudden anxiety, frustration, and thrills churning in my stomach.

"Happy Birthday, baby," I squeal, my anger at his tardiness dissolving as I playfully slap his rear from behind.

With such furiousness, a rough hand pushes me away so that I tumble back onto the sprinkler-soaked lawn. I peer into the dazed eyes of a stranger with an identical mustache to my husband. He also has the same haircut, the same clothes, and he is the same height. Only it isn't my husband at all.

"Oh my goodness, I am so sorry, Madame Anna," a voice rasps back. "Oh, my goodness. I didn't mean –

With a startled look on my face, I scramble to close my sprawled legs.

"Oh, never mind. I am okay," I croak, motioning the stranger aside.

I float to my feet and back away soundlessly from the unfamiliar man with an almost frozen face to match Saif's hollowed-out, deer-in-the-headlines expression. As I spin in a psychedelic air castle, every face forms into mine, a wild hallucination that lasts seconds. Or minutes.

My life, even though I cannot fully grasp this right now, will be impacted greatly by security decoys from that point on.

I make my way in a daze to the kitchen and toward the bewitching round barrow of moist cream and dangerous delight–inviting me, accepting me.

Saif calls to tell me he must stay in Moscow a little longer. Oligarchs invited him to the Miss Universe Russia pageant, and the co-owner also owns a prominent defense manufacturing company. Saif says he needs to spend more time rubbing shoulders at the beauty queen affair.

"Why do you need Russian weapons? Don't you have enough?" I ask.

"Just in case the Americans come here next after Iraq," Saif responds casually. "Washington cannot be trusted."

I guess the effort to build better relations died before it really began.

I have strange visions of my husband cavorting with blue-eyed blondes in a five-star hotel room near the Kremlin, a pricey present from the FSB. I picture them on top of him, all over him, the images multiplying before my eyes. Identical and everywhere. Disturbing acts. I propel the thought from my mind. How un-First Lady of me. But it doesn't go away.

I sever off a piece of the birthday cake and gouge it into my palms–the spongy texture is lighter than it looks–and it crumbles in my bare hand. I do not pause to find a fork or even to taste. I eat.

Cream springs from my lips, and I sever off another slab. I eat to forget how I miss Saif and because I have no choice but to miss him quietly. But I should not complain. Saif gave me the opportunity to run away from this life back in New York, and I volunteered to stay. He gave me this beautiful life. Beautiful on the outside.

I cut another gigantic slice and subconsciously celebrate myself for no reason. And then I carve off another, more enormous this time, and plop down on the breakfast bench, seductively licking the fresh crème off my lips.

A full figure appears at the kitchen door. It isn't my reflection, but it could have been me at that moment—me trapped inside a funhouse swallowing swords of sugar and fat, swallowing without chewing.

"Oh no, Madame Anna, I cut for you," a spooked Millie says. "That is me to do, my job!"

Busted. I can't run in humiliation, but being caught is, in an odd way, thrilling. I do not want to be alone.

"Sit," I demand, hushing her with the white-tipped finger of silence over my lips. "Sit with me and eat."

"Oh, Madame Anna, I cannot do that," Millie responds eccentrically, gripping her wobbly cheeks. "I am not allowed to do that."

Dark sweetness defiles my lips, and I argue back, possessed by someone I'm not even sure is me.

"Millie, you must eat with me!"

Her furrowed brow flits from side to side. She glances from side to side and then relaxes. Millie nestles in close and chisels herself an equally large portion. As I watch intently, I want to make sure someone else is eating the same amount as me.

"I have been working here at the Palace kitchen for more than twenty years, and no one has ever asked me to eat with them," Millie continues, her eyes sparkling. "Thank you, Madame Anna."

If there is ever a silver lining to a binge eating burst, it is that food forges a bond between two distant people that no words can conquer.

I rise early, too early for a Sunday, in a glucose-drunken stupor with cake crumbs sprinkled on Saif's unslept side of the bed.

I swallow, trying pathetically to produce some saliva to water the parched throat burn, my recollection soupy, wedged between a dream and a painful tangibility. In the Fanta-colored sunrise reflection, my bones seem to peep out through dehydrated skin a little more than the day before. Of course, I pledge to myself that the cycle will stop now and that this will never happen again.

I close my eyes, and when I open them, the pure white walls lurch forward, delicately closing in on me—a choking, suffocating sensation. I must get away from the Palace. I jump up and wriggle on a pair of jeans—Gucci tags still attached—and mask my unwashed hair beneath a baseball cap. I text Taya to hurry up and come with me, and when she arrives, I instruct the driver to drive. It is technically Taya's day off, but she never minds being at my call. Taya is irreplaceable to me, and she knows it.

I remove a file from my oversized Hermes Birkin and stare blankly at all the different hospitals, clinics, and institutions in Cyra that could be suitable for a surprise First Lady morale visit. Or, from Taya's lens, appropriate photo opportunities.

I love that big, pricey bag that can store so many fat files. It is a learned love.

I run my finger down the milky pages and land on one.

"The Pistachio Center," I announce to Taya. "What is it?"

"Let's find out," she says with a shrug. "Tucana has some of the finest nuts in the whole region, and there are a few shelling factories around there, it is kind of a desolate slummy area. But I'm sure the workers will appreciate the visit."

After circumnavigating the choked city streets and descending a narrow canyon, my sphere opens into a cathedral of run-down shops and dun-colored homes of suburbia, which I had never seen before. Small children pedal rusty bicycles, and women roam barefoot in grimy gutters for whatever food scraps they can find.

The macrocosm outside the Palace sees my husband's face much more than I do. Perhaps I hadn't noticed, or maybe it happened overnight, but suddenly, at least to me, his image is everywhere. Each billboard along the tree-lined streets features Saif in a different pose. There is Saif, the steely military commander; Saif, the primitive mountain man with an axe on horseback; Saif in the villages, arms filled with flowers as small children sit dotingly at his legs; and Saif with his head bowed in prayer as lepers yearn for his touch.

Saif is just like his father—the antithesis of the contemporary leader he promised we would both be.

We drive past the amber crescents of sand along the shoreline, next to waves that do not move. Over the hill is a small hut with sepia colors, like an old photograph from when Rasa was the only spoken language of the Tucanese. It shimmers on a khaki mound of earth with a crippled fence.

But as our car approaches, it is clear that the property is anything but shimmering. Instead, the outside shell appears stripped back into the cracked, dun tones of a pistachio shell. Only it is not a shelling factory at all.

We stop. And I step into the most dismal parcel of a place I have ever been. Palace officials would probably rather forget this place exists than spend a little more money on it.

Although we are not expected, a nervous caretaker—a plump older named Eva—welcomes us. We are VIPs, she has no choice but to welcome us. On the other side of the decrepit office and kitchen, a dozen women mill around in a dead garden, caged by high concrete walls, between craters in the dust and debris that no one had ever bothered to clean up.

I do not need to exchange glances with Taya to know that she is far from pleased about my choice of coming here. I can feel the burn of her perfectly shaped eyebrow, but I do not care.

Some women twirl in hitched-up, homespun skirts, their wavy bodies whizzing like the spinning of their minds, paragons of neglect. It is as though everyone is drunk on despair, neurosis, or some potent combination of the two, except for one woman. She sits alone, far from the others as possible, behind a curtain of disheveled inky hair like a child who refuses to deal with the pain of de-tangling.

"I remember her," I whisper to nobody but myself, yet I cannot pinpoint where or how.

An official Palace photographer suddenly appears behind us, snapping away as we stand in the center of this circle of mania.

Taya grouses.

"I know you are new, but I called you up last minute, and I expect you to do a decent job," she barks to the young man. "But don't ever photograph me again. I'm the flak; you only ever photograph the principal."

The trembling young man lifts his long lens closer to my makeup-free cheeks.

"Stop," I insist, motioning for him to lower the lens, uncomfortable. "No photos today, please."

"But Anna, we need photos of you for the press release," Taya objects. "It's your duty. People need to know you care."

"Not in here, not today," I reply firmly. It all looked wrong, exploitative, and too dismal to allow the big world to see.

"Fine, Ans," Taya says haughtily. "Don't waste too much time here if you have nothing to show for it. We'll wait for you inside."

I tepidly approach the woman with the long black hair, hugging her dirty bare feet and rocking. Back and forth. I maintain a respectful distance, conscious of penetrating the circumference of her private space. She seems surrounded by a mist of innocence that compels me.

The young woman's view of the world intrigues me.

She flicks her long dark eyelashes open and closed. After that, they stay closed, as if she were trying to buffer herself from the horrors of reality by escaping into imagination. It probably wouldn't have mattered if she was in a room by herself or in a space alongside ten thousand people. This poor lady will probably always be alone.

"The baby," she says, dazed, sensing me in her circumference.

I take that as my cue to inch closer, moving a rotting plastic chair to the side and sitting on the cracked concrete beside her.

"I couldn't save the baby," she continues.

I clutch my chest, winded. The phrase, the familiar phrase.

"I couldn't save it either," I whisper back.

A fly on the wall might call the conversation crazy. But it does not feel like two mad people conversing. It feels perfectly normal, as though two barely functioning people now have a place for their madness to go. Like a child who plays with soft toys until they fade and fall apart, wilted petals rest on her lap.

The woman's eyes flutter open, and huge green eyes descend on me, enameled with tears. I see huge emerald eyes identical to mine as if I were looking into a mirror. We both take a sharp breath.

Is she my ghost? She wears my face with a few more years of a much more tortured life.

Seconds. Seconds more. The young woman will not break her stare, so it is me who jumps up with dusty knees and pounces away without so much as a goodbye. I must leave the so-called garden of the insane before I fracture.

I realize then that calling it the Pistachio Center is a subtle way to describe the nuthouse for the insane.

"What's that lady's name? The one sitting by herself?" I casually ask the caregiver Eva, an overweight and emotional woman with bushy eyebrows, back inside the office where Taya is texting and tapping her heel with impatience.

Eva jumps to her feet and bows.

"Yes, your honor, I mean maj–ah Madame Anna," she babbles, rummaging through a notebook. "Forgive me; I am new here . . . H-Hala . . . Her name is Hala. She comes to us from Vea."

Eva talks in almost gibberish for a while, thumbing through disorganized notes of loose filings. I offer a handshake and a thank you before bolting toward the waiting car.

I want to go back. But I do not want to go back. The Pistachio Center feels like that terrifying rabbit hole of our childhood nightmares, a place you collapse into and can never return. I do not feel ready, but not ready for what? My right temple pulses. I need to stop thinking. So I do what I do best right now. I dress up, say very little, and swan around in soirees and pretty places.

Soon the summer surfaces—divesting us of heavy coats and thick clothes—and I slip into a series of flights and facials, flutes of champagne, orchestral evenings, and dress fittings. But there are also many sniveling nights alone in my quarters—tears dripping into Cliff's microphone. Josie's voice grows raspier with every call, etched in worry and evidence that she is smoking again. Or drinking. Or both.

"Have you talked to your father? Or Lolita? Has he told you anything?" she often asks in heightened desperation. "Any news? Anything new?"

Saif, my Ulysses that cannot be caged, comes, and he goes.

"Sorry, Anna, I thought I would have time for dinner tonight, but we need to push up my flight to Caracas before the storm," Saif notes one afternoon with a distant kiss on the cheek.

I smile with a pang.

"Venezuela, how lucky. I wish sometimes you would take me with you," I mutter.

"I promise soon. We have a lot of business to do, you know, new governments take many months, years, to get all the footing in place," he explains. "And President Chavez likes to get right down to business."

"If you have time when you arrive, you should see how he goes to the square sometimes just to be with the people, to read poetry with them," I continue. "Being the President requires charisma; it is more than just appealing to the wealthy and the elite."

Saif cocks his head for a second and then leaves in an imaginary cloud of dust.

A few times, in flashes of intoxicated bravery, I try to return to the saddest place I have ever been. Each time, Taya waves her hand and declares she has something different, something more important scheduled. Nobody dares talk about mental health in Tucana, and nobody speaks openly about the Pistachio Center. Perhaps other Palace people know it is there. But if they do, no one says a word.

My solution to temper the maze of thoughts is to get outside the confines of the Palace more often. I must show the Tucanese commoners that I am doing something, even if I am doing nothing. It is usually for a few photographs, mounds of miniature food worth more than an average person's annual earnings, and then I zip out again. The visits only exist in Taya's mind if there are discs replete with press photographs. Sometimes, bored men in cloven leather jackets and down-turned mouths show up in places I visit.

In Cyra, the new amphitheater features big names like Beyonce and Bocelli. The after-parties overflow with champagne, conversations about the weather, and consistently full flights to Dubai.

I am doing all these glorious things, but am changing so very little in the scheme of things.

"You don't look so great," Taya remarks one morning, genuinely concerned as we head off to an Amsa Foundation-sponsored cello recital.

"I don't know what is wrong," I reply carefully. "But if I knew what it was, I would fix it."

Taking a deep breath, she pulls me close for a long embrace.

Although I know what is wrong, I am still unsure of my Palace place and how much more I can protest. With all these outfit changes and cheek kissing, I'm losing weeks of my life. Can I ever amount to anything more than this? Surely, I have the power to make a difference. There was a time when I believed this leadership role would have meaning for me. Don't I belong to a plot that leads somewhere? Although I try cleverly to unravel the faux bow of my life, it remains tight and veiled.

I am in my Palace office on the morning of Friday, October 8th. I remember the date because it is Lolita's birthday. I miss her in a series of pangs; she is so close to me, yet so far. After the lost email debacle, I had taken to calling her at random times. Sometimes she answers. But most often, she does not.

I can only discern a few huffs of stifled tears when she does.

"Only because I love your delicate voice, Anna," she would say so quietly that I could hardly hear.

I worry for Lolita. But my concern for her has, over time, slipped down the priority ladder. Most importantly, I am trying to be a wife to a husband I rarely touch, trying to be the First Lady to a country I still do not understand but love defensively all the same.

I switch on Cyra24 in my office to see my husband alone in Verte Square. He sits cross-legged on a traditional embroidered blanket near the fountain, which sprouts diamond-shaped dots of bubbly liquid. He is holding a small black book titled *The Essential Rumi*. That was my bedside book I had never opened.

At first, I think it must be a decoy, but the camera zooms in closer. No, it is Saif.

"Don't be satisfied with stories, how things have gone with others," Saif states, with strength and somehow sincerity too. "Unfold your own myth."

It reminds me of a film I saw as a teenager called *Forrest Gump*—the scene in which Forrest is running and running, and one-by-one word gets around, and more people join him.

Then, a few pundits appear on Cyra24 to praise all the praise that the President Doctor is supposedly receiving from around the globe—no longer chartered as an ugly enemy by default of his father. He has fundamentally transformed Tucana, they say. I do not know who they are, these pundits.

I peer out from my office window to spot Taya kissing a beefy man, one of her chiseled creatures whom I assume earned a temporary security clearance to visit her suite late at night. She waves him off and walks away.

"A rugby player from South Africa in town for a few days, forget the name," she says breezily a minute later, waltzing around my office, marks of love still shining on the nape of her neck.

Taya stops, examining the Cyra24 footage of Saif pretending to be an all-person leader for a moment.

"Oh, the doctor. Look at that," she says with a laugh. "I bet he has never read anything poetic in all his life."

Perplexed and inspired faces watch their President Doctor reading whimsically alone in the square, and they, too, sit on the pavement, cross-legged at a respectful distance, repeating Rumi. Word spreads through the area; hundreds of commoners descend to join the reading, and then thousands. But the President Doctor is now hardly visible as an armed security formation files in around him.

Then, like Forest, he stops. He stands up, turns around, and announces he is going home now.

"How Hugo Chavez of him," I retort, remembering how I told him off-handedly just before he left for Caracas about how the charismatic President attracted crowds in Bolivar Square with his surprise sermons.

Taya flips back to face me and slaps a newspaper from her oversized purse down on my desk.

"More news for you, Ans," she asserts, not responding to my jab yet never missing a beat.

Taya extends her arms out, fingers caressing my back in light massage motions along my neck and shoulders. Then her long, magenta-tipped fingernails dig superficially into my flesh. Minor scratches, like bites between friends, I reason. It is strange, yet not strange when it is someone you love.

"Too much tension," she purrs, cleavage pressing into my shoulder. "But, you know, I will always be that person who will release it for you. You know that."

Here I am, a poker-faced Queen stranded in a game of chess. Taya has a way of making herself irreplaceable in my life. Then she straightens up and gestures to the *Tucana Times's* front page.

"Soooo, your hubby also won the Nobel Peace Prize. The committee just announced it. The *Times* prepped this front cover in advance, just in case, but it is being distributed across the country as we speak," Taya proclaims. "Can you believe it?"

I should be happy for him. His victory should feel like my victory.

"For what? He hasn't done anything," I grumble.

"The Norwegian Nobel Committee has decided to award the Nobel Peace Prize for 2004 to Tucanese President Saif Stephane Rian Amsa for his extraordinary efforts to strengthen international diplomacy and cooperation between peoples. The Committee has attached special importance to Amsa's vision and work for a world without nuclear weapons," Taya says, as if she has memorized the article verbatim. "Thanks to Amsa's initiative, Tucana is now playing a more constructive role in a tumultuous region rife with conflict and destruction. Furthermore, we are strengthening the fundamental principles of democracy and human rights. President Amsa's diplomacy is founded in the concept that those who lead the world must do so based on values and attitudes shared by the majority of the world's population."

I internally gag, like so much of what my character has become–felt but not heard.

"That says a lot without saying anything at all," I declare in irritation. "I'm going to tell him that the right thing to do is not accept it. That would be the noble thing to do, to tell the world that the prize is so esteemed that he cannot possibly take such an honor without achieving something truly noteworthy on the ground."

The President Doctor stumbles home a few nights later, drunk on attention and fine wine from European leaders. I still try.

"Honey, I think it might be too soon to accept such a big humanitarian prize like the Nobel," I suggest soothingly. "We're still working on repairing–

Saif laughs with a flip of his hand. He laughs me away. He used to take me seriously, didn't he?

I take a few steps back from him. I have mutated into his possession, whereas once we were equals, shielded by New York City skylines, studying and earning and slipping on sidewalks. We were little people in a prominent place and in a lot of love.

"A decoy can always make the trip if you don't want to support me," he barks back.

So I travel with him–annoyed–to Oslo, mainly under the urging of Taya and O. They both worried that if I didn't make a proper appearance, the tabloids would run wild with rumors that our relationship was on the rocks. So I don Cowdray pearls and assume my position in the front row. My husband touts the notion of honoring individual freedom and pledging to join the international community to shut down Guantanamo Bay.

Saif purses his lips and nods his head as the audience applauds him. Yawn. More food. All rich people do is eat.

We miss our first wedding anniversary. During the flight home from Oslo, with some other stops along the way, we come into that ward of timelessness between time zones.

Since I moved to Tucana last December, the life we once shared has dissipated into his and mine. The President Doctor goes about his business, and I go about mine. Occasionally, we come together like the storms of our past. But Saif can no longer do anything in a small way. His love is large and full of vigor, and increasingly, so are the fits of fighting that temper the tender times.

"I've been in this role almost a year, and I still haven't been granted permission to make a public speech or give a one-on-one interview where I'm not your prop," I huff, staring out the window as we make the short drive from our private landing strip adjacent to the commercial airport to the Palace, the "Welcome to Oslo" brochure still poking out of my new ostrich-skin tote.

The traffic halts to an instant standstill.

Saif looks irritated, scrolling through his BlackBerry.

"Why is this taking so long?" he flares at our driver.

"I'm sorry, sir, it is the same route we always take," the driver replies cautiously. "I don't know what has happened."

"Well, I don't remember it taking this long," Saif groans. "I will see tomorrow that this is changed, and you are changed."

I glare at him—irked mainly by his ignoring me more than his treatment of the driver—until he has no choice but to meet my gaze.

"And as I was saying, I'm simply letting you know this is changing," I state. "My role is changing."

We come to a red light at an intersection not far from the Palace. It feels familiar—the same one where I had seen an old man bludgeoned to death on that first visit. I pause. In bright blue letters in front of us, across a nondescript cement building, are the spray-painted words we cannot avoid: *"Down with the dictators. Doctor, you're next."*

Blood rushes to my ears.

Our faces freeze: the driver, the guard in the passenger seat, myself, and the President Doctor beside me.

Next, I register Saif's twitching, the forehead vein popping, the uncontrolled rage I can recall seeing just twice before: 9/11 and the time when I told him our baby was gone.

My first instinct is to crouch and press my body against the bullet-resistant polycarbonate glass.

Saif and the guard trade riled glances, but neither of us say a word. I do not tell my husband not to worry about the vandals, to let it go. Should I tell him not to worry? Would it make a difference in what is to come?

CHAPTER
TWELVE

As a gesture of defiance, taking one of many Mercedes SUVs replaced every six months with new custom models, I rise and leave before anyone can stop me. I disappear into the dawn darkness down the lonely Vea Road the following day. I don't tell anyone my whereabouts, not Taya, my husband, nor the security team. My life is mapped out for me like a ship I cannot steer, and I am tired of being watched and followed.

If my father does not respond to me from his residence just a block from the Palace, then all I can do is assume he was out in the field. I will find out what he is doing outside of Cyra.

I peel recklessly through the elegant, curvaceous streets, remembering the rush of freedom that comes with driving myself. Construction has already begun on a new airport road, as quickly as possible after my husband's angry outburst at the traffic coming back from the airport. In most major cities, airport roads tend to zig-zag across the landscape, respectful of people's land and homes. But Saif demanded there be just one straight line slicing directly from the airport to the Palace.

Powerless peasants, individual property rights . . . Never mind. Saif's men will raze these squalid homes by day's end.

After squealing onto Vea Road, I do not dare to stop, zipping through the washed-out hues of gray, beige, and oceans extending beyond where water and skies submerge. I pass pockets of voluptuous beauty on a gentle winter morning, occasionally maimed by giant oil wells that cast a space-like silhouette across the early light.

In some places, rockets have crushed livelihoods like sheeting rain and ripping chunks of the earth. I could not have seen these sights from my buffer of smuggled Dior dresses and restricted internet access and state TV.

Farmers—with their summer sunburn and wrinkle-rimmed eyes—trudge through pastures garnished in snow. Now and then, there are neat squares of filmy color where blossoms shoot wildly from the earth. I accelerate onto a private road leading to the oil ministry's remote office and attempt to take photographs inside my head. I approach the copper gate, where two men cradled AK-47s in a shack the way some men carry a child, half snoozing by a small fire to stay warm.

"I need to see Bobby Russell," I snap curtly, stunning them from their slumber.

The men look at me curiously, rubbing their eyes as if trying to discern why this woman is all alone in the middle of nowhere. My red eyes and raw complexion, free from curation and war paint, are the best mask I can muster as the ever-together First Lady.

"Do you have an appointment?" one of them asks, voice stern.

I want to tell them that he is my father, that I can surely see him any-time. But no one here knows he is the man who half-created me. We never even shared the same last name.

"It's Sunday," the other guard interjects more forcefully than his com-rade.

I smile sweetly, leaning in—subtle seduction—and lower my voice.

"Minister Russell works every day, that I know; all he does is work," I denote slowly, drawing a fat wad of cash that would be the healthiest bribe waved their way in some time. "So now, is he there? Where is he working today?"

The men pause, both waiting for the other to speak, until finally, the less gruff of the two comes forth.

"About forty more miles down the road, there was an incident at the pipeline," he responds, looking the other way as I hand over the freshly printed stack. "The Minister is there, assessing."

With a spluttering of soot, I tear away.

At first, the cluster looks like flowers in a far field, but as I drive closer, I realize they are people, tens of them. I observe from a distance for a few minutes. Then hundreds emerge. Villagers, young and old, are dressed in their Sunday finest: white dresses and plaid pants, likely the only nice clothes they own, now streaked with inky dabs running to and from their beaten-up vehicles and camel-drawn carts with buckets of black.

I realize that part of the pipeline has ruptured, coating the vegetation with oil-like water. News of the pipeline fissure quickly spread to neighboring villages, and the poor and desperate came to the feast. It isn't the first burst, and I am sure it won't be the last.

I carefully walk toward those faces, swollen with excitement. Nobody claims to recognize me; a green scarf is swathed around my body. My BlackBerry starts ringing–a cheesy harmonic chime with Taya's caller ID. As I move closer to the people, however, the last bar of cell service dissipates into a calming silence.

With unfamiliar faces filling my sight, the desperation to see my father simmers for a small space of time.

I notice one woman, sixtyish with a gaunt face and oval eyes, with a little boy of two or three on her hip, whom she explains is her grandson.

"Good morning," I say with what I hope is a kind smile.

In return, she smiles warmly.

"You look like Madame Anna," she tells me softly. "But prettier you are, natural with no makeup. I'm Simone."

There is a romanticism in her throaty, halting English, and she has all the answers without me having to ask questions. Simone remembers when explorers first discovered oil in Tucana in the late 1970s. She was a teenager who left school at ten to work in her father's butcher shop.

"We thought we would be rich," Simone continues, almost apologetically. "Daddy closed the shop and learned how to work on the rig, but we didn't see a penny. President General Rian and all his men took all that money. The men are still in charge—that American they just made Minister—his company brought in the first tools, only to benefit themselves and the regime."

My heart skips a beat.

"Bobby Russell?"

"Yes, he has been coming in and out of here for decades, taking all the money from us to go home to Hollywood, they say," Simone notes, staring off into the distance. "RUSCO is still here, taking away all our things."

My mind meanders to my privileged tender years—splashing in the Beverly Hills Hotel and our medieval-like mansion on Mulholland Drive. At what cost?

"But the oil boys working here say he got in trouble with the Americans about a decade ago, questioning his business practices, so he stayed here for good and can't go back anymore," Simone explains, kissing the forehead of the little boy.

I gulp, disoriented by the flowing black oil, glossy as wet paint and seeping into the earth like water, meeting a cracked tongue. I wish that were me—that the ground would swallow me whole or suck the darkness away.

"Is he here?" I ask. "Is Minister Russell or his team here to stop the leak?"

Simone waves her hand cavalierly.

"Sometimes, he lets us have our fun for a while. Take some buckets home," she asserts. "Then, they'll send in the guards to stop it all with a hail of bullets when the game is up. I carried my grandson, and we ran along Vea Road to escape them. The road does end somewhere."

With the complexity of my life increasing, the right side of my head hurts even more than usual. I stoop further into the void of uncertainty just when I think I have it figured out. Nevertheless, I am not sure if the worst is yet to come. My eyes swivel around to study the slim, snaking road lined with forests and claypans, covered with a dusting of snow akin to icing sugar.

"The road ends somewhere," I whisper out loud, repeating what Simone had said. Vea Road ends somewhere. Hala's home.

"I want to go to Vea," I blurt out, worried that the longer I stay here, the more I would say, eventually giving myself away. "Am I close?"

It is as though a drape opens across Simone's face, and the fine lines around her eyes stiffen.

"Are you alone? Do you have any men with you?" she asks.

"No, I mean, yes. Yes, I'm alone," I quickly reply.

"There are no men allowed in Vea. There were no men left and no more allowed," Simone informs me, tenderly weaving her fingers through the small boy's uncultivated mass of ringlets. "That is why my grandson now lives with me in Rocca, a few miles away."

I don't understand. But a surge of determination—intent on sewing together the complicated patches of this layered quilt—bursts forth from my soul and settles somewhere in my head.

"Why are no men allowed?" I ask.

Simone's face clouds over, and she drops her eyes to the floor. Just as quickly as I utter the question, the answer dawns on me.

The UN book I read as a teenager while nursing a backside gunshot wound in a Los Angeles hospital bed broached one alarming event—the Vea Massacre of 1981—although very few details were given. A criminal gang from the city in black robes had come in, and Vea's male population had died in droves—but there were only a few sentences; no context, no information. It was a paragraph unfinished and half-scratched out. I was so raptured by the book's courtly descriptions of Arabian horses galloping through the orchids, the faultless azure waters, and the charismatic President General Rian—who I now know was not so appealing after all—that back then it did not occur to me to try to dig a little deeper.

"I- I have to go," I mumble and kiss the child's forehead before swooping back to my black Mercedes.

On my way out, I catch a glimpse of my father shielded by binoculars behind a camouflaged Humvee. He would never be camouflaged to me at 6'5 with cowboy boots and a hat. I want to speak to him. But I also don't want to speak to him at all. I freeze.

Bobby limbers a few feet forward. The Saigon stomp. His body seems to wear guilt like some men wear armor to battle. He doesn't try to intervene; perhaps this is what Simone meant about giving them time to take the prized oil. It is his way of handling remorse, or it is his way of playing a game: cat and mouse. He is the grand master in control, calling the shots.

I rush back to my car before my father sees me and drive deeper down that lonely road, holding myself together, determined not to break. Our dusty, dainty land is still the most picturesque on earth, foliated gallantly in winter white. Then I mentally slap myself. Should it have been theirs? Only it feels like ours, this land. Rural Tucana feels bizarrely like mine.

A piece of tattered, sun-discolored underwear encrusted on the roadside looms into view. I slow the car and shudder, but I cannot move that sorrowful symbol from the earth. The discarded underwear must be related to the brutal massacre of 1981, I tell myself solemnly.

In the middle of the island, just before I reach Vea's steep mountain, a metallic "RIP" plaque embossed into the rock and accompanied by withered flowers diverts my attention.

I step out into the open air and crack off a dead petal, my fingers touching the spot where Firas had plunged into the gorge in his new Ferrari. Firas's life paralyzes me for a moment, an intense sorrow searing my heart. If Firas had ruled, I would have had my love and freedom far away. Then I close my eyes and imagine what life my husband and I would have lived together: winters in Palm Beach, summers in Cape Cod, and bursts along Manhattan's shoreline in between.

Then I drive on. I drive until Vea unfolds before me—a secluded village at the hoof of our mountain. I maneuver the car to the side and watch for a minute. Or many minutes, suspended in the fallacy of time. Clusters of beautiful women with raven hair sway about with an innate sensuality, some carrying baskets on their heads and others collecting water from the stream. I slowly step out and float forward.

I expect them to gather and tilt their heads at me, an outsider entering their tightly closed land. But they do not.

It seems as if I am dead and have risen in an afterlife with these women in angel white dresses, several with identical rings subtly tattooed into their temples. Clay homes created with latticed reed walls dot the panorama, but it is not until I move closer that I realize those structures are decayed—slumping with neglect. Behind them, a short distance away, headstones also sink into knolls of snow and a cracked piano the color of snow languishes nearby, submerged in the earth.

Secretly, I still want to look inside.

The women glide like ghosts in the sunshine, vulnerable yet protected by one another. Vea should feel like the hems of the earth, a place so detached from all I have ever known. Only there is nothing foreign to me about it.

Have I read too much as a child? Have I become too wrapped up in the make-believe?

I continue roaming through the little market, passing bare-footed little girls already oblivious to the chime of donkey bells and listening to the soft sounds of Rasa melting into modern English. Did an outsider teach the native Tucanese the "new" language?

A small crowd assembles by the dock, and a fisherwoman with long black braids casts a pole into the malaise of the stagnant water. In my peripheral vision, I see an overturned raft drifting. No sound can be heard.

As I join the group of white-clothed and raven-haired women milling about beside the glassy surface of the water, I realize they are not fishing for Tucana's famous cod. Rather, they are fishing for the people from the overturned homemade raft, sinking into the low-growing bushes by the water, pulling out plastic bags crammed with belongings and broken shoes with their long poles.

"Refugees," a middle-aged woman says in truncated English, rippling her fingers into mine as she lifts a tiny lifeless boy from the gloomy depths. "But Tucanese. They wanted freedom. Only they never made it out."

She shakes her head despairingly, speaking in staccato, devoid of nuance and emotion.

My mind shouts at me, "*You are First Lady! Do something!*"

I fixate on the sinking raft. Sinking, sinking. I won't admit to myself that my fancy title has little meaning, that my life has little meaning.

How little control I have over my life. Every luxury is lavishly thrust upon me: designer outfits, banquet-quality food, professional hair products, and stylists to do the styling. Nothing is of my own making. I don't even have my own money—I only make requests and send servants off to fulfill them. Everything must be scheduled into a template in a system somewhere, approved, and re-approved by the very individuals who are supposed to work for me. I am supposed to tell them what to do, but somehow, together, they have managed to turn it all around.

I have lost my grip on life, existing on a daily hum of missing my husband, my first country, the tattered manuscripts in Cliff's wood-scented office, and myself. When had I surrendered myself?

"When did you come home? I didn't know you were coming home," the woman choruses, dropping in a few sing-song words of Rasa to blend with the slivered English.

I must have looked back at her in such a quizzical way that she drops my hand and steps away.

"I'm sorry," the woman continues, slightly rattled herself. "I thought you were somebody else."

Perhaps she realizes I am the President Doctor's wife.

"Never mind. We lost her long ago," the voice whispers. "You look like my cousin. The prettiest one. They took her away long ago . . . but we can't talk about that, they could be listening."

I glance around and do not see anyone else but the girls and women of Vea. Of course, it is the ones you do not see that you must watch out for, as Willard once warned.

Like an apparition or a dark angel, the woman sashays off into the blur of light.

An emaciated, watery winter sun glistens on the still sea below. It is the rescue mission and the bodies with quiet hearts I must focus on. The sea stands still, open, and empty. One lifeless body after another lies on the shoreline, telling a story I cannot see.

Painful silence drags on after the women recover each of the dead–twelve souls tenderly sheathed in blankets and carried away–and then I feel it. The sensation of a terrible death. The burned baby. It has been a while, and I dare not look back, but I feel it rolling in flames down that granite mountain road behind me, a creaking, wailing shadow.

Before I hear the baby's cries over the rapid pounding of my pulse, I can feel its hot breath streaming across my neck. Yet most pronounced of all, I can smell it. Sweaty, burning, bloody–the peculiar scent that sticks inside the folds of my skin. It wants me from the inside out, like the soul that has gotten away. But this time, I do not fear it.

The sky blue of the flawless day quickly dissipates to reveal charcoal streaks. A storm is coming out of nowhere, rushing closer. I need to get back to Cyra–back to the existence where I am supposed to belong, smiling and waiting for my husband to come home to his rarely used side of the bed.

Putting one foot on the pedal, I fly, waiting for the sky to shatter at any moment. Only the storm, gaining momentum behind the gloom, does not come.

THIRTEEN

After I return to the Palace late in the afternoon, I ignore Taya's endless questions about why I didn't answer my phone, why I didn't care about how worried she was about me, and where I was. I know she knows where I was–there is not an inch of the island I can explore without somebody following or reporting back.

I did not see any leather jackets, but the Shush–the Shush are the ones you don't see–report directly to Tig, who then files reports to the President Doctor. The Shush can haunt me, but all I can do is let them fall from my paranoid mind.

In the lonely eclipse of the Palace–inside the sadness that clings to a Sunday night–I scurry down into my office. I frantically open my laptop, searching for anything I can connect to the Vea Massacre of 1981. *Search results cannot be found*, Google announces. Alta Vista doesn't open. Wikipedia gives me a 404 error, and AOL turns an endless rainbow wheel that never leads to anything.

"Most search engines and social media sites have been disabled as a precautionary measure to avoid problems, protests, and Amnesty International," Taya explains. "Those human rights groups don't think too highly of the Amsa region, but you knew that."

I wait a few moments for my heart rate to return to normal. I had not even noticed Taya following me, out of nowhere, appearing at my shoulder.

Then she breezily sits on the couch, crossing her legs, giving me a few more seconds to recover from the startle.

"I guess you decided to skip a day in your life when you are supposed to be up-to-date and by your husband's side," Taya continues dryly.

Taya is still angry that I left for Vea without her. I can't blame her. She must have been bombarded with angry questions by the security apparatus and O and all those watching my every move.

"Intel analyzed the street surveillance video and tracked down the two teen boys who vandalized the wall," Taya tells me cautiously. "They were arrested at their homes last night."

I look over at my beloved bookshelf and observe for the first time that a furry button of mold is growing over the spine of the 1977 state-sanctioned Tucanese history edition, a book worn by water and time.

"I just thought you should know," she elaborates in a near-whisper, jumping up to nervously shove a newspaper into my palm, disguised by a manila folder cover. "Things might be problematic for a while."

In only a few short hours after the arrest, *The Cyra Examiner*–a more tabloid paper than *The Tucana Times*, and one which refuses to accept any State funding and is thus routinely raided by Palace authorities–obtained ghastly photographs. The pictures are from deep inside the 301 prison: the chipping ivory building on the edges of the city slums, featuring boys at the hands of the Shush.

In rough-hewed night vision color, two bone-thin juveniles–resembling children far more than they paralleled seasoned rebels–are beaten up by their feet until their pores burst black and blue. Another photo shows one boy–his longish blonde hair falling into his blood-wet eyes–with two front teeth ripped out from blackened gums.

An additional image inside the newspaper, too under-exposed to tell precisely what is going on and too graphic for the cover, seems to shows a child forced to rape another as a bevy of leather jackets and plain-clothed men with bellies bulging over trouser tops hover around them.

The frail newspaper slaps onto the floor.

"There is no way my husband would have condoned this," I shakily proclaim, more to myself than to Taya.

Her nose wrinkles, and her open palms beckon, emanating a bohemian spiritedness I rarely see from her pragmatic and robust self.

"I don't know," Taya says, her eyes widening. "But the paper has been shut down, the editor arrested—as per the President Doctor's orders. After that, just the government-owned networks and newspapers are allowed to operate. The others had their media licenses revoked. It's still all a work in progress."

My first thought is that they should not have published such disturbing images. My second thought is that I must figure out what all this means and what will happen next. My third concern is what will happen to the editor when security forces reach him if they haven't already.

In part defiance, part desperation, I text Saif a question mark. He knows exactly what I am probing, and he writes me back immediately, declaring the photographs are fake.

"The tortuous interrogation sessions never happened," Saif asserts with the typo that makes me think it is cut-and-paste. "The newspaper needed to go because it was spreading fake news."

My husband does not bald-faced lie to me; I remind myself. He repeats only what he knows to be true. Well, what his circle tells him is true.

I worry a bit about the fresh Russian weapons coming in on trucks most mornings; yet I block it out. Defense, after all. We cannot be sure the Americans will not invade here too. But what will I do if the Americans come?

"Trust me, Anna. I looked at those photographs. I know real injuries from fake ones," Saif writes. "I'm a doctor, remember."

Did he forget he had never completed his degree? No one reminded him of that, I suppose. An hour later, Saif attempts to butter me up, promising in a flurry of messages that he is coming home late tonight from somewhere—only to be with me.

But I realize then that as the year's twilight weeks rise and sink, we have not done one of my favorite things in the world—we have not gone together to the Christmas Markets. We have not drunk mulled wine to forget our troubles, nor roamed the pavements to the echo of carols from the stony towers littered with lights the way we did a year ago.

Only I do what I have become accustomed to doing. I let it go.

Outside, a snowstorm fractures into a million fragments. Sometime after midnight, my husband slides into the bed beside me, nuzzles my neck and falls almost straight to sleep. I hold back tears and pine for him, missing him as he sleeps beside me. Saif's boyish face appears peaceful, but his fist is clenched beneath his chin. I warily release his fingers, inhaling the long-lost smell of his breath so close to my nose. I will do everything to keep him. I have nowhere better to go.

Saif stirs a little and, with eyes still closed, gropes my sable hair as it tumbles around us.

"Beautiful," he whispers against the roar of nature's lair so intense it could shatter the glass.

"How do you know when your eyes are closed?"

"I'm an eye doctor, remember? I see everything like it is second nature."

Again, I let that annoying exaggeration go. I close my eyes and drift into dreams, much less complicated than reality.

The morning after Christmas, news erupts that one detained boy died overnight from internal injuries sustained in a brutal interrogation. Less than thirty minutes later, a pebble cracks one of the glass windows near the tower at the Palace gates. Hours later, protesters descend upon the streets outside with chants about holding the Doctor accountable.

From the balcony above my office, I can vaguely make out a swell of people indenting the manicured lanes beyond the gates. I can hear them too. I can hear my name, but I can't entirely decipher what they are chanting. I return to my office and turn on the television. Demonstrators hold photographs of the incarcerated boys, a jarring memorial to the one who lost his life.

Cyra24 abruptly cuts away to the frazzled studio anchor.

"And as you can see, the terrorists are trying to spread fake news to the international media using actors and a false narrative," the wide-eyed blonde chokes out, worried about retaliation over footage that should not have been aired.

Taya left a rolled-up *Cyra Examiner*–sheathed in a Prada shopping bag at my door–and a post-it note with her signature, two exclamation marks and instructions to open the back page. The paper's rear contains images of people crowded in the streets outside the Palace, engulfed in passionate protest, timestamped the previous day.

I try Saif's cell phone, no answer.

I examine the photographs again. They all look like kids, not much younger than me–from the local university and high schools. They have books and little bunches of baby's breath in their backpacks. They march, and their mouths hang open in chant, armed with little more than hand-painted signs seeking "free and fair elections" and "equal access to education." Some throw up their hands with two fingers parted, the classic peace sign.

I do not know who "they" are, but I do something I have never done before. I telephone his assistant; he tells me they are in the Guerra Room for the daily intelligence briefing.

I rush across two Palace wings and demand that the suited guards approach my husband to grant me verbal permission to sit inside that rayless, underground room with the sculpture born out of the Spanish Civil War. Saif does so with reluctance, sensing I won't walk away without terse words this time.

I take a seat at a stretched-out table among a dozen men. A few drop their eyes, refusing to meet a woman's gaze. A few more glare at me with mild indignation, unsure whether I am first a woman or a First Lady. Willard winks. My stomach jingles.

Woodenness washes over the static air. Smoke from thin cigarettes lingers in the fuzzy light, afraid to cut–or fully dissipate –in the cold room, stripped of emotion and light.

"We are bringing back conscription," Tig Amsa, the Defense Minister, announces, not bothering even to acknowledge my existence. "Males between eighteen and thirty-two must serve at least three years in the Tucana Armed Forces. Starting now, military personnel will round them up."

Emboldened, unafraid, hallucinating–just a tad.

"Saif, don't you think that is a step backward for Tucana? We are supposed to be edging toward choice and democratic values," I observe.

"They are terrorists, Anna," he responds tersely. "Terrorists who have been lurking in this country for too long."

"Can't you stop this? The killings?" I continue.

"I am here, aren't I?" Saif replies, glancing around the stiff room. "This is why we are here, figuring out what next to do."

Tig stands up and clears his throat, signaling it is his turn to speak, not mine.

"Number two, we are declaring a State of Emergency," Tig continues. "That grants us a lot more leeway–we can detain without trial for up to two years, and we can move money into military spending. PM and President have signed."

Tig smiles triumphantly for a few seconds, his thin lips drooping into a more half-smile of amusement.

"It's just a simple protest, Saif," I state, reminding the room that he is the one in charge–not Tig. "Demonstrations happen everywhere, all the time. They are youthful voices that want to be listened to, so go out and listen to them. Address the complaints. There is no need for a State of Emergency."

Saif slams his fist on the table. The angry twitch. The September 11th twitch.

"How can I meet their demands? They want elections; they want a new President. They want to undo all the hard work of the Amsa family," he bristles. "They say they want freedom. I gave them their freedom. They want to bring in the Salafists from Saudi Arabia, and in time, they want Tucana to become like Iraq or Iran and run the Christians from their home. We've all seen this slippery slope before."

I do not respond with words, but I carefully examine each image on the stack of intelligence photographs of the table. There is a list on the back of each picture of the detainee's family members, along with their names, ages, and occupations or studies. I do not turn them over. There is safety in knowing only heads without names and occupations. Impassioned young faces stare back at me, equipped with anger and signs. Those bodies that do not want war. Those bodies seek revolution.

Dismissing my husband as occasionally bad-tempered is too easy. He is not crazy. He is not two-dimensional, either. Saif is not his father. He is not the President General. He is the President Doctor. I convince myself that he is loved much more than he is feared.

I look him dead in the eyes, and the memories of a young man who would wait with an umbrella on a New York corner for as long as it took to hail a clattering yellow cab flood back, a man who studied hard and brought me deli flowers and whose sadness and happiness clicked with mine.

But is there something slightly evil in his bones? As quickly as it comes, I shove the thought far away.

"I agree with Anna," Willard suddenly chimes in. "I think we can manage this without going to those lengths."

Willard. Ever my defender in the drowning cesspools of power. I smile at his earnest face from across the mahogany table. He smiles back.

Still, there is no further debate on the matter. The President Doctor listens to his younger brother without really listening at all. Saif signs those two presidential Executive Orders, and the meeting is over. After the men exit, including Saif who does not bother to say goodbye to me, Willard lingers, his eyes wide and worrisome.

"I don't know what is happening, Anna. What a bothersome situation. I don't know who is filling the Guerra with truthful, verified information, and where this all leads and why," he says, staring up into the military fixture affixed on the low ceiling. "The State of Emergency means the return of executions in the Square . . . I hope this conflict can end soon. For all of us."

We hug for a long time. I cry a little into Willard's shoulder, wanting to stay frozen in that frame forever.

"He was far from a good man at the calmest times," Willard whispers. "For all the negative passages and perceptions out there about him, my father knew this place better than anybody I know; he knew what to do to stop tragedy from escalating to this annihilating point–I do miss him."

I don't want to ask him about my husband, but I do. And I can't stop myself.

"I don't know who or what to believe, Willard. I don't know who is killing people, but people are dying. I'm trying to do my own research but– I hope Saif knows what he is doing," I admit, trying to shake off the shadow of moral darkness.

Willard holds my hand for a long moment, centering me as I dip in and out of my smog of disbelief.

"It is okay to feel overwhelmed, Anna. Tucana is overwhelming. This is a disturbance Tucana has never had to deal with before, at least not on this scale. And to answer your question indirectly, absolute power can corrupt. It is only natural," he says soothingly. "But I am working for the best and safest Tucana. And you are his backbone, every man is only as powerful as the woman he loves."

I sniff back the infantile tears and thank Willard over and over for being such a rock in a floating pool of calamity.

The Executive Orders do nothing to keep the young in their homes before or after nightfall. On that dwindling day of 2005, the demonstrations
bring more demonstrations–now they are happening out of Cyra, funnel-
ing through the villages that generally have better things to do than protest. Or perhaps the people realize they have nothing left to lose. I sit in the
murkiness of my office bathroom, watching live streams of baby-faced Tucanese–some with tears streaming down their faces–swarming the streets,
in the winter of their lives, in the winter of our lives.

Despite the internet restrictions, VPNs enable explicit cellphone videos
to spawn social media, and almost all international press latches on with
squawks of outrage. I have one, courtesy of Cliff. Another of our little secrets. It has become my lifeline in transmitting the recording back to him
and scanning the internet beyond the Tucana bubble. But I am scared even
to acknowledge I have a VPN in my head. What would they all do if they
found out? And if the Shush knows—I don't think they do—they never
reveal it.

I jump when my phone rings, the kind of jump you do when the teacher
comes up behind you in a test and catches you cheating, with the math
formulas scrawled across your sweaty palm.

"Anna, are you okay? What is happening over there? Is the regime going
to take more action?" Josie asks.

I pause. The regime? The phrase hits me in the heart.

"I am fine. Everything is fine," I retort. "Busy entertaining, got to go."

Josie continues to call back. I decline the call twice before allowing it to
just ring right through as I remain engrossed in watching Cyra's stream of
protests and pleas from my laptop, feeling lost in a labyrinth of love and
nagging fear.

Weeks earlier, my husband assured me that the police would maintain
as much order as possible, and that law enforcement was strictly instructed

to apprehend only those inciting violence or damaging public property.

But something has shifted, something so big that intelligence briefings can no longer ignore. Earlier that morning, December 31st, military vehicles mowed down demonstrators, and government-issued ammunition sliced the air. Youth waving signs in the cold city died on the glutted streets, youth I can imagine did not want to lose their country because that meant they would lose lives far beyond their own. Anyone with any connection to the protests was dragged out of bed and disappeared into the 301.

Saif genuinely appears astounded by it all, projecting that deer-in-headlights expression over our gourmet lunch set against the backdrop of bombs and bullets, sinking so fast and so far from his surface of comfort. Yet he temporarily calms me, with the assurance that he never issued such an order to law enforcement and security personnel.

"I would never tell my troops to take people from their homes," Saif insists, pushing around a medium-rare lamb chop.

While Saif has done many hurtful things, he has never bluntly lied to me. He is too far away, at the other end of the long table, for me to pat his trembling hand.

"I believe you," I respond.

Saif still holds the top job. But as our little lunchtime ends and I walk away, I can't tell if the power is slipping from his fingers. Has the old guard overshadowed him? His father's cronies? His uncle? Is someone in his—in our—inner circle running rogue?

That night, we stand together on the central Palace balcony and watch overhead as everybody dances by the pool and sips champagne beneath the twinkling fairy lights. It is the New Year's Eve fundraising gala for our Amsa Foundation. Saif attempts to memorize at least parts of the keynote address someone else wrote for him.

My husband's hand quivers even more as he skims over the typed speech. Then he shuts his eyes like a slumbering infant who has no control over the images around him and can only wrestle with supervising his thoughts. Finally, the MC calls Saif's name over the speaker, so away he goes.

In the sky's murky glow, I see him as a child in a maze of monsters. It is impossible not to love that child.

Below me, the guests in fine furs sample the caviar and champagne, and two pageant princess-types in high heels proceed into heavy intoxication. One tumbles into the pool and yanks in the other amid a splash and raucous laughter—all as plumes of smoke rise into the witching hour on the city's outskirts. The DJ's increasing volume drowns out the sirens, the heaviness of life beyond the Palace gates. Nobody notices, or if they do, they don't care.

Nevertheless, the columns encircle us; Cyra at its periphery is on fire. How long can the gold and gleaming things, statuesque towers, and perfect patches of flowers last from my first visit? We are all observing the same stage show unfolding before us, with the same cast of characters, props and dialogue. But I am watching something completely different from the rest of the people here.

If I keep my mouth closed, my version may dwindle.

I sneak back inside, adjudicating my reflection in the bathroom mirror—almost like a chameleon, morphing into whomever my husband needs me to be. I dab a little water over my cheekbones, but what I want is to submerge my head in a full sink, smudge my eye makeup and let the crimson of my lips drip around my chin like blood bursting from my tired pores. So instead, I do what any respectable First Lady would do. I ride the elevator down to the party, accept a fine glass of bubbles and loop my arm lovingly through my husband's elbow. The party drifts on, and we all pretend we do not know that bodies are piling up in the streets, that the floodgates are wrenched open.

A barely five-foot man with red-rimmed glasses and a fuchsia suit comes energetically bounding toward me, bowing excessively and showering me with praise over my looks and smarts.

"I want to pick your brain about everything, Madame Anna," he enthuses, introducing himself as Phil from Boston but living all over the Middle East as an 'artist.' "What do you think about global warming? Is it the biggest problem here?"

I smile politely and reply that it seems we have warmer days in the winter now than even a few years ago, trying to move away delicately.

"And the video? You saw the movie everyone is talking about?" Phil continues, leaning in a little too close for comfort.

"I don't have a television," I answer, trying to politely evanesce into the crowd.

"Is everything okay here?" Willard suddenly asks.

Phew. The man who always comes to my rescue, much more than my husband ever does.

"Can I help you, sir?" Willard asks Phil.

I daintily shuffle away, and when I turn around, the men are shaking hands and conversing jovially.

I drink until the only plumes of concern are in my hungover mind as I stir from a restless sleep as the next day's alarm clock strikes midday.

At the polite request of Willard. in a handwritten note delivered to my quarters, he begged me to have a one-on-one luncheon with his mother, vowing she had some important things to share. I meet with Madame Sara alone in the dining annex of the Versailles Baroque ballroom.

"She wants to tell you something, and it would mean the world to me," Willard wrote. "The family needs to be unified through these challenging times. You are our family, Anna."

How could I have said no?

Madame Sara greets me with a rigid cheek kiss—only one—and we sit almost in silence, the ringing of cutlery and glasses the only ambiance, our conversations always on a fault line that could spasm at any time.

"Millie prepared us sirloin steak at Willard's suggestion," Madame Sara asserts flatly. "Yours with pepper sauce, mine without . . . I prefer simple sea salt."

"I prefer simple sea salt too, but you didn't ask," I counter.

"Willard selected the menu for Millie, I wish he had chosen a classic French bordelaise sauce," Madame Sara concedes dryly. "My son should know I disdain pepper sauce. Sea salt is better than sauce that is not freshly made. Anyhow, Willard told me you wanted a private lunch with me because you had something important to share."

That little charmer. He gets me. He gets us.

"Some First Lady bonding," I reply curtly.

"Very well," Madame Sara haughtily remarks, taking a small sip of her martini.

We slice through our rare steaks without a word, cutting the pieces into blood-seared cubes. I watch as Madame Sara pierces through the wrinkled flesh, neatly carving the carcass into perfect cubes of crimson, trimming all the fat away with the seared blade. Those twenty-five antique Solstice Comete chandeliers shake, tingling for a few seconds in the suspension of time.

BANG. We hear it. But we do not see it.

Some kind of bombing, I numbly evaluate in my churning head. Madame Sara's eyes seem to reach the same conclusion. At the Palace? Near the Palace? My radar still needs to be developed enough to know. Madame Sara's jawline only hardens, staring through me. Unwavering. Chop. Chew.

My heart hammers. I am too stubborn to show Madame Sara I am scared. Or I am not scared at all. An undeclared staring contest unfurls between us. Neither of us loosen our focus, and my eyes still cast daggers into hers. Chop. Chew.

She scowls at me as I chew and chew, that creamy sauce rippling around my burning tongue. Chew. Chew. Chew. Cough. A chunk of meat lodges into my throat and stops wedged against my airway. It does not taste right. I try clearing my throat. I try again to cough, but everything I have to say is clenched shut.

Sirens yelp outside the aftermath of a close bombing, alarm rising so close to home. But in the elastic seconds, the immediate panic gives way to peace. The chandeliers obscure. They blink. Opaque light spins and sinks into the ceiling. My muscles ache, then float, and my body drowns in the temperature-controlled air. It is so easy to give in, to slip . . . I grasp my throat with my hands, the prickles of panic reemerging. I try again–and again–in desperate vain to swallow.

Madame Sara ogles me curiously, her thin, painted eyebrows rising. Her Botox-poisoned face is doing its best to crease in confusion. Haven't I been struggling for breath for minutes? Or is it only seconds?

Then something sinister glimmers and dawns across her face, like awakening from a dream to be propelled into a nightmare.

"Oh, my goodness," Madame Sara murmurs, pouncing towards me. Like a sorcerer with magic hands, she clenches her fist and presses into my wheezing abdomen, yanking my feet up from the floor as if to lure me closer to heaven.

Once, twice–the forsaken steak cube comes flying, and I collapse back into my seat with misty eyes.

Madame Sara composes herself, looks down at me, wipes her hands on my napkin, and instructs me to drink some water.

"My goodness, Anna, get it together. The last thing we need here is another family tragedy," she says quietly, brushing my shoulder with a gentle tap as she strolls out.

I do not know what is more arduous to comprehend: that I had almost choked to death or that Madame Sara sincerely thought my death would be a tragedy.

In perfectly sequenced timing, Taya rushes in.

"Where did Madame Sara go? Willard told me you were having lunch together," she comments, glancing at the mostly uneaten food and back at my puffed cheeks.

"We aren't hungry," I respond hurriedly, sounding high-pitched and pathetic. "And the steak was far too undercoo–"

"A suicide bomb hit the south wall of the Palace. A man posed as a sanitation worker and detonated. Three of our guards are dead. Shit is getting real here, Ans. Not good," Taya informs me brusquely. "What else is not good is that you did an interview at the gala last night without telling me."

But I had not.

Taya waves a printed-out Gawker.com article from her clipboard and hands it to me. I have never even heard of it. The headline blares, "Tucanese Dictator's Wife Declares Climate Change the Biggest National Threat, Blames YouTube Video for Civil Unrest."

"While violent turmoil grips the nation amid the most brutal government crackdown in its history, Tucanese First Lady Anna Amsa told Gawker during a New Year's Eve fundraising gala that her biggest concern was not the horrific human rights abuses in her country, but global warming."

I hand it back to Taya, unable to read anymore. So, she takes it upon herself.

"'The drunken First Lady also contended that a low-budget YouTube film from the West, while prohibited as part of the YouTube prohibition in Tucana, sparked the demonstrations that turned deadly late last month,'" Taya continues. "'The homemade movie, titled *Filthy Tucanese*, centered on the long-running ruling family as profanity-laced cabbage patch kids and mocked the Tucanese outside the elite circle . . . The video was disgraceful and disrespectful, and unfortunately, some people believed the video was a true reflection of Palace discussions.'"

Then I remember that a little pipsqueak of a man in the pink suit and red-rimmed glasses asked me over a Moet if I thought climate change was a big problem–maybe he said the biggest problem. I had not even known the nameless face was a reporter, much less working for the west. I wasn't drunk, either. I drank after that. What an asshole.

"Then he asked me if I had seen the video. I asked him what video. He said if I had not seen the video, it must mean I did not care about the people of Tucana and how they viewed the Palace," I rattle off in self-defense. "I politely moved away, saying I did not own a television. That is true. Technically, I don't own anything. Even my lingerie purchased here belongs to the Palace."

Taya opens up a grainy, low-budget movie on her Blackberry. Puppet-like characters pop up and down, one with Saif's signature mustache, and one with long dark hair and a red suit I occasionally wore.

"Just so you know, terrorist protesters made the terribly low budget *Filthy Tucanese* and it is doing the rounds on the internet," Taya explains. "It's supposed to be a comedy, although I don't take fondly to anyone making a mockery of my best friend . . . But Saif wasn't happy. It is why he ordered the police to go all-out in shooting back."

The twin cherubs stare down at me from their faintly painted position on the roof, urging me to do something. Say something. Not just to sit there in a helpless mess.

"But anyway, these Gawker guys made you like, not so smart, even though we all know how smart you are," Taya says, tapping away at her Blackberry energetically. "They do this to women. Terrible patriarchy, but don't worry Anna, I will fix this with some better press. Give me a day or two to–"

At that moment, with a scorching throat and a throbbing right temple, I can only zero in on the red blink shining through the chandelier's web of illumination.

"Taya," I state, trying to sound more authoritative than I feel. "I don't like this ballroom. It is old, ugly, and doesn't represent the new, young spirit of the Palace. We must change it."

CHAPTER

FOURTEEN

At the stroke of midday on Valentine's Day, I visit the Palace clinic for my once-monthly checkup and B12 shot. I pee in the cup as I always do.

"Madame," the doctor reenters the small room, taking my hand. "You are pregnant."

Time suspends for a moment, the words sinking into the pit of my stomach where I imagined the life now brewing. Well, my period is a week late. I had put it down to stress. After all, Saif and I had hardly had any intimate time in the past few weeks. And I was on birth control.

Internally, I weep. I weep so hard on that table.

More than that, I worry that I am now forever tethered to the man I love but fear being stuck to him all the same. But I love Saif, don't I? It would never have occurred to me before to want out in any way.

"I will take excellent care of you," the doctor assures me. "My life depends on that."

Externally, I pull my shell together and smile a dazzling zoom-whitened smile as I sail back to my quarters. I find myself longing to throw up violently, but I acknowledge that now belongs to my past.

"It's not just about you anymore," I say to myself through gritted teeth.

When I return to my– our –suite, I find Saif has left me a Valentine's Day gift: a set of opal-engraved goblets from Dubai. There is no card.

The earlier talk of dinner plans wither away without words. Saif is stuck in the Guerra Room again. I want to tell him. But to do that, I would have to join them. I want to scream at all those men to stop before it hurts our children and escalates into a full-scale war. Only I can't do that without saying too much. I want to hold my secret close for a little longer.

I switch on the television, immediately captivated by the breaking news of an oil pipeline that exploded just a few miles from where I had stood on Vea Road. The anchors all screech about this emboldened theft and "act of terrorism." My father issued a written statement to the newsrooms confirming that "terrorists" had nicked the pipe to extract oil, but as "hundreds of terrorists" swarmed in to "steal government property," a fire ignited. Over the past hour, that violent inferno has claimed many lives, leaving piles of blackened bones and broiled, empty faces.

Only these Tucanese villagers do not look like terrorists to me. Instead, they look like bone-protruding bodies desperate to stuff their stomachs in a country where you either shop in the Madame Sara towers in snakeskin boots or you roam barefoot, dodging the snakes that sliver through decaying spaces. There is little in-between.

A few seconds of hue-drained footage flashes across the screen: children squat in the dirt, holding the hands of their dead mothers. In another flash, a contorted, sobbing woman holds a motionless infant, the skin on her arms appearing to drip and melt with the burns. In the smoky mist against a divine landscape drenched in darkness, the pinched face of the baby lies untouched, like an angel sleeping, dying, dead. I recognize those raw and frail arms clutching the little life as Simone's, the woman I had met at the punctured pipeline weeks ago. She howls so intently it sounds as though she is half-woman, half-wild.

Suddenly, the footage fades out and another "expert contributor" appears, explaining how the terrorists' actions have mercilessly killed the Tucanese people.

These news people do not say the pipeline is far older than the recommended fifteen-year lifespan. Less money spent on upgrades means more money for the Amsa loyalists in control. Fire can start from the tiniest fissure.

The charred remains, I am sure, will be buried in shallow graves with headless stones, and the media will move along. Yet something else is off, something I cannot ignore.

Among the swell of the distraught are mourners bellowing into the ash landscape with cries for freedom, throwing up peace signs, bony fingers shaped like a V in the burning air, all in the name of peace and victory and free and fair elections. Is there a growing anti-government sentiment among the Tucanese?

How many are fueling the anarchy we were all trying to shut out? I turn off the television. I shut out what I do not want to know.

I wander through the manicured Palace grounds, sucking in the final remnants of sunlight on a day supposed to be all about eternal love, clutching my stomach but still feeling empty, with no real symptoms of pregnancy, and alone. I had spent most of my early life by myself–running up Mulholland Drive in frilly dresses, resting against Dad's steel-bulging waistband in a bid to occupy his distracted mind, or reading in solitude–a self-imposed withdrawal from a world I could not understand.

It was my wedding day, however, one of the most exciting days of my life, that made me understand what it means to be more than alone. I understood, as soon as the bleeding began, what it meant to be lonely.

Laughter–genuine laughter–emanates from the central Palace patio, and I curiously rush toward.

A small pool of people hover around a set-up of lights and a camera on the patio, specially designated for press conferences. I realize my husband is in the wide-span director's chair, and I recognize one of the Cyra24 anchors in a form-fitting skirt suit sitting cross-legged across from him.

O, the makeup artists, producers and the Palace press corps banter and laugh–laughing and musing about their personal lives. They ignore the searing fact that hundreds of Tucanese people have just lost their lives, and with each passing second, security forces heave hundreds more into secret jails. At least, that is what the news on my VPN tells me.

"A few terrorists from outside the country started the fighting. The accusations of a military crackdown are patently false," the President Doctor reiterates to the state television network. "This is not civil unrest. There is no civil war here. Let's be clear. The CIA and other outside groups are funding these people to cause problems. All these outside countries want to create problems to get to our oil, just like they are trying to do unsuccessfully in Iraq."

Saif has become so polished, so prepared. I idle at the outset of the patio, close enough to hear but far away enough not to be noticed, as my husband rehearses the lines spoon-fed to him by O and Tig.

"Unfortunately, we have lost many Tucanese lives, the lives of state supporters loyal to the government," Saif continues, not waiting for the next question just in case he lost his train of thought. "The terrorist militia took pictures of these deaths and uploaded them to the internet with VPNs. They then accused the government forces of ordering and committing these crimes. These so-called terrorist pictures were staged and conducted by the terrorists as a rouse to stir trouble for the Palace."

I half-expect the leggy anchor to break out into flirtatious giggling. Well, the President Doctor is still handsome in his own way. That is a compliment to me. I have always had impeccable taste, if not the best judgment. That is the excuse I give myself.

"These are terrorists who want our oil and want to create chaos and take away the great freedoms we Tucanese people have," the President Doctor says solemnly. "But I want to let everyone know that the situation is under control."

It is Oscar-worthy. But the following line—the following line I know is off-script.

"And remember, the people inciting this violence against us are not Tucanese," Saif says.

A part of him is so steeped in denial that he cannot conceive of the notion that vast segments of the population hate him. Saif knows nothing but a life in which the island belongs to him, to his family. He is not ready to play with the possibility that Tucanese people could turn against him.

The lights come down, and O watches the footage carefully, barking at the producer to delete a few lines and add some post-production softener to give the President Doctor a compassionate quality.

After everyone has hurried away, I follow the young cameraman out into the garden as he heaves his equipment back into his van. I batter my eyelashes at his apprehensive face and tell him I am working on a project for the Amsa Foundation, which requires all the newspaper archives from August to October 1981.

"The project requires a bit of digging through the news archives, but it's very secret for the moment. So please do not inform your colleagues about it or mention me," I caution, discreetly handing him a folded-up note with my direct cell phone line as I shake his hand. "You know what will happen if I find out you told anyone of this request . . . So let me know when you have it, and I will come to you to collect it."

The veiled threat that has just come from my lips shocks me. It is as though it emanated from a woman who looks and dresses like me but is not me. The young man nods, shakes a little, and stutters that he is eager to help—he does not want to let the First Lady down. There is no way for a civilian to say no to the Palace elite. I should straighten my spine, or at least pretend to exude confidence and power. Yet I feel small and desperate, like a kid scheming to start fires in the sandpit.

Out of the corner of my eye, I count two–three, four–women who look eerily like me and dress like me, wrapped in identical Givenchy coats to mine. They mill around Palace vehicles, the same ones I ride in.

"Yes, Madame," the cameraman says before he vanishes beyond the sword-like gates. "I will get to it right away."

When I look back at the decoys, Neo hands them silver suitcases, probably stuffed with designer shoes and lingerie like mine. Odd punches of envy and anger rip at my heart, and I long more than anything to charge on over and demand Neo explain to me why they are getting all these nice things and yet have to do none of the First Lady's jobs, or hold none of the pressures.

Saif does not belong to me, I repeat to myself. I do not even belong to me. Over my shoulder, I see Neo and the decoys are gone. I stumble back inside, dizzy, and sick. But not sick enough to do anything about it.

The cameraman calls me the following afternoon to say he has something. We meet an hour later in my office. As the sweating Cyra24 employee babbles, I draw the blinds, saying little.

"Most of the archives for that time are gone," he admits despondently. "But I found two article clippings accidentally archived in more recent folders."

"Thank you," I mouth, handing him another folded-up $100 bill in yet another obscure hand-off handshake. "The Amsa Foundation thanks you for your time and dedication to supporting this important cause of Tucanese culture and history."

I forgot to ask his name; it is better that I do not know. For his sake, more than mine.

Most of the print is smudged and faded, and to my disappointment, I can make out truncated phrases of the text, a middle-page article dated August 30, 1981.

"*On August 15, 1981, the small coastal village of Vea is believed to have come under attack by armed insurgents . . . Little information is available as the matter is under investigation, but early reports indicate no male survivors . . . At least 23 girls and women are believed to have been kidnapped . . . President General Rian has offered personal condolences to the survivors in surrounding villages, vowing to find the assailants responsible and bring them justice.*"

I pick up the second article, blotted in the yellow streaks of a time gone by, dated September 21, 1981.

"Oh my goodness, Ans, buckle up, the article is here," Taya booms, flinging open my office door and forcing me to jump just a little and turn the article over. "I told you I would make that terrible New Year's Eve article right—and I did."

She struts into my office, handing me a Styrofoam cup filled with espresso shots. I put it to my lips. I touch my stomach. Still flat. I put the cup down without sipping.

"It's such a win," Taya gushes, flipping over a glossy copy of *American Vogue*, which features my face and figure in a vintage Versace blouse, looking ever so Photoshopped and porcelain, staring powerfully into the lens. A flash of my trademark Christian Louboutin red soles are visible to the discernible eye as I sit cross-legged on a bronzed throne, Photoshopped extra tiny into my favorite high-waisted J.Crew pants, just for a relatable measure, naturally.

"Just what we needed. A counter to everything," Taya continues giddily. "Some incredible press!"

I flip open to the profile piece, running my finger along the bold font headline: "Anna Amsa: An Island Orchid."

I had almost forgotten about the interview, which began the morning after the choking incident on New Year's Day when the awful chandelier and the bomb blast in the distance still tormented my mind, just after Taya promised to repair the damage of the Gawker article.

It was, without saying, the budding days of the all-out anarchy.

A tall British woman spent the day with me, taking notes and snapping photographs as Taya shuffled me from place to place, having negotiated with Fashion Week stylists on all the right things to wear. Designer, but not too designer.

"Sharp, smart, compassionate," Taya coached as we drove toward an orphanage on the edge of Cyra, where I would first meet the *Vogue* writer, Lucia. "Humble, driven. Remember, First Lady of the people."

I know Taya had been filtering through and declining a bundle of U.S. press requests for months. She turns most of them down not only to maintain my air of a leader more focused on work than publicity, but also because she secretly fears the worst: reporters will turn the misdeeds of my husband or my husband's father against me. Commentators in the West had been running wild with editorials about his "undeserved" Nobel Peace Prize.

Yet the *Vogue Magazine* interview, Taya insisted, would be different. She said she knew the communications director from her days as an intern on Capitol Hill, and had garnered reassurance that the piece would be flattering and make no mention of Saif's critics.

"The article will be all about you, an American offering to the Tucana people," Taya told me at the time. "A vision of glamor and grit, an oasis of a woman fighting from freedom, peace and service."

I let the words of the published article seep in, numb.

"'Anna Amsa is magnetic, her style is not the opulence of Middle East royalty, but of chic minimalism and tailored perfection,'" I read verbatim of the article. "She is loved in Tucana, where women earn as much as men and all religions are tolerated. Despite Tucana's troubles, the first couple has turned a new leaf."

The glowing piece details my all-white office in a nondescript building within a residential neighborhood.

"'Humble and simple, bringing Madame Anna physically closer to the people she is here to serve,'" the article continues. "'Yet the office is so untouched, it is like a museum collecting dust.'"

The truth is that I never use that office. It is a show for fools like Lucia. Her words wax praise for how I drove myself through the city in an SUV, refusing to have bodyguards at my side. She was evidently impressed by my swerving from one maternity hospital to another philanthropy center. In reality, I didn't know specific addresses and locations. I barely pay attention when drivers shuffle me from one place to the next. The directions all came through my earpiece.

Taya's derivative is to show that Cyra's people are the victims of past terrorist uprisings now under control. Never mind that shrapnel continues to slice the homes of the innocent and sometimes slice their skin. But any skirmishes are the fault of the terrorists against us. At the same time, we must show that the resilient people of Cyra live life as usual, soldier through uncertainty, go out joyfully in the safe zones at night, and bring their babies to the parks for picnics.

"'My early career was very much cutting my way through a man's world. I never let being a woman hold me back,'" the magazine quotes me as saying while I water my private patch in the Palace garden. "But my finance career has made me who I am today. I have transferable skills and the ability to think analytically. Moreover, my understanding of the business side of a company is paramount to my ability now to run an NGO and oversee critical projects. We are all about diversity in Tucana, which you want to see in the Middle East. What people don't always know about our island is we are very secular."

The "Island Orchid" story goes on and on about my quests to preserve the culture of Tucana. I had apparently described it as a "financial asset we needed to invest in." I told Lucia that I prefer to cook meals for my family to ensure that my future children only ingest products cultivated in a cruelty-free environment. Then, during a walk-and-talk through Cyra's oldest museum, I "confess" that my husband is planning to advance his medical degree "on the side." But the priority will always be to be "of use to his people." I don't remember saying that at all. It isn't something I even knew to say.

Still, one part feels particularly gratifying in writing–surreal, even.

"'While her husband was the one to have won the Nobel Peace Prize during his first year in office–albeit controversially, as critics have questioned whether he had done anything significant to deserve the honor–First Lady Anna Amsa might have been the one in the family genuinely worthy of the dispensation. With a long neck and an energetic grace, and when she thinks nobody is watching, Anna reaches to her husband for a kiss,'" the article concludes. "'The First couple waves goodbye to me from the foot of the tarmac, a vision of a couple deeply in love and in the throes of modernizing the Middle East into a land of peace and equality.'"

That last phrase sends something glacial through my veins.

"Isn't it fabulous?" Taya buzzes, high off her formidable work. "You know, my friend, the *Vogue* communications director, told me the writer was a bit upset when she returned to her hotel and opened her laptop to discover that someone had tried to get into the server. I warned those idiots to stay discreet. She wanted to mention it in the article and how a random assortment of guys in leather jackets and dark glasses followed her everywhere she went. But my friend, at my request, told her not to. Isn't that great?"

I feel elated and nauseous. The notion of being so glamorized in my homeland certainly makes me feel as though I am somebody. I made it in this life. But there is something wrong, something nagging.

Taya's vibrating Blackberry fissures the silence.

"Yes, I am with her now. We read it. What a fabulous article. Honest and well-written," she gushes.

Moments linger, and her face contorts. Taya hangs up, slowly placing the phone into her blazer pocket. Again, it starts reverberating. She ignores it.

"I am so sorry, Anna. I don't know how to tell you this, but *Vogue* is removing all the magazine copies from the shelves and has already deleted the article from the website," Taya says apologetically. "I– I guess many news outlets were very upset with the portrayal and failure to acknowledge the– the, ah, situation, the abuses that the human rights groups complain about. It's, ah, causing quite the outcry over there."

I pause, trying to wrap my head around the whirlwind of emotion.

"Can't I issue some statement to defend myself? I had no idea about the server breach or politics," I contend, wanting to cry.

Taya's eyes dip to the floor, and she melts into official mode.

"I will handle any comment requests with no comments, and I suggest you don't discuss the topic with anyone or mention the article," she states carefully. "Let me take care of this, Anna. We won't let these naysayers in the U.S. who don't understand this country ever make you doubt yourself."

With that, Taya clicks her stilettos and exits. I am left alone in the big office, depleted, divorced from the things, the feelings, inside me. I propel the glossy magazine into the trash and, for good measure, pour myself a glass of red wine. Pregnant and all. But only to smell it, to take in the earthy aromas and escape for a few seconds. And then I return to the old articles that the cameraman found for me.

"'According to local witnesses on the ground, the 23 girls and women aged between 14 and 28 held hostage by armed bandits were returned to Vea sometime in late August following government intervention and President Rian's demands,'" the second article glares back at me. "'One female, around 16 years old, and her mother remain unaccounted for . . .'"

Glamour is fleeting.

Half a photograph, torn and blurred in the low light and crooked frame, accompanies the report. Women clad in white, captioned the "Vea villagers before the massacre" . . . A young mother cradles a black-haired child, almost poetic in its untouched processing. Those eyes. Familiar eyes. Unforgettable green eyes.

I storm out of the office, vowing to leave the troubles I have inside it. But I cannot. I storm back in and lie down helplessly on the floor, holding my stomach as a wave of nausea and fatigue hit all at once.

O calls an urgent meeting later that day to devise a crisis communications blueprint to contend with the mess unfolding in the international press over the article that the outside press claims "glorified a brutal dictatorship."

"This is worse than it was under President General Rian," huffs one press secretary, a Palace staffer for years, but whose name I had never learned.

I push a pen so deep into my palm that drops of blood trickle out. I wonder how something so benign could have morphed into something so disastrous.

For hours that afternoon, I immerse my shaking body in warm, froth-like cotton candy bundles that sweeten my skin. I dip in and out like that little girl who swam unsupervised in the fairyland that was the Beverly Hills Hotel—until my fingers shrivel and the music stops.

In the dead of that night, with my husband in a snoring stupor, shadows from moonlit trees looking like angry scars across his face, I creep into the adjoining bathroom, armed with a laptop and VPN. My face falls as fuzzy images emerge of soldiers swarming bloodied streets to shut down the factories that illegally produced cheap replicas of "the First Lady's outfits" are shut down. The *AP* wire runs a story that fan blogs fawning over my style and how to copy my clothes are all now blocked and deleted.

"'The Prime Minister's office issued the decree,'" the report states.

What? I can't wait for the first hints of sunlight to talk to Taya. I sheath myself in a thick terrycloth robe and loafers and march over to her quarters. She answers smoky eyed at the door, opening just the crack as a subtle warning that she does not want me venturing inside, coughing over the cough of someone inside. Since when does Taya not tell me about the company she keeps? Have we stopped being best friends and instead only become working women?

"Taya, we need to talk," I stress. "About these factory raids and the ban on the blogs."

"Anna, it is not the time right now. But long story short, I discussed it with Willard, and we both agreed all this copycat clothing is bad for optics—silly and superficial," Taya explains, not apologetically. "We need the world to see the depth we know you have."

So Taya knew this was happening and never thought to warn me. But that is not the part that climbs into my nerve center and irritates me the most. I didn't know Willard and Taya even talked, let alone talked about a strategy involving me. I am bothered neither of them mentioned that. I want to ask Taya a million questions. I want to know how well she knows Willard and why she just now mentioned their conversations. But, instead, I nod meekly and shrink away. What happened to the ambitious woman with a spine?

Saif is gone from our quarters when I arrive back, evidently lost to his world of power and puppetry.

I wait days for him to return, but he does not. So, I keep the pregnancy news close and return to the doctor for my first-trimester ultrasound scan alone. I float down onto the table, neither happy nor sad, and shut my eyes. *Thump. Thump.* The heartbeat that vanished around my wedding day is back. But it is a different beat this time—a life conceived in a vastly different time and place.

"Pregnant with twins," the doctor states, bereft of emotion in his bushy eyebrows.

I do not know if I can bear another seven to eight months of waiting to bleed, waiting for it all to go up in smoke. Can I cope if one does not make it? Can I manage if both do not make it? Will I go crazy waiting for something to go wrong? Can I tell the difference between spotting and a miscarriage? Will I even cope if both do make it?

I grieve for my twins while they are still here. I am grieving them if they go away, and I worry they will be born on an island where everyone is suffering—confused about the suffering, or denying that the suffering exists. Three more days pass, and I give up and text Saif the news that I can no longer hide the secret I can no longer keep.

"I'm pregnant," I write.

"We're pregnant," he writes back two minutes later. "I wondered when you would tell me about the twins."

Nothing is sacred to me anymore. The President Doctor already knew. When I married a man that belonged to everyone, it had not occurred that I would be property to everyone too. My personal information passed around as others see fit.

I break the news to Taya later that morning. She smiles, embraces me, and excitedly tells me that the press release is already in O's hands, running final approval. She says she has already arranged an exclusive deal to sell the first photos and use the proceeds for the Amsa Foundation. I do not break the news after all.

"Come on, Anna," Taya says tenderly, staring into my half-startled expression. "Everyone knows. The Palace doctor would have been in serious trouble if he did not immediately report it. You know that."

I place two hands over my belly and close my eyes, for the first time feeling–really feeling–the minuscule beans that are only half mine.

"What if something happens to them? Isn't it too early to tell the world?" I stammer.

"Then you'll become a potent spokesperson in fighting the stigmas around pregnancy loss," Taya answers, almost a little too bubbly, silently patting herself on the back for her quick crisis thinking.

She pauses.

"Oh my gosh, Anna, I am so sorry. That came off not the way I wanted it to," Taya says hurriedly, reaching for my hand and kissing it. "Nothing bad will happen. You are safe here. You have the best possible care that the entire Middle East can offer. And this is wonderful for your image. Who could hate a new mother in the press? Pending motherhood will make you even more relatable to the press. Everyone will be talking about this. The *Vogue* thing is old news now; this could not have come at a better time."

"But I was on birth control," I blurt out in nonsensical self-defense. "I saw the doctor every three months for a shot and–

I catch myself. Would it be possible for the doctor to have administered a phony last shot?

"Birth control isn't foolproof, Anna. Besides, you need to be a mother for your image to win over the Tucanese. It is your sole duty and purpose," Taya notes with a little too much confidence. "You will be a gorgeous mother, and the world will know you are a gorgeous mother."

As the breaking news feathers into gossip on the Tucana streets over the next few weeks, my husband arrives home every night in time for dinner and kisses me lovingly at night, coming back to me. If only a little. For this morsel of time, Saif is the kind doctor who rubs my feet and warmly instructs me to take good care of myself and Tucana's future leaders.

Weeks pass, and my stomach begins to descend a little more each day as my mind swishes with an ascending list of distractions. Each morning I check for blood between my legs and lay there waiting for the stench of a burning baby. The stench grows with my stomach–trailing me, kicking me everywhere I go.

I often wonder what our lives would be like if we were still in our Manhattan loft. I wonder if I would even have lived in Tucana if it weren't for the first pregnancy that did not make it. If that had taken place earlier, would Saif and I have even gone through with nuptials?

Now, when Saif and I are alone, we are never alone. There is always someone watching, some security guard sweeping a place before we arrive, someone always two steps ahead and two steps behind. They pretend it is an invisible God protecting us, but someone on a monitor deep in the Palace's bowels is watching us have sex, sleep, shower, fight, kiss, make up, talk, not talk.

I am beginning to crack under pressure. No, not beginning. I have long been cracking. But I will not crack in a way where you suddenly shatter or even in a way where you get dropped enough times on a veneered floor that, eventually, you become so weak that the shells break apart.

I am cracking the way an aging foot cracks. It starts baby soft, and then you keep treading on it and then pounding on it. There is moisturizer, but the pores suck it up over time and it no longer has any effect. So you apply more and more, but the result still wanes. Then one day, you realize your foot isn't soft anymore, and the cracks are too deep to be repaired; the calluses have become an extra limb. So you must keep standing, pounding, and you can never turn back the anti-aging clock to the time when it was soft.

If you remove that new limb, you will bleed out. But I am not about to bleed out. So, you stand firm on that bonus limb, and each day it becomes more hardened, and you don't even notice. Then you wake up one day, and it is so hard; it is a rock that will never soften again.

I do not know the man I love, or maybe I always loved the wrong man.

FIFTEEN

Sometime in late March, the military progresses from bullets on the ground to dropping bombs high from the sky. It is necessary to squash the uprising; everyone around me insists.

If only I could believe them, believe all those staffers with fancy titles and even fancier cars and suits. I want to believe them because I lived through 9/11. I was right there, spinning naked in the fog of debris of depression, and I know what terrorists can do.

"If you give them an inch, they want to take a mile," Saif would always say.

Sometimes the warplanes hover off in the distance. I listen to the whirling sound, and it chills me. I always thought you could only hear that sound just before impact when it is too late to run or hide. But I hear it.

Then the rumors that chemical weapons are decimating entire neighborhoods–coming from our side–begin.

At one of my prenatal checkups, a nurse whimpers from the back room of the Palace clinic. I tip-toe toward the open door, her lips tremble, and she sobs softly into the phone. The nurse tells the person on the other end that she just returned from another medical clinic in the countryside, detailing how triplets brought in that morning were frothing at the mouth, wheezing, and struggling to breathe.

"When medical staff ripped off their tiny clothes, their little frames reeked of chlorine," the nurse continues in a teary whisper.

"The witnesses all said the same thing; different-looking shells landed in a thud of yellowish smoke," she quivers, too upset to care that she is breaking protocol and repeating information that the government does not want to be exposed. "Cylinders that did not explode but smelled like . . ."

The nurse suddenly snaps back into herself, looking at me as if to plead forgiveness for saying too much. I try to question her, but she runs from the room in fear.

I rub my stomach, feeling gentle kicks. I do not wait to see the doctor. Instead, I wrap a soft shawl around my shoulders and storm straight over and past the guard, stomping down into the ongoing Guerra Room meeting. I demand to know if it is true.

"Propaganda and lies from the terrorists," Saif assures me calmly. "They make chemical weapons, bringing in materials from Iraq. We must seal the border. No more refugees; we cannot afford to put our people at any more risk."

Silence swoops over the room. Then, my husband's jaw drops as he acknowledges what he has just said: someone using chemical weapons on Tucanese territory is a party to this battle.

"The terrorists are coming from other places with funding by extremists in Saudi Arabia and the United Kingdom," he rambles. "The Tucanese people are with us, this isn't a civil war. We need to step up our response."

I don't know exactly what that means, but I know it means the worst is yet to come.

"It will be rough for a little while, but the war will end sooner this way," Saif says in half-hearted appeasement. "Anyone trying to overthrow an official, elected government is a terrorist."

I sense a heightened tremble in the President Doctor's voice; perhaps it is part fear and part anger. I have the terrible thought about what would happen to Tucana if the terrorists got to him. Would the bloodshed stop?

Is it possible for one man to turn it on and off like a switch? Would all this end if Saif were to step down as they want him to and sever the multi-decade rule of the Amsa family?

"We are a peaceful nation; these people are extremists," Saif proclaims to the group, gaining energy. "They won't stop here. People who want to destroy our beautiful island will fill the vacuum. These are outsiders. The Tucanese people want me; they want us here to protect them the way my family has always done."

Hardened faces look back at the President Doctor. I should have the guts to yell at all of them. But that won't bring me any closer to understanding.

At another meeting at the end of April, Saif calls a snap presidential election. He thinks it might curry his favor with the international community—the perception of a free and fair leader letting the people decide in the midst of a raging storm. Predicting that it will only worsen things, I advise against it.

"Madame Anna is right," Willard conjectures from across the long wooden table. "It could draw more attention."

The President Doctor does not bother to address his younger brother, or come to my defense.

"Anna, no more Guerra room meetings," Saif suddenly says sternly. "You need to protect the twins, no need to expose yourself to these things. Besides, there is nothing to worry about. We have the turmoil under our full control."

"If there is nothing to worry about," I respond, my voice quivering in anger. "Then why are you pushing me out?"

I mentally shake off the nagging turmoil in my gut and make several solo campaign appearances to support the President Doctor. But, with at least a hint of courage, I inform Taya and O that I will only go to places of my choosing. These are the small moral victories.

For one, I will not go to a military hospital. Would I be able to tell the difference between those who are forced to serve and those who choose to? How would I know which of the wounded had not wounded someone else for no verifiable reason? Is there a possibility that terrorists are hidden among the ranks?

I will not watch the state orchestra play, either. I don't want to sit in the grand theater and listen to the romantic music of Tchaikovsky while our spellbinding little island sinks. It reminds me of the musicians who played on the Titanic after it hit the iceberg until the very end. And only the rich survived.

With my approval, Taya and O arrange for me to visit the Amsa Girls School, which was opened by the Amsa Foundation a year earlier. The school is supposed to specialize in information technology and teach young girls to code from an early age. But when I ask to see the curriculum, the principal anxiously grabs a fistful of her cotton dress and tells me there isn't one.

Suddenly, she instructs the small girls to sing to me songs they have written about the marvelous heritage of the Amsa leaders.

The students show me pictures of the "hero President Doctor" personally saving a mother and newborn from being stampeded to death by a mob of indignant protesters. I do not have the heart to tell them that it is just another decoy, a staged stampede set up across the Palace lawn.

A few days later, I request a campaign stop at the magnificent 15th-century monastery on the mountain, the one I had toured on my first visit to Tucana. It is still there, sprawling over the aqua hills on Vea Road, now pot-marked with a few bullet holes from the fits of a war that the Palace does not dare to call a war at all.

It is Good Friday.

The sisters hold my hand. We pray for the Amsa family and its future—to the burning candles, we offer the Litany of Humility.

"That others may become holier than I, provided that I may become as holy as I should," I repeat the last line many times over, a little louder with each iteration.

Sister Mariam, a ginger-haired woman with dark-rimmed, owl-like eyes, takes me by the hand because she says she has something I need to see. She wants to show me how a rocket landed in the garden, burning a hole in the mystical green and shattering the statue of an angel that had stood hallowed there for hundreds of years.

"You must know, and your husband must know, that not even a church is safe," Sister Mariam whispers, her voice cracking. "Our faith tells us to forgive the terrorists, but when will it end?"

"Soon," I lie. "It will all be over soon."

I stay a little longer and observe as the nuns move about their day, lighting candles, and cooking meals for the orphaned children, and then returning to the pews to pray again—their backs bent over, their bodies bathed in sincere devotion to the only thing that matters to them in the end.

I can't help but feel envious of these women and the simplicity of their calling, of the lives they lived—free from the tangles of careers and power, money and fame, looks, clothes, men and marriage, family, and the lost abdominal definition that comes with pregnancy.

I am exhausted and emotional the next day: election day. I would stay beneath the plush covers forever if I had my way. But Taya insists that I need to stand beside my husband and celebrate his victory in ruling Tucana for another five years.

"You soften him," she muses, wooing me with a maternity dress custom from Burberry—washed-out purple and lovely. "We don't want people looking at him as a dictator. He is a family man, and you are the Jackie to the John."

It doesn't take long for a so-called "independent" team to tabulate the votes brought into the Palace from the polling stations outside popular cafes and local schools. The President Doctor wins with 98.9 percent of the vote. But, of course, there is no real opposition party. If there was ever true dissent, and if there had been, they would have been jailed by now under the banner of terrorism. I never asked. Should I have asked?

I can already conceptualize the international headlines about the elections being a farce and all a complete sham. It is none of "their" business anyway. These international press people think they know everything, but they are not Tucanese. Many articles about me are grossly inaccurate or blatantly untrue. What else are these so-called reporters saying that is not true? Those press people oceans away do not understand the unrest these terrorists are causing. It was fine before all these college children–paid off by the CIA and foreign forces–demanded change. These dissenters will not stop until the oil is in their possession, right?

Saif tells me these things. If I can repeat it enough times, it may become my truth.

Begrudgingly, I step out into the breeze, holding my husband's hand and waving to the thousands who braved the elements of the early evening. The crowd roars, and it plunges Saif into ecstasy, a wave that becomes more physical and a smile that beams a little brighter. But when I kiss him for the cameras, all I can taste is his shame. Or am I tasting my shame?

The sky opens into a magical myriad of fireworks, and the intensity of the crowd sprouts.

And then a gunshot whooshes by my nose, by my husband's nose, landing into a nameless loyalist celebrating below. It happens so quickly that there is no time to gasp, freak out, or duck. One moment we are waving and smiling. The next, security flings us into the back of the armored vehicle and maneuvers us away from the scene at breakneck speed.

Saif breathlessly reaches for my little belly, asking me if his babies are okay.

"Our babies," I correct him automatically, smoothening the wrinkles the security men had put in my dress. I look around at the plush leather interior for the seatbelts; how does an official armored vehicle not have seatbelts?

Strangely, the gunshot barely rattled me, but my confusion over this war–and it is a war whether the President Doctor chooses to use that term or not–has peaked. There is no good and evil, or perhaps there is all good and evil. I do not know who is fighting, who and what it will take to stop the fighting.

"I told you. They call themselves freedom fighters, but they are terrorists," Saif says, pulling me close to him. "Only terrorists would try to kill unborn children. These are incredibly malicious, mentally disturbed people we're talking about."

"Do hurt people create war? Or does war create hurt people?" I ask.

If Saif is listening, he doesn't reply.

In the dead of night and after the disarray of the day placates, Palace senior personnel whisk the President Doctor away–to Tehran, I think. But now I am not listening.

I can't sleep in that colossal room as hail bounces in from the open window that I have no energy to close. I sit up, staring into gray nothingness. Shadows stray across my face, and then the horror movie unfurls–barely audible sobs of a dying infant prickle my bare skin, smoke layering my nostrils until I struggle to breathe. I could scream; I could turn on the lamp. Only I sit there, my heart thudding, the tips of my fingers reaching out to skirt the empty darkness.

My phone rings with a loud, piercing shrill. Who has the nerve to call me at two o'clock in the morning?

It is Josie.

It is not a call littered with the usual questions about where I am, who I am talking to and whether I feel safe. It is a call without questions, just a statement that she is dying and that I need to come immediately so she can explain. There are no theatrics to her tone.

I wake up Taya, and stare into the rainy skies as she oscillates about making arrangements. I don't bother telling Saif. He will inevitably learn from his litany of spying staff and technology, if he doesn't know already.

CHAPTER

SIXTEEN

The skyline shutters behind me as the private jet touches down in Los Angeles, becoming another dot where the sky meets sandy highways. Here I am again in my childhood hometown, a place that carries a wealth of memories that belong to me but also belong to a stranger who once lived a free and unencumbered life.

Less than twenty-four hours ago, I was worried about the rebellion that had only ratcheted up after the elections—and if the croissants Millie had prepared were as low-carb as she vowed. The texture was more fluffy than usual, but I promised I would not harm myself anymore through pregnancy.

The private car cruises from LAX along the Pacific Coast Highway, cutting through the mid-morning, gauze-like haze that blankets the entire Westside until afternoon. I expected it to be like I never left, but Los Angeles no longer belongs to me.

Josie is all that remains of my old life, and going back to her feels more confronting than navigating my island gnashed by war. War is what happens to everyone else in Tucana and many people in many countries. But back in my old country, my old state, my hometown, I am forced to confront a battle of a different style.

Josie's only instruction is to meet her at Saint John's in Santa Monica.

Entering the hospital, surrounded by a mass of aberrant faces and smelling of antiseptic, is, in many ways, like coming of age. Of course, I am married with children on the way and have a job with a fancy title, fancy things, and no salary. But venturing into that hospital is when the burden of adulthood comes crashing down on me.

But all that is the responsibility of someone else. It would take me only a moment to make a call and someone would be on the way to help or rescue me. It may not be possible for me to access money, but all I need to do is phone what I want, and it miraculously appears on my doorstep. There is no paper money in that game of life, only requests masked as demands.

This time, carrying a flimsy bouquet of 7-Eleven roses into the blinding white room, I have to adult alone. In the waiting areas, shafts of light pour through the windows, creating ponds of light across the gloomy faces. This is the grown-up world, and no amount of money or power can solve the problems.

Tap. Tap. Tap.

The click of my stiletto heels along the linoleum and vinyl composition tile seems as loud as an electric guitar invading a silent meditation. People's eyes slither all over me; at least that is what it feels like, and then they resume their daily chores, unsure whether to acknowledge me or look away. Most probably have no idea who I am, too absorbed in their own lives to care about the goings on of a country a world away.

Still, I kick myself for not wearing a more suitable footing. Every step echoes and bounces off the walls of the quiet and sterile place as the nurse slowly leads me to my mother's private suite.

I remember Saint John's Hospital so vividly from the days I spent here after the gunshot, entombed beneath blankets, immersed in the *Books of Tucana*. But nothing here has changed too much. The artwork still features the Santa Monica pier nearby with watercolors. The doctors and nurses still have chic haircuts and frozen foreheads, their offices are still adorned with thank you cards and photographs of rock star wives and swimsuit models treated here.

But I have changed. Josie has too.

The nurse—young and plump with eyes full of remorse—propels back the sallow curtain.

Strings of pearly tubes wrap around Josie's wrists, and a blue, shapeless gown deepens her blanched complexion. Shining bald skin replaces her artificially blonde ringlets, and her lashes and brows are no longer there. The fillers in her cheeks have long diminished, her breast implants removed, and the curtain appears to have fallen on the stage makeup she once would have never been seen without in a public setting.

For the first time, I see Josie without a face full of that dancer's eyeshadow and liquid cat eyes, without some carefully curated outfit that hugged her willowy silhouette and turned every head in the room. What is left is a sick woman somewhere near fifty, returning to an infant-like state with delicate bones pushing against the skin of her childish frame. Josie is all alone and in the terrifying twilight of her life.

She gasps at my oversized belly, bulging through my form-fitting pink and white suit dress.

"Not one, but two," I point out.

Pause. Long pause.

Josie places her dried-out hands on my stomach as if to protect the tiny humans inside me, the small humans I so wanted once upon a time. The truth is that I am no longer sure what life they will have. I love them, but they materialized at a time when they are not wanted. And with them burgeoning inside me, I cannot leave. Even if I want too.

Josie holds her breath as we embrace as if to savor every ounce of her decaying energy. I fold myself elegantly into the enveloping side chair, ensuring my posture is upright and my palms folded neatly into my lap. You can never trust that a long lens won't fixate on a crack in the window. I am still the First Lady somewhere.

"You are quite the star now, Anna," Josie emphasizes, her French accent still as strong as I imagined it was the day she stepped off the plane from Paris. "You were always going to be special."

The talk starts small–the weather in Cyra, the designer stores, the Palace interior, the in-house hairstylist, and Neo's shopping skills. I tell Josie how much I miss Lolita and how confused I am that she never comes around. I tell her that, to the best of my knowledge, Dad is doing well but that we rarely speak.

"Saif has frequent calls and meetings with Dad, but I have mostly given up," I confide. "And I have given up on Lolita too–it is like she is hiding from me, and I don't know why. She lives so near but yet so far because I can't ever reach her."

Josie looks firmly into my eyes, shaking her head the way a schoolteacher would at a naive child.

"Anna, the chemo isn't working," Josie suddenly divulges. "Tomorrow, they will take out my ovaries–and all the parts that make me a woman. I know at my age, you know, mid-fortyish, menopause is around the corner anyway."

Her words drift in and out of my consciousness. *She's lying about her age again.*

"But Anna, they are going to take them away," Josie continues in a gravelly whisper. "That means no babies of my own. There might have been a way–"

Before I can even register the strange rant, a howl from down the corridor startles me to my feet. I hear it. We all hear it; a scream so wild and so primal. It sounds so inhuman and yet, simultaneously, jabs me with an electric sense of remembrance. The bellowing goes on and on, like a wolf amid slaughter–a long, excruciating severing of the throat with a sword.

Josie covers her ears, trying to armor herself from any more pain and heartache.

I wait almost a full minute for it to stop, and when it doesn't, I interlace my fingers with Josie in a silent apology and rush out into the stale corridor. *I am First Lady, do something!* The staff continue their duties as if the scream is the soundtrack to which they live out their vocations.

The raw howls emanate from the open door at the far end. At first, I run, clutching my midsection, squeezing my bladder as I jostle along. But as I get closer, I slow. Goosebumps wash over my body.

I tepidly approach the door frame, incline forward to peek around–and then silence. The curdling cries dissolve in an instant.

I hesitate. My heart drums so hard in my chest that I worry it will burst through my skin. I ready myself and count down five slow seconds as I lean in with my eyes closed. As I count another five, the silence is so enveloping that I am sure every person inside that ward can hear my pulse.

I fling my lids open. The first thing I see is an empty, unmade hospital cot. I breathe a sigh of relief. But then, from some kind of hell from above, a burned baby drops down from nowhere with a loud splatter onto the stiff mattress.

I shriek and scramble in; the little head had hit the bed so hard; surely it is hurt. Only when I extend my fingers to touch the charred flesh that the baby evaporates from my sight. What remains is a young woman–around my age–distraught on the floor, her back against the other side of the metallic bed frame.

Forgetting the appropriate etiquette of a First Lady, I straddle over the bed cot in my dress–and kneel beside this blubbering girl. My eyes flit to and from, searching for the suffering baby, while trying to comfort the stranger beside me.

"Natalie," I say gently, glancing at the name scrawled on her patient blue bracelet. "Natalie, can I help you?"

The young woman possesses a baby face and strawberry blonde locks to match the sprinkling of light freckles across her cheeks. There is a pile of UCLA textbooks on the floor, and a framed picture of a mildly pudgier, younger version of her at Disney World, holding on tight to who I assume is her mother.

"I'm only twenty-two, and the doctor said they have to take everything–my ovaries–everything," she sobs. "I wanted to be a mom. I always wanted to be a mom. But I'll never get to."

Natalie nuzzles her shattered face into my shoulder. I imagine she is far from home.

The tragedy of her dense cries launches me out of my shiny royal status and down into the matte reality. I have nothing to offer this sobbing girl, no words of comfort. No warm hand on this planet can assure her it will all be okay.

I am thinking about myself, quietly relieved that this is not me. I press my palm down on my burgeoning belly, consumed with guilt and graciousness. I am lucky. Josie, too, should count her blessings. At least she could have one child. I snap out of my self-indulgent trance and hold Natalie. I hold her until her wails dull into exhausted huffs, and a nurse enters the room. I kiss her forehead like the mother I will soon be.

I touch my pop belly again, and for the first time, I acknowledge that I want these babies. I want to give them everything I have. I want to love and protect them, and I vow to do whatever it takes. Whatever that takes.

"Give yourself twenty days," I whisper, forcing myself up onto shaking legs, kicking myself for such an insensitive remark. I walk cautiously back down the quiet passageway into Josie's room.

She is still in the same position, staring into the same blank wall.

"Why did you never have any more children after me?" I ask bluntly, resuming my upright position on the side chair.

"We tried," Josie divulges. "But none came."

I think about the odd phrase that had lurched from her mouth earlier: "*That means no babies of my own.*"

"None or no more?" I follow up, unable to prepare myself to trickle deeper into the unknown. "Is there another reason you only ever wanted me to call you Josie?"

The woman I have known all my life, or perhaps did not know, chafes me with fragile eyes. But then, the dam breaks, and words flood from her mouth in a way she cannot contain.

"I loved you like my own. I love you like my own," Josie rambles pleadingly. "I was just a young ballerina in a new country I didn't understand. It just happened too quickly with your father. I should not have done it. I should not have dove down the stairs."

Josie's mind meanders as if entering a transient holding place of which she would never return to the full living. Gone, but not all the way gone. I confirm from the horse's mouth what Lolita spilled to me as a little girl. Josie chronicles her demand that she and Dad move to the palm tree-lined streets of Hollywood, the tacky Vegas shotgun wedding, and her refusal to change her name. Dad capitulated when she drunkenly berated him for not changing his, all as she chain-smoked cigarettes in the drive-thru chapel before they made it official.

Darkness dances over her eyes as if sifting through the regret of what came next: the intoxicated, dramatic stomach-first plunge down the concrete fire-exit stairs.

"Blood was everywhere, and I knew our baby was dead," Josie says, heaped in moral weariness. "I should not have done it. I should not have thrown myself down the stairs . . . And immediately, I wanted it back. I made your father promise that if he wanted to keep me, he would get it–get you back. I made him promise to do whatever it took . . ."

My mind strays back to that night in our Mulholland Drive home, when Josie drunkenly whimpered about the wrong child dying, wailing that I should not have been born, until Lolita, rattled and sweating, led her into the sounds of a running shower.

I clutch my stomach with one hand and use the other to block an ear, worrying that such words could take my babies from me too.

Josie closes her eyes, retreating into her dimmest days.

"I was not the one who had twins, Anna baby. There was only one baby, one girl, and I killed her," she babbles on. "Immediately, I regretted it. Straight away, I demanded your father promise that to keep me as his wife he would have to get me another baby. I did not trust myself to be pregnant again, I did not trust that I would not hurt myself again . . ."

Josie collects her harsh recollections for a moment.

"Bobby said he had the highest-level connections in Tucana. The child would be his, mine, ours, from the beginning," she continues. "I made him promise to do whatever it took."

The look of panic that must have fluctuated between my eyes and mouth only stimulates Josie–she understands that she has only a small window in a race against time to get it all out.

"So Bobby went back to Tucana, where he set up his oil business, where he said he was tight with the government. So the rules were he had no rules. I waited months and months . . . then one day, Bobby said the birth was approaching. The plane ticket came, and off I went to Tucana," she explains. "I went for the birth. November 24, 1982."

I gasp. That is my birth date. I lean forward, trying to make the jagged jigsaw fit somewhere in my burning right brain. There is a part of me that wants to tell Josie to stop talking because I am worried the Shush are listening in. My need to know, however, is too powerful.

"So, Dad had me go to someone else in Tucana, and you went there to get me," I respond slowly, filling in the wide-open spaces with some words.

"The President General had Lolita reassigned from the Palace housekeeping staff to be bound by secrecy as our private servant. She came with me to the forest to take care of you as I had no idea how," Josie says, her throat croaking. "We couldn't go home right away. Bobby wanted to wait, do some work, and make it seem like Tucana was a place to call home. He would have preferred to stay there. He knew the scrutiny on him would become worse and worse in the U.S., so we stayed in our forest home, our secret garden. We fought and fought for more than a year about staying there or returning home."

"The twins were in Tucana," I state, like a slap across my face. "I had a twin brother in Tucana."

"You cried so much, Anna baby. The doctors kept you down so much, so many sedatives for a small girl," Josie details, more to herself than me. "Lolita always worried you would not wake up. But you did. You are so strong and I loved you. I always loved you."

Josie's eyes flutter. But there are no eyelashes left to bat and no eyebrows left to raise.

"And then Bobby had enough. He got sick of me complaining about that isolated house in the woods when I could be in Hollywood," Josie explains. "He agreed that it was time to separate his work from the family and said we should be far away from Tucana, far from his work, and far from this big mess. And the President was worried too, he worried with us all there that the Tucanese would find out and it would spark another violent uprising."

Josie draws a long, reflective breath.

"The shadow came with you. The baby's shadow, I knew it," Josie says, turning her shoulder away from me. "He came with you, but only you can see him. When it upset you, I told you it wasn't real. But I know that it was."

The brother. The shadows. The twin. Nothing can kill a twin connection, not even death.

How dare the President General order his men to invade and massacre a village to find a victim for my father? It was all a dramatic, sick dictator's game to show who held the power. What a lame man he must have been to also kill all Vea's men, to fear their retaliation. And what a horrible sin my father committed. It is no wonder he sought forgiveness from that little Santa Monica church by the sea.

There are many things I should say. But I do the universal thing all lost people do when there is too much to comprehend. I say nothing. Josie promises to write me a letter detailing more so I can read it before my next visit. She lightly pats me on the head, as she did when I was her little girl.

"I'm tired now, Anna," Josie sniffs, dabbing her tears. "I have to find some strength for tomorrow."

Tomorrow, the doctors will take away what remains of her femininity, she says, the feminine parts. Perhaps her ballerina grace will be gone for good. I think it went long ago, but she held it with a loose sequined thread for too long.

I am not about to let her dim into an escape so easily.

"If you aren't my real mother," I murmur as low as possible, wracked by fear that the Shush is listening. "Who is?"

Josie had already descended into her holding place, a slumber so deep it teetered on death.

I glance up at the bouquet languishing on the wooden table. I forgot to ask a nurse for water for the roses I had brought Josie. They are already dying as I sit in her room. Let them suffer, I tell myself bitterly. Let the flowers die slowly.

The way someone leaves the scene tells you everything. I float out in a wasted state, unable to find a voice to cry or a backbone to shake her, wondering when I will be back at that hospital and under what circumstances, wondering what she will tell me in that letter she had promised to write.

Outside in the silvery corridors, Josie's doctor approaches me. I try to pull myself together; he insists she still has months.

"This is a rough patch. It will happen, but it will not happen right away," the doctor says earnestly, pushing up his slipping glasses.

I do not need to ask the doctor what he means by "it"—for Josie, this is it.

Everything at this moment is unbraiding around me. The doctor suggests I plan to return sometime soon, just after my babies are born. He promises to keep me abreast of her condition, but I am not really listening.

All I want is whiskey. I evade the waiting driver and instead take a taxi to the Beverly Hills Hotel. For old-time's sake, I sail down the red carpet, into the time-capsule blush lobby, and then into the Polo Lounge's garden spiced with the rich and famous.

I disguise my bump beneath a big black coat and my guilt behind oversized dark glasses. I order a Jack Daniels at the bar and dig out my laptop.

They say you should never Google yourself, and even with a VPN in Tucana, I avoided typing in my name directly. I realize very quickly that, for too long, I immersed myself in an ignorant bubble.

The first article published only forty-eight hours ago is from *The Washington Post*, referring to me under the ominous headline of "Lady Macbeth." *The Sunday Times* claims I am the "First Lady from Hell." They portray me as some malicious witch that goes along with my husband's clampdown, quoting anonymous Tucana sources as the covert force behind the damaging story.

"It isn't me. It is the terrorists," I protest a little too loudly, prompting two old-money, white-haired heads to stare quizzically from a nearby table.

Even if I had tried harder to stop all this misery, Saif probably would not have listened. Or maybe Saif would have listened. I can't make him do anything he does not want to, although I wish I could.

The wives of the British and Swedish ambassadors to the United Nations made a joint video, posted after the first group of demonstrators were rounded up and murdered with a series of bullets to their brains. In the clip, the two women dramatically appeal for me to "take a risk and not hide behind my husband" and to "demand a stop to the bloodletting."

I haven't heard anything about a mass execution, not even on the news. Nor was I told about this video. So those who make up these crowds are merely demonstrators, or are they terrorists?

Never mind. The old guard fanning the President Doctor would have laughed in my face if I tried to intervene. I don't know who is making these decisions anymore, and if my husband is really the one in charge.

Like a moth to the flame, I continue reading. A new *Human Rights Watch* report with witness testimony claims government forces are conducting random home checks. If each Tucanese living does not feature Saif and Rian's official portraits front and center in each living room, the report states, the automatic assumption is that the occupants belong to an underground opposition movement.

"'*Every home is subject to random checks by security forces, and authorities will detain the head of the household, subject them to torture if those portraits are not in prime position*,'" the report continues.

It seems ludicrous, but it does not seem impossible. Saif is following in his father's footsteps, after all. Still, I know nothing about this either. At least here, however, I doubt most people would believe me.

Someone also leaked the story to *The Daily Mail* about how Saif and I met when I was underage, boozing in the Silver Legs Hell's Kitchen strip club, and that we had gone home together that night. I am shocked–so few people have any awareness of this real story.

Taya is the only person I had told, but then again, I wonder who Saif might have informed. He was always too embarrassed to talk about it, and he made me swear to secrecy. I had nearly started to believe the official narrative about our chance meeting reading by the pond in Central Park. Other biographers have more recently claimed it was in a hailstorm that struck just the west side. We had both fled into Tavern on the Green to escape the rains, instantly connected, and when it stopped that evening, we shopped together at Bloomingdale's.

Those carefree days of childish abandon feel like many lifetimes ago. I make a mental note to talk to Taya about it, have her issue some corrections to these silly papers, to try and salvage whatever remains of my tattered reputation. *Vanity Fair* also features an expose under the headline "Bad First Lady was a Bad Girl Long Before" chronicling my expulsion from Beverly Hills High School after brining a gun to school and later shooting myself amid a blustery escapade with an older man in Venice Beach. Well, I never even told Saif about that one.

My indignation rises. Why am I painted as the nefarious one?

Then it pops up on *Yahoo! News* that the President Doctor and I are on a luxurious vacation by the beachfront in Muscat. A long-lens paparazzi photograph shows me in my favorite floral Balenciaga strapless sundress.

There I am on the balcony of a private villa, basking my smooth legs beneath the golden rays, my long hair unraveling in a cascade of free love, surfer-girl kinks. My husband is love-biting my neck with his hands lovingly pawing my bump.

It is him. But it is not me.

I recognize the girl as one of the decoys, the one they use the most, the favorite of O and Neo and the minions behind the scenes. She was one of the beauty queens who hung around Firas and then at the parties when I moved to Cyra. I think she became a little obsessed with me or sensed a work opportunity, or she just wanted to fuck my husband. I don't know. She underwent several surgeries to look like me, Taya once gossiped.

"She studies videos of you wherever she can find them," Taya had said as we watched her mingle from afar at an Amsa Foundation brunch. "Sometimes we need to dress her up in copies of your clothes and send her out in advance of appearances or for distant photo ops; it is all for your security."

And now that decoy has copied–or stolen–my favorite sundress. She is also trying to steal my husband. I push the thought from my mind. Instead, I already know that I will do anything other than admit that the things we surrendered everything for are things we can no longer, or never could, control. I do not know what the President Doctor does on his days and nights away.

All of it, this pink Beverly Hills Hotel facade, feels like a lie. I don't have time to wait for the private plane to return, so I call for an assistant to book an immediate first-class flight home. Lingering in the airport lounge, camouflaged in my oversized sunglasses and hat, I research more about Vea in 1981.

Little comes up. The news may not have made it this far. There is one snippet, though. The BBC reported in 1982 that two low-level employees from the country's major oil company, RUSCO, were identified by two victims. They absconded before the trial started, and the case merely shriveled away.

I hold the whiskey to my nose, suck in the aroma, and dial Cliff. He does not answer, but my voicemail is short and to the point. I give him the password to my encrypted file on his server, of which all my private, VPN-buried memos have long been syncing too.

"I am ready for the truth to come out soon," I inform Cliff's voicemail. "And I'm uncertain if I should leave while I can."

A kick myself for the last, irrational part and wish I could take it back. Where would I go? Who would I be? Would they come here in the night and take my babies away from me?

There is something urgent in the way the wind outside is picking up. It will be too late if the plane does not take off soon. I will not be able to go anywhere. To be stuck is a terrible thing. I wish I could say I felt free here, but I do not. I could never get away with not going back. Somebody would always find me.

The speakers sing out the call to begin boarding. I casually stand up and drop my laptop and the BlackBerry onto the hard floor with vigor, watching in twisted ecstasy as they smash into hundreds of miniature fragments.

"Whoops!" I exclaim to the surprised faces around me.

The Shush would undoubtedly troll through my electronics upon return when I am not watching, given I had ventured to an enemy nation abroad. They would certainly want to know every little thing I had seen and done in my brief excursion to the United States.

This is one round I will keep them from winning; it is the small victories, after all.

In numb inertia as we soar above the fluffy clouds, I think tearfully about my mother and brother lost to the unknown. I think about Lolita and the crooked cemetery of knowledge she keeps. I think about my father, but I no longer think of him much at all anymore. I think of Josie and the letter she would write, and how ghosts of the daylight wait to take her away. I think about the babies in my belly and the burbling warzone to which I am returning. I think of the secret garden and the sedatives, and

I question if I am part-Tucanese after all. I think about the world pegging me as the war crimes instigator rather than the arm candy who willingly gave away all her strength. I think about all the decoys and wonder what their job description entails. I think about my husband and Taya and how much of this I should share.

I think about all these things as if staring into a mosaic of color, a stained-glass window–all the dazzling, ever-changing colors only make sense from a distance. Up close, the random patches of contrasting color make no sense at all. I touch my stomach and think about the nurse from my prenatal visit, the one I had overheard detailing the chemical attack victims. With a flinch, I realize that I never saw her in the clinic again after that tearful encounter.

I wish I could stop thinking.

When I land, Taya is waiting with a new laptop and phone. I can't escape.

"I heard you lost your comms devices; well, we can't have that, Anna," she says with a knowing pluck of the tongue. "I guess you wanted to start fresh, so here you go."

I don't bother to try and defend myself. When I reconnect to the outside a day later, Cliff replies with a voice message, assuring me he is working on my request.

"Head on a swivel and powder dry. Your Hotel California is that you can't loathe someone once you get them, once you really understand them," he says. "And keep in mind, true change doesn't always require big announcements. If you want to do it, show the world, don't tell them."

I wander back into my living quarters. I smell Saif's cologne, but he is not there to greet me. Instead, he has left a large bouquet of yellow roses. I ruminate for a fleeting second on who else has stayed in this room with him–I'm endlessly wounding, wrecking, wondering. *He can have those wom-*

en, I tell myself. He can have all the women he wants, but they will never be us. They will never have our connection. They will never be me.

I take in the mild scent of cloves and lemon and soften. Saif still loves me. I slip into my favorite sundress, the same one the decoy wore in the picture of them together. Instead of hurting him back, I slowly begin to hurt myself more and more.

CHAPTER

SEVENTEEN

For two days straight, I repeatedly call Dad and Lolita. I email them, too, begging them to call me back. They do not. I give up temporarily and set about plotting ways to unravel the mystery of my life by myself without getting too far.

Then, two weeks later, just after my early evening shower, the dreaded news arrives in a handwritten note left under my bedroom door from O's office.

Soon after being discharged from the hospital to her home in Malibu, Josie's frail body went into unexpected cardiac arrest. I imagine she slipped away after just a short outburst of theatrics that nobody was there to see. All alone.

The way someone exits tells us everything. Josie had come through and left me hints along the way, but there are still so many unanswered questions left in her wake. I am distraught. One can expect that death is coming, but it still comes as a tremendous shock when it does. Perhaps I naively believed in a miracle right up until she took her last breath.

O's office must have notified Saif. He hurries up from the Guerra Room.

"The doctor was wrong," I tell him testily, as the note in my hands smudged with hot tears. "He told me there was time."

Saif sits on the deck as I whimper into the predawn. He lets me sit with the pain and holds my hand. It is the worst time of day to receive such news, the loneliest time of day when the sunshine is so far. But what tortures me the most is wondering if Josie managed to write me the letter before she left. Despite my ever-puffy ankles and night sweats, I intend to return for the funeral and pay my last respects to the woman I knew, but not well enough.

Saif vows he will come with me to Los Angeles. It has been months since we have gone anywhere together. But just hours before I am to leave for the airport, Taya rushes into my room with more news.

"O's office just received a notice from the U.S. Treasury Department," she says steadily, her eyes wide. "Anna, you are listed on the new economic sanctions list–along with the President and most of the ministers, including Bobby."

Prickles shoot through my entire body, and I raise my voice for an explanation.

"What did I do? I've been the only one trying to stop this mess," I argue. "I don't even know what it means. What does this mean?"

Taya is also visibly shaken.

"Anyone involved in the oppression of the people or human rights abuses," she laments. "I'm so sorry, Anna. I know they are wrong about this. We'll sort this out. We will show them."

Images of Josie's decomposing body in a plush white coffin, alone in a big church, race through my mind. I have unanswered questions. Even though she is dead, somehow, I figure I would find the answers by seeing her one last time.

"It's just too much of a risk for you to return to the U.S. now," Taya cautions. "Remember, you aren't a citizen anymore, and the feds will most certainly arrest you when you land or make you turn right back around."

I close my eyes and massage my right temple, which throbs like I have been bruised and battered.

"Anna, cry," she whispers tenderly. "You know, it is okay to cry."

But I will not. I must not. Taya moves in to massage my shoulders again.

I step away. Human touch in this second will break me.

It takes a few days for my name to appear on the sanctions lists issued by the European Union and Arab League. The United Nations also tried to sanction us, but Saif and Putin had a long call, and Russia vetoed the resolution in the Security Council. A minor achievement, I suppose.

So I do the only thing I can to keep my mind active in this last epoch of brain-fogged pregnancy: I work. Taya stresses to me, over and over, that I need to stay as busy as possible with the Amsa Foundation to save the country and its reputation. Working is the only thing she, too, knows how to do.

"Optics," she would often chorus. "The world needs to know you care."

I plan to launch an appeal to help victims of the burst pipelines, whose limbs and lives blistered into oblivion. However, Taya rolls her eyes.

"You know I can't get approval for that," she stammers. "Besides, nobody in Tucana, the people that matter, really care."

I wish I were brave enough to return to the Pistachio Center. But I am not. Not yet. So instead, in a scud of hormonal nesting and Josie-grieving mania, I throw up my hands and declare that I will host the most magnificent parties.

Only that ugly Versailles Baroque ballroom needs fixing first and foremost. I do not wait for anyone's approval. I take out the foundation's checkbook. It is, after all, a business expense. I have Neo phone for the best designers and contractors from Moscow to arrive on the next flight armed with design delights. I send them off to take hammers to those ugly twenty-five antique Solstice Comete chandeliers. I order woven glass from Istanbul and assign Neo to fly over to collect them personally, and return with suitcases of John Q. Shearer gloss for the walls.

To ensure my new ballroom will come to life, I inform the contractors that my deadline is three days. They will also receive double the pay if they work around the clock. I rename it the Anna Ballroom, because Cyra has not yet named a boulevard after me.

When the millions in the fluffy Amsa foundation account hit zero, I demand Taya talk to Willard and pull from the Prime Minister's state-of-emergency funds. I could have asked the President Doctor, I guess, but he would scold me for being ridiculous and insist I rest before giving birth to the heirs. If Saif has heard about my blitz, he does not bother to say anything. I pass Madame Sara in the hallway as the renovations are ongoing. She shoots me a steely gaze, but keeps her mouth closed. I am holding the heirs to the totalitarian hereditary dictatorship, and for a little more time, I have a power that will never come again.

Willard releases the money with a cedar-smelling note advising me to take care of myself. I grow more energetic as the building, painting, and theatrics twirl on. I supervise each waking minute of the work, ignoring the horrified gawks from Madame Sara who lurks in the backdrop as the contractors throw her design legacy into the piles of plaster and trash.

At this point, Taya figures better than to try to stop me. But she does not ignore my unraveling circus.

"Nobody says no to me," I emphasize, even before she opens her mouth. "I've sacrificed all my freedoms for this place. I am at least going to have it looking how I want it."

"It just doesn't look so great. Terrorists are out there hurting the Tucanese people, and you are spending money renovating the ballroom because you never liked the décor," Taya says as the new interior glitters across the freshly painted room. "I called a contact at *Architectural Digest* to see if we could do a feature. That way, I can administer the spin in the name of arts and culture, but they won't touch you . . ."

She walks through the vast space in her signature black Cavalli suit, like a supermodel strolling into a photo shoot.

"The aesthetic, though—you are so on point," Taya marvels. "This looks incredible. Chic and Frank Lloyd Wright meets Mies Van der Rohe. We will have some fabulous events here."

My anger over being unable to travel due to the mounting sanctions slowly subsides. Even the loss of Josie numbs me more than it wounds me. I mellow into the anxiety of a different species–continuously checking the mailroom for her letter, praying she sent it before she died. Maybe a palliative care nurse kept it to send to me. I dwell little on my pregnancy. I prepare for my First Lady assignments with much more enthusiasm and attention to detail than I plan out how I will mother.

Cosmetically, the U.S. sanctions are terrible for Tucana. But nothing grossly changes–for me, at least. Some staffers complain they are not able to travel far and wide. Others lament that our currency is dropping, making it harder to attract foreign business. Yet mostly, it feels like the convoluted political talk I do not want to comprehend. My budding financial career was clipped lifetimes ago.

In something akin to heightened mania, party season is my priority.

On a warm early fall afternoon, I ready myself to host an upcoming summit for the wives of global leaders–North Korea, China, Iran, and Russia–the nations that have not relinquished diplomatic ties. It is more of a protracted tea party, but the word summit sounds much more important and worthy.

However, as I inspect the tiny 19th century cups tinged with gold streaks woven into the porcelain, fixated in a time warp about who has sipped from such a delight, it occurs to me that Millie must know something more about Tucanese history than she has ever shared. She had, after all, lived in the ghostly Palace grounds for decades.

Straight away, I corner Millie in the kitchen. I ask her emphatically if she remembers the Vea Massacre of 1981. Millie's fat face contorts into myriad emotions, resting in wide-eyed worry, and she says she does not. I press again.

"Did it make much news? Did they find the missing mother and daughter?" I ask, feigning my best air of dispassion.

"No," Millie creaks. "No, no one talked about it. We weren't allowed to–I don't remember it all."

She hurries away from me, fingers pressed eccentrically over her trembling lips. Why does nothing make sense? I let it slide for now, but I will not let the issue go.

My new set of solid gold cutlery arrives just in time. I pick up a fresh Prada coat between the morning's ribbon-cutting displays. When I come down with a mild sore throat, a Palace nurse lays bare a collection of therapeutic concoctions before me like a covey of fine wines.

Preparations for the summit are perfect—except for one thing: I must inspect the selection of cheese.

Three hours before the First Ladies' summit in the poolside glass dining hall, Millie knocks at my living quarters' door in trepidation. With my hair in rollers and a cucumber mask plastering my face, I am busy inscribing handwritten thank you cards for each guest, now irritated by Millie's distracting and unscheduled presence.

"Madam Anna, I don't know how else to tell you this," she sputters, her forehead swimming in perspiration. "It's terrible news, and I am so sorry. I honestly did everything I could–

"Millie, what is it?" I press.

"I placed an order for the Swiss cheese, the finest La Maison Du Gruyere as you like, Madame, many days ago. I also placed an order for aged Granito," Millie digresses in her broken but improving English.

I cross my arms.

"Millie, I know you know Granito isn't quite the same. It's tougher in its consistency, more robust and nuttier, and better served with dessert wine than as an appetizer," I retort.

Millie frowns–a deep, downcast frown like the circus clown puts on when the show is over.

"It should have arrived at the beginning of last week, but it did not, Madame," Millie continues, tremor tinging her tone. "We have been calling and calling to find out where the holdup was, and last night, we found out that Europe-"

I raise an exquisitely curved eyebrow. I know it is exquisite because I just had them shaped and perfected.

"Let me guess. Europe has halted cheese exports to Tucana over concerns about the wording of the sanctions, which they have interpreted as rendering their companies in violation of the U.N. sanctions," I surmise.

Silence cuts the air.

"Go on," I reply indignantly, motioning for Millie to get to the punchline.

"So yesterday afternoon, I sent a team—including me—to hunt down any existing La Maison Du Gruyere, Granito, or even Bregaglia or Emmentaler Echaukaeserei or No Name pasteurized two-year-old Cow's-Milk Cheese from Tschlin or really any Swiss cheese we could find," she explains, tears welling. "Entire teams in every neighborhood contacting every fine dining restaurant, a gourmet supermarket, security forces even went door-to-door, but nothing . . . The imports haven't arrived in many weeks . . . Nobody has any . . ."

"What are you telling me, Millie?" I ask, my voice quivering up and down like a kid-friendly rollercoaster.

"I am so sorry, Madame Anna, but at the summit tonight it's best we have local smoked goat's milk ricotta. I can assure you it comes from the Sahar Mountains in Tucana east and is pasteurized, so it is safe for pregnant you," Millie says, her fingers trembling. "It has been smoking in the juniper wood chamber and is wonderfully aromatic. I have no doubt the lovely ladies will be much impressed by what we here in Tucana can produce."

"Don't tell me what my guests want! This is un-fucking-believable," I yell, standing up and wiping the pencil tin off my desk in an angry furor. "I cannot believe on such an important occasion you would fail me like this with the wrong fucking cheese. This is the Presidential Palace, not some honky-tonk, crappy, rat-infested diner in the slums."

My vision frosts and my eardrums burn as I pace the room, cracking and screaming in a way I had no control over–berating Millie, throwing papers in a disorderly mess, my hair rollers dropping to the floor as I stomp up and down from wall to wall.

Fuck the sanctions, fuck Millie, fuck all this nonsense.

I draw a breath, regain my composure, and lengthen my neck. I storm over to Millie, staring rabidly into her watery eyes.

"Quit the crying, go downstairs, and make the best damn fucking dinner of your life," I bark. "Because it will be your last here. You got it? This is your last night working here. Now, get out of my face."

Although it is not the first outburst from a person I sometimes do not recognize, the viciousness of my own words amazes me momentarily, as if I am outside looking in at myself. I am playing some role or plunging into a stereotype of a character I think I have to play.

Tears roll down Millie's plump face, and she runs off without saying a word. I hear her trip and tumble down the wooden staircase in her haste, letting out a helpless yelp. I hesitate, but I do not go to see if she was okay. Millie resurfaces later at the event with thick white bandages bound around her ankle. She carries the overflowing trays with a wincing limp.

I look away, partly angry at the sanctions and embarrassed about my outburst, stripped of empathy. The real reason I resent Millie at that moment is because she should have told me about the 1981 Vea Massacre when I questioned her.

The veneered summit whips past in a blur, punctured with goods for my unborn children. Strangely, the other first ladies are not really there to talk to me, they are there to talk to each other. The women are all polite, at a distance. Has my reputation as the wartime wife even become too damaging for them?

The next morning, I smell the sweet scent of fresh bread emanating from the traditional oven as I walk to the gym for my prenatal personal training session. Millie must be hard at work counting ingredients and preparing for the days ahead.

"What are you doing?" I ask.

"Good morning, Madame Anna. I prepare for you gluten-free Ezekiel bread for after your gym and have the most delicious avocados brought for you from Bogota. Madame Anna, I will carve it onto the warm bread for you topped with your favorite super fine diamond crystal sea salt," she beams proudly. "And a vanilla protein shake of which I am right now ringing out the cashews for the fresh cashew milk. I remember you switched from almond ten days ago."

I remove a bottle of cool pH-balanced water from the large refrigerator.

"Tell me what you know about Vea 1981," I demand.

Her eyes slither to the polished floor and she shakes her head, wracked in a shoulder spasm.

"That is what I thought. I told you yesterday you were fired," I declare. "And I meant it. So, finish this meal, leave it for the servers to serve to me, pack up all your belongings out of the living quarters, collect your last paycheck from the financier's department, and go."

"But I thought last night was such success," Millie protests. "You maybe were just upset that you didn't mean it."

For once, I can play predator and not prey.

"You thought wrong," I retaliate calmly. "I have a new chef moving into your quarters this afternoon, so hurry up and go."

I almost apologize for being a monster. Nearly all of me wants to apologize. Only I can't bring myself to do it.

As I cross the lawn after my precisely forty-minute personal training session, twenty minutes of prenatal yoga, and then seven minutes of meditation in the sunshine to up my vitamin D intake, I spot Millie struggling all alone with her two heavy suitcases. She is still limping on her bandaged foot, making her way toward the empirical gates. A thirty-year dedication to the Presidential Palace fills those boxes.

My guilt twinges until I reach my suite and realize I do not have a chef on standby to assemble the lunch meal.

"Resumes now!" I snarl at Taya. "New chef, can't keep the same boring food forever."

I stride in my sweat dotted Lululemon sports clothes to my office and lift out my hidden file with those media clippings. I scrutinize that old, half-a-photograph of *Vea Vogue Magazine*—torn and blurred in the low light, a green-eyed mother cradling a black-haired child with green eyes.

Through wistful eyes, it clicks: the young woman cradling the baby. That was my Lolita.

Knives puncture my stomach, a thousand of them all at once, and I drop to the hard ground, struggling for air. A trickle lumbers down a pale leg, and I glance away, afraid I have been stabbed or shot or would drown in a pool of blood the way I almost did as a rebellious teenager by the Venice Boardwalk.

When I peep over my mid-section mound, the puddle is all clear.

"Oh my goodness," I pant, reaching for my desk phone. "The babies are coming."

Our babies arrive ten minutes before midnight in the Palace clinic across the lawn, two minutes apart, three weeks early. September 10, 2006. It is long and terrifying, but surprisingly painless, almost euphoric, as the epidural propels me into a dreamless bubble bath as I push. Saif makes it just in time.

Afterward, when the medical staff takes the babies away for medical checks, I kiss my husband; he tastes different. Sweaty and separated from the reality now upon me, I don't ask where he has been because I already know the answer deep down. I smell the Dior Hypnotic Poison perfume I stopped wearing two months ago.

But the President Doctor showers me with kisses and praises me on how well I did because our boy came out first, then our girl. Our boy arrives with my green eyes and the President Doctor's curly, coarse, milky brown hair. Our girl possesses his almost colorless gray eyes and my dark mane.

Trumpets blow in the streets, and canons fire large tufts of blue smoke with smaller clumps of pink toward the heavens. I want to call our little ones Neptune and Kanaloa, after ancient gods and goddesses of the sea.

"Don't be ridiculous with those American New Age things," Saif laughs dismissively. "The birth certificates are already being printed—Rian and Ella. Ella was my grandmother's name. I thought it would be a nice touch."

But when I glimpse at Saif, he is staring at our sleeping children, still half-laughing. It is as though he is laughing so that he will not cry, a semi-depth to him I had never seen.

CHAPTER

EIGHTEEN

The sky is a perpetual, mutated gray for a month after the twins are born. Every time I peer out the window, a few holes let a glimpse of light in, but it mostly looks like it wants to rain. However, it rarely does. The typical fall sunshine had evaporated along with the silence. Instead, gunshots, bombs, and wails rip through the air—sometimes all through the night and sometimes just in brief smatterings.

I love my babies in a way I never thought possible. But I cannot stop weeping when I am around them. I am their first home, but they no longer belong to me. They, well, Rian primarily, are next-in-line for a life from which I cannot protect them.

Having children has made me obsessively deliberate on who my blood belongs to and who I am. The roaring internal debate is making my bones weak, wearing them out. If only there were a way to end the mental anguish. I want to finish a part of me, but not all of me.

When I investigate my reflection, cast against the tinted windows between me and the characterless lawns below, I barely recognize the face and body that slouches back. I do not recognize the woman with cracked hair and eyes of liquid sadness. I once had perky breasts, small and sphere and natural. Now they sag a little. I don't know her, this bleary woman. Is that a stretch mark? Holy shit, what was the point of ordering all that virgin coconut oil if all I was going to get was stretch marks anyway? It may be an impression from the sheets against my skin. But, no, it is a stretch mark.

Saif comes and goes as he pleases. But with the war gaining steam, he can no longer safely leave the Palace grounds. So he spends most of his days and nights in the Guerra room, and it isn't always for professional purposes, I assume.

O and Taya refuse to schedule me for any engagements, insisting that the people's princess must devote all her time to motherhood in the early phase. But there is little for me to do. Someone else does everything. I am the people's princess, yet I am not supposed to be human.

One grim afternoon, Taya patiently sits on the heated bathroom floor with me as I try again to breastfeed Rian and Ella. Eventually, I give up and hand them to the nurse for a formula feed. Then, divorced from myself, I light a stale cigarette from an old packet kept stashed away at the back of the medicine cabinet for no reason other than a rainy day when it all becomes too much.

"I'm bored," I tell Taya flatly.

"To live in boredom is to live in luxury," she responds. "Take a break, Anna. It is okay to take a break."

I hear the nurse re-enter the main bedroom and place the twins in their cribs. A few minutes after she leaves, they both begin to cry.

Let them cry until someone in uniform swoops in to take them away, I figure.

"I can arrange someone for you to talk to, a professional. You know, a shrink. A therapist. I think it would help," Taya says, picking up where our conversation left off and touching my hand.

"No, thank you," I reply without hesitation.

How can anyone be trusted not to blab about me to the press or the feds? How can anyone be trusted not to gossip about me for a buck or two? Therapy is an American thing anyway, I reason. It is not for people here. In Tucana, there is the quiet nuthouse in the slums; nobody talks about it, and then there is nothing. I wonder about those women in the Pistachio Center; I wonder how Hala is doing. I wonder how the decrepit House survives all the city's mayhem and turmoil.

"People here did not have mental problems," one uniformed army officer told me at a dinner event early in my First Lady tenure, after I casually broached the issue. "It is just not a thing."

But if these men had seen their comrades die, watched blood splatter across the shocked faces of children over and over again, and could still be fine afterward, then I could be fine too.

On another day, Willard–who stops by on his excited uncle duties–also tries to soothe me. I want to drown out my babies' piercing howls with a bottle of Pinot Noir. Instead, he guides me over to the Palace spa so I can float through the foam in the pale light. He joins me in the warmth, in the bubbles.

Willard wants me to know I am not alone, reiterates his brother is a difficult man, and confides that things have become so untamed on the streets that even the President Doctor can do little to stop the gushing wound of Tucana.

"I yearn, I wish I could make all our problems vamoose, go away," he utters in the spasming light. "But, Anna, you must take care of yourself first before you can begin to take him–and the unfathomable depth of Tucana's obstacles—on."

There is a spark in how Willard always looks out for me–brotherly or romantically. I haven't quite figured out what that chemistry is, but it zaps like electricity, as though he knows so much about me and sees me in a light that I can't see myself.

My mind bounces back to my last visit with Josie at the hospital.

"But, Anna, they are going to take them away. That means no babies of my own," she sobbed.

"We tried," she said softly. *"But no more came."*

Then to my earliest memories in the storied hotel pool. I am a little girl hugging my father's gun-poking leg, and later the burned baby—the one from all my daydreams, nightmares, and real-life—chases me down the driveway. And I can't forget Lolita and Bobby's Rasa exchange at my bedroom door one morning before he tells me I am going to boarding school.

The faces of Palace staffers shift in and out like a blur. I do not greet anyone; soon enough, they decipher that they had better not greet me, not even with a "Madame" or a nod, bows and curtsies.

It is still warm outside. Yet for the next few weeks, I bury my bag of bones in a hoodie the color of oysters and timeworn denim jeans. I do not bother to slap on an ounce of makeup as I burrow myself into a corner of the bedroom with my notebook to write. I seesaw between scrawling and whispering into the recorder.

A patch of light drifts across the window one day, and a spout of life peeks through. I press my broken nail over the buzzer until a maid comes in to seal it shut.

Soon, a brittle winter creeps in, draping the gardens in a grim white. And still, the twins scream and scream. Sometimes I go to them. Most of the time, I leave it for the nannies, nurses, or unfamiliar faces that morph with every passing day. They work around the clock, darting in and out of the extraordinary Disney-themed nursery we built directly below our master quarters with a private elevator to go up and down.

One of the workers on the schedule is that decoy woman, the main one in the paparazzi pictures cavorting with my husband in the private villa, emerging from the sea like the hippie mermaid I could have been in another life. She is the one Neo showered with duplicates of everything I owned, from my signature scent to the slight ding in my red-soled stiletto. She does morning shifts three days per week.

I ask my husband one night if he had hand-selected her. Saif claims she has a nursing degree. I doubt it, but I am too tired to object.

In the dying light of most days, during the afternoon nap time, I watch over my babies, wrapped in white like sleeping angels. Legally, I have no rights to them. At any moment, if my husband wants to, he has the constitutional power to take them from me and give them to someone fitter than me. The decoy woman, even. I am the vessel that brought these tender lives to the island for someone else. In my imagination they have both my good and his evil in them, and I fear it will pulsate through their veins more as they grow into a world at war and fractured by confusion.

What began before Christmas years ago as graffiti on a wall and a spout of protests, bedeviled by the fables of freedom and equal opportunity, is now a worsening war that the Palace can no longer control.

I often think of Josie. She picked me, but I am not hers. I do not know to whom I belong. My brain can no longer connect the pieces of obsession and where to turn next to fit it all together.

One day in the garden, blood seeps below the crack of the high-security walls and runs through the shards of grass—deep, fresh, red blood.

Cyra24 declares burly men arrived on boats brimming with arms, leading an insurgency to overthrow the government with religious radicals. The government had no choice but to fire back. Nobody wants to believe that it is Tucanese doing this to other Tucanese.

I remember what Cliff once told me after 9/11 when we talked about statistics and the finish lines to suffering: Did my husband know where the finish line would be? What would it look like? Would we know if we reached it?

There is no finish line—no goal, no real victory.

Then one night, I am meandering through the suite, speaking gibberish into Cliff's microphone under an ever-changing assortment of VPNs, when I am overwhelmed by a choking sense of someone or something closing in—almost ready to bust what I have been doing all this time, to unseal my sealed story. I don't have forever to figure out the mystery; I only have now.

Security refuses to permit me to leave the compound to cut ribbons at new hospital openings or even meet Neo on Madame Sara Boulevard to select new shoes. I probe visiting the Pistachio Center, but Taya claims that is off-limits too.

"Why?" I ask Taya.

I know why.

"It's better you stay here for now," Taya emphasizes diplomatically, but not answering the question at all.

One clear afternoon I peek out through the iron curtain of the high gates. Through the slits, I see trucks loaded with the disfigured. Flashes of street clothes and banners are ripped apart with bloodstains, producing eerie eruptions of color. A normal reaction would be to flinch, but I do not.

As the season transitions, I cut myself off from all the things I know are right and moral, like being a good mother, a good person, and a thinking animal. Saif waits for some months, until early in the New Year, to say it. And then he does; if he is scared, he does not show it.

"Why don't you go to Russia for a little while? St. Petersburg is a lovely city; my babies will be safe there. You didn't sign up for this," Saif says. "You deserve a better life. Free from this danger and calamity. I'm worried about something happening to Rian and our daughter."

"And me?"

"Of course, you too. I could never forgive myself if anything ever happened to you."

This is my chance. The President is permitting me to go, to escape this jungle of crazy that has characterized my life.

For a moment, I envision a life of Porsche and the Bolshoi, of black fur coats and anonymity. I could build a farmhouse in Siberia and read under yellow winter lights like I did as a child. I am jealous of the imagined self, but I am also jealous of my past self too–the one who looks after herself in the New York streets and pours every paycheck into a walk-up apartment that smelled of fried Chinese food and old furniture that smelled of 70's discos.

In Russia, I can seek asylum at the U.S. Embassy or earn amnesty in the Netherlands by testifying against the President Doctor at the International Criminal Court. Or I could hide but never seek forever in the forests of Bosnia.

This is it.

I look at the President Doctor's doe-eyed glare. His face is still that of my husband. Sometimes hardened, but I fell for him when the front was still a baby face. I knew the person who lives beneath the layers of power and weakness.

What would happen to Tucana if the terrorists got to him? I jump a little at the mere thought of it. What would I do then? Would the bloodshed stop? Could this one man turn it on and off like a switch?

My heart sinks. I imagine my devastation. I understand, really understand at that moment, what Cliff meant when he said it is impossible to loathe someone once you understand them. Isn't that what we all want? To be understood even more than loved?

Cliff is right. I gave up everything to enter the beguiling oasis in the middle of the madness that is the Hotel California. I can't give up more than I already have, which means staying. I'm not going to give up Saif. We have come too far. The pain he is putting me through will not go away even if I were to walk away. I could do everything to keep him, but only if he wants to be kept. It does not even make sense to me why I want to. But I still do.

"No," I respond. "I committed to you, and I am committed to this country. Tucana is my home; you are my home, and I am not leaving."

I can be stubborn.

War, bullets, broken bodies–those things have become so familiar that they no longer frighten me. I want more than anything to go out into the world. Being at home with children–being a wife and a mother, and feeling trapped in a pretty castle–those are the things that drag me below and make me scared that this is the climax to all there is in my life.

Yet when the offer to leave from my husband came, my ticket out, I did not want it. It's obvious why. I worry that if I flee, the puzzle will never be solved. It would never be over. And I would always be left to wonder.

Out of the blue that January, Lolita sends me a small card and finely woven, almost weightless, baby-sized gold bracelets for the children, sent with regards from both her and my father. But I am sure it is only Lolita who put the energy into it.

Still, neither of them sought a clearance to come over, and when they do not pick up the phone, I do something I am growing more eager to do again–recede into the streets all alone, even if that gets me into trouble.

I scoop up the napping babies with crinkles carved from the pillows into their fluffy cheeks. I wrap them in cashmere blankets, but I don't know how to do it right. Awkwardly, I put them in the stroller, praying they will not slip out.

Then, I push the double stroller on a frozen afternoon down the Palace lane, ignoring the confused questions from the guards who swap worried glances and walk a few steps behind. I stroll a manicured block to the Oil Minister's Cyra residence, Dad's Texan-style ranch, the place I visited only once before on my first visit to Cyra with Saif to announce our engagement.

I continue past the little camel-colored hut of guards and straight to the door, banging furiously until Lolita's round face peeped back.

"You," I said, whirling back at the men with a menacing stare. "Stay."

Lolita looks at the infants curled up in fetal positions and bursts into tears. She cries so hard I worry she will stop breathing. Lolita picked up a newborn in each arm, and I follow her through the warm mansion to the back where she lives in an affixed cottage that is blanched with rouge windows and a terrace replete with pot plants and an overhanging orange tree.

I sit for a few minutes as Lolita nurses them with bottles that smell like vanilla soap, just as she had nursed me. She had not expected me, her hair—always parted and braided down the right side of her face—is slicked back in a simple chignon. But I see it. That circular scar on her right temple. Thin and angry. Had I just never noticed it before? Or is it that I had never known to notice it?

"Lolita," I press on, knowing that time is not on my side, that Taya or the Shush or a driver or Saif or somebody will soon peel me back to the Palace. "What can you tell me about the Vea Massacre of 1981?"

Lolita's unkempt eyebrows droop, and the color seems to bleed out from her olive skin. Her expression transitions through many mental states, stitched together by a heavy flood of scenes inside her memory, her terrorized memory. For a second, I think she might hand me the babies, and then run away. But she hands them back gingerly and sits upright. Lolita's face settles on disgust and despair, too rundown to keep running.

"Vea is haunted," Lolita admits. "They came. I still remember the morning they came. August 1981. Collecting water from the well. The black cluster was coming through the only road in and the only road out."

As Lolita speaks, her throat becomes more wizened, and she cannot stop—because to talk is to keep her nostalgia awake; it is a way of holding on and letting go.

"I tried to hide my daughter. I tried to hide Hala because she was so young—just sixteen—and so beautiful with our family line of green eyes. I knew they would want her," Lolita says, her eyes wet with retrospection. "But I could not save her. I could not save my husband, my father, my sons."

She remembers the smell of gunpowder as it battered their bodies, as all the males in the village crumpled like dolls into the cavities of the gorge below. She remembers how they loaded the young women into the backs of cattle trucks, propelling the burning muzzles of their just-fired guns into their right temples as the men in black flung inside—they were bawling and petrified as the trucks swarmed into the density of a dust storm.

"I held her on the truck, my daughter. Hala was so afraid. I was so afraid," Lolita says. "I did not know where they would take us and if we would ever return to Vea."

Then Lolita stops. She hesitates and etches a single fingernail into my palm. But she does not run from her memories. I examine those flat fingers, remembering how they would race across the piano before Josie had men and a truck remove it from the Mulholland Drive house. I realize then that the lovely, velvety language she sang in was Rasa.

"For days, maybe weeks, they kept us in the basement of the RUSCO office, several miles down the road from our village. The men examined us, touching us all over. They wanted the prettiest. I tried to make her ugly. I threw dirt on Hala's face," she continues, hotfooting to find the words out of worry they would dry up. "But it was her green eyes. They sent everyone else back to Vea. Except for Hala and me. They brought Hala to the one man . . . This is why I always wanted to protect your green eyes."

I brace myself for what is going to come next.

"President General Rian was there, waiting to present Hala like a shiny new present to his friend," Lolita sobs. "Then Bobby Russell was there. I could do nothing. They sent Hala home with him. She was the chosen one."

Lolita cries that she could only tell her frightened daughter to make it through.

"They kept us Vea women submerged in the dungeons, down twenty-two crooked steps. I counted them as I cleaned for them, the President General's men, every day," Lolita breaks into whimpers, punctured by infant-like hiccups. "It was not until months later that they let me go to stay with her under guards' watch in Bobby's house in the woods. She screamed so much for me I think they worried if I did not come, she would go mad and destroy the babies inside."

She draws a battered breath.

"But Hala, she was a brave girl. She kicked and fought the whole time she was in captivity, every time Bobby came anywhere near her," Lolita says. "And then Josie arrived a week before the birth . . . You came; the other one came," Lolita says.

"The twin came," I correct her, heartsick. "My twin brother came."

"Josie only wanted the girl because that is what she killed on the steps. Hala was sent with the other baby back to Vea," Lolita whispers. "The President General's people told her it was her gift that she could keep the unwanted one . . . I knew too much. I knew it all. The President told me I must stay with the family. I was now Bobby's slave for life. Josie did not know how to raise you."

Lolita does not pause to breathe or wipe away the swell of tears, talking faster and faster.

"If I told a soul what happened, President General assured me personally he would slaughter every woman and child in Vea after they were all raped and tortured," she divulges. "But even if I had a choice, I would have still chosen to stay with you. Even if you never knew what happened, I could watch over you silently. I wanted to be close to you, Anna."

Lolita's body enters a dark place, battered by the secrets in the ancient hills and her mind.

"One time, just a few weeks after you turned one, I escaped with you back to the mountain," Lolita continues, pulling me close in a terrified whisper. "I don't know what I was thinking; it was a moment of haste. A car crowded with women from Vea stopped outside early one morning. I thought it would be my only chance."

I remember what Josie had said in her hospital bed about Bobby wanting to lead a private life in the Tucanese woods as long as possible, worried that someone would find out if he returned to the United States. In Tucana, President General Rian's iron-fisted rule protected him. The rest of the world was a different story. But eventually, and after more than a year of fighting with Josie after my birth, he conceded it was time to take the family out of that tumultuous place.

Lolita pauses, taking another shallow, ragged breath.

"But it didn't take them long, a week or so, to find us. I had nowhere else to go but Vea. We tried to hide moving from tent to tent," she says. "They, the guardsman, found us in Vea just two days before Christmas. They punished us by taking Peter. What they did to baby Peter, I . . . it hurts too much. Hala was the one who found him in the fire. Christmas Eve came, and we woke up in the morning . . . And I never saw my Hala again. I suppose she died too. By late Christmas morning, the guards pulled me away too, with you crying in my arms, back to Bobby's house in the woods."

Like the oil pipelines, it was all a sick game, the guards watching Lolita and Hala enjoy a moment of freedom and waiting for the right moment to rip it all away.

I think, at that moment, this is what it must feel like before the plane crashes down–when the pilot loses control in the storm, and there is nothing you can do but wait to meet fate. The lights flicker and dim, and the oxygen masks fall. While the plane is dropping, everyone starts screaming their deepest confessions, their regrets, and the dark secrets that have plagued them for so long come gushing out.

And then it suddenly ceases. The air becomes precipitously static, and the lights flash back to bright. The plane cruises onward. But the remnants of what almost transpired cannot be taken back.

"Hala always worried you were half evil, but I did not. You were you," Lolita stammers, staring down at her own great-grandchildren. "And your babies are too. They are not your husband, they belong to themselves."

Through the white, lacy curtain, southern-style and scalloped at the edges, guards with folded arms moving across the front lawn catch my eye. At least a dozen of them.

"Your whole life, I wanted to tell you everything, but I knew what they—the guards and Bobby—could do if I told you. I was not allowed to say anything to anyone," Lolita cries. "Everyone was you."

"Hala is not dead," I steadily object, remembering the woman with a face that mirrored mine at the Pistachio Center. "Your daughter, my mother, is not dead."

"What do you mean?" Lolita asks quizzically.

Before I can open my mouth, ash flies across Lolita's face, a mixture of fear and panic piercing her eyes. The aftermath. The only survivors of the crash.

"Anna, please take the babies and go home now," Lolita says breathlessly. "They will come for me now, and I do not want them to come for you too. Please, Anna, go now. Keep yourself safe."

In an oddly formal tone, as if in shock at her own doing and the knowledge that someone out there behind the walls was listening, she waves me away. Lolita insists my father is not home; he is at the remote office, but is due home tomorrow. She says she will send my regards and let him know I stopped by.

My blood. Lolita is my blood. We both understand what is bound to happen next if we continue this conversation.

Obediently, I stand up, place my sleeping babies back into the stroller, and stumble out into a world that has changed.

Twins. Like me.

I love them in a way I did not before, perhaps because I understand them. The tiny, crying little innocent forms of life.

I feed the babies fairytales the second we arrived back at the Palace. I always thought I would be one of those parents who would never read my children fairytales because I did not want them to learn lies. But as the reality of my world darkens, all I can do is read them fairytales that they are too young to comprehend. Lies, lovely lies, will be their bodyguards, protectors from the harsh outside.

I read my babies fairytales when they should be sleeping and when I should be sleeping—the ones with magic are my favorites because they seem like they could become real. Then, with the first streak of daylight, I order an artist to the nursery to paint the characters on canvases so they can spring to life before their eyes.

The following morning, I send for actors to arrive in costume by lunchtime to mime and narrate, and then for an orchestra at sundown to give meaning to the melodies that dictate when to be excited and when to be scared and when to laugh and when to cry. It is a lovely construct of everything that isn't real. The wild war goes away when the play is playing.

When I am not reading tales, my mind plots how I can return to the Pistachio Center. To Hala. To my mother. To get her to Lolita. Her mother.

After the actors leave in the afternoon and the curtain comes down on my mad moment of make-believe, I sit in the nursery and buy a giant wooden tower, wooden piece by wooden piece. It will be years before my babies can properly play with these children's building blocks O gave as a gift to the new arrivals.

But they sit in their baby seats, observing in a cacophony of tired tears.

That night, I try to make sense of it all. It is all still confusing. It is all still sitting on top of the brain and not quite seeping inside. It is part denial too. The life I am living in, the life I have always lived in, is a lie. Maybe sometimes we try too hard to make sense of things that really just do not deserve sense in them at all.

I return to the Oil Minister's residence the following day, the same trail of guards in my wake. Bobby must be back from the oil fields by now. He must know a lot more than he had ever let on he did. I also figure that he has figured out that I will not let him get away with this for a second longer.

Before I can even reach the door, Bobby is already there, his brooding body and features extra harsh beneath that evil yellow porch light.

"Anna, you can't be here," Bobby says, his stoicism breaking into something akin to a beg.

"What did you do? What did you do to Vea in 1981?" I seethe, low enough so the guards behind cannot hear. "Why?"

Bobby looks around, anxiously ushers me inside and slams the door with a thud.

"Anna, I wanted you to have a happy childhood. I wanted you to grow up loved with nice things in a safe place. I didn't mean for any of this to happen," he stammers.

The Texan cowboy splinters–if only a little.

"I never brought you back here to visit. I didn't want you in Tucana because I was scared of hurting you even more; I was scared of what they might do to your honor because of what I had done," he whispers. "You'd already been through enough. I just wanted you to have a happy little American dream. This island is horse shit."

So, to keep me away all those years was to protect me, but also to protect himself. This is Bobby's way of telling me, as his daughter, that he loved me, but it is his way of loving himself too. And to not have to look at me every day, to not be there as my father, he did not have to remind himself constantly of what damage he did in the once idyllic village on the edge of the earth.

"Cut the bullshit," I stammer back. "You never wanted me to find out what you had done."

"I did not know President General Rian would help me like that. I did not know what he would do to all those people," his voice trails off. "I did not know he would send his men in like that."

The President General's black-clad forces paraded those lost and lonely women each at gunpoint, the muzzle tattooing round and nasty scars into their right temple–branding them like cattle, to be discarded faces without names. And then, they killed all the men.

Bobby swears he did not know what took place until later; he swears this over and over. He swears that the President General and his men picked the prettiest girl to bring to him and that she wanted to be there. He vows that the terrified girl wanted a beautiful life of beautiful things for herself.

"I loved Josie," he insists. "I would have done anything for her. And I did do anything for her."

Bobby's strong voice plummets into the subdued, and he spits out the tobacco he had been chewing.

"Go, Anna," he croaks. "You have to get away from here. You've done enough."

His lips quiver. Is it swelling anger? Or swelling guilt? Is this how he stared at Hala that day he violated her too?

It makes sense to me now why he covered me angrily when I was an almost teen attracting the eyes of older men at the Beverly Hills Hotel. He knew what his kind could do to the young, the innocent, the green-eyed and long-legged.

"The Shush already came last night and took Lolita. I'm sure I'll be next," Bobby asserts matter-of-factly. "I can only sit here and wait . . . Please go and be with your husband. Let him protect you. Please, I don't want them to take you too."

His eyes dance with desperation, a slow dance of death.

A life of lies will come back to us all, eventually.

"There was no Saigon stomp," I spit at him. "You were never anywhere near Vietnam in the 1970s. You were drilling for oil in Tucana. And you were injured when she–when Lolita's daughter–fought back."

There is a moment's pause. My father says nothing.

"Fuck you, Bobby," I spit again. "You're a fucking criminal."

I walk away into the sea-blue morning, and I never look back.

CHAPTER

NINETEEN

Nothing will shift if I stand still. The burning baby will continue to break through the ornate cage posing as a palace. So, I cannot stand still.

I wish good morning to my two slivers of sunshine, the helpless little humans I love but am learning to love more and leave them in the good care of the day's nanny. It is time to step out. It is time to revisit the most dismal parcel of a place before the clock runs out.

My mirror of a woman has been nibbling at my nightmares, much more real than any decoy, and I cannot rip her eerily recognizable eyes from my mind. Hala is more than just another woman in a concealed nuthouse. She is me. She is Lolita. She is the blood of my veins and the pains in my brain.

Under the radar, in a blue baseball cap and jeans, before anyone can stop me, I jump into a freshly cleaned Palace car with my babies and accelerate off. I no longer recognize the city I once thought was the most stunning in the world, the short drive to the city feeling like a long and despondent voyage.

The previously esteemed billboards of the President Doctor have almost all been defaced or blown to bits. I flee deeper into the desolate streets, streets strangled by skeletons of charred cars and storefronts, streets that reek of burned rubber and decomposing bodies, where bombs have drained away all the color and napalm has gouged roofs and windows. Every home is stripped naked, guttered by relentless air raids. Only one side possesses air power, and that is not the side of the rebels or to whom Saif refers as terrorists.

From where I sit, figurines faraway look like dots inside a house of horrors, little lives unraveling like a braid–tight at first. However, as I get closer, I can see how spread out they are in the open air, trapped on top of lifeless plots. Gaunt faces dig deep holes into the earth, and I have a strange thought that they are digging their own graves.

Then I realize they probably are–this is life beyond the Palace bubble. Do they wonder what will be written on their tombstones? Probably nothing at all. Would anybody care to afford them such dignity?

The vehicle skulks along until it reaches that forlorn place perched amid Cyra's slums, one of the few brittle buildings still standing.

The Pistachio Center's caregiver, Eva, the same woman with the expressive face–thinner now, perhaps from the reduced food rations from war–looks panicked by my arrival. But she hurriedly bows down and opens the door into my garden, apologizing profusely because they have run out of tea and no more will arrive anytime soon. I hardly register what she is saying.

"Hala," I state. "What's wrong with Hala?"

The woman shakes her head glumly.

"We don't know; she has been here for a long time," Eva continues. "She says she is from Vea and was taken away in some kind of massacre and had twins–a boy and a girl."

Eva glances side-to-side and drops her voice to a hoarse whisper.

"Apparently, one died, and one was taken away from her," she says, hiding her words even from the walls that could always be listening. "And she lost her mind."

I feign a gentle nod of concern, but underneath the layers of my skin, my stomach is scraping up against me in torment.

I request–perhaps more demand–to see Hala's chart, but there is little to see. The rough notes show she was born around June 1965 and was brought involuntarily to the clinic on April 1, 1983. She was released to go home again on October 5, but on Christmas Day that year, government workers brought her back with the mandate that she is characterized as a "lifer."

Holding my breath, I move out into the garden, and it is as if nothing has changed since the last and first time I visited.

But time has stopped for all these women. Hala sits alone in a corner on a broken plastic chair underneath the streaks of sunlight, the same place I left her last time. As I inch closer to her this time, I notice something has changed slightly. She is weaker, smaller, more like a little girl, closing back into herself a little more as time grinds. And the smell. It isn't the smell of body odor or unwashed hair; not a single stain maims Hala's long white nightgown. It is more like ammonia–part rotten eggs, part fishy.

Self-cannibalism is a smell that can only stem from a body so feeble it breaks down, with toxins nowhere to go but out through the wasting muscle and the frangible pores.

I sit beside her on the unkempt, sunbaked grass and, for a long time, stare up at the reflection looking back at me. Then, something of a small smile shatters the emptiness of her doll-like face with pulsating green eyes.

"You came back," Hala says demurely. "I couldn't save your brother, but I could save you."

She closes her eyes again, safer somewhere between dead and awake than in the memory that haunts her reality. When Hala opens her eyes again, she looks at me lovingly. It is clear to me that she is not crazy, but so profoundly traumatized and lost. She has no place to wander but in her mind.

Hala is deeply traumatized. But she is not mad. Hala doesn't profess to know who I am–as in the First Lady of her land–and is hardly concerned with any status symbols. And when I am beside her, I'm not either.

"I'm Anna," I remind her.

"That's a pretty name, like my little girl's name," she says airily. "Anna, I have something to tell you. Nobody believes me."

A precursor before the rush.

Hala massages a dirty, peeling fingernail around the right temple scar, the size of a pistol's muzzle. Perhaps that is why Bobby's gun never scared me—the memory of blood having survived it. Hala narrates in broken English, punctuated with words of Rasa, inducing a movie through my closed eyes.

I picture Hala hauled into a cattle truck after the armed guards open fire, her green eyes plucked as the ultimate victim of the Americans who wanted a child. Raped, giving birth to twins in captivity, eventually allowed to return with only one child, only for that child to be handed the most brutal death at the foot of the craggy mountains as a punishment for her mother fleeing captivity with the twin daughter.

"Peter," Hala whispers. "I could not save my son, Peter. And then those men brought me here, and I never saw my daughter or mother again."

"The people of Vea have no books, but the village possessed one old faded-white piano," Hala continues, slinking into a stream of consciousness.

"Sometimes my mother would play," she says in almost a sing-song tune.

I remember through my fevered lens of nostalgia how Lolita was terrified at first to teach me to play—perhaps to her, melodies can heal, but they can also curse with a cemetery of memories. Maybe it was the same for Josie; when she stopped dancing, she could no longer listen to beautiful music. I understand now why Josie had that lovely instrument taken away; her guilt, her connection to that past, still spiking every moment.

Peter was the only little boy in the village, the one who would be the last. After the invaders killed all of Vea's men in the massacre of 1981, and as the surviving girls shrank in fear that the black army would return, the Vea elders imposed a permanent ban on males of any age entering Vea. The girls who want to marry must move to another village miles away. If they want to return, they can only return with their daughters.

"I always wondered about the twin, Peter's sister. I did not get to name her," Hala says whimsically. "The other woman named her after a dancer. I did not care; she was still my Anna."

Hala's emerald eyes light up.

"Then it was like an early Christmas gift; my mother came back and brought my girl to me. I held her," Hala continues, her body oozing with infectious love and energy before crashing through the valley floor of her recollections again.

I dwell on what Lolita had told me–how she had once escaped Bobby and Josie's hold and taken me back to the mountain.

"Then the men entered Vea again . . . The first thing they did was take away my Peter as we slept," Hala whispers, covering her open mouth like an exasperated child.

Her story reads like a tale of psychological torture, destroying a woman inch by inch.

"They burned my Peter," Hala says flatly, her shoulders slumping. "Then they took me away. All alone."

She stops speaking. The story is over without a happily ever after. I flick open my eyes as Hala beckons me closer, and I huddle beside her rotting feet. She holds her broken fingernail again up to the ring seared into the flesh of her right temple.

"You," I say to Hala. "You were the woman in the crowd."

The inauguration: the woman who stood out like a sore thumb, with disobedient, wild and distracted eyes. The memory reinforces Hala is no fan of the First Family. But she knows what it has done. She understands what the fault lines of power have done.

The pathetic Palace even bused in those from the Pistachio Center to serve as propaganda symbols of regime support that day.

"Everyone is here, everyone is here because this is a nation that adores the Amsa family," O told my fascinated face, whizzing by and barking orders to his staff.

Hala shrugs as if to say not by choice.

Hala. Lolita's Hala. My Hala. My mother. Lolita's daughter. The timeline is like a spider's web with a center. The invasion. The capture. The birth. Twins. Hala sent back to Vea with the boy.

"You came. The other one came . . . Josie came, and Hala was sent with the other one back to Vea," I state out loud.

Hala's twin boy. My twin brother.

"But even if I had a choice, I would have still chosen to stay with you. Even if you never knew what happened, I could watch over you silently. I wanted to be close to you, Anna," I remember Lolita's words. *"One time, just a few weeks after you turned one, I escaped with you back to the mountain,"* Lolita confesses, pulling me close in a terrified whisper. *"I don't know what I was thinking; it was a moment of haste. A car crowded with women from Vea stopped outside early one morning. I thought it would be by only chance . . . Christmas Eve came, and we woke up in the morning . . . And I never saw my Hala again."*

Palace guardsmen sent Hala to Pistachio.

"I'm sorry to interrupt, but the Prime Minister is here for you, and he says it is urgent," Eva says quietly, her trembling hand tapping me on the shoulder.

I allow the lady to guide me away from my paralysis, promising Hala I will come back. I can taste how close I am, like the little girl who wanted to look inside pianos instead of playing and rip off Barbie heads to examine the insides. I will not stop until I understand. Inside the decaying waiting room, Taya and Willard say little as they usher me into the back of their self-driven SUV.

I haphazardly reach down into my breast pocket to ensure the small switch is on, holding it against my heart, hoping Cliff will someday transcribe every word this fog of emotion will take from me.

"Anna, we need to save you," Willard says cryptically as we screech back toward the Palace, distant mortar rounds growing closer and closer. "The Shush is going to get you. Remember, Uncle Tig still runs the Shush. He knows what you know and a lot that you do not."

"What do I know?" I ask him calmly.

Taya and Willard trade knowing glances. There is no further discussion until we hover over olives and rapidly warming beer, even though it is still morning, in Willard's private living quarters.

Cherry blotches of anxiety surface on Taya's flawless skin, something I have never seen on her, not in all our years of sisterhood.

"Saif knows about the 1981 Massacre; he knows it happened. But I don't know what else he knows," Willard continues. "But what I do know is that the Shush will get you before you can question him or tell him the rest. To stop them from getting you, you need to get to him first."

I fixate for a few seconds on the fact that I have never entered Willard's living quarters. It is different than I expected, with posters of his late father in full military garb and Stalin quotes inscribed like poetry on the midnight navy walls. Why are Taya's suits and stilettos bursting out of the open closet?

My mind desperately seeks distraction.

"You see, Saif doesn't know it was Uncle Tig's militia who took the girls at my father's orders to find the prettiest. The one most likely to be a star," Willard continues smoothly. "But my father wasn't taking them for himself–he was taking them for his friend and oil tycoon. I know everything; I have always known everything. So, when our mother found out Saif met you, she panicked and told me everything about you, where you came from. Dad told her everything."

Willard glances over at Taya and touches her arm, signaling that he has already told her everything I do not know but am only just finding out. Maybe Madama Sara never disliked me. Perhaps she didn't know how to like me or act around me. Perhaps it was always about fearing how her world would unravel with me in the middle.

And just when the sting could not sting more–

"By now, you must know why Josie was never 'mom' to you," Willard adds.

"I loved you like my own. I love you like my own. I was just a young ballerina in a new country I didn't understand. It just happened too quickly with your father," Josie had told me. *"I should not have done it. I should not have thrown myself down the stairs . . . I wanted it back, and I made your father promise that if he wanted to keep me, he would get it–get you back. I made him promise to do whatever it took . . ."*

Taya rubs my shoulder, mascara tears stuck to the glass of her Chloe tortoiseshell frames. But in a few seconds, her face morphs from sympathetic to impatient, from personal to professional, the way only Taya Taylor knows how.

"Anna, you know what you need to do. You know that if you don't force your husband to step down–all this will come out. Do you know what happens to children of rape in the Middle East? It is still a dishonor. You know what happens to dishonored girls–you aren't an American anymore. You have nowhere to go," she presses on, her words dripping against my ear. "But with Saif no longer in charge and Willard stepping in to fill the shoes, he will protect you. We will protect you."

I examine Willard and Taya side-by-side. They are holding hands. I gape at them both. When did Taya start to keep such secrets from me?

"The safety of your babies is the only thing that matters to you, right?" Taya asks.

"Well, yes– ah, of course," I stutter back.

"You have to save yourself first, Anna. We know the Shush is coming for you. They want you out of the way. They want you silenced and not to talk to the President Doctor about this. I don't want a First Lady filled with such bad blood," Taya proclaims. "But if Saif is gone, you save yourself and many innocent lives. But unfortunately, he is making the military do terrible things."

I gulp for air like a fish panicked outside water, and Taya maneuvers me closer for a tight hug.

"Aside from saving your own life, you will save many lives. It is the right thing to do," she says demurely. "We know about your VPN, that you are well aware of all the deaths your husband has ordered and the deaths of innocent people you did nothing about, but you can turn the tide. New leadership will bring peace to Tucana, and you are the only one who can ensure Saif is gone. Nobody but us will ever know."

"And if Saif isn't going to go on his own accord, you will do whatever it takes to give your babies a future, right?" Taya notes, more a statement than a question.

My knees buckle, and I almost tumble to the floor like a broken fish.

"It will be easy, there will be a silencer on the gun, and we will make sure the cameras are all turned the other way. It will be a terrorist attack because it's not the first time someone has tried to shoot down our President," Willard emphasizes. "But this must happen now before more lives are lost by barrel bombs and chemical attacks."

My shoulders are not that strong. I cannot take on the weight of this world.

"Per the constitution, I will only be the interim President until your baby Rian turns 28. I will protect you and the family," Willard pledges. "I will not let anyone hurt you. Uncle Tig and the Shush will all be out of the job; they will be nobodies in the 301 jail. We can't have peace here with them around. And we will reform Tucana once and for all. Alongside you."

What is my responsibility in all of this? How much am I supposed to carry?

"Try to remember you aren't the only one with troubles and decisions to make, Anna," Taya says, sounding soft and stern simultaneously.

When Willard speaks next, he speaks so faintly that I have to lean in to make out the words from his mouth over the buzz of the Swarovski-speckled ceiling fan. I am dealing with a different Willard than the one who held my back.

"There is video," he purrs. "Video of you . . . and my eldest brother . . . in the gym."

My heart suspends, wounded.

"We don't want Saif to ever learn of the video, the press, or anyone else . . ." his voice trails off. "It is most imprudent and highly injurious to the Amsa Family. Terribly bashful on your behalf."

"I think you mean baleful, Willard," I sneer back. "And I don't think a little video like that will destroy the family's reputation. You all have managed to do that successfully on your own."

I glare at Willard and into a face no longer boyish but something more like a menacing man I do not know. Or never knew. I had never noticed the resemblance to his father before. But with his narrow mustache twitching, hair combed over, and a cigar moving up toward his lips, they look almost one and the same.

For the sake of it, I want to explain to him that nothing transpired with Firas that morning other than that his pig of an older brother had forced himself upon me. But had I done enough to push him away? Anyway, nothing happened. I left before anything could, didn't I? What does it look like in the video? What would Saif do? Who else had seen it? How does Willard know it even exists?

"Listen, Anna, the video won't end up anywhere if you do the right thing. The right thing is Saif cannot remain. He will not remain," Willard says darkly. "The damage he has also done is catastrophic, and you are either complicit in continuing it, or you support us in the next chapter. Lives are depending on you to stop this ruthless calamity."

My brain freezes, like the childhood intensity of inhaling an ice cream too quickly. I cannot comprehend.

"Can you give me until tonight to work this out?" I squeak back, my voice trapped in a shell of fear and weakness.

Willard and Taya nod in unison. But Taya's lips tighten with urgency.

"We know that there are more attacks on the way. On top of all the chaos happening already, the United States made this big deal about not crossing red lines and threatening intervention if the chemical line was crossed, but they did nothing. That was months ago, and we can't let it continue," Taya says, a slight pleading in her tone. "You are the only one who can do this, and we can have this taken care of by tomorrow."

A tear rolls down my cheek. This time, neither of them offer a hand or a word of comfort. Taya glances down at my simple, rough engagement diamond, contrasted against the much fancier thick rose gold wedding band passed down through the generations.

"You could have said no," she pronounces impatiently as I turn slowly to walk away.

I swim through a sea of confusion to the master's quarters. Would the Americans kill me too? I am, after all, no longer an American.

As soon as I return numbly to my quarters, unfazed by the screaming babies that mimicked all the things I am too numb to convey, I instruct the night nurse to go home, and I pace up and down the nursery, a child in each arm.

Rian and Ella are part me, part Saif, and part audacious individuals who will become somebody different altogether, their own people, if I raise them right.

The mailroom clerk tucks a letter below the door, a wax-sealed envelope with a return address made out to Extreme Press. But when I open it, it is not from Cliff at all. I recognize Josie's handwriting straightaway. This is the letter I have been waiting for, the one she promised to send before she died.

How smart it was that she sent the letter to Cliff, evading interception.

"'I wanted a star. I wanted you to be a star, but not this kind of star,'" the letter begins. "'And so, your father selected the prettiest girl. But I only wanted the girl, the prettiest girl. I only wanted you . . .'"

The handwriting becomes looser and less readable, but I persist.

"'Soon after I brought you back, I received a ton of calls from the U.S. government about the birth certificate, questioning my medical care, probing its authenticity,'" the letter continues. "'I would have gone to jail for the rest of my life, and they would have taken you away. I loved you. I had no choice if I wanted to keep you. It took several years, but I was notified I was under investigation, and there was only one way out . . . So, I flipped for them. I became the U.S. government's top Tucana informant.'"

Then it clicks. I remember Josie waking up breathlessly and early one Monday morning, dressed like Farrah Fawcett in a white pantsuit almost the same color as her drained face. And then she climbed into a black helicopter, which hovered for a few minutes in the backyard, and then chopped up and through the Los Angeles smog.

"'Your father did not know at first. I worked for his business, I traveled there, I reported back, and I drank because it was all I could do to console myself for spying on the only man who loved me,'" the writing went on. "'Lolita always seemed to know something was not right. She always worried you would be taken away from her.'"

Lolita, who usually plucks her tongue and nods whenever—or however—Josie flitters from home, swallows stress with every breath. There is something different this time.

"'But with all the information I had provided, the government finally had what they needed to prosecute,'" Josie wrote. "'They were piecing together all his war crimes with the old Rian regime, the ones which I was immune from, given that I had not directly participated, and I had flipped for them. He could feel it. Now, the Feds were closing in on him.'"

We attend Bob Seger's holiday party in a private room at the Beverly Hills Hotel. I assume Dad knows him from whisky nights in the Polo Lounge. I sit quietly in the back, observing the expanse of tuxedos and swinging dresses swish before me as their well-dressed offspring wait in line for the fake Santa Claus photos.

The night is only getting started, the ballroom filling with famous people drinking champagne in flutes and glancing over one another's shoulder for the next person to rub elbows with when Dad declares we are leaving.

"Those two men not drinking near the stage," I overhear him mutter to Josie. "I've seen them before. At the airport lounge, down the bottom of Mulholland

Drive, at Tony Romo's café garden on a random day."

It is the first time I have seen the Bobby Paradis mask crack a little–he stomps a little more heavily than usual, and I worry his shaking leg will buckle beneath him.

Dad proclaims again that we are leaving.

Josie rolls her eyes.

"You're losing it, Bobby," she responds curtly, sauntering calmly toward coat check to collect her giant mink wrap.

"'It was me; it was me who secretly cautioned him to go to Tucana and never come back. I could not have lived with myself if I had not at least warned him to run. If he didn't, I would have to kill him,'" the letter continues.

"I have a lot of business there now, little. It's booming with oil," he says, with what I detect as mild pride. "Bigger and bigger every day. The only foreigner allowed by their government to stay."

"I would like to visit there someday," I press on. "It seems like an interesting place."

Again, Dad looks through me–no "yes," but no "no" either.

"When it's safe and steady enough, I will try to send you a ticket," he fumbles. "Regardless, we will have to meet somewhere outside of here."

"'Bobby gave me you. He did everything I had asked,'" Josie scrawled. "'The least I could do was warn him, having spied on him almost all our romantic lives.'"

My mind leaps back to that last visit with Josie at the hospital, then back to Café Lalo when I was still in boarding school.

"I am selling the Mulholland mansion," Josie continues, looking out the frosted window into the wet streets and the black umbrellas piled up beside the heaping black hills of trash. "To retire in a small beachside studio in Malibu."

"Retire from what? I didn't know you ever worked," I remark with a quarter smile.

"'I did retire after you went to boarding school. I thought with you on the East Coast and Bobby and Lolita gone, I could somehow find time to reconcile what I had done,'" Josie's words endure in the letter. "'Complicit in accepting a child from rape, forcing the victim's grandmother into silence and into our home, then snitching on it all.'"

Through the ups and the downs, Josie drank her demons away and loved me as much as she knew how to love me.

"'It was the least I could do, warn him not to come home. He made Lolita go back too,'" Josie scrawls. "'I never told him why. I never told Lolita, either. But I think somehow, they both knew. But later, the U.S. government came after me. They came to the house in the helicopter, and we went all the way to H.Q. They knew I was the one that had tipped Bobby off not to return and ruined the case that they had spent so many years on.'"

I suppose he loved her, always loved her. They could no longer communicate–but they never did divorce.

"'They forced me out of retirement when they found out Saif was coming for studies. I didn't have a choice but to work a little more. Otherwise, I would be in prison on death row,'" reads the letter. "'I just wanted you to get to know him a bit, share a bit of what you knew so I could report back and give them at least some intelligence they wanted. Truly, the last thing I wanted was for you to fall in love with a dictator and lose your American Dream.'"

"Anna, I was doing a little–well, research–looking ahead to your wedding, and I didn't know before, but," she pauses. "It's in the Tucana Constitution that anyone who marries into the First Family with foreign citizenship must relinquish it; they can only be Tucanese. So, this wouldn't be good for you. Nothing is worth losing your U.S. citizenship and ability to be here and safe."

My goodness, Josie had worked. The snitch. I understand now why she was so excited when I connected to Saif–her access to intelligence information would be unprecedented. But on the flipside, she worried I would fall too deep and find out all the things nobody wanted me to know.

"'I didn't want to spy on you. I didn't want to hurt you. I loved you, and

I thought if I cooperated with what the government asked of me, asked you all those endless questions and made a visit or two that I could surveil you and protect you,'" the ink wanes. "I will send this to Cliff, the man you told me about doing work for, and hope he knows what to do. The Shush won't suspect him the way they started to suspect me . . .'"

And that is all. Vanity led her to me, it kept her going, and when there was no more left, she went.

I recognize Cliff's writing on a separate post-it tucked inside.

"I've got you," is all he penned.

By that, I understand he has archived the years of memos and the confusing mosaic of my life. I exhale, knowing the words had all flowed through and feeling somehow safe in the belief that that is still the one secret that this hell of an island could not take from me.

The clock ticks a brassy tock, grinding against the glass with the synchronicity of the pulse behind my knees. I will not buckle. I have made up my mind, and I march across the lawn to tell Taya and Willard. There is no right thing to do. But in that, I will do what I believe is the most right.

When I return to our living quarters, Saif is home. He rarely makes it back this early, and I can't hide my surprise. His body bows like an old man, and I let him put the children to sleep alone. The children's building blocks crash down, sending a shudder through my spine. His accidental knock.

Perhaps Saif has no idea about the monster who fathered him, the operation his dad ordered upon that innocent mountain village. I suspect he would not have been able to love me if he had known. I glance at his stooped silhouette in the night light and back at the photo by the bedside, the state-sanctioned wedding photo of us together in Paris with our first child still living inside of me, and I want to howl in agony.

"I need to know what you knew. I need to tell you what I knew," I whimper, half into his shadow and half into the tiny metallic chip resting by my beating heart. "Even if they get to me before you."

I can't help but love my husband, the fresh-faced medical student. I love him, the person he was before this thing–the dictator thing–happened. But I stopped liking him long ago.

And for the first time, I have a whiff of what it must mean to sort of like oneself. After all, I come from the lineage of two of the strongest women I ever knew in the winter of their lives.

CHAPTER

TWENTY

It could have been just another cold, indifferent morning in December. We rise, shower, dress, and head out to rule our little world.

I calmly watch, my nose pressed against the bathroom door crack, as his naked body steps out from the adjoining gold-tinted shower curtain and into the gothic swirl of steam. My mind spirals with questions about what he knows. I want to ask before it is too late.

Suddenly, a muffled cry and a single gunshot shatter my silent movie.

Several sprays of blood erupt from my husband's flesh. The man I once loved crumbles onto the tiles of snow-white marble. My palms—which had been sweating all night—are now dry.

I am unable to scream. There is no way I can cry. One tear. It isn't a tear of pain, anger, or relief. It is of emptiness. Can I save him? There is no way to save him. I should have told myself that a long time ago. My husband—lifeless on the bathroom floor—the ruler of our country, can no longer hurt. He can no longer love.

The life I knew is over, the ordinary moment we think will never come, but I did not want it to end this way.

I push against the ruby-rimmed door handle, marching into the thickening pool of blood and pieces of heart staining the dramatically figured Pavonazzo marble, an endowment from the Ottoman Emperor a century ago. Organ meats an animal could feast on for days.

I crouch over his shell, hollowed by globs of missing flesh. I take a deep breath–straddle his lifeless body and lean my lips into his blood.

May I ask? Is it too late? Where did I come from? Had he known?

A figure entangled in steam catches my eye. For a moment, it looks like me. A mirror? There is no mirror on the shower curtain. I squeeze my eyes shut, waiting for the seconds to pass. One, two, three.

I open them again. Still there. A nauseating wave passes through me as I watch myself frozen behind the frosted curtain, a gun to my right temple. The dim light makes my dead-still silhouette slip into obscurity. Although I am moving, I am shaking. Aren't I?

Am I holding a gun? My sweaty palms are empty. Did I do this? I could not have. I did not. Did I?

All of a sudden: panic, chaos. My drifting mind snaps back with a thud. Babies wail. I need to speed into the forest. Far, far away.

Soon they will all be here, and they will all know. Holy hell, the dictator is dead. The dictator's wife will be next. Before alarm bells ring, I am in one of the readily available Palace vehicles, my babies fastened in their car seats, praying to and for what, I don't know what.

Even in the most bombed out of places, there is beauty. But you have to look for it, just like if someone tells you to look around the room and look for all things red, your eye will find all things red that it would never have noticed before. It will attract all things red into sight. Opportunities besiege us, but we will not find them if we aren't looking for them.

Vea Road has changed significantly since the last time I took it. Now, soldiers, rag-tag protestors, oil pipelines, and poverty have seeped through every inch of tar and burned the once mythical passage alive. It has been burned alive by greed and hatred.

"I will not be like my father," Saif pledges, looking me dead in the eyes.

He glimpses through the window into the browning trees, frosted white, and stretching into the thick tendrils of morning mist.

"I will be proud. I am proud. But Tucana will be a free place. I will address the concerns of the dissidents. Nobody has ever really listened to them," Saif continues.

In the eyes of the world, Saif isn't like his father. He is considered much worse.

Looking through the flying glass at the world around me, the broken bodies, blood, and bits of buildings wedged into breathless beings do not shock me. Once a place has been bombed into nothingness anyway, it is marked off the list. There is naive beauty in believing it wouldn't need to be attacked again, which means we are one less patch from winning the war and moving on with our lives. Maybe this doesn't make any sense. Perhaps it isn't supposed to. My husband is dead; it makes sense, but no sense at all. Is this a bad dream?

I reach Vea in record time. To a naive eye, it would look like the one deposit untouched by the ugly hatred that had seeped into Tucana's capillaries. But not everyone remembers that the isolated village fought a battle decades ago and is still fighting it.

The women in pure white wrest before me, oblivious to the twilight, the war, and the death of the dictator, which will soon ooze its way into the airwaves. I can feel the dry rustle of the trees in my veins, and I savor the aroma of the loamy ground. I understand why men are no longer allowed in the mountain village of lush greens and sea that stretch so far.

I imagine in this quiet little place that you can row a small boat so far into the distance and gently tilt off the earth all in silence, Mother Nature serenely swallowing you up, never heard from again. Vea is so far removed from the ghosts of Mulholland Drive, the shades of pink tacked on the walls of the Beverly Hills Hotel, the narrow hallways of Athena Academy for Girls and from the whirlwind of watching New York City transform in a matter of minutes from pre-9/11 to everything after that.

In Vea, it is as though nothing has changed since time began—a pale green and crystal blue land as weightless as a cloud, sucked into the sunshine.

I pick up my sleeping children from the backseat and carry them into the village. Even though they are too young to remember, I want them to know that they once visited Vea—the place on the edge of the earth—even my son.

"You're back," observes the same middle-aged woman I had seen by the dock last time. It used to be an endless body of sea blue water, now drastically drained and splattered with ink, tarnished by oil spills. The woman still speaks in staccato and moves like a sphinx toward me. Her feet barely touch the earth, and she waves me down the way an angel must wave down those she treasures.

"Hala is back," she continues, her pale face cracking with a small but curious smile.

I shake my head.

"I'm not Hala," I respond softly. "I'm Hala's daughter."

Her face lights up, and the women gather, fingertips reaching for me—for my children—but not touching, not daring to touch.

"It's the first baby boy in Vea since Peter," the woman says, not unkindly. "Hala's grandson?"

I nod.

"What happened to Peter?" I ask prudently, knowing the answer but desperately hoping the information is wrong.

A hush descends over the growing crowd of curious faces. I ought to have known the silence would lead to what would amount to the end. A faint siren roars over the hinterland.

"The big men came again and took him," the woman states solemnly.

"Into the fire."

The feeling of losing something inside you engulfs me. Despite some claims that the soul slips peacefully into the spiritual realm, I have come to believe that death will always be violent and frightening.

"The next morning, the men took her too," the woman confides.

The sirens boom louder. A glance over into a deep gorge and know that must be the site of the mass grave, where all Vea's men perished long ago.

Nobody will say Hala is disturbed. Nobody will say she has been abducted, violated, enslaved, released, and had her son murdered before her, and that President General Rian's men sent her back to the Pistachio Center—to the nuthouse—for good.

The sirens scream, the flashes of red and blue light strobing against my ashen skin.

I look at all of the surviving women of Vea. They no longer flinch at the sight of authority with all these weapons drawn. Never mind them. They all lost something long ago in the summer of 1981. I lost something long ago too.

I pivot around as a multitude of police vehicles approach, familiar uniforms springing from the cars with guns drawn, bellowing down on me that I am under arrest.

I raise my hands. A few women lunge forward toward my babies, but security forces send them reeling with gunshots tearing through the traumatized skies.

I do not fight it. I do not fight it when the men grab my babies. I do not fight the handcuffs or resist guards projecting me like a ragdoll into the bowels of the 301 prison. All that is left is hope.

"You are charged with assassination," derides Tig with a gun pointed at my placid face, almost smiling.

Only they are wrong. I never killed Tig's brother. I never killed the doctor, the president, the dictator, or my husband. They are wrong. And if I did not do it, the real killer is still out there.

CHAPTER

TWENTY-ONE

Tucana is under a State of Emergency, which means the Palace has stripped the people of even the facade of due process. Therefore, they do not need to provide me with a trial. So long as the emergency veil is in place, the government technically can detain me for up to two years without even charging me with a crime.

But the sooner they do, the sooner they can render me dead. So, they orchestrate a sham court hearing less than two weeks after my arrest.

The kangaroo court, now relegated to the judiciary's dusty basement to avoid attacks, lasts only a few minutes. Then, in a fraudulent trial closed to the public, my government-sanctioned lawyer is allowed to meet with me just five minutes before the court session.

"I'm sorry, Anna. Unfortunately, there isn't much I can do. They have all the evidence they need to pin you for assassination," says the man who never even told me his name.

However, his quivering lip tells me that any word in my defense could also send him to the gallows. Thus, he does not say a word. Uncle Tig sits in the back, taking notes. He, too, says nothing.

The prosecutors show the judge surveillance footage on an old-fashioned projector. Colorless and grainy, there I am, emerging from the nursery elevator with my perfectly contoured, rose-tinted blush line. I spend precious moments crafting in my satin robe the color of blood, holding a small handgun. I am hiding in the bathroom. Minutes pass until my husband enters for his morning shower . . . And then the President Doctor crumples to the ground, a single blow to the chest.

However, the culprit that looks like me is not me, the still shadow I saw wedged behind the shower curtain that morning.

"It was the decoy nanny and mistress," I instantly protest, slapped into silence by the guard with his gun pressed against my hip bone.

"Then why did you not call for help? Why did you get in a vehicle and flee to Vea?" a prosecutor asks.

I open my mouth to answer and realize I do not have an adequate response. Shock, I suppose. I could never have pulled the trigger on Saif. At least not until I asked him what he knew about my past and Vea. I could not have killed him until I put the pieces together.

And Saif's knowledge of my past is the one piece I will now never know. But his father knew exactly who I was–and so did Uncle Tig.

The President General does not bother to introduce himself to me. But he stares at me uncomfortably for a long stretch of time, his brother Tig whispering something into his ear that causes him to glance at me and then the exit multiple times over.

Further, I could not kill someone I still, maybe a little bit, love. What is human life to these people anyhow? I will simply be another number erased from the population data. There are many people I thought I knew in my short life, I am only 24, but it turns out I know none of them.

"I hereby sentence the defendant to death by hanging," the judge fumes, but without the guts to look me square in the eye.

It does not seem real. It is not right. But I will not let these people see me cry. Will my war be over before the one all around me is complete? I think about how I was at war most of my life with someone or myself. Now I know why.

I beg the guards to tell me where my babies are, but they wave me away. One haphazardly surmises that the heirs to the Palace are safe; of course, they are safe. But how can I believe them? Not seeing the twins hurts me more than a pending death sentence. I cannot fathom never seeing them again.

In handcuffs, the guards walk me back to a new cell, this time positioned on the far west side, marked for those on death row. Cockroaches feast on the decomposing limbs left on the floor of those tortured so severely that they never even made it to their official execution date. I step over it, refusing to shudder or let the cameras know I am afraid. Through the narrow bars, I notice an older woman bruised all over with a swollen face pushing through the rusted bars; goodness knows how wounded she is from the inside. The muzzle-induced scar on her right temple is now more pronounced than ever.

Lolita. My grandmother. Oh, what I would do to rip away the wrought iron to hug her. I wait for the guards to leave.

"Hala is not dead," I remind her, no longer caring to lower my voice. "They took her to the center for mad women on the hill. The Pistachio Center. They thought nobody would find her, and she would never be free. But you must fight for her."

I hoped I could bring them together. I hope, even without me, they will find each other again.

Through the slight cracks, Lolita looks into me. Despite having had her hair shaved off, she doesn't seem bothered. Lolita learned from the wild. She traces my cuffed hand with her index finger–fingernail chillingly removed–pressing into my palm the last letter.

"They will catch us if we speak, Anna. But I wrote this for you," Lolita cries. "I did not think I would have the chance to give it to you . . . and I wish it was not like this."

Huddled in my cell corner under a few streaks of dying daylight, I piece the puzzle together with Lolita's words.

December 24, 1983. The slice of time before one's memory has adequately started to patch together the threadbare fragments of a life too young to recall.

You were just thirteen months old and living on the edge of the earth; a place that only a small number of people even know is the village of Vea . . .

And so it goes.

Like a spider's web, the timeline develops a little more: the 1981 invasion. Hala's capture. The rape. The captivity. Josie arrives. The birth. Twins. Hala is back in Vea with the boy. I stay with Bobby and Josie, and Lolita. Lolita escapes with me. In an act of revenge, forces burn the twin boy and, a day later, send Hala to the Pistachio Center for life. Forces recapture Lolita and me. Eventually, Bobby and Josie, Lolita, and her Anna fly to the U.S. to live a life of lies until federal investigators open a case against Bobby and Josie for her involvement in a crime abroad. But Josie flips.

"So, I flipped for them," Josie tells me from her hospital bed. *"I became the U.S. government's top Tucana informant."*

Memories flood into my veins, electrifying every hair on my filthy body.

As a little girl, I sit at the foot of the stairs, listening to Lolita's silhouette make endless phone calls to all the bars, cafes, and clubs Josie frequents. I listen to her yell to nobody in particular that this is not Josie's normal departure.

"What if they take Anna away?" Lolita sobs to herself, scarfing down chunks of pound cake.

Lolita, who usually plucks her tongue and nods whenever–or however–Josie flitters from home, swallows stress with every breath. There is something different this time.

Lolita knew then that it was the beginning of the end, but she was too afraid to say it.

"'Your father did not know at first. I worked for his business, I traveled there, I reported back, and I drank because it was all I could do to console myself for spying on the only man who loved me,'" read Josie's final letter delivered discreetly through Cliff. *"'Lolita always seemed to know something was not right. She always worried you would be taken away from her . . . But with all the information I had provided, the government finally had what they needed to prosecute. They were piecing together all his war crimes with the old Rian regime, the ones which*

I was immune from, given that I had flipped for them. He could feel it. Now, the feds were closing in on him.'"

Out of guilt, Josie warned Bobby not to return to the United States. She gave him an out he never deserved.

Eventually, Lolita and I decay into an unnerving slumber on our frail mattresses. And when I rise before the first light the next day, my grandmother is gone.

For a reason I can only accept, but struggle to comprehend, the universe brought me back to the birth of my life. To Tucana. My true home is slowly dying. In a strange but mellowing way, my mission feels almost accomplished if it weren't for fear of what will happen to Ella and Rian without me. I fear the people they could grow up to be.

Over the next few days in prison, I learn to slip into a one-eyed sleep as the echoes of those screaming in torture broil my ears. The first days vacillate between deep dreaming and sleeplessness, lost in the grim fascination of what the human body can withstand. Then one morning, the house of horrors becomes normal. How rapidly we grow comfortable with being so uncomfortable.

I can't see it, but I can always hear it. And smell it too. The smell of fear and the rotting bodies pile up in this prison below the earth—tongues plucked from terrified mouths and eyeballs yanked from sockets. Then there is the sizzling sound of bare wires dipped in water and zapping human flesh and metal pipes beating heads so hard that they twist. The drills. My brain freezes inside my maddening head when I hear that menacing sound. Each time I slap my right temple, trying to slap away the horrific pain of a drill through my scalp that is not mine.

New detainees are almost always dressed in someone else's blood when security forces drag them down from the warren alleys above. Sometimes they carry bits of burned flesh in their hair, but they are always with grit on their face, bearing testimony to the type of evil I should have defected from long ago. I could have run to the U.N. or stayed in the U.S. when I went to see Josie. I could have begged for a refugee raft to row to another country. But would anybody have listened? If I had fled any earlier, my babies would not exist. The thought zaps me more than my own failure to run away.

If I had defected later, what would have become of Lolita? My children? The torture lingers like the harsh hallway lights that are never switched off or replaced, even when they blink furious fluorescent. I can take the physical suffering. The psychological torture, however, is far more brutal. How much longer can I hold it together? How many more days until they plan to push me to the gallows? Nobody will give me answers. Nobody knows.

I expect to see Bobby dragged into a cell in this deep dungeon of depression, but I never do.

When will the end come? Will Tig dare rape me after interrogation the way he often hinted at when nobody else is around? He has already ripped my fingernails and caused purple bulges beneath my watering eyes. For him, violating me would be icing on his wicked cake.

And this is what the interrogators also claim is light torture. I am lucky. I am still a VIP, after all.

"We will let you keep your hair for now," Tig spits one night after returning me to the cell from a session. "But we can shave it at any time and make you eat it."

I later ask a rotating guard if the Red Cross is coming to inspect conditions.

"You know, to check on the detainee and ensure their rights are not being infringed upon," I continue sarcastically.

The gruff guard at my door, the one with the overzealous eyes molesting my weakening frame, indeed thinks it is funny I would ask such a question. I can hardly blame him.

"The Palace judiciary would clean you up and put you on house arrest at the Four Seasons before they let them in," the nameless guard roars with a mess of missing teeth, slapping his knee in stupid laughter.

Days and nights drag on, and nobody comes to see me; perhaps nobody is allowed. One afternoon, a voice that sounded like O's grappling with the guard in that clipped English tang yells my name.

"No visitors," the guard insists.

"Anna needs to know the Prime Minister is the one behind this; he is trying to bring us all down for power," the O voice remarks.

"No visitors," the guard repeats, louder this time.

O's intonation eventually withers away.

I scream to O, pleading for him to come back and tell me who is taking care of my babies. But he is gone.

In those dying days, all alone with a hidden microphone down my bra and some scraps of food, I recognize that the summary of our lives comes down to a few sentences that begin and then end. My lineage stems from the waters where life began, a child of rape. It has taken a long time for the spider's web to form, but the last string is still dangling: how will it all end?

"You cried so much, Anna baby. The doctors kept you down so much, so many sedatives for a small baby girl," Josie details, more to herself than me. "Lolita always worried you would not wake up. But I loved you. I always loved you."

Josie's eyes flutter. But there are no eyelashes left to bat and no eyebrows left to raise.

And when Anna's childhood memories return to concrete life, it is almost five years later, her existence revolves around a faraway and dreamy property called the Beverly Hills Hotel.

They kept me down and tried to erase the early memories, but they had not succeeded.

And everyone says there is this special kinetic connection between twins: the earth cannot separate them even when one is gone—and the shadows and burning breath begging for a hand never left me for long. Of course, I can't bring Peter back, but at least I will not die without the world knowing all of what occurred. Perhaps that is savior enough.

That was the beginning. And soon, it will end. Rape was the start of my mother's sentence. My death is coming sooner. But it was the woman I had always thought was my mother that got me here: her insistence in my meeting Saif, so she had enough material to keep her spy bosses from throwing her behind bars, led to the strip club, injected me with the grit to stay, the maternal instinct to love, and into the dark blindness of love. I put up with Saif's ceaseless affairs and his secrecy, fearing the repercussions of speaking out and losing touch with the right time to walk away.

The tabloids will make what they want of this life. They will feast on me until their stomachs burst like foie gras, and their insides will be dead like mine. However, my story is my story, and they can never take that away from me. Cliff has kept the memos safe, and I know he will compile them all together and publish this memoir. The dictators cannot erase my story. They can spread all the lies they want about me, but my story will be there for everyone to read. The Palace cannot torch the truth. The truth will torch.

My children will someday know who I was and the line of women who gave them life.

"My voice will not be taken from me, even after I have gone," I whisper into the battery-dying microphone against my heart where it rests against the folds of my skin permanently puckered from the days, weeks, perhaps months I have spent contorted into this tiny cell.

I am still determining if it is day or night. Worse, I no longer care. I hear rumors from the 301 guards that a lavish Palace funeral took place for Saif, followed by an even more lavish inauguration of the youngest Amsa and his stylish, blonde American bride followed the mandatory twenty days of mourning. I could never be accustomed to that time-controlled ritual of grief.

All the lives lost in the bid for freedom, I am told tens of thousands had died in this war, and for what? Who has twenty days to mourn them? Mourning is a luxury for the elite. Those trying to get by and survive another hour do not have time for that.

CHAPTER

TWENTY-TWO

I have reached the swan song.

"Last meal?" the guard asks brusquely.

I shake my head.

"No last meal," I reply sternly. "Just one last wish."

The guard cocks his head, amused.

"When you take me out of here, just let me walk without cuffs," I continue defiantly. "I have nowhere to run, so let my hands be free one last time."

"I'll ask the boss," is all the guard mumbles. "No chocolate cake? No burger?"

I shake my head again and dwell on the years I spent watching my weight, engrossed in food, consuming too much of it and purging it away in the toilet. Now I am wasted to the weight of a small girl, almost in the same way Hala withered to the bone. Self-cannibalism. Life devoured us alive, one way or another, and there is nothing romantic about bones breaking out from one's cracked and bruised skin.

"I'll go to hell light," I respond calmly.

Those small acts of revenge, those fleeting moments, have held me together all these months. When I turn back to the broken back wall, a burned baby emerges from the crawling floor beneath a razor-thin beam of light. There are no burns, squeals, or licking flames around my feet.

"Peter," I say softly, scooping up the warm infant.

He finally looks at home, eyes tightly closed and tiny mouth slightly agape. Asleep with the angels. Somewhere in a place of starlight and dust. Around an hour later, or it could have been ten minutes, Peter disperses into the dim air, and the concentrated ray of light vanishes. My brother, like Peter Pan, will forever be an infant, his life frozen in the fields of time and soon in the books of history.

The guards yank me from my dungeon, and I ride on a windowless bus through the prettiest but ugly countryside, once my obsession. Sunlight cascades into my eyes as townsfolk push wheelbarrows along broken roads and fruit rots in the open market. Everyday life continues against the backdrop of bombing and bloodshed. Only this time it feels like a movie, and my character no longer has a place.

And then thick crowds and the eerie quiet of Verte Square uncoils before me. There are so many people; I suspect the Palace has again bused in the Tucanese far and wide to pretend this is what they want, forced to shout, "down with the dictator's wife!"

I walk barefoot along the concrete like a piece of cattle marched to the slaughter. Crowds wait and faces blur together into one mystical water painting through my teary eyes. I draw a deep breath. I will not cry. I pass Taya and Willard in the center front row as an unexpected whip of sunlight lashes my fading skin. Dust to dust. Ash to ash.

I stop, narrowing my eyes at Taya.

"You fucked up, Anna. You didn't even try to stop your husband from doing the awful things your VPN told you all about," she says confidently, although I see her hand shaking. "Remember, I told you I would stab you in the front if I thought you deserved it. Well, I guess this is now."

I did not forget. Taya told me that in boarding school, the first day we met. When someone tells you what they will do, believe them. For a second, Taya's diamond ring accompanied by a solid rose gold band blinds my weary eyes. But Taya stabbed me in the back, too. She promised she would not do that, and she did. Saif's ending, my ending, is all the product of Taya and Willard's scheming, a secret and convenient love affair corrupted by power and money and the self-aggrandizing that they can do better.

My closest confidante is now the newly inaugurated First Lady. Taya cleverly married the once relatively powerless Prime Minister, now the almighty President.

Even if I could have shot daggers through my eyes at her, I would not bother. Even if I had stopped my husband from ordering attacks and coming clean about the chemical weapons, it would not have made a difference. The two of them have been plotting to get us out of the picture for a long time, the dirty power play. My gaze shifts to Willard.

I think about the graffiti on the wall that sparked this civil war and the teenagers who were blamed, arrested and tortured to death. But had anyone ever seen the tape of them painting those words "Down with the dictators. Doctor, you're next"? Who issued the orders to interrogate the boy to his death? What about the "Filthy Tucanese" viral video, supposedly made by anti-Palace protesters? That was all Willard's doing, I suddenly realize.

Soldiers were sent out into the bloodied streets to shut down all the factories that reproduced cheap facsimiles of all my outfits. The Palace banned blog sites featuring my style from the internet under a decree issued by–the Prime Minister.

This was Willard's way to steadily chip away at my public persona while appearing as the beacon of support.

I had lunch with Madame Sara on New Year's Day in the ballroom–that was Willard's idea. He had begged me to make amends with his mother because, in his words, the family needed unification during this difficult time. So, Madame Sara and I sat together in awkward silence against only the clunking of cutlery and glasses. Madame Sara pointed out that Millie had prepared the sirloin steak with pepper sauce, but she did not like pepper sauce.

"Willard selected the menu for Millie; I wish he had chosen a classic French bordelaise sauce," Madame Sara commented. "My son should know I disdain pep-

per sauce."

Willard tampered with the sauce. Willard was then the one who had tried to poison me. And at some point, he romanced–and recruited–Taya to his team. Even that first slither of bad press–the *Gawker* reporter at the New Year's Eve Party–was Willard's thick wallet.

"Is everything okay here?" Willard suddenly asks.

Phew. The man who always comes to my rescue, much more than my husband ever does.

"Can I help you, sir?" Willard asks Phil.

I daintily shuffle away, and when I turn around, the men are shaking hands and conversing jovially.

I think harder back to that handshake–Willard discreetly passes the reporter something. Money. Willard gave him money. Furthermore, Willard was the instigator who brought back capital punishment without me even noticing.

"That grants us a lot more leeway–we can detain without trial for up to two years, and we can move money into military spending," Uncle Tig had said at the meeting. "PM and President have signed."

Yes, the Prime Minister brought that to the table with a careful plan in mind and convinced the President Doctor to sign.

Then I remember the random gunshot after Election Day.

The sky opens into a magical myriad of fireworks, and the intensity of the crowd sprouts.

And then a gunshot whooshes by my nose, by my husband's nose, landing into a nameless loyalist celebrating below.

Someone did try to shoot Saif. It was not an embarrassing figment of my imagination; it was Willard's doing. He probably also poisoned his father, sending his aging body into cardiac arrest. I wouldn't put it past the whip-smart university kid to have fixed his biggest brother's new car for an accident, either. And just a few years later, he organized for someone who looked like me to put a bullet through his other brother's head.

But maybe I should have unraveled all of this much earlier, I think, remembering my very first visit to Vea and how it was only my notes about Willard that were deleted from my laptop.

"We knew you would not have the guts to go through with it by the morning," Willard menacingly whispers as if to read my mind. "We had a backup."

He and Taya had ordered the decoy to do the dirty work just in case.

"We will protect you," I imagine they told her.

"It's easy to get people to do what you want when they have no other choice," Willard continues with a low laugh.

The guards, hanging back to at least allow me the dignity of one final private conversation, step forward and push me toward the noose that swung beneath the scorch of the intense sunlight that left no patch uninvaded by its brightness.

Willard and Taya deserve each other. Taya was never building all those high-powered media contacts for me; she was always building them for herself, for the day she would seize the limelight. She—they—were also sabotaging me at the same time.

Someone leaked the story to The Daily Mail about how Saif and I met when I was underage, boozing in the Silver Legs Hell's Kitchen strip club, and that we had gone home together that night. I am shocked—so few people have any awareness of this real story.

Taya is the only person I had told, but then again, I wonder who Saif might have informed. He was always too embarrassed to talk about it and made me swear to secrecy.

I think about all those nasty headlines and realize Taya engaged in tarnishing my name with Will for much longer than I first thought, right down to *The Vanity Fair* article about my high school expulsion and shooting. I confided in Taya, and only Taya, about that at boarding school. But first, before the destruction, Taya controlled me—every inch of my image, possibly right down to my getting pregnant again.

Would it be possible that the doctor gave me a phony last shot?

"Birth control isn't foolproof, Anna. Besides, you need to be a mother for your image to win over the Tucanese. It is your sole duty and purpose," Taya notes with a little too much confidence.

I turn and lock eyes with Taya one last time. I stretch my fingers up and out into a V sign–for peace and victory–and smile. Her feline gray eyes drop to the concrete.

In those ensuing seconds, the crowd swells. As I walk, I think about all the time I've had since my arrest to contemplate this moment. Remember how everyone loves you when you're dead? Somehow, I think I will be the exception to that rule.

Deep down, I never thought this moment would come.

I should be thinking about something with depth and richness, yet in truth, I am captivated by the growling of my hungry stomach and confusion about why I am here.

Why am I here? I started this dictator's wife life for love, but the commitment to continue down this path I started had tainted that love. I have not lived perfectly. I have made many mistakes. I turned a blind eye to things I should have fought for and rallied against, but life is easier from the outside looking in. Life is easier from hindsight too.

It occurs to me that Taya and Willard have my babies. My eyes scan everywhere for them. They are not there at the Square, yet I know she will try to wash their brains with her lies. But my babies will not only know of the fabrications from Taya and Willard. I can only hope there will be a way out for them somewhere north of my life, and they will take it before it is too late. I would do anything to hold them right now. Only I am relieved they are not here. I would not want them to see this. As a product of rape, I know how the DNA of trauma lives in the blood, even when we are too young to remember.

I peer down at my ragged gray jumpsuit. Cliff's microphone is still tucked inside my bra, holding on to my heart, my words still floating back to him as the red-light flashes that there are just a few more minutes of battery life.

Cliff will edit and compile, and the world will know all I can tell them of the Amsa family. The world will also come to know the little girl, the idealist, the lover, the mother, and the woman behind The Dictator's Wife. I can't make the pangs of sorrow for all the things I have not done, not said, and not tried to stop as Tucana turned into a blood bath behind the sword-like Palace gates go away.

But when I try to remember, really try to remember, I can't pinpoint precisely when and how so much went wrong and where it all fell apart. I suppose that is what pain and power do to you—days drift. Tiny things change day by day, and then suddenly, you wake up, and everything has changed. You have lost, even when you do not fully understand the game's rules. Aren't we all just compiled sums of our past and the pasts before us?

There were a few times I nearly left, but nearly is the saddest word in the English dictionary. Nearly ends in a lie.

I want to tell the people of Tucana that I am sorry, that I should have been bolder and braver and done more to stop the bleeding. But will anyone listen?

With or without me, my babies will find the truth. Just like I did. Putting all the puzzle pieces together cost me my life, but it was worth it. If my children inherit anything from me, I pray they keep going until you have the answers.

I observe the giant statue and fountain, with water spouting from the mouths of the giant cherubs. The national arts symbol of twins no longer frightens me; it comforts me. I step up to the platform of my own free will. I do not need a guard to force me. I will not die on my knees for whatever it still might be worth.

Although it might seem odd, but as I face death, the silence is over for me. Not many people get to see what I see, walk in such sick, expensive shoes. And I won't let my side go untold.

"I am done with not having the last word," I retort as the noose fastens around my neck.

From my dimming lens, the hordes of faces all dissipate, and what unfolds before me is an empty place, bereft of all humans, at the edge of the earth where civilization began.

I draw a deep breath. I push my shoulders back.

"The way someone goes tells us everything," I whisper into my microphone as it dies.

Before the guards can push me, I gracefully spring into the air.

EPILOGUE

Based on years of recordings, I compiled this memoir with the words by Anna Paradis, with gaps filled in by editorial research and historical footage.

I first met Anna in 1999. She was a university freshman in New York City with a rucksack of books and burning eyes. Anna struck me as a lonely soul who longed for adventure, love, and as a young adult who witnessed September 11, dreamed of a career in finance that could somehow contribute to a better world.

When Anna left for the vast skies and scarlet seas of Tucana, she was, in many ways, still a forlorn child with a superficial knowledge of what she was getting into and the kind of life I do not think she chose. Instead, it was the life that chose her.

I did not listen to these recordings until after she died. I knew that if I did, I would have tried to bring her out–to intervene–to interfere with a destiny she was supposed to have on the edge of the earth.

It was a difficult decision, observing the red light in my office flash and not turning on the sound, but it was a decision that I, as the compiler and editor of this book, cannot regret.

When Anna first told me she was marrying the son of the Tucanese autocrat, I resisted the paternal urge to bluntly caution her not to do it. I had my own experience with this regime. I backpacked through Tucana in

1980, just a few years after the massive discovery of oil. The Palace commissioned me to write *The Book of Tucana*. I wrote the book like any historical and narrative guide–the good, the bad, the bruises, and the truth. Unfortunately, the regime of dictator Rian Amsa did not appreciate such a factual account and edited out and guttered the work to be of their twisted liking. I insisted they remove my name as the author, and the Palace blacklisted me from returning to Tucana.

I know Anna fell in love with that book as a little girl, and I could not bring myself to tell her of my dealings with the dictatorship and that the Palace PR team butchered and manipulated so much of the book. One time, she almost guessed when she saw some of the old photographs pinned on my office wall of the early tensions. I almost told her. However, I chose to stay quiet. Sometimes, we must learn life's lessons in our own way, the hard way. Anna was the type of person who–like myself in my more adventure-seeking days–needed to be out there on the edge, learning on a tightrope with no net to catch the fall.

I learned that Anna was on death row only through press reports. I booked a ticket to Cyra, but was denied a visa because of that long-standing ban. I attempted to get the prominent human rights groups involved in calling for an appeal in her case, yet they would not take it on, claiming donations would dry up if they appeared to support "the dictator's wife."

"She is the enemy," they all wrote me back, if they wrote back at all.

I still resisted the urge to listen to her transmissions, questioning if she was the monster much of the media depicted her to be. Nevertheless, I loved Anna because I understood Anna.

Flawed, but a victim of the very system of which millions of people–not only the Tucanese–are still victims around the world. In this case, they are victims of a continued dictatorship, with all the vestiges of power still flowing inside the small, evil circle that is the Amsa family.

In one way or another, this world will build you up to knock you down. It will have its way. There is a global need to hear Anna's story–because without stories, we die. We forget the molecules that make up life. We forget who we are here for and why. We fail to seek the truth.

I will not write rest in peace, because Anna is still without peace. Instead, I will write rest in revolution–as this is what I hope this memoir inspires–a real, lasting revolution this time. A global revolution for every citizen under the sun to live free. Everybody has a part to play.

And above all, Anna was a mother. I hope her children learn the truth of their early life much earlier than she did; before it is too late.

HOLLIE S. MCKAY

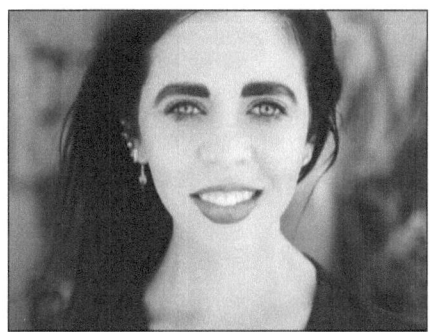

HOLLIE S. MCKAY is an investigative and international affairs/war journalist with over fourteen years of specialized focus on warfare, terrorism, and crimes against humanity.

Hollie has worked on the frontlines of several major war zones and covered humanitarian and diplomatic crises in Iraq, Afghanistan, Pakistan, Syria, Iran, Turkey, Yemen, Saudi Arabia, Burma, Russia, Africa, Latin America, and other areas.

Her globally-spanned coverage, in the form of thousands of print articles and essays, has included exclusive and detailed interviews with numerous captured terrorists, as well as high-ranking government, military, and intelligence officials and leaders from all sides.

She has spent considerable time embedded with US and foreign troops, conducted extensive interviews with survivors of torture, sex slavery and forced child jihadist training, refugees, and internally-displaced people to communicate the complexities of such catastrophes and war crimes on local populations.

Hollie's columns have been featured in the Wall Street Journal and her writings referenced in innumerable mainstream publications and academic journals. Additionally, she has won numerous foreign press and humanitarian awards.

ABOUT THE PUBLISHER

Di Angelo Publications was founded in 2008 by Sequoia Schmidt—at the age of seventeen. The modernized publishing firm's creative headquarters is in Los Angeles, California. In 2020, Di Angelo Publications made a conscious decision to move all printing and production for domestic distribution of its books to the United States. The firm is comprised of eleven imprints, and the featured imprint, Reverie, was inspired by the long-lasting legacy of fiction and adult literature.

www.ingramcontent.com/pod-product-compliance
Lightning Source LLC
Chambersburg PA
CBHW030408030726
47497CB00002B/531